MY MOTHER
GETS MARRIED

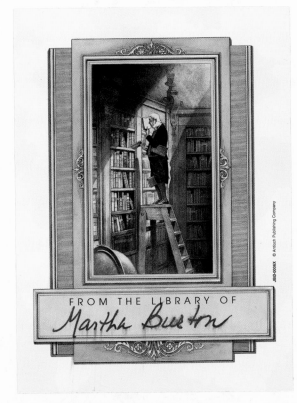

MY MOTHER GETS MARRIED

Moa Martinson

TRANSLATED AND WITH AN AFTERWORD BY

Margaret S. Lacy

THE FEMINIST PRESS
at The City University of New York
New York, New York

Published 1988 by The Feminist Press at The City University of New York, 311 East 94 Street, New York, N.Y. 10128
Distributed by the Talman Company, Inc., 150 Fifth Avenue, New York, N.Y. 10011

Printed in the United States of America
91   90   89   88   6   5   4   3   2   1

This translation of *My Mother Gets Married (Mor gifter sig)* is published by agreement with Bokförlaget Legenda AB, Stockholm. *Mor gifter sig* was first published in 1936. Moa Martinson wrote the foreword for a new Swedish edition in 1956.

Library of Congress Cataloging-in-Publication Data

Martinson, Moa, 1890–1964.
  My mother gets married.

  Translation of: Mor gifter sig.
  Bibliography: p.
  I. Title.
PT9875.M39M613   1988   839.7'372   88-21405
ISBN 0-935312-99-4
ISBN 0-935312-81-1 (pbk.)

This publication is made possible, in part, by public funds from the New York State Council on the Arts. The Feminist Press is also grateful to Alida Brill for her generosity.

Cover design: Gilda Hannah
Cover art: *Portrait of a Girl* by Paula Modersohn-Becker. Reproduced by permission of the Von der Heydt-Museum, Wuppertal, West Germany.

Foreword

The main person in this book is my mother. She died, age eighty-five, on a foggy day in November, 1955. She left me with an emptiness that was devastating. In the course of my life my mother was my best and most trustworthy friend who possessed that cultivation and experience that never can be learned in schools or the university, only from life in its bitterest form. For her sake and in her memory I must put this question: Did my mother's life, my own, and millions of other anonymous lives in our country need to be so hard in spite of peace, in spite of hard work and the eager, unceasing search for work that hardly paid for daily bread? With good reason I ask this question for my mother's sake, my own, and in the name of two-thirds of the people of Sweden.

Part of the question can be answered by the reception my colleagues and I received with our early books about life in Sweden's anonymous circles. My book, *My Mother Gets Married,* was called in a review "food for the dump." I let my mother read the review, and her comment follows: "The wretches cannot understand life like this; it is better you stop writing. There's no use in trying. I think they're embarrassed to have your name in the papers with theirs."

Ja, that was her view of critics and "popularity." My generation didn't think much of advertising in the papers. Besides, we were brought up to believe that you had to work for every öre. To get something for nothing was as embarrassing as to advertise yourself in the newspaper. Possibly that upbringing was wrong in a time when iron-hard laws, both written and unwritten, which decreed that work determines a human being's right to exist, put a barbed-wire fence around any possibilities for most of us. (Like so many others, half of my numerous relatives are in America.)* That it was an honor to work for your bread was nearly the only enlightenment we were given; the rest we had to learn from life itself. The part of my mother's and my life that is described in this book is not singular. It was common for hundreds of thousands of mothers and children in our land. Without having a vocabulary to interpret in words their strong, irresistible love of life and children, mothers fought their battle in silence. If the children and fathers starved, the mothers starved even more. That was their unwritten law.

Few of the "educated," few of the well-to-do, never anyone from the Swedish throne, and hardly any on the part of government noticed those anonymous mothers' battles, or else pretended not to see the terrible poverty and conditions described in this book.

The reviewer who called the book "food for the dump" continues still today to belittle everything I write. Of course, words are free. For myself, I'll go to the grave with the indignation and the disappointment that an academic education and a warm and cozy life did not shape those who had them with a broader viewpoint and more sympathy for the majority of citizens who fought their battle for life on life's outermost edge.

Paradoxically enough, I am mostly indignant not because I was denied the possibility to get a university education, but because I landed right in the same anonymous hell as my mother. Maybe it was even harder for me, for I was fully conscious that it was hell. I was clear about the injustice against all of us, and powerless. Once my mother said, "You cannot possibly write about *everything;* they would die of shame." Yes, she was right; it wouldn't do to tell everything, that would be too much, and some of the bad things should probably be completely forgotten; I don't know, maybe not.

In any event everything in this book is true even if some of the things too sad to tell are left out. In the beginning I tried to camouflage a little, but that didn't work. The result was that I wrote "Old Island Road" instead of "Daxberg's Road." Hundreds of letters came from Norrköping, "We know where that farm is, and it's on Daxberg's Road." The letters thought I hadn't remembered correctly. Mother and I finally had our first room where we got to be alone together, which was described in the book's first chapter.

---

* To escape the hard living conditions in turn-of-the-century Sweden, many Swedes emigrated to America.

The house still stands today just as it was at Ljura farm, which now is in Norrköping.

No, to camouflage in a biography was not my idea; that won't do, but perhaps you have a right to leave out the worst, if you see that it can harm someone who never harmed you or meant ill.

I hope you get some good from the book. Perhaps you'll get a little idea of how necessary the fight is when it's fought for something truly worthwhile: to endure.

Your
Moa

1956

OUR MOTHERS

"There burns a fire, it burns so clear,
it burns in a thousand rings.
I will go through the fire and with my darling dance."

So we sang in the dusky alleys
where the twilight hid our paleness.
Our dance was so quiet at night
waiting for tired mothers.
Our faces were so naked
and our eyes were so clear,
like those of lung-sick death-doomed priests,
for we were illegitimate children,
our mothers were unwed women.

Our mothers went through the fire,
and found on the other side
the high dark wall
of German wool factories.
Our mothers went through the fire
and found on the other side
prisons and spinning houses and punishment
and some found certain death.
We saw our mothers cry on lonely nights in the alleys.
We saw them at night go "on the street"
when the landlord wrangled about rent.

Alone they came back
long after we slept at night.
We are our mothers' daughters
and still we sing the song:
"There burns a fire, it burns so clear,
it burns in a thousand rings."

MY MOTHER
GETS MARRIED

Chapter 1

I remember so well the day Mother got married. We lived with her sister in Norrköping. It was a Friday. Mother got the day off from the factory. She wore a black dress borrowed from a friend, for Mother's money problems had never really cleared up after she'd paid off my expensive treatments for "English sickness."* The money Mother had got "once and for all" from my real father—who was, of course, too fine to marry my mother, for it was taken for granted there was a big difference between marrying and being a father—that money Mother had given her father so I could always stay there. That same year my grandfather got T.B. and died.

My grandmother could keep me only one year; then she had to go to the poorhouse, for she had become blind. So my mother had to take me along to her servant's jobs as best she could until she got work at Brück's factory in Norrköping.

My "child support" had long since come to an end, because at some time in his life, grandfather had put his name on an IOU for a neighbor.

But now Mother was getting married. She had on a black dress and a long necklace of oval, unpolished pearls around her neck.

I got the necklace afterwards. I still have it. Mother sat in Aunt's single room and waited for my stepfather. It was so strange— Mother dressed so fine on a week day.

Mother and my stepfather were away an hour; then they came back and were married.

"Now you must say Papa," Mother said.

My stepfather hemmed and hawed, stretched himself, and twisted his mustache. "*Ja*, now you must say Papa," he said.

*An expression for rickets.

1

I said Uncle long afterwards.

We lived with my aunt awhile. I saw my mother becoming fat and ugly, but I didn't understand anything. One day she quit the factory.

"Tomorrow we'll move to our own place," she said, taking me on her knee and looking happy.

The next day Mother and I plodded through town and out on Old Island Road to a farm that was only a little way from Norrköping.

We struggled along, each of us carrying a lot of stuff.

I lugged a new window shade Mother had got from her friends at the factory. A fine window shade. (Much has been written, both verse and prose, about the patterns and pictures on those old window shades. I think they certainly played an important part in exciting a child's imagination.) On this window shade a girl on an arched bridge was carrying water. That seemed to me like a lot of trouble. I lay wondering many nights afterwards how things had turned out where that girl lived, if she'd scrubbed that day, for her skirts had been tucked up, and how I could get ahold of such nice clogs as she'd had on. I have never seen the like of such a thing, not even in big marketplaces after I'd grown up.

We walked along on the wide old road, Mother and I, an old, old road, one of the oldest in the land. It was in April, sunny and warm.

My stepfather was already working on the farm. Mother and I would get to be all by ourselves the whole afternoon. For the first time since I was born, we would be alone with just each other. I would soon be seven years old.

My stepfather's foster mother had given us most of the furniture. Good stuff of birch. A dresser, a bed, a table, some chairs, only the settee was new. It was painted brown, and a row of acorns decorated its frame, sixty-four acorns. The settee was bought for me to sleep on.

Now Mother and I were on our way to our first home.

We came to a white plastered cottage, with a big, high flight of stairs, set in a wooded hillside. In the windows we could see faces peeking curiously at us through the curtains.

Taking out a key, Mother unlocked the first door to the left in the entrance hall.

"Oh—oh—oh—oh!" That was all I could say.

Mother had been there already, putting everything in order.

There were long white curtains at the windows, *two* of them in the room. Old curtains she had got from Grandma, now mended and blue-starched. A white spread on the yellow Gustavian bed, a white cloth on the table, new rag rugs Mother had woven herself when she spent evenings with Grandma after the whistle blew at the factory. I had often cried when Mother trudged there, for Grandma lived in Vilbergen outside of Norrköping, and it was too far for me to walk, but now the new rugs lay here. Juniper twigs in the stove.

Mother explained that there was a common kitchen at the other end of the hallway where those who had only one room could cook and bake as they needed.

"And that's wonderful," she said, "we get out of the smoke and smells."

But those who had been at the farm for a long time had all got their dibs on the kitchen. Mother was new and came from the factory—"bag of bones"—that was the high and mighty country-wives' name for women factory workers, and they had to fix their food in their own rooms.

On the birch dresser was a pair of small pictures I recognized, for I had seen them at Grandma's where I'd been a few times. It wasn't hard at all for me to call my stepfather's foster mother Grandma, as it was to call him Papa. There was also a pair of fine vases. In them Mother had put alder branches with their little black cones.

(Now, nearly forty years later, I have the vases with alder branches and black cones here on a shelf. My mother was always so anxious about her things, for she had to pack and unpack so often. The vases are over a hundred years old, because Grandma had got them from her mother-in-law when she married, and they weren't new then either. Five generations of poor folks for sure have inherited these vases.)

And there was my new settee of spruce with acorn trim.

I sat quietly in the room the whole afternoon. It was so completely different from my aunt's; she had only the one room with noisy kids and wagon drivers who boarded there and a great hullabaloo constantly on the stairs, and the terrible racket of horses and wagons on the cobbled streets.

Mother also sat quietly. We didn't go out. I sat on the settee that would be my own, my very own bed. So often my bed had been on the floor or shared with someone else.

And then Mother would always be home, would be there all day, and I could talk to here whenever I had anything to say, and that was nearly all the time.

3

It was the loveliest afternoon in my whole childhood. It was the only time I experienced the words "home, Mother taking care of me," and it became a memory for life. We drank coffee together quietly and ceremoniously. Mother didn't have any proper cooking pots. I remember that the pan we used for coffee was tin, and it cost fifty öre.

In the evening my stepfather came.

Mother and I had had our home one afternoon.

I could never stand my stepfather, mainly because he felt he owned my mother, and so he was mean to her, beat her, and then she had other kids that he was the rightful father of so I couldn't stand them either. When they died, for none of them lived a year, I cried in despair because I didn't like them.

One day when I was nine years old, I said to Mother, "I remember that I sat on someone's knee who wore an apron with wide red stripes, and I got raspberries and milk. Where was that anyways?"

Mother's face got white as chalk.

"What are you saying? You can't remember that!"

"Oh, *ja,* I remember there was a big table and a flower pot with yellow flowers, a whole tree it was with yellow flowers, and a stove with leaves in it, and a pipe that went from the stove to the ceiling."

"You don't remember who held you on the knee?"

No, I didn't remember that.

"Well, *ja,* it was me. It was the same day I took you from your grandmother's. You were only one and a half, the tree on the table was your grandmother's slipperflower, famous in the whole parish; it isn't possible you could remember it."

"*Ja,* but I do," I insisted. "I remember it, and if it was you, you stood with one foot on the floor and the other on a stool, and I sat on your knee, and you fed me raspberries and milk."

Mother looked almost scared. That's the trouble with little witnesses that you take no account of. Here it was only a question about something as pleasant as raspberries and milk, but life has so many sides.

I saw how preoccupied Mother had become, and instinctively I assured her that I didn't remember anything more, only that I had once sat on a floor and high above me were many black men. Although I saw only their legs, I knew the men were black. Then Mother looked even more scared and said, "It was the place where

4

we stayed the day after you had those raspberries. I got you room and board with a family next to the Bersbo mines, and the wife fed the miners. How much do you remember really?" she asked a bit sharply.

She had got red in the face. She couldn't believe her ears, thought I was a disagreeable kid who remembered what I ought not to know about.

"I took you from that place fast," she fumed. "You had to always sit on the floor in a draft, and you got the English sickness."

"I don't remember any more," I said diplomatically when I saw how upset Mother was.

I couldn't walk until I was three years old. I had, as my mother said, got the English sickness through neglect.

When Mother began work at the factory in Norrköping, she found a pediatrician, Doctor L., who cured me. My aunt maintained that my mother starved herself for two years so that she could pay for the cure. "There was such mollycoddling with that brat, it'd been better to whip her like you did with the other kids. They found a quack out at Qvarsebo."

Doctor L. had me at his own home for three weeks he was so interested in the case. It wasn't often that a doctor with a big practice does that for a factory worker's illegitimate child. And as if that wasn't enough, when my mother came down with typhoid at the same time, the doctor got me into Mamre Children's Home outside Norrköping.

I was there almost four years. I don't remember anything about the doctor or the cure of salt baths and good food and cod liver oil I had to take, but I do remember at the children's home that I got a whipping every day for all the bad words I said. And the more they beat me, the more I yelled and swore and said the worst words I could think of that I had heard from wagon drivers and gangs of boys.

There was good food at the children's home and really good care, but one day at dinner I didn't get any gooseberry pudding because I had sat at the table flicking bread crumbs with my thumbnail, just as I had seen a woman who boarded and roomed there slapping fleas.

I had to stand in the corner by the stove with a strap around my neck and look at the others shovelling that wonderful gooseberry pudding into their mouths. I yelled the whole time and said dirty words so they had to carry me out. When the doctor came the next day, he had to take me to town again, for they wouldn't keep me at the children's home.

I never told Mother I remembered that.

I was afraid she would think I remembered much more. I had seen so much of grown-ups' doings that I had a hazy idea Mother didn't want me to remember much, not even about her. But I'm convinced I hadn't become a "frost-bitten flower" through any possible sins she'd committed.

By her marriage with my stepfather, my mother acquired curious relatives.

They called themselves—the whole lot—"well-off" and they put on airs, or as they said, they were "educated." To be "educated" meant sitting on the grass and eating sandwiches and potatoes and meatballs and drinking beer and brandy while singing, "Here it is heaven to be."

Those relatives who weren't well-off were all of them decadent, black sheep. My stepfather was a black sheep, and all the relatives sighed with relief when my mother married him.

Now they'd be through with him. All the lies he'd bombarded them with, standing there, looking so foolish, in their shining kitchens, just to cadge the one and ten that a liter of brandy cost.

But now all that was over, now Albert was a married man, and if there was anything to the woman he'd got, Albert would be well-off and educated, too.

They managed the education themselves. We lived so handily close to town that it was an "idyllic" Sunday promenade for these "educated" town dwellers to walk out every Sunday and eat sandwiches and drink beer and sing, "Here it is heaven to be." The well-off part they helped out with, too. They dragged cast-off clothes, rinds of cheese, and bread crumbs, everything like that they could, out to us, "for in the country you can use everything."

One of them, an old spinster—the whole parish called her "Aunt"—was a seamstress who sewed for the most aristocratic families in town, going from house to house. One of her special friends was, of course, a very intelligent, esteemed Dean's wife, and "Aunt" was very fine and educated. I remember that she talked a lot about hot flashes and dizziness and that she fainted easily.

"Aunt" and the rest of the relatives who got the honor to be in her company came out on Sundays the first summer my mother was married and ate up every bit of our food. Everything that we would

6

have for the week. My stepfather was a day worker on the farm, earning eight kronor a week.

My mother worked out in the fields as long as it was light for seventy-five öre a day. And I had to take care of things at home as best as I could. But every Sunday sure as ever those fine relatives came, and you couldn't keep getting so many sandwiches and meatballs on eight kronor.

They usually had some cheap coffeebread with them. The male relatives, who were beer drivers or foremen at the factories, sometimes had a liter of brandy along. Those times, since the men didn't want the coffeebread, Mother got to keep what they didn't eat.

I remember so well the first time "Aunt" came. It was about two weeks after Mother and I had had our afternoon together.

I got a bag of cloth scraps "for your doll" and five öre.

"Poor Albert, who has to support a child who isn't his," the old lady said, shaking her head at her friends who were with her.

"Albert," my stepfather, and my mother didn't hear that, of course.

None of those people ever spoke out like that to the folks they spited; to their faces it was nothing but thanks and praise.

She pulled out Mother's dresser drawers, snooped in the cupboard, rubbed with her fingers to see if there was any dust exactly like the original mean old mother-in-law.

"Hedvig is very capable," she nodded when she saw Mother's little supply of tea towels, three sheets and other linens well pressed by the mangler, and nicely ironed men's shirts.

I was not yet seven, but I was hopping mad. Not any of them cared that I heard their gabbing and saw their shameful inspection.

A seven-year-old, especially if illegitimate, doesn't understand more than a three-month-old pig was their obvious opinion. All of those "educated" relatives were dying out; none of them had children.

My mother had slaved with all her might in order to have it like "Here it is heaven to be," and it was a blessing she got to borrow the kitchen because the oldest of the farmhands' wives in the house knew some of the fine guests and was impressed that a factory "bag of bones" had such grand company. And Mother prepared the food and got everything all ready, my stepfather helping, too, and soon there it was, the spread laid out on the cloth in the grove, all that eight kronor could get, and they sang, "Here it is heaven to be," the relatives picking flowers and being Bellman shepherdesses* and la-ti-da-ing all over the place, as my mother said afterwards.

"Get rid of that bunch, Hedvig," Grandma would say when Mother happened to see her. "Throw them out; they eat you out of house and home. You need to watch your pennies now."

Mother was expecting a baby soon, and she worked in the fields every day and had that "educated" lot every Sunday to wait on and feed, the food we should have eaten ourselves.

"Send them packing, Hedvig. When Albert was little, those high and mighties sashayed out every Sunday to see how he grew. He wasn't much to look at and they didn't care about the kid anyway; no, it was the food and being waited on they wanted. All of Vilbergen swarmed around those fools with their bouquets of flowers, exactly as if this burg was now a really big town, they became just like children, old people, all of them, when they caught sight of those shrivelled sticks coming to Vilbergen. I advise you to throw them out, Hedvig. They only lure Albert to drink again."

But Hedvig wasn't as sure of herself as Grandma. Hedvig had an illegitimate child, had slaved most of her life, had learned to curtsey and hold her tongue before fine and "educated" folks, and now soon she'd have another child and was so awfully tired she didn't have the strength to stop them. And anyway you couldn't treat guests that way. Mother kept on having the company until the baby came. A whole lot of stuff went to the pawnbroker's in town on account of those guests, for my stepfather thought everything became rosier with "Here it is heaven to be."

The baby was born on a Saturday, and Grandma stayed with us over Sunday. It was in August, and it is among my life's most agreeable, most triumphant memories when Grandma turned back that "educated" tribe filing down the grove. Seventy-two-year-old Grandma glared over her spectacles on her well-shaped nose. (Grandma had been one of Norrköping's most beautiful factory workers in her time—she was related only by marriage to those "educated.") She gave them her very worst scolding, asking if they didn't have any more sense in their numb skulls than alley cats when they let themselves hang around folks who had so little money and who worked so hard. "Hedvig lies there in bed, which I gave them myself, they certainly got nothing from you, though you were glad when your Albert finally got married. She lies there thin

*Bellman was a popular sixteenth-century Swedish poet.

8

as a rail, and her newborn doesn't even weigh two kilos, and it's your fault, for she has worked every day and would have had plenty of food, if she hadn't had to stuff it in you. Today anyway you don't come here."

The "educated" shrugged their shoulders. Albert's foster mother they knew well enough, she had no common sense, no education. And so they walked back to town again with their sack of twenty-five öre coffeebread.

We got out of having them the rest of the summer, and that was lucky, for my mother recovered slowly from having the baby. The doctor said she had been overworked and was half-starved. "That happens with factory workers," he said, "living on their watery coffee and bread, they slowly starve themselves to death."

The doctor knew that my mother had worked at the factory, but he knew nothing about those "educated." You can find a remedy for factory workers' bad food, for that's something that can be openly discussed, but you simply *have* to treat idiotic, pretentious people, for it just isn't polite not to give the last you have to "educated" guests. I have found it hard to tolerate well-off, unbidden guests ever since that time. You will find other people who probably aren't so "educated" and not so well-off that you'll gladly share the last you have.

At the same farm where we entertained all those well-off guests, one of our neighbors was a big, stone-deaf old man with a coal-black beard and fringe of hair. He was a binge drinker and had the d.t.'s a couple of times a year. He and his wife lived in an attic above us. The old man's name was Jonsson, but he was just called Jon. At every one of his drinking bouts, the farm workers said that Jon celebrated like at a wedding.

An insatiable curiosity seized me about that big old man who was as silent as a stone when he wasn't drunk. For a long time I stalked him, following him around, hard on his heels, not because I liked him or was interested in his "celebrations"—I had seen a lot of his kind of "celebrating" when I'd been roomed and boarded in those old ramshackle houses in the north for two years.

No, I was determined to inspect his ears close up.

Mystery had come into my life. Here lived a man who couldn't hear, who talked silently and never cared about an answer, for he didn't hear you. Only his wife could move her lips so that he understood words.

Of something like compassion for the old man I wasn't conscious.

9

Instead I was jealous about his interesting defect, and I had firmly decided I'd have to look into his curious ears that I'd seen sticking out from his black hair and beard. I had concocted a theory about Jon's ears.

The old man was accustomed to my being at his heels, sometimes giving me candy, and his wife, a bent old woman, who was also dark, became friendly toward me only because of the old man. He was so seldom friendly to any one, least of all his wife. On one of his binges, I happened to bump into him, but he only stood there, mumbling, "Little girl, little girl." The old woman who had been inside the entranceway had hurried out, for when he was drunk, he threatened to kill her. Now she stopped in her tracks, looking surprised. But the old man, catching sight of her, began roaring about death and the devil, and the old woman disappeared.

So I was able to follow him when he swayed up to his room. My theory was very simple. The old man just didn't have any holes in his ears, and now I would behold that phenomenon. Maybe I had a vague idea that I could talk the old man into letting me bore holes in his ears to his head. I thought it would be easy enough. Then he would be able to hear.

The old man filled a whole row of brandy glasses that were lined up. If it was water or brandy he slopped into the glasses I didn't know. Some of them he put on the mantel of the fireplace, and then skoaled to imaginary guests, shrieking, pretending to fence with his arms, sometimes fighting right out in the middle of the room with a chair. At last when all the glasses were empty, he sat quietly by the fireplace.

I knew my moment had come, and stealing over to Jon, sitting there with his eyes shut, I peered right into his ears.

There *were* holes in them. They were like anyone else's ears, and losing all interest in the old man, I wanted to get away. It was so dark and junky up there in the attic. I had a sudden longing for Mother's fine room with the blue-starched curtains, the vases that now had leaves in them, and my settee with the acorns.

But now it turned out that I couldn't get away. As fast as I neared the door, he babbled, "Little girl, little girl."

And I didn't dare to go, for he looked creepy. Now, since I had lost interest in him, I thought he only looked disgusting and scary, drunk, dirty, and ugly, and I had heard a lot about how he had cut the little old woman with a knife and how mean he was. My fright overpowered me. I crept into a corner.

Jon began skoaling and bellowing again.

I heard Mother calling for me down in the hallway to bring in the wood, but I didn't dare to answer. To carry in wood was the worst thing I knew. I would rather trail along in the fields the whole day than carry an armload of wood into the room. It was so unspeakably tiresome to carry in wood. But now I promised myself to keep the woodbasket full and do everything Mother told me if only I could get away. Mother called several times, and I dared not answer. The old man would probably strangle me, and if Mother saw that I was here, I'd get a whipping.

Now the old man sat by the fireside again. Every time he lost his balance, swaying on his chair, he swore and yelled and beat his fists on the chalk walls so that big chunks fell down, and the dust clouded over me in the corner. I sat huddled there a couple of hours. Twilight came, and the old man tumbled over onto the floor and began to snore. I sneaked out then, heading right to the woodshed and coming in with an armful of wood just as Mother was getting ready to search for me. She grabbed my braid.

"I walked down to the field to Unc—Papa," I said to mollify her.

"What were you doing there?"

"He wasn't there; I don't know where he is," I answered to avoid further digging in the subject.

"You don't go there without permission anymore, or you'll get a whipping." Mother looked stern and cross.

I tirelessly carried wood and didn't even hint for midday coffee which I'd missed, though I was so hungry that my stomach growled. "Confounded old man who has ears like that," I mumbled to myself. The next time the old man had gotten out of hand, the old woman came running, wanting to borrow Hedvig's little girl who could manage her old Jon when he had "delirium."

But Hedvig didn't loan out her little girl, asking instead if the old woman weren't out of her mind after all the "celebrations" Jon had held.

The deaf man who even so had holes in his ears was nothing to me.

But once something really strange happened to me. It was at the same farm when the "educated" clan was there in full splendor on Sundays, and Mother was a little tired and inattentive.

I wasn't any the worse for lack of food. Meals were always nothing but meager. If I got a fair-sized chunk of bread I could get along a whole day just so my playtime wasn't interrupted. There weren't any kids at the farm, mostly older couples and migrant men. But kids came from other quarters, and life was wonderful for me, for we had all the fields and forest to play in, and that meant something to you if you'd been used to only a corner in a town yard and hardly that.

Food couldn't, as I said, entice me to any grand prizes, but there was one temptation that could drive me to the path of crime, and that was hard candy to suck on. It was every kid's source of corruption around 1902. The rich as well as the poor. However much was displayed in the windows of treats and delicacies, hard candy was number one; after that came toffee. Hard candy's power depended, I think, partly on its enticing colors, partly on the shapes of the pieces. They weren't precisely or uniformly made, which might set them over other sweets. The pieces were roughly shaped with countless edges that secretly glimmered and looked as if they'd stretch to eternity to suck on. There was something generous about hard candies that kids understood who were used to sharing— careful, mathematical sharing.

One day I was sent to buy five öre's worth of yeast. It was nearly a mile to the store, the little store where the farm workers had credit. The town was nearer, but for children to walk there was too dangerous Mother had told me often enough. It was the town's outskirts themselves that were dangerous. The circus grounds lay by the tollgates, and just before the circus were the calf scales where the farmers weighed their calves on the way to the butcher's, and where they carried on something awful.

It was a tiresome, boring walk to the little store. I wasn't used to walking such a long way either, for in town you always had a store around the corner. It was a hot summer day. The heat quivered over the fallow fields and the corn. A flat, nearly straight path without a tree the whole way. It looked as if it'd never end. Exactly five öre I had, too, not even so much as one öre to spare. Four öre's worth of yeast you couldn't buy, for the storekeeper would think you had stolen it.

Tired from heat and thirst, I finally reached the store and drank water from the yard pump with its long trough underneath for the horses.

On the counter in the store gleamed a big glass jar of yellow hard candies. I wasn't sure if I had got sunstroke on the way, but I very coolly bought five öre's worth of hard candy and walked out without the yeast.

I knew that I had done something absolutely dangerous, but it felt as if that meant nothing. That I couldn't go home without the yeast I knew, and I didn't go home either. I didn't have an inkling about how I would solve the problem, as I sucked greedily on the candy, letting all else become something to think about later. I set off right over another field, coming out on Old Island Road which led to town, but I decided not to go on that road either. Perhaps I had got cross on that tiresome, long walk to the store, and the unreasonableness of not getting to go to the nearest store by the tollgates. What I would do in town I didn't know. Maybe look up some of the "educated" or my aunt whom I had lived with, and try to get ahold of five öre.

I perceived the hopelessness of that plan. Aunt lived on credit, never seeing a penny, for Uncle took charge of the cash. The "educated" would take me home. I still wasn't quite seven.

The hard candies lasted past the calf scales which were closed just then. They lasted past the circus; there wasn't a sign of people, the tent was empty, swings and merry-go-round, too. Everything looked sinister and so terribly lonely with only the ramshackle stands, their paint peeling off, the scuffed, lopsided animals on the carousel, and then the mysterious closed calf scales.

I sat on a bridge that went over a small stream on the way out of the circus and sucked the last of the candy.

A farmer drove up from Sankt Anna or Drothem or some place. Stopping at the calf scales, he took out a key, unlocked them, laid a little narrow gangplank from the threshold of the scales to his wagon, opened the calf stall, and dragged the poor animal by its tail to the scales. Then he dragged him by the ears to his wagon again. The calf bawled hoarsely as if it knew its fateful hour was struck, which it was, for in an hour a butcher in town would take its life. I sat there awhile, crying over the calf's bad luck and forgetting my own crime. When I realized that I couldn't just sit there forever, my tears stopped.

I began to reflect as I sat looking down through the spaces between the bridge planks, seeing things down there, cigarette butts, cards, rubbish. A thought came to me. I had never been to the circus, had no idea that poor folks ever since circus performances in Rome used to hunt for valuables dropped by the rich. So careless the rich were, they didn't need to take such care of everything. Here were big gaps, here perhaps people had lost money. That was one thing that all town kids were on to, and they crawled and hunted

13

under the bridge after every performance, but I believed I was the only one in the world who had happened upon this great idea.

I scrambled down in the dried-up stream and crawled under the bridge. I had always been terrified to crawl in any dark place. My aunt had never got me to go willingly down in their horrid root cellar for potatoes, not before she had soundly whipped me. She said I was lazy, but that dark hole truly scared me out of my wits. I trembled like jelly and could hardly pick up the potatoes from the basket, feeling sick for a whole day after such a journey. But now I didn't have even a thought of danger or uneasiness, though it was very murky under the bridge and all kinds of trash lay heaped there. I was seized with a zest for discovery. Snakes and frogs didn't exist, who were otherwise my night's horrors and my day's dangers since we had come to the country. Inch by inch I crawled under the bridge. And I found a twenty-five öre piece. I wasn't the least surprised that I found it. It was as it should be. I should find *something* after such an idea.

It was as if I'd been changed. The world had become another at one blow. Life wasn't as it was before; you could manage your affairs without grown-ups poking their noses into your business and standing with whip in hand and fingering five öre. A bit of hard candy wasn't impossible to get, but a voice warned nonetheless, and I walked to town and bought first yeast for five öre and then rolls for twenty öre. You could get quite a few rolls for twenty öre then, good rolls with cinnamon and sugar. I didn't buy any more candy, but I ate a roll, only one. What I would tell Mother, I didn't know. I ran as much as I could on the way home. It was already long after lunch time, and Mother had wanted to have bread for my stepfather's afternoon coffee. He who quarreled, and kicked up a row, and swore over the least thing. I sprang home.

Mother was boiling mad. She had made some pancakes and was rushing out with coffee to my stepfather in the field. She had torn off a big branch which she had ready. A whipping it would be, for she had got that from her father and she had become a well-behaved person. *Ja,* the illegitimate child was, of course, a minus, but maybe since she hadn't got whipped enough, she didn't spare me from them. Now I came along on that forbidden road to town and had been away five hours to boot.

"Are you going to whip me when I have these?" I asked.

"I'll give you this for that, *ja.*"

I held out the sack of rolls and the packet of yeast.

"Where have you been, young one?"

I made up a story that just popped out of me. I had come across "Crazy Oscar" (the parish idiot who was harmless and went free). He had sprung after me, and I had to run off the road to the little store, and I had lost the five öre and cried so awfully that a nice "uncle" had given me twenty-five öre, and I had flown to the tollgates and bought yeast and rolls since Mother didn't get to bake. Mother blindly believed me.

She had read, of course, as later in my life I had, about those obligatory nice "uncles" who always gave unfortunate girls the coin they'd lost. And so it was with poor Mother just now when her mouth watered as soon as she saw a sweet roll or anything unusually good that didn't come from their salary of eight kronor with those "educated" guests coming and eating up their food on Sundays. I saw that she took a roll and chewed it with a dreadful speed. Then she gave me the coffee basket, putting in three rolls but forgetting to take out the pancakes. I got to go along to my stepfather with coffee, and Mother gave me a roll on the way; I was forgiven and in high favor. And when my stepfather saw both rolls and pancakes in the basket in the middle of the week, he also was put in good humor.

"Hälsa hem och tacka!"* I had never heard him say that before.

Ja, so that day ended and ordinary days came again.

Most curious was the twenty-five öre under the bridge. I have often wondered about that as a grown-up, for at least a hundred children would have searched under the bridge after the last circus performance.

Perhaps it was another seven-year-old who had been sent to buy yeast and had lost her coin on the bridge and hadn't dared to crawl after it all alone. My inclination for mystery got elevated to unimagined heights from the incident, things of higher rank than a deaf ear that hadn't any hole. This was sheer enchantment, a help from above or from some troll under the bridge. I never made another attempt; in fact I became scared of the bridge as long as we lived on the farm. The day had been too many-colored, too much of a feeling of guilt in some way overshadowed my adventure. The only gleam of light was the twenty-five öre, and it was unexplainable.

*A hearty Swedish greeting, literally meaning "Greetings to the folks at home and thank you!"

Chapter 2

After living a half-year at the farm beside Old Island Road, we began moving here and there, and at that time I had to begin school.

I hated my first teacher from the first day when Mother enrolled me in school. I could read well and write a little before I began school, and both Mother and I were exceedingly proud of that. But the teacher questioned Mother in a superior tone about why I should go to school at all since I was so gifted.

"It isn't at all good that children learn to read at home, I must say, Madam. I am not happy at all about it, let me inform you, Madam."

Madam! No one had said Madam to my mother in all her life. The title had fallen into disuse. Only really old women and old broom sweepers at the market square were called that. My mother was just twenty-seven, carried herself well, and was young looking in spite of overworking at the farm and the years she'd starved herself at the factory. The teacher was fifteen years older at least than my mother.

The whole way home to the paper mill where my stepfather worked that fall, Mother crabbed about the teacher. I helped feed her irritation as much as I could.

"I ought not bother with school at all," Mother said.

"*Ja,* that's right," I agreed.

"He's begun to drink, so we certainly won't be here long," Mother said. "You can begin school at the next place."

"I can do that for sure," I said.

"But there would only be a fight about it, of course," Mother said, brushing away all the support I was giving. "She's now, of course, already got a grudge against you, so you must try to behave yourself as best as you can. Never answer impolitely, do always what she says, and learn your lessons! Whatever you do, never answer impolitely!"

"No, I won't do that," I said. And so we continued to fuss about

16

the teacher, Mother and I. We walked homeward so downhearted. We had set out to enroll me in school and get praise for having already got hard-won learning, but instead we had got mud in our eyes. It wasn't good to see so quickly how things were probably going to be.

I was quite clever in knitting and crocheting even though I was so young. Mother had been gone so much at work ever since I'd been born, and I had taught myself rudimentary handwork, knitting and crocheting, just as I had learned to read, a bit from one neighbor and a bit from the next, for the days got so long when Mother was away.

Even my ability in knitting became a minus for me with that rigidly proper teacher.

Most of us new beginners were from the paper mill, but some of the other students were tenant farmers' and hired hands' kids. They didn't have it easy. We kids from the paper mill were too fine to play with them—me, too, though I had just come from a farm. I caught on quickly. In some ways I was more of a town kid than any of them from the paper mill, though I had certainly thrived better at Old Island Road farm than in town. People usually aren't thankful for the blessings of nature.

The kids from the farms mostly played by themselves except in the fall when the apples got ripe. Then it was they who played high and mighty with their schoolbags full of apples, and we who had to stoop and be friends—you just couldn't find words for how we catered to them.

The school was held in a ramshackle house. Every year the factory owners talked about building a school, but it never got done; I don't think they built it even now.

The house had been an old-fashioned tenant cottage, having three big rooms. It had three entrances at the front. A family lived in the first room which was as large as the schoolroom that was in the middle. The school teacher lived in the third room. The school had thirty children in all. The room was six meters long and five meters wide. The desks were long, once painted black that now was mostly worn off. Six sat at every desk. When the one who sat innermost at the desk had to stand beside it and be disgraced or had to ask the teacher's permission to go to the toilet, all the rest had to stand and shuffle into the aisle so he or she could get out. We all stood there, making our disapproval obvious as well, adding to the kid's misery. I sat at the end, and that was lucky, for I had to stand by the desk

17

frequently. At the very first things were all right with the teacher and me. She had a tough job at the beginning to get the farm and factory kids together, for from the farm mothers she got thick cream and patties of home-churned butter, and the factory wives invited her for coffee. The one was as good as the other. She didn't have time for me at first, for she got neither coffee nor cream from Mother; we had nothing left over for that.

Behind me at the next desk was a boy named Alvar.* And truly no one fitted that name better. I never saw him smile. He was the tallest of all of us, his face deathly white with deep black rings under his eyes.

Tuberculosis flourished enormously at the mill.

The family who lived in the schoolhouse had two children afflicted with t.b., one in the lungs, the other in the hip. The girl who had it in the lungs was present sometimes, for she was of school age. Her face wasn't white, but yellow, and the skin was stretched over her cheek bones.

She never had strength enough to play with us. At our lessons, when she hoarsely coughed, the teacher sat looking constantly irritated at her, two fire-red splotches on her neck. All of us turned and tried to look as irritated also at the poor thing who hacked. I must admit that not one of us was noble, no one thought about that yellow wretch, so she suffered at disturbing our lessons and that exacting teacher who got those red splotches on her neck at the least noise from the children. We did as the teacher; we glared at her for her everlasting coughing. I never looked but I have a feeling that Alvar was the only one who didn't turn his head and stare with the same harshness as the teacher. He wasn't so anxious about having his lessons disturbed as the rest of us. One such impatient teacher often prepares the ground for a hundred other impatient teachers. When you're seven years old, the teacher is just about the only great authority you have to imitate.

Frequently, after such staring, the girl was gone for several days. In the spring that same term she died. We contributed to a wreath and sang at the graveside.

The teacher had two roses that she laid in that thin little skeleton's grave. The roses were like the red splotches that climbed up the teacher's neck when the girl had coughed.

Then there was Alvar. He never knew anything. He never learned

*"Alvar" means serious.

18

to read right. His clothes were so pitiful, always too small. Buttons were always off so that his shirt hung out of his fly.

He was so foolishly sweet, so angelically stupid that you could tease him to any lengths. I teased him only once, but that was more than enough. My cheeks still flush when I think about it. It was really pointless, but still I knew he'd get into trouble. And however it is, you try your best to get others into trouble especially if you, yourself, are often in it. It was nearly all the teacher's fault. And I turned against her from that day. She put an idiotic question to us. Here we were just beginners and she asked us what a domestic she-ass's foal was called. None of us had seen a donkey, not even in a picture. What a donkey's foal was called we for sure didn't know.

"It is either a ewe or a ram," I turned and whispered to Alvar.

In a flash he stood, holding up his hand.

"Oh, so you know that; that is certainly curious." And the teacher smiled sourly.

Red as fire I looked back at Alvar. His face was paler than usual. too late he grasped that I had whispered something crazy to him. He mumbled softly.

"Speak up, what is it?"

"A ram or a ewe," he said and sat down.

"Come here!"

Since Alvar sat in the middle, the others had to scramble into the aisle. I saw her pick up her ruler and how Alvar bowed his head, holding up his arm to shield himself. Jesus, if it only had been one of those well-dressed boys, it wouldn't have been so hard to confess, but this ragamuffin. I hesitated a second, but when she raised the ruler to strike him head on—she was, of course, too fine to hit him with her hand, not wanting to touch him—I yelled, "Stop, stop, it was me who whispered that to him!"

The red splotches spread up her neck, her face white and hard. I think it was that hard, frozen face that riled me the most. I can't stand hard faces to this day.

"Come here, you, too!"

I leaped up, sprang quickly as a rat out to the little entryway, snatched up my schoolbag, and ran home. "She was going to beat me," was all I said to Mother, who was in the washhouse doing the laundry for a foreman's wife.

"I'll give her a beating, I will," Mother said furiously. She knew at once who it was who had thought to beat me. Just then the foreman's wife appeared.

19

"Heavens, is school out already, and I haven't warmed up Anna's lunch."

"No, school isn't out. Mia ran home because the teacher was going to beat her," Mother said bitterly, rubbing the soap so hard on the cloth that the other woman probably thought she was being wasteful.

"A beating, no, our Anna never gets that, and Miss Andersson is such a wonderful woman. We couldn't get a better teacher. She often comes in and has coffee with us."

"*Ja,* coffee makes her neither better nor worse," Mother said. I saw how angry Mother was. She had no other choice, or the foreman's wife would have had to do her washing herself. But my stepfather had taken to sitting in Skull-Jon's tavern in town on Saturday nights, and there was just no money left over for home. So Mother said no more while she did the washing, though the foreman's wife lingered on, prattling in the teacher's defense. I munched on the sandwiches I had in my schoolbag, and then helped Mother, so I thought, with the washing.

The next day I had to sit in the "shame" desk the whole day, but I didn't tell Mother that. Instead I made up a story that I knew my lessons so well that the teacher patted me on the head. Mother hadn't asked why the teacher was suddenly going to beat me the day before, so I didn't have much difficulty getting her to believe me. Alvar wasn't there that day or for many days. He had had another lung hemorrhage.

Soon it came time to move again. Skull-Jon's tavern, the beer drivers, and my stepfather's job at the paper mill didn't go very well together.

Two weeks before we moved I really clashed with the teacher. She taught us handwork two days a week along with the bigger girls from the so-called folk school. We younger girls would knit mittens, the older girls stockings. Having already knitted my mittens in two handcraft hours, for we got to take home our work, I asked if I could knit stockings. The factory owners provided the yarn and other materials for handcrafts.

Though I had been in this school for four months, I had never got to recite my lessons. I was quick, very ambitious, and always knew my lessons. I was better at answering "free" questions than the rest, but the teacher most often pretended she didn't see that I had raised my hand. I sightread, the other kids spelled and sounded out the letters. I thought it sounded so lovely but it was just not possible for me to do that. One day when the teacher worked with me at least fifteen minutes trying to make me sound the letters, she got so angry that she hit me in the face, bloodying my nose. I said nothing, shielding my face if she should strike me again. She calmed down at once, hurrying out for a hand basin of water, and told me to wash my nose.

"Mother would get scared if I came home like this," I said, and the tears came.

Then she washed and carefully dried my face, turning to the class. "I didn't mean to do such a thing, but, you see, children, how disobedient Mia is. I *cannot* be patient with her." And then she sat down and cried. I immediately stopped crying. I went to my desk, sat down, and turned up my swollen nose. Not one more tear fell. While the teacher snuffled awhile and the girls stared disapprovingly at me, I got up and said,

"I won't tell Mother about this. I'll say that I fell down and hit myself."

I thought she was afraid of my mother. I was all wrong about that. She didn't care about my mother, she was afraid of other people's judgment of her. She rose, saying I could say whatever I wanted to my mother, and that if I weren't obedient from now on, I would be expelled from her school. After that day she hated me openly.

At a craft hour just before we moved, I asked her to help me turn the heel of my stocking; it was done a different way in school from what Mother had taught me. She took the stocking and began to unravel the heel. Leaning over to see better, I touched her little hair bun. "For shame," she shrieked, "keep your distance!" I went back to my desk without my stocking and sat down.

"Come here, and see how you should do this!"

I got up and went to her again. The other girls looked doggedly down at their work. "What have you done to your knitting needle?" she asked, drawing one of the needles in and out through the stitches.

"Nothing."

"The needle has hacks in it. What will this be for a stocking? The yarn is all tufted."

She showed me the needle, and there were really deep cuts in it. I knew that the needle had stuck in the stitches during the last craft hour, but it didn't occur to me to wonder why they did.

"Answer! What have you done to the needle?"

21

I was silent. I had done nothing to the needle.

"I am responsible to the factory store for all the things here for handcrafts, and you will learn to speak the truth. You have been an animal ever since you came here." She talked fast, the red splotches on her neck spreading all the way to the point of her chin.

I had to sit at my desk all afternoon. The teacher didn't get a word from me, not even a lie. I didn't know anything to say; I didn't know how the needle had got that way. It was at the most worth only two öre, but I was surprised about the hacks in it. The teacher forbid me to knit the stocking as long as I wouldn't confess; when I did that, I'd get to knit. I was completely stumped. It had happened so fast. If I could only have hit on something, even said that I had wrecked the needle, but I couldn't think how it had happened. I knew that I'd have to admit just how I had ruined it, but my ability to figure out how it might have been done must have dried up that day.

I didn't get home until it was nearly dark.

Everything at home was at cross-purposes. Mother was red-eyed from crying, my stepfather dejected and miserable; no one noticed when I came or if I had come at all. Finally Mother gave me a drop of coffee; that I hadn't eaten supper she didn't notice.

My stepfather had got a woman with child at the factory quarters where he was used to hanging around in his free time, and the woman had no better sense than to officially accuse him. The laws were rigid at that time that a mother with child could *not* get support from the father of the child if he was married to another woman.

The accusation papers had just come that day, and my mother was wild, for she hadn't had an inkling about the affair.

Ja, it was a dog's life. I saw my well-behaved Mother hit my stepfather again and again, and he gave as good as he got. The neighbors came and broke up the fight, but my mother had completely lost her usual modest way with the neighbors, driving them out and calling them names. That day the mill wives got to know how they stood.

"Holier-than-thou, you stuck-up apes!" Mother yelled. "Your kind doesn't even wash themselves once ever, out with you!"

My uncle, Mother's brother, had to vouch for my mother at the District Court, and the lovers, my stepfather and that poor woman who had four illegitimate kids already, were lucky that they didn't have to go to jail.

"The law would have put you in," Mother said to my stepfather. "But for Alma's sake who I worked side by side with and know how bad she has it, you'll get away with it. But if you do that ever again, you'll land in the hospital. You listen, do you hear? You'll be laid up a long time in the hospital!"

"Is that a speech for a wife to make?" asked my stepfather, who could be very plaintive when the situation required it.

"That is a speech for a wife to make," my mother said very firmly. "Think if you should take your fine Aunt, she who sits in the same pew as the Dean's wife, or, at least, on the same john, and the paper mill masters and all your fine relatives out to Alma in the south dumps where she lives with her kids in a hole, and tell how you got fired at the mill, and show them that last kid which is yours. I believe that should be enough for all of you." While Mother talked from the depths of her heart, my stepfather gave up the fight and shut up.

The next day Mother walked to town for the baby who already was six months old, but the little one couldn't stay with us, for my stepfather became like a crazy man, yelling and swearing, so that the neighbors came again. My mother had to take the baby back. It was a girl.

The whole time I had my own battle with the teacher. The stocking needle had become an obsession with her. Now I like a twig must be bent properly and become an obedient, decent child. She hung on for a whole week with me. I had to stand in front of her at her desk for all the lessons, and at every break she incited the others to shout in chorus, "Tell the truth, tell the truth!"

I couldn't eat or sleep. No one noticed at home, for they were always fighting about the law and the new baby. Every day I was glad to get away from that row, hoping that the teacher had forgotten the needle. No, indeed, each day I had to go up front and stand there.

"Shall we say morning prayers before you confess?" she asked. I was silent.

"Ja, then you won't get to say prayers with the rest of us, but just fold your hands!"

The kids were curious, wondering what in heaven's name I had done with the stocking needle. Stuck it through a cat maybe? Or stuck a person with it? They couldn't understand why only a needle had caused such a calamity. It must have been an attempt at murder at least. I refused to explain. I just kept silent, crying at home in my acorn bed at night. The story about my stepfather's baby had also got around the neighborhood, for one day in that week of hell when

23

I had to stay in as usual for the whole recess, one of the girls stuck her head in, saying in the most infernal tone, "In the morning you'll have to stay home and rock your sister."

That was the foreman's Anna. She hadn't lost her baby teeth, which hung like little loose tips in her mouth. Her hair stuck out every which way, and she had a little embroidered Dalarna bag that held a hankie, hanging from a red belt. I couldn't stand her because of that bag. I would never have one like it, so brightly colored. Only rich kids had such a treasure. Organ grinders' monkeys also had bags like that. They belonged to that black fur. I thought the foreman's Anna looked like a devilish monkey with her sharp little teeth when she stood in the door, making faces at me after her slurring remarks about my sister.

Toward evening on that same day, two of Anna's baby teeth were missing from her mouth, her purse strap was broken, and the purse was dirtied with clay, for I had trampled it in a wheel track.

The day after that the teacher got *her* idea. I had now had more than enough, never answered, threatened to fight as fast as any of the kids came near. Anna didn't dare to tease; she was afraid of another beating.

When school was over, the teacher called me. I think she was as tired of her everlasting fuss about the stocking needle as I. It sometimes happens that small-minded people get tired of themselves. Or maybe she decided that she could never drag out the matter if she didn't get off dead center, when I was stubbornly mute before all her questions. She had decided to put an end to the thing. She hurried the others so they'd be out of the way. They looked really scared, thinking I'd get whipped. She herself went out in the entranceway, watching to see that everyone had left. "Why are you standing here? Go home now!" I heard her say.

"Don't hit her!" That was Alvar. I could tell by his voice how frightened he was.

"Pfu," I heard the teacher sniff.

"Don't hit her! I can manage to get a stocking needle," he said high and clear.

"She won't get whipped. I want to talk to her about something. Go home now." And she stood there until Alvar had gone.

My spirits didn't lift at all by Alvar's defense. He was a no-account, trashy and sick. If it had been any of the other kids, the fine ones, it would have made no difference. A stocking needle, a lie about a stocking needle! It was such a pitiful thing I thought maybe

24

I didn't even remember it that well. A lie, that was when you bought hard candy with Mother's last five öre which she had to have for yeast, about such a thing I went home and lied. I knew nothing about the stocking needle. The whole crazy thing was so trifling I couldn't lie about such a scrap. That would be like admitting you took bread crumbs from chickens, *ja*, not even as much as that.

The teacher came back into the room and up to me at her desk. The stocking with the famous needle in it lay before us. She took out a big carving knife. That startled me, but I quickly calmed myself. It would be as it had to be. At home it was quarreling and here unbearable. I'd be lucky if only my head were cut off.

"You had the needle on the desk like this," she said, drawing the needle from the knitting.

Then I responded for the first time in my trial. "Now my stocking is wrecked as well!" I yelled. "Now it's unravelled!"

She looked amazed. That a kid could be such a monster she had never thought. I ought certainly to be meek now after a whole week's punishment. I saw that she kept swallowing, and I waited for a blow or a knife cut.

"I will thread the needle in and pick up the stitches if any have fallen out," she said softly. "You had the needle like this on your desk," she went on, "and you sat there thoughtlessly and made these cuts with your mother's knife in the needle, as you've perhaps forgotten," she added appealingly.

"Mother hasn't got a knife like that," I said grimly, but I began to catch on.

"Try to remember!" She spoke in a low, hoarse voice.

I was quite a long time.

'Well, *ja*, that's so," I finally said. Then she boxed my ears twice, and I got to go home for the first time that week while it was still light. We were well along into April.

My mother was home alone. She was red-eyed from crying and miserable. I was red-eyed from crying and miserable.

"It's just as well he's been fired so we can leave here," she said. Then she really looked at me. "Are you sick? Heavens, little one, you must have the measles."

I fainted. For several days I lay sick with fever. My head ached, and round and round danced stocking needles, knives, and Dalarna bags with showy roses.

When my stepfather heard the story later, he became quite self-

25

important. Here at least was a debt he could pay up. He had made the hacks, himself, in the stocking needle for his pipe. He'd tell that to the teacher so she'd hear it in both ears. He was almost fatherly to me, sympathizing with me, and promising he'd more than make up for it, it'd be the least he could do. A baby who had come unlawfully into the world and insisted upon his fatherhood, well, that was something else—he couldn't do anything about that. The law had freed him, though the law hadn't said a word about how he'd make peace with Mother or what that baby would eat. But both Mother and my stepfather had gotten tired of the whole sorry affair; there just wasn't anything to do. If money could be found for the economic side of the story, that could be managed; the ethical side is one in such situations that can never be worked out or explained.

Mother thought that the stocking needle was a good diversion evidently, for she said nothing when my stepfather dashed off to the teacher.

He came home at last and was all smiles. Oh my, oh my, the teacher was so sorry. She had invited him for coffee (my stepfather was very handsome, according to all the grown-ups), and she had cried. He had brought the stocking home, as well as cookies she'd sent for me, and she had begged my forgiveness through him.

My mother snorted at all that. I certainly wouldn't have to go to that school any more. I didn't eat the cookies.

So ended my experience with my first teacher.

The story was good for something—it was quiet at home for a while. Soon we would move and I'd be in a new school. I decided never to learn a lesson in that school.

Chapter 3

The next teacher was famous for her strictness. The school was called Holmstad and lay a mile and a half from Norrköping. My stepfather had taken a job as a ditchdigger at a farm near the school. The paper mill was about two miles father away.

There were children from the very poorest of homes, dock workers' and migrants' kids together with all those from the parish, and some from wealthy homes, too. So many of us weren't well-off that those "fine ones" had to follow us. Especially for me who had been an outcast for such a long time it was really uplifting to get favors from girls who wore lace collars and had those colorful Dalarna bags swinging at their sides. The boys here were mostly a ragged bunch, washed out and pale, but not like Alvar, serious and generous. They had learned their society's hard arts as helpers to the large gang out by Sandbyhov, that big flophouse for tramps from Sweden and foreign parts who taught these ten- to fourteen-year-olds English slang and their proudest art of rolling cigarettes. My male schoolmates, eight- and ten-year-olds, were already crafty scouts when it came to warning gangs of older boys of the police on horseback, who came riding, two by two, out by Sandbyhov as soon as it began to get dark. I was fascinated at first.

I came in the middle of the term at Holmstad with no expectations but also unworried about how I'd get along with this strict teacher. Looking me over, the kids drew back to comment, finding it hard to place me. I was fearless and outspoken, knew their jargon well, but most of them thought I was too fine.

My mother always kept me neat; only the Dalarna bag was missing, or I would have crossed over the line to those rightfully fine kids. But Mother never bought such a bag. She couldn't stand gaudy show. My hair was so long and thick for my age that on that count alone I would have been considered fine. A girl with a long, thick pigtail would always be accepted in the outskirt neighborhood.

The new teacher was a slim, tall woman of forty. Her hair was brown and curly, clipped short like a man's. A snow-white part right in the middle. Was the teacher beautiful or ugly? I thought she was very beautiful. To me she was the most beautiful being I had ever seen. The room was big, but run-down and smoke-filled, and I thought my first school looked splendid compared to this one. Big chunks of plaster had fallen off the walls. When I stood by the map of Jerusalem and Nazareth, which, of course, is a beginner's first acquaintance with geography, the pointer wanted to keep moving out on the wall among the plaster cracks and point out new, afflicted towns for Christ to heal, the whole wall was so much like a map.

I sat alone at a desk. Here the desks were only for two, and that it was no privilege to sit alone I understood from every kid's eagerness to get her friend beside her so no one would be tempted to sit beside the new schoolmate.

I had heard there would be another newcomer, but I didn't know if it would be a boy or a girl.

It didn't bother me to sit by myself or with a boy. The first teacher had used that as a punishment. When a girl misbehaved (it would be for only a slight offense), she had to move to a boys' desk.

But a boy never had to move to a girls' desk.

The short time I had her for a teacher I never understood why sitting beside a boy should be a punishment. It happened to me two times. I thought it was a happy change, for I got to sit right by the window and could look out. The teacher soon noticed that her punishment was a pleasure to me. The last time I offended, as I've said, I had to stand in front of her desk.

I quickly grasped why it was a shame to sit alone in this new school. Those who had lice had to sit by themselves until the teacher deloused them.

It sounds grim, but her method was just. What was she to do? So many kids with lice went to the school. Both body lice and head lice. The teacher took action at once when she saw that someone was crawling with lice. Washed their hair with sabadilla vinegar and had a change of clothes for them that she'd got in one way or another. So many poor little kids with lice she took down to her washhouse and cleaned up, got them clean underwear or shirt, putting their old clothes in boiling water. And then, of course, a note went along to their parents or the matron at the poorhouse or to the farmers who had foster children to "var så god* and don't send the children to school with lice." That was why the rumor got around that she was strict.

I sat and looked at my new teacher while she sat waiting quietly for the class to come to order. For the first time in my life I perceived a woman. An unknown woman. I experienced a feeling of anguish and chaos.

I had simply fallen in love with that dark, serious woman, and I felt this as a possible betrayal of my mother. My mother's little hollow face with her thick, blonde crown of hair flickered up, but I thought she was so awfully ordinary and gray beside this vision. I sat squeezing the note Mother had sent with me, a soiled note with poor handwriting. Everything Mother had ever done was more important than what had been abscribed to God, but now I suddenly could not hand in the note. I thought it was so dumb that I stuffed it in the desk. At the same time tears came to my eyes; I remembered Mother once when she cried.

I had seen her cry many times, but just this one time came to me now. She had sat at the table, her head on her arms, the little hairs on her neck straggled down, her bun of hair had fallen to the side, and when she lifted up her face to me, for she had heard me come in, it was so strangely twisted with anguish that I screamed. Just now I saw Mother's anguish-filled face so clearly that I thought I heard her sobs. Shyly I looked at the teacher and kept myself from crying. My mother's poor twisted face, the one I had seen a year ago, won over my new love for an instant. I took out the note from the desk and went up to the teacher. It just said that Mother was away doing washing and didn't have time to come with me. Next I gave her my report from my first school. It stated coldly that I had been there for five months. She read both it and my mother's crumpled note while I stared bewitchedly at her short curly hair and its white part in the middle. In a flash I decided to give Mother no peace until she chopped off my hair.

The teacher bid me welcome, taking me by the hand and looking searchingly at me with her serious eyes. I shivered with happiness. On the spot I would have done whatever she wanted me to do, but

*"Var så god" is the Swedish expression for "You're welcome." Literally, it means "Be so good."

she told me only to go and sit down. From my desk I fastened my eyes on her. To think that the next morning I'd get to come here again and the next and the next.

Just like that the stocking needles and all that foolishness vanished into thin air. In an instant Mother became only my servant who worked, made my lunch, starched and ironed my pinafores. I had three of them. My best one, to my misery, I didn't have on this day. It was dirty. Mother used to take them along with her in a little package and wash them when she did the washing for people, but today she certainly hadn't the package with her. Thinking about that, I became very annoyed with Mother. She should surely have seen to it that I was as fine as possible when I began a new school.

"There will be another newcomer," the teacher said in her sweet, perfect voice. For with the one you love everything is perfect.

"Are you there, Hanna?" she called out to the corridor where the door to the schoolroom stood open.

A little figure appeared in the doorway.

Little Hanna. Never have I forgotten you. You came into my heart, which was blooming with unselfish love for the first time. (Love only for a mother is always selfish. Mother is that necessary, everyday person, and my mother just now was only a washerwoman, a washerwoman red-eyed from crying who had wisps of hair straggling down her neck from her thick hairbun, while my new love had a snow-white parting in her curly brown hair. Feverishly I begged God that night for curly hair.) Hanna! A little figure stepped across the threshold and stopped in the doorway, her eyes looking down at the floor. I had never even caught a glimpse of her before; she had certainly hidden herself the whole time before the teacher called us to order.

Her hair was nearly white and so tightly braided that a little tail stuck straight out from her neck. Her face gleamed white as a flower the sun shines on, a flower that soon will be cut. Her face shone with light, a thin little face. She had on one of those jackets that was fastened in front with about thirty hooks. First you hooked its lining with fifteen hooks, and then those on the outside of the jacket itself. The skirt she wore reached nearly to her feet, much longer in back than in front.

Her bare feet stuck out, small and white, under the edge of the skirt. It was the end of May, summer heat in the middle of the day but a bit frosty as soon as the sun went down. None of the other kids were barefoot, and this was Hanna's registration day. She held

30

her hands tightly, tightly folded across what would be her stomach if any indication of it had shown in that snug skirt. I remember that her hands were folded so tightly that her knuckles were white. She was maybe three feet tall.

"Come in, Hanna, You have a new schoolmate you can sit with."

But Hanna didn't dare to move from her spot. The other kids leaned forward, nudging each other and whispering. They knew her. She was from the poorhouse at Vilbergen. Broom-Mina's Hanna, who used to trudge along to the marketplace and run with Mina's brooms to the houses because the women who shopped were too fine to carry home such a thing as a broom.

I looked at Hanna while the kids whispered and the teacher sat waiting for her. As if in a trance, I got up. I think I believed she was a beautiful little old troll without wrinkles (since I already read whatever I happened on, my reading matter was very strange). I went to her, taking her hand which she reluctantly gave me, laughing and talking the whole time as if I wasn't in school at all with an unknown teacher and unknown kids but alone with Hanna. Leading her to my desk, I whispered to her when I saw the teacher's smile, for she looked at both of us and smiled.

"You have to go up and show your report card. Do you have a note from your mama?"

"No," Hanna whispered.

"But your mama should certainly have written a note," I said in a reproachful tone.

"She can't really write," Hanna began, her lips trembling, for I had looked so strict.

"Come," I said, and that little barefooted figure in her ragged jacket with those thirty hooks trotted with her hand in mine up to the teacher.

The other children looked a little pale and scared. This had been a most unusual interruption; they should have had Bible reading for at least fifteen minutes by now. A pupil who talked without asking the teacher's permission they had never seen before. This would end dangerously.

I whispered to the teacher, "Hanna's mama can't write, and Hanna hasn't any report card. Please, kind miss, let her stay anyway."

"*Ja,*" the teacher said. "You needn't worry. She can stay." And she patted Hanna's skinned-back hair, so tightly braided.

31

I only wished that the teacher had chosen to cut off one of my feet or a hand.

We walked back to our desk again, and the Bible reading began. I don't know how Hanna had the lesson prepared, but she knew it. She stood there with her hands firmly folded, a tiny little person in a long skirt and warm jacket with puffed sleeves, rattling off in a single breath: "Abraham dwelt in the plain of Mamre. . . ."

I was in an uproar all day. I sat for hours, secretly pinching my arms, pulling my fingers nearly out of their sockets to prove how much pain I could stand. Some instinct told me that you had to endure pain without blinking or screaming when you loved someone who was so perfect as my new teacher. I had bruises on my arms long afterwards. My first day in school was definitely lucky, but I didn't feel triumphant. Deep clouds had rolled up in my mind. Outer success and attention had no value now. You don't crave attention from those you don't care about. I lay in bed that night, counting my acorns for a long time and pinching my forearm so that tears came.

"What are you doing, child? Say your prayers and go to sleep," Mother said crossly while she sat broodingly staring into space.

"I've said my prayers."

"Well, go to sleep then."

Just like that, according to the command. But though my eyes were full of sand, I pinched my arms still harder. The Catholic church's flagellating and telling one's beads had come to me without my even hearing talk about the pope. After love comes into the world, no church is needed. Love brings forth both confession and mortification.

No one, not even a child can go to sleep on command.

I, like so many others who have just fallen in love, lay awake the whole first night after such a wonder. I was so tired in the morning that I had to stay home from school.

I think it was lucky for me that Hanna came and shared some of the violent infatuation my new teacher kindled; otherwise it would have become a disaster. Even so, for a few days I was an egoist of the purest sort. I got a whipping from Mother, and that restored me a little bit to my usual self. It hurt enough that I could stop my self-torture. Quite simply I had asked her one afternoon about a number of things, for example, why did she no longer have alder cones in the vases? Why didn't she have cottage curtains for the only window in the room we now had? Why was our home never tidied up?

"And my best pinafore you haven't washed. I want to look like somebody. . . ."

"Like what?" Mother asked threateningly. "What are you talking about? Are you getting to be like 'him'? Shame on you! Is that what you're learning in school, to come home and be nasty to your own Mother?"

Now Mother was really mad. She couldn't put up long curtains here, the window was too little. Besides, the stove smoked, and she couldn't make the room as nice as the one at Old Island Road. No one was more unhappy either than she with the room. And so she took my criticism so much harder. But I had fantasized about having coffee in a fine room with long blue-starched curtains and a white tablecloth, and dreamed of seeing my beautiful teacher in that room on my acorn settee that now began to look really scuffed.

"What did the teacher say?" my mother asked suddenly. "Did you give her my note?"

"The teacher is so fine, she has short curly hair, she looks like the queen in Grandma's picture" (That was Crown-Princess Victoria).

Mother said nothing for a while.

"Couldn't you make it a little nicer here, too?" I ventured carefully. "And can I have a Dalarna bag? I want to look like somebody."

"I'll give you this for somebody," Mother said, giving me a couple of hard blows on my seat over my skirts. "Be satisfied with what you have, and be a bit ashamed of yourself. Every day I'm out slaving for folks washing all kinds of crap just so you'll have enough to eat."

Ja, so that was it! Having enough to eat, that really wasn't so important. The fight wasn't getting anywhere. I sat and sulked a while.

"You could have taken another guy, someone who would've taken care of us," I finally said. Once I had heard my aunt say that to another of Mother's sisters.

"Now you'll shut up," Mother said, and with that I got soundly whipped with a birch branch.

Hanna became my go-between in all my love for the teacher. There was no need of beatings or standing in the corner or anything like that here; the teacher never used such methods. The kids

33

obeyed her anyway. But I thought that no one loved her more than
I.

Hanna and I took over carrying in the wood when one of the boys
allowed us to. Hanna couldn't do much, but I had a good physique
and was sturdy in every way. What, for that matter, wouldn't I have
done for the teacher's sake? On every day we brought in the wood,
Hanna got to eat lunch with her. She never invited me for that. I had
coffee once with her, but I was in such a state of excitement over
being alone with her in her fresh, fine room that I began to cry, and
it was hard for me to cry.

"Little child," she only said, stroking me on my cheek. "Little
child, don't cry. Today you can recite 'Spring has come.'"

I went without drinking the coffee; she didn't insist that I drink it.
I often got to recite:

Spring has come, her garland weaves
the meadows. Blue lights the sky,
Willows bear yellow-gold sheaves,
Juniper cradles the elves' lullaby.

The poem was like a legend, and with the teacher's dark eyes
resting on me, as interested each time I recited, it became a legend.

A couple of the other girls tried to learn verses by heart, reciting
for me in the school yard and wanting me to ask the teacher if they
could perform. Oh, no, they had to ask the teacher themselves. If it
had been Hanna! But Hanna didn't like verse.

I didn't need to spell or sound out the syllables ever in this school.
When the teacher noticed that I read on sight, she encouraged me to
practice at home.

"Don't read carelessly. Don't read silently. Read aloud and
enunciate every word." I blindly obeyed her. And Mother thought
they were terribly long lessons that I sat rattling off late at night,
until she saw that I was reading a cheap paperback entitled *The Vestal
Virgins*. It was about ten American girls who were on a world tour.
Their secret lovers searched for them all over the globe, and they
were ambushed by Indians and grizzly bears, and they were
sometimes killed and then raised from the dead, and everything
happened that could, until in the last part, their lovers found them
and they all got married. It was a wedding of ten couples, and their
husbands were all discovered to be lords, even though they were
born in America.

34

My mother took the book away from me. I didn't get whipped, for the novel belonged to Grandma.

The fourth day I came home from school, Grandma was with us. She was then seventy-four years old. Grandma lived at Vilbergen, a little village quite far from town, squeezed between bare little rocky knolls. Old women who sold flowers and made brooms lived there, battling it out. Already at the end of May everything green was swept up. Not a windflower, not a straw could be found on the knolls. Straw and grass were picked and colored and sold to the housewives in town for their vases which stood beside plaster statues and savings banks. Pine needles, spruce branches, juniper twigs—everything was sold. The village would have been like a desert but for the garden patches around the houses. Little houses, little gardens, little flowers. There wasn't room for bushes and trees. Mignonette and sweet peas in garden after garden. That was their specialty. The other, more expensive flowers the gardeners brought in big wagons to the marketplace. Pines and hardwoods grew all over the countryside, stripped bare like the knolls after the thieves had gone over them.

The trees' fate is often like people's. The trees depend on the place where they stand, must let themselves be handled in whatever way just so they can remain. The root-grown is plundered for bread for the "free." All are dependent upon their roots. Even the winds are rooted some place. The wind doesn't go where it will. It was only that melancholy king of Judah who asserted that and was believed because he was king.

"Last night they stole my wormwood," Grandma said, dishing up potatoes and pork for me. Mother was out scrubbing. Grandma had wormwood and salvia, some crocuses and jack-in-the-pulpits. Year after year, however carefully she watched, her flowers were stolen and brought to market. Her lilac bush which was unique in Vilbergen—it was a Persian lilac—was plundered every year. The flower women couldn't let it stand there in all its splendor in the midst of devastation; it represented bread, newspapers, a cup of coffee, or some necessity. Grandma spit to the left as soon as she met an old market woman, looked critically in her basket, and didn't answer her greeting.

"They'll become fat enough now they've stolen my wormwood," Grandma crabbed while I ate. "How are you getting along in your new school?" she asked, turning away from her feud that she knew well enough I wasn't interested in.

I told her how wonderful everything was and about the teacher and Hanna.

"Who is Hanna?" Grandma asked sharply.

"Ja . . . they . . . her mama is Broom-Mina," I answered, hesitatingly.

Grandma's old cheeks reddened, and she didn't say a word. I got scared. What in heaven's name was this now for craziness? Hanna couldn't very well help that Broom-Mina sold brooms and lived in the poorhouse. I got mad at Grandma.

"Hanna is very nice," I said loudly and defiantly.

No answer.

"The other kids think so, too." (That wasn't really true, but what can you do to convince people?)

"You'd best do your lessons," Grandma said, still looking cross.

Grandma was always kind to me, and she was very close to my mother. My stepfather, her brother's son and her foster son, she regarded as the most pitiful being who ever walked in a pair of shoes. She wasn't a biased mother-in-law. But, as she said, blood is thicker than water.

"Poor you, Hedvig," she often said to my mother. "He couldn't be anything else. Such a mother as he had and a father who never was sober."

My stepfather's mother was a factory worker, a half-sister to one of the "educated," that highly esteemed seamstress whose good friend was the Dean's wife. That half-sister, my stepfather's mother, "got more bad habits from those rich, overdone birds than she could handle," getting involved with Grandma's brother, who was a chimney sweeper, when he came to see Grandma. It was in that way that Grandma had gotten those strange relatives. The two women, Grandma and my stepfather's mother, had roomed together and worked at Drag's factory in Norrköping.

It was very funny to hear Grandma tell Mother about it. "'God, your brother's so marvellous! God, he's so handsome! Your brother's so sweet to me! God, but your brother's wonderful!' You watch out for my brother! Be careful, and don't receive him when I'm not here! There are many who thought he was handsome and got soot for it. Sleep with a drunk chimney sweeper and you'll get only soot for your trouble," Grandma had warned.

Both women worked night shifts at that time, and when Grandma was on her shift, the chimney sweeper obviously was received.

"Only a couple of months afterwards, I didn't hear anything else but wailing," Grandma related.

"Your brother doesn't come anymore. Have you seen anything of your brother? Now he doesn't come to see me anymore."

Grandma stopped talking and spit three times to the left.

"He had more kids, you see, Hedvig, but those other women at least took hold of things better. They managed quite well, marrying other men, but this here jade was the silliest woman I've seen in my life. I was a widow for the second time, childless, and was going to marry again. When she had the baby, I took him and wrote to the Captain [Grandma's oldest brother was a captain] through the consulate, explaining how things were, and he helped me with some money for the baby's care. Although it'd been better if I'd thrown the kid in Motala stream and done my time." She used to end the tale like that, looking grim.

Grandma always expressed herself dramatically. "Otherwise," she explained, "people won't listen to what you say."

"They had no other kid than Broom-Mina's to sit beside your girl in school," Grandma told my mother that night.

Mother looked embarrassed, her face getting all red. Then I knew that something was really wrong.

'I'll go to school in the morning and change that," Grandma said.

I was beside myself. I began to scream without crying. At the top of my voice I screamed, hitting my clasped hands on the table and stamping my feet.

"Are you mad, child?" Mother said, shaking me. But I just screamed until I got a nervous shock or whatever it was, beginning to hiccup and vomit. Both Mother and Grandma got frightened and talked soothingly to me. Grandma would *not* go to school; I would get to keep my Hanna.

After I had vomited, I calmed down, and putting my arms around Grandma's neck, I said, "I like Hanna so much, so very much."

Then Grandma began to cry, but Mother looked cold and unmoved.

Through quarrels and gossip at home, I later got some inkling about how the matter lay. At one time my stepfather, too, had gone out with Broom-Mina, and everyone believed that Hanna was the result.

That was several years before my mother went with him. Grandma though had to bear the brunt of the scandal from all of

Vilbergen for the sorry tale. Grandma had forced him to enlist in the army right after Hanna was born, so he'd learn how to "behave."

"And he can behave himself if he wants to, for he became batman for a captain, staying with him the whole time he was in service," Grandma sometimes said with a certain pride, looking full of hope. That you could just move about as you wished even when you were in the army Grandma believed, of course.

"He would have gotten on well with the regiment, there are so many lazy bones," Mother said once.

"*Ja*, he was lazy enough after he'd come home from it, fat as a pig he was, too, but he'd got a fine report. He tried being a policeman for awhile." Grandma's tone was still a bit proud.

"*Ja*, go and pound the pavement and stand on the corner, he's shown he can do that," Mother sniffed.

"He can work if he wants to, Hedvig."

"When he wants to, *ja*, but hardly ever when he's had to. I've learned to work whether I want to or not. That's what all of us must do who don't own anything."

Grandma nodded, looking determined.

Life was work; that much had become clear to me.

So they sat, each with her own thoughts. I was really cross that now they seemed so preoccupied with my stepfather. I felt left out. For sometimes in the evening when Mother moved silently, quietly about the room, Grandma would talk about her life. She became so big and strange then that I understood she was old, many, many years old.

Grandma talked about her brothers. This was more than a fairy tale, this was life, strange, curious life. Think of having such brothers! In Grandma's house their framed pictures hung on the walls.

One of the brothers, an old man, wore an American captain's uniform. He had four medals on his breast. (I have the picture on my cottage wall now. Though it is faded and much the worse for wear, the American eagle is clearly visible on the four medals.) He had won them for merit on land and sea, having taken part in the Civil War. He had also sailed a ship for many years for the East Indian Company. He was twenty years older than Grandma.

The other brother wore a chimney sweep uniform. He was younger than Grandma and my stepfather's father. He also had medals, two of them, on his sooty frock.

"That I know life, you have to believe, Hedvig. I know what life is. You don't have it easy, Hedvig, but . . . We lost Father and Mother at the same time when cholera swept the town. My brother and I had to go to that devil for a relative who took everything from us. My older brother, the Captain, had already gone to sea. Though he was our father's flesh and blood brother, he took our parents' farm and everything. *Ja,* you've seen the farm, Hedvig, you know the ones who live there, inheritors for three generations, but there isn't much happiness there, as you know. [I knew where the farm lay, on the outskirts just before you got to Norrköping. Snowball bushes and a pear tree with the yellow hills behind them.] For me to have a sweet sister, Hedvig, oh . . . she was seventeen years old, and one night she stayed out late with her friend, and she got whipped for it."

("Only one night she stayed out late with her friend," I used to whisper to my poor, homely doll.)

" . . . she was whipped. I was twelve then and my brother was nine. My uncle beat her with a rod on her naked back. She was grown, but she was beaten naked, for that Satan was religious. We heard, brother and I, how she cried and groaned, and we began to yell, and then we were whipped, but she, our big sister, was whipped naked. 'You whore, you will be on your knees for three hours and pray Our Father, you will go through your Gethsemane, you will be cleansed. . . . Your parents died of cholera because God was angry with them, and you are a sinner and bring bad luck to our house.'"

Grandma spoke in a deep hoarse voice when she imitated that zealous uncle.

"'Lie there and sweat blood, you whore!' Everyone in the whole neighborhood heard how he roared and carried on, but mostly just poor folks lived thereabouts, no one dared to come to her rescue, no one, no one.

"Late at night sister climbed up the stairs to us. 'I'll go down to the river and wash my back, it burns and hurts so I think I'll die if I don't get some water on my back.' She climbed out the window. We had been whipped, brother and I, and didn't dare to go with her. All alone she dragged herself there. We thought she'd go to see her friend. But she didn't do that."

("We thought she'd go to see her friend," I wove it here and there when I told the tale to Hanna.)

"No, she didn't do that. She went all the way to Abacka and jumped in. All that way she walked in agony, three whole miles.

Folks used to go and drown themselves there, so the police had their eyes on the shallows just before the rapids, for they found her the same day. But do you think, Hedvig, that the police said anything about her back that was shredded to pieces? No, nothing."

("Do you think that the police said anything about her back that was shredded to pieces?—no-o-o, nothing," I said to Hanna. And Hanna sobbed while I thought revengeful thoughts against the police.)

"They carried her to the morgue and we had to go down and look at her and identify her as our sister. Her back, Hedvig, never will I forget it—I am seventy-four years old now, I was twelve then—like a washboard her back was, big weals, one after the other. But no one had seen that. No one wanted to see that. Children were whipped in every home at that time, a back that was shredded to pieces, well, they thought that wasn't anything special.

"It was because sister was whipped naked by that devil that she took her life. Her friend didn't dare show himself. She was buried without her friend, where I don't know, for brother and I ran away the night after they found her in the river. No one looked for us. They were glad to be rid of us, that's for sure. Then the farm would become theirs, for no one knew where the Captain was. *Ja*, Hedvig, what I have since walked through, crawled through, sprung through—mostly tried to slip around, but that never works—always you must go through it.

"My youngest brother was a chimney sweep by chance just as I became a weaver by chance. I was very near to becoming something else. . . . After brother was fourteen years old, he wasn't sober a day. Then he drifted around as a journeyman in Belgium—for that episode, I scraped together money, going in an old tub of a boat, and took him home again. *Ja*, drink had completely ruined him. He couldn't live without drinking. Couldn't really work without brandy. I tried to drink, too, for a while that first year. I was thirteen years old and taking care of the pigs at Stegeborg, that was my job, pig-maid. At that time brandy was dirt cheap and there was plenty of it. But it's good that drink isn't the way with us women."

("It's good that drink isn't the way with us women," I used to instruct Hanna.)

"My brother was all I had, the only one that remembered Father and Mother, who knew that the green-painted farmhouse was our home. But he only drank, sang and drank. He was handsome—you could see his fine looks in the kids he'd fathered. He never owned anything more than what he stood in, his chimney sweep uniform, but the women, both better and worse, were crazy about him. He got medals, too. He rescued folks from certain death in raging fires. In Linköping, he carried a priest out at the very last moment. 'It wouldn't be right that you, a priest, should burn up like any other poor devil in hell,' he'd said with the priest on his back, and folks had grinned. "Lasse in Bråvika"* wrote about him. There were no fire departments then, chimney sweeps were firemen. My brother never knew what he was doing since he was never sober. He burned to death in a fire in Malmö when he was thirty years old. He died for a mutt. The dog barked and howled in the burning house where they'd been lucky to save most of the stuff. A woman who looked after the dog cried, begging him to try to save the dog. He was like wax for women, and both he and the dog burned to death. That was also in the newspaper. Albert here was then a little over a year old. Just the year before, the Captain had found us through the police. Thanks to the chimney sweep's brave feats, the police had managed to find both of us, and that was lucky, for we weren't in the public register. Our robber of an uncle had seen to that, but he was dead by then and couldn't, of course, be called to account. According to the official guardianship papers, everything had been used up for 'the children's upbringing.'

"You should have seen my brother, the Captain, Hedvig. What a man!

"He was gray by then, had medals and a uniform so he did, but even so he cried like a baby when I told him about my sister's back.

"'My sister whipped like a black slave,' he yelled. 'I was in the war to free the slaves, and then I find the same white devils here at home. Our own uncle, old prayer geezer we called him when we were little, for whenever he came to see us, he always was saying prayers. That was why he prayed, he wanted to have our father's inheritance, too. He prayed well, he got everything. He wanted you dead, too. He intended that, sure as can be, the mad devil. If they'd lived, he and his cowardly mouse of a wife, I'd have hung them on the yardarm of the ship that lies here at Arkö, hung them as a warning to the whole town. We were related to the town magistrate here—couldn't anyone do anything, couldn't anyone help you?'

"'No one who knew anything would do anything for brother or

*Moa explains in a footnote that "Lasse in Bravika" was a well- known feature writer in the newspaper *Ostgöten.*

41

me. No one troubles much about a couple of kids. Folks value only what they can claim, can lay their hands on. You know that well enough since you lived here in this town once,' I told the Captain.

"If you'd seen my brother, the Captain, Hedvig, then you'd have seen a man for once. He's been dead a long time now. He couldn't stay that time more than a few days. I never saw him again. He sailed ships in all the world's harbors, and in America they wanted to pay him good wages to be in their army. Before he left he gave me a savings account of one thousand kronor to bring up Albert, our brother's son. I've taken care of him as good as I could. But there's the stock he comes from, and then his crazy mother's relatives who poked their noses into everything. They never gave him anything, just the opposite. They wanted to handle the savings account I got from my brother. *Ja,* Hedvig, that's life for you, for all us folks. . . . Albert is the only blood relative I have left, and he's not much, so he isn't . . . but there's something sweet about him; his father, the chimney sweep, was sweet in spite of his drunkenness. Drink and loose women destroyed him. Albert wants to go the same way, but he's married to you, Hedvig. I believe it will be good in the end, you're so different from the women he's gone with, he'll come to steady himself. You have to get through it whether you want to or not, or else do as my sister. I've often gone to Abacka, Hedvig, stood there staring down in the water . . ."

("She didn't go to her friend," I whispered, when I should have been asleep.)

"Say your prayers out loud," Grandma said. But then I pretended to be asleep.

I can't remember that I had ever been so close to a playmate as Hanna. And even so she never could play.

When finally, by endlessly pestering Mother, I got to bring Hanna home, she just sat quietly in my play corner, listening to my chatter, looking at my simple toys so seriously. I had turned the commode into a doll cupboard. I had something that could be taken for a doll, of course, but that didn't interest me much. I had other things, a lot of cards and shells about which I told such strange stories that Hanna was completely paralyzed. Mostly the stories were about sea captains and chimney sweeps.

Mother had outdone herself in making that ugly room look good, and she was so nice to Hanna. We had settled on a day when we

42

knew Grandma wouldn't be coming, for you could never know how she'd have taken it.

Mother gave Hanna one of my outgrown dresses, already doomed to become carpet rags. Patched and worn and just cotton but at least not sewn thirty years before like little Hanna's old dress with its thirty hooks that had been taken from the old clothing barrels at the poorhouse. A white apron that Mother had sewn not long before she got, too. It was already too little for me, for the remnant hadn't stretched far enough. Mother dressed her, combed her hair, and tied a posy in it, letting a little curl hang loose.

She looked so sweet. That she was barefoot meant nothing, for all the kids went barefoot now in the heat, Sundays as well as weekdays.

We showed her the mirror. She looked quietly at herself for a while.

"Mia is best in school. The teacher likes Mia the best," she said to my mother. I saw how her mouth trembled with shyness.

That was her thanks. And Mother knew that. I had become so closed-up and stingy toward Mother about everything that concerned school since my first beloved day there, but now I began to feel warm and generous again to her. Mother's friendliness to Hanna made me happy.

Mother gave us ryebread sandwiches and cocoa. Not ordinary cocoa but real stuff from cocoa nibs. We bought them by the sack near the harbor in Norrköping.

The next day Hanna came as usual to school, her hair drawn back, its stiff little tail tied with a piece of yarn. She was wearing the ancient top with its thirty hooks and the old woman's skirt.

At lunchtime I asked her why she wasn't wearing the dress and apron instead of these insufferable clothes.

The matron of the poorhouse had told her that those clothes should be kept for graduation ceremonies and that it was sinful to wear your hair loose.

We were powerless, both Hanna and I.

One day Hanna wasn't at school, or the next day either.

I roamed about all alone. The teacher needed no wood now in the warm weather, cooking her food on a kerosene stove. I scuffed about, sulking and refusing to play. The kids got fed up, and one of the "better" girls said that I was "simple" since I wanted to play only with Hanna.

"Simple?"

"*Ja*, because Broom-Mina is simple, and Hanna is, too."

A refreshing fight then followed, for in my school days and in my surroundings it wasn't only boys who fought.

The next day Hanna came, red-eyed and sorrowful. She wore my old dress and the white apron, and a narrow black band that looked like a shoe lace was knotted around her stiff little tail of hair. Her brother had died. She had gone with her mother to his burial.

Hanna's brother was Alvar.

I was very quiet the whole day. I never told her that I had been to school with him, teasing him to say that a donkey's foal meant the same thing as a ewe's. But I doubled my tenderness to Hanna. I cried with her as if it had been *my* brother, and my rare tears made the other kids serious. The poorhouse warden had apprenticed Alvar to a tenant farmer who also worked at the paper mill. "I can give her a stocking needle," he had said. I remembered his voice. "Don't hit her."

Now he was dead.

That night I prayed to God properly, not about curly hair, not about any advantages at all. I asked Him for forgiveness because of Alvar. I think I mourned Alvar more than Hanna did, for she had never done him an injustice or played the bully. I had. That's what makes sorrow after a death bitter.

Chapter 4

"White horses stand in the stall,
Stretch, spur, spear in hand.
Minne mashes all her cakes.
Apples, raffles, root, toot, shoot."

"Ester's hid. Use another count, Mia."
"No, then it'll be uneven. You have to use the same count."
"No, use 'Annika, vannika.'" It was Hanna who yelled.

"Annika, vannika, Södervalje,
Heckle, hackle all the judges.
King Karl, general,
Wanders through the silver hall.
Eight days till the knot's tied
Dance, Annika, vannika, bride."

"Mia's hid. Hanna, you count!"
Hanna knew only "Eenie, meenie."
"Heck, we're not playing that game. We can't use that. Hanna just can't count. Mia, count, even though you're hidden."
Hanna's face was blood-red; her little pigtail nearly drooped on her neck. But it was always the same. Before I could stop it, someone always saw to it that Hanna had to stand there and be made fun of while my skills were touted.
"We won't play hide-and-seek. It's so dumb. Let's play a dance game!" I yelled.
I was often taken into the ring in the dance games, and then Hanna got in, too, for as soon as it was my turn to choose, I took her. But it was hard for her in hide-and-seek. She never could find a hiding place and was always caught. She sprang on her bare feet so you could see how her heart pounded in her tight jacket, but she could never get away. I suffered with her when I saw how Hanna would hunt for a place and always be caught.
"We'll play a ring game; otherwise I won't play."

45

"You're so stuck-up."

"Recess is nearly over. We won't have time to play hide-and-seek. Teacher gets cross when we hide ourselves and don't hear the bell." Some had already begun clasping hands, forming a ring. Even the ones who had hesitated joined it, but Ester, who had called me stuck-up—she was one of the leaders—stayed out of the ring and pouted.

"You begin, Ester. Let's do 'Fair Lads.'" And Ester couldn't resist, skipping into the circle and choosing the storekeeper's daughter, a sweet, quiet girl who belonged to her own class, for Ester's father was the foreman on the same farm where my stepfather was a ditchdigger. Ditchdiggers hadn't been ranked yet; you didn't really know where you stood. Draindiggers were nearly skilled workers, but a ditchdigger wasn't quite the same—my rank was up in the air in that school. That we were very poor they saw easily enough, but I had no brothers or sisters and always had a bit of food with me. They didn't know exactly where I lived.

It was plain as day with Hanna. No storekeeper's or foreman's daughter took anyone like her in the ring, not anyone with that rat tail and long skirt and crazy jacket.

When it was her turn, the storekeeper's daughter chose me.

"A fair lad needs a friend
—peonies and red roses—
for roses red and lilies blue
were all my heart could offer true
—peonies and red roses."

Hanna became numb as usual and remote when she came into the ring. The song was nearly finished by the time she got hold of herself and chose, some of the kids calling eagerly, "Choose someone, Hanna, take someone!" At the last second when we were singing the last line in the verse, she made up her mind, and always it was me she dragged again into the ring.

There were kids almost as poorly dressed as Hanna, kids who greedily hung close to you, their eyes begging when you ate your margarine sandwich or, like the storekeeper's daughter, a fine liverwurst one, but Hanna never dared to venture near, either to rich or poor, no one but me, and even me she was scared of sometimes.

One day something awful happened to her. She had forgotten to go to the toilet during recess, and already at the beginning of the hour it was urgent for her to ask to go out. And that she dared not do. I saw something was wrong with her and whispered, "Have you a toothache?" She shook her head.

"We will write now and not whisper," my slender idol said at the front of the room. She was very strict with me, stricter in fact than she was with the other kids, but in return was much closer to me than to them. I never felt sad about her reprimands. I think I liked them. I think I only cared that she paid attention to me even if I were reprimanded.

Now I wrote industriously, not looking at Hanna anymore. Suddenly Hanna got up, stammering something, and we all heard how it ran down her legs.

The teacher's face became dark red. "Go out, Hanna," she said only. "Continue to write," she said strictly to all the curious kids straining to look at Hanna, some of them grinning. Hanna tiptoed out. We wrote and wrote, the teacher walking between the rows of desks to observe our writing. We couldn't get a chance to look back toward the door that stood open if Hanna should come tiptoeing in again.

But the hour went by, and Hanna didn't come.

When recess came, I ran around searching for her. No one helped me. The others stood in clumps giggling, and a boy yelled to me that Hanna went home to get dry underpants.

"She doesn't have any underpants," the foreman's daughter screamed.

But I scarcely heard their taunts. Anxiety was nearly choking me. I imagined that Hanna was dead. I didn't hear when the bell rang. I ran farther from school, searching the bushes down by the privy, scrabbling into a deep ditch, tramping up on the road a long way and calling. I asked a fellow I met if he'd seen a girl with a long skirt and a little braid. No, he hadn't, but even if he had, I belonged at school, for the bell had long since rung. I ran back as fast as I could, maybe Hanna had come during recess.

Red-faced and sweaty I came in. The others were at their desks, their slates in front of them. I didn't look at them or the teacher either. I saw only that my desk was empty, that Hanna wasn't found.

"Go to your seat, Mia, and take out your slate. Write the numbers that are on the blackboard."

I obeyed mechanically, getting out my slate, but then I just sat there staring. The teacher said nothing. She didn't come down to me to see if I had done anything, didn't ask about Hanna. All of a sudden I began to hate the teacher. For about ten minutes I hated her so that I wanted to spring up and scratch her face, pinch her, force her to ask me to go and look for Hanna, go to the poorhouse and see if she had gone home. Hanna was surely dead lying at the railroad crossing where a child had been found a year ago, and where a farmer from Å parish had been run over. Or maybe she had been eaten up by the dog at the storekeeper's—she had to go past it on the way to the poorhouse. A dog so big and bad-tempered that he'd been written up in the newspaper *Östgöten*.

I sat there hating my beloved teacher for her indifference to Hanna's misfortune. I knew how afraid Hanna was of the dog. Often I had walked her past his place; I wasn't afraid of short-haired dogs. This one was smooth as a calf. For long-haired, shaggy dogs I was endlessly afraid. I knew how terrified Hanna would be to come back here, and now the teacher was like a stone and was mad at Hanna only because of the terrible thing that had happened to her.

I decided that as soon as recess came I'd go out and look for Hanna and not come back until I'd found her. When the hour passed, my slate was empty, not a number had I written. I was so disturbed that I just let the slate lay on top of the desk, a witness to my indifference.

Just as I was on my way out, the teacher called, "Mia, come here. I want to talk to you. The rest of you go out."

I hesitated. Hate flared still, but I couldn't resist that voice. I turned so fast in the doorway that I knocked into one of the girls who began to cry because she'd hit her nose. I felt no pain myself, though my cheek was blue the day after and was tender for a long time.

"What happened?" the teacher asked. The girl only sobbed. I thought she was just showing off. At that time I thought everyone who cried and complained like that did so to show off. "Is your nose bleeding?" the teacher asked.

Dear God . . . I paced back and forth while the girl sniffled. "I think so."

Taking my apron, I wiped her nose with it quite roughly. "It isn't bleeding," I yelled. "Go down to the pump and put cold water on it." I pushed her out into the corridor.

That looked mean. The teacher followed us out and saw now that the girl's nose wasn't bleeding. Then I had to beg her pardon. "You ought to do that when you bump into people," the teacher said seriously.

"I'm sorry I did that," I said, trembling with anger and impatience. I suspect most folks ask for pardon in that state of mind.

The teacher and I went back into the empty schoolroom. "Mia," she said. Then she looked at me and was silent. She didn't say another word.

"I'll have to go now," I said after a while.

"Where will you go?"

"To look for Hanna. She's certain to be dead now, the train's run over her or the dog at Helmsta has chewed her to pieces."

"Mia, was it right that Hanna left like that, and is it right that she hasn't come back?"

"Hanna is so scared. She is just *so* scared."

"*Ja,* but I'm not angry with Hanna. You, Mia, must not be so self-willed as you are."

So. Just so. I calmed down. It was the same old tune. Now I'd be in for a hard whipping. I began to hate the teacher again. She was the same as the others, she was like Mother. And Mother sometimes didn't whip you, though you probably should have been. What had I done now? Hadn't done my sums. I couldn't do them when I couldn't *think,* when the numbers on the blackboard jumped here and there so I couldn't *write* them because Hanna lay dead under the train.

"Did you hear what I said? You must hold the reins on yourself, Mia. You like Hanna, but you must let Hanna be Hanna; she can never be you."

I didn't understand what she meant. I certainly wouldn't get whipped. What would it be then? Something new, something I hadn't been subjected to before?

"I must do what's right for Hanna. No one cares about her."

"You were going to leave without permission. Why did you want to do that? Why didn't you ask for permission? I was waiting for you to ask permission, Mia."

Now I sat there, blown out like a candle flame. Why hadn't I asked for permission to look for Hanna?

"Do you think I am unkind?"

"No, no," I cried out.

"Why didn't you ask for permission instead of planning to run off? I saw that you were thinking of doing that."

Well, you just never get anything by asking. Never, never. The whole time I had the stocking needle teacher in front of my eyes.

"You have never asked me for anything."

This was worse than a whipping. I couldn't clear this up. What should I do? Now I didn't hate her, didn't love her either. I was afraid. She was like that dangerous God I read about in Grandma's book of sermons. He who saw in the darkness. He who journeyed everywhere, punishing folks and living like a tyrant all over the world. He who had permission to do exactly as He pleased without anyone punishing him.

I was scared. And always when I got scared, I started to think clearly. In moments of utter terror I had the clearest thoughts. My instinct for self-preservation was enormous.

"You could have asked me to look right away for Hanna," I said calmly, though I shivered and burned with eagerness and with anxiety of what would happen and because I couldn't get out to look for Hanna.

The kids came, peeking in the door. The recess had been long. The teacher sat, looking straight ahead. Her cheeks were dark red. Now she's angry, I thought. Now everything is finished and Hanna is dead. I got up. I felt how cold my cheeks were.

"*Ja,* Mia, I could have asked you," I heard the teacher say, "but you must learn not to be so worried beforehand and imagine everything possible. Hanna isn't dead. Hanna is shy and doesn't dare to come back here today. Now I'm asking you to go to the poorhouse [it was *called* the poorhouse then] and find out about her. You are free the rest of the day."

Now God was forgotten, that stranger who travelled around in the clouds and judged. He had nothing to do with my teacher. She was a new god that no one had known before. But what can you do when you stand before a new god? I didn't know of any advice. I had only to go, but I couldn't do just that. I had to say something.

"I must call the children," the teacher said.

I hesitated. What should I say? "I don't know, I—I beg your pardon so much," I said, although now my voice was humble, and I thought what I said was so dumb.

"*Ja,* Mia, but this hardly comes under any laws, that is to say any laws of courtesy. Even so I understand you. But you must not let yourself depend on asking pardon or forgiveness too often. That can so easily become a habit. One who often begs for forgiveness often does wrong."

I think I always knew that. I made a deep curtsey and said nothing. When I got as far as the school yard, the bell rang. I ran past the kids as if they weren't there, out and away to Hanna. For she lived, my new god had said that she lived.

In the poorhouse there was chaos.

Four older women stood on the porch steps, quarreling so fiercely that none of them could possibly hear what the other was saying. Broom-Mina was one of them, a big coarse woman with a smooth rosy face though she was over fifty. The quarrel was about Hanna.

"Is the brat to go and piss in her clothes like that when she's eight years old? Shall she then? Isn't she my kid? Don't I have the right to whip her black and blue?" Mina screamed.

"You big ox, hitting that poor little kid like that!" yelled a thin old woman. "Shame on you! You don't know how hard you hit. When "frun"* comes home, you'll have the devil to pay."

"Frun" was the matron, I knew, who must have been out someplace now, and Mina had beaten Hanna. I crouched down a little so they wouldn't catch sight of me. I had to think of what I would say so I could find Hanna. She was lying somewhere, badly beaten by that huge Mina. My anxiety began again. My new god didn't count any longer, and the old one I had always considered a punisher, nothing else.

"You go there and piss like that yourself, though you're an old crone," a tall woman yelled, walking toward Mina and knotting her fist. "You're a dirty old tug, you're so big! I don't know what God's doing when He lets you have kids! A harbor roughneck is what you'd pass for! I'm sure you broke two of the girl's ribs."

Then I screamed high and hysterically, rushing into the house. Around and around through the big living room, up to the second floor, then down again and out into the kitchen. And there Hanna sat! I saw that she had been crying, but she could move and was eating. A woman was holding a cup with milk and in it Hanna dipped a rusk.

All the usual order of things in the poorhouse seemed to be completely upset that day, for in the kitchen in the women's section, where men would never be seen, was a man, a tall, stooped old man. He stood beside Hanna, talking in a jolly, child-like voice. Hanna ate, sobbing now and then. The woman who fed her couldn't talk so anyone understood what she said. She had snow-white hair,

*"Frun" means married woman.

51

white brows and eyelashes, and her eyes were red like those of a rabbit. She wasn't thirty yet.

"Hanna, Hanna, teacher let me out of school to come to you. You're free today, too. Teacher isn't angry, not one bit, for you couldn't help it." I stretched the truth a little. "Teacher said that. I'll stay here with you now."

Hanna blushed and took the cup from the woman. She was ashamed she had let herself be fed. The old man turned to me. "Such a nice girl—it's so kind of you. Hanna doesn't have much fun. Mina, she . . ." *Ja,* then he seemed to recollect that Mina was after all Hanna's Mother, and so he didn't say anything more but left.

Hanna told me then that the old man had come in just as Mina was beating her black and blue because she'd come home wet. "It was because that devil Sjökvisten saw it; otherwise Mama wouldn't have beaten me," Hanna cried. "But Sjökvisten gossips all the time about Mama, says she's nutty, and that we, her kids, will be, too, and Mama got so mad she beat me so I thought I'd die. But then "Uncle" Berg came and knocked Mama down and the other women helped him. Because when Mama gets mad, she beats you to death. She beat the cat to death that she got mad at."

I was very interested in all this I was hearing. Here it seemed that life was really lived. Cats were beaten to death when you got mad at them.

The albino woman babbled something I couldn't understand. Suddenly she let her apron fall off. Then she sneered, picked up her apron, and said something to Hanna. Hanna stuck out her tongue. Never had I seen Hanna behave like that.

"She fancies that guys think about her just because she lets her apron fall off. She unties the sash ten times a day, and then she runs around yelling, 'See, see, see, me, me, me.'"

Hanna looked so mean when she imitated that poor woman who looked so awful with her white hair, like a plucked chicken. One of the women from the fight on the steps came in. She saw the albino standing there with her apron in her hand. "There you are all set to do your crazy act again now. Out with you. You're no company for kids." And that bent old woman shooed the poor idiot into the hall.

I couldn't understand what bad thing she had done or what fun there'd be in guys thinking about you. But Hanna winked knowingly. I saw that the Hanna here amidst all this loose living while "frun" was away was a whole new Hanna who knew things, secret things that I thought were too dumb to understand.

"How do you feel now, Hanna?" the old woman asked after she'd got rid of that poor lovesick albino.

Well, Hanna had a lot of pain, Mina had beaten her so dreadfully. The thought suddenly struck me that Hanna was showing off, and she was, too, for when the old woman limped out of the room, Hanna whispered, "She has money, you see, and I always get some when anyone is around to see; she does it to tease the others who don't have any money."

It wouldn't be easy to bring up your children in the poorhouse. Had Mina an inkling about what bringing up children really was, she would have despaired. Now she clung only to her owner's rights to Hanna, and they were undisputed, for nearly all the old women there had waited outside the door of the room Mina'd been in the night she gave birth to Hanna in the poorhouse.

Nearly all of them were angry at Broom-Mina, for she was the youngest of the old women and went to the market every Saturday and still could snatch for herself a bit of fun which for the others was finished—only pain and bitterness remained—all of Mina's enemies defended Hanna as soon as Mina opened her mouth to utter a word of admonishment to her.

The very least thing could set off the worst commotion, and no one could stop the row without "frun."

But today she wasn't home.

I took Hanna out to the old garden, overgrown with moss. The trees were full of green apples, forbidden fruit from on high. The apples belonged to the chairman of the poorhouse.

Hanna pulled down several apples anyway, and I felt a little sting of jealousy. Never would I have been able to pull down a green apple at the house where I lived and done it so nonchalantly. There never were any apple trees even nearby where I lived.

"Does it hurt much where she hit you?" I wanted to bring Hanna down to her suffering again so she'd be a little dependent on me, although I had certainly seen how many she had who made much of her.

"Not so bad. Do you want to see?" She unhooked that everlasting jacket and pulled it off. Unfastened the skirt, drew the faded yellow vest over her head, and stood there, little and thin in the sun. The skirt's rough waistband had cut into her naked skin. Over her breasts the skin was stretched, her ribs showing every hook of the jacket. She was so frighteningly thin.

53

"Don't you get any food?" I asked.

"Oh, *ja,* but I never want any. I eat only on Saturday when Mama and I are in town," she said carelessly. "Look here."

Right across her back was a broad swollen welt. That was from Mina's big fist. And she had blue bruises from old blows and pinches on her flanks.

"My back hurts all the time, Mama's so heavy-handed. And then one of the old men pinches me as soon as he sees me. Look here, too." She lifted up her thin little arm; the under skin was completely black.

"Grandma's sister was whipped so her back bled, and she drowned herself. Show teacher before they kill you," I pleaded, full of dread. "Otherwise I'll tell about it."

Hanna's eyes darkened with fear. "Don't do that." She began to cry. "Don't do that. I won't go to school anymore if you do that."

"No, no, I promise, but that old man mustn't pinch you."

"He gives me money, too. All the old men are sweet, you'll see that." She pulled her vest over her head and put on the jacket without hooking it. 'It doesn't hurt so much if it isn't hooked," she said knowledgeably.

She drew me into a corner where a whole clump of wild plum trees grew. Crept in the underbrush and came out again with a handful of five and ten öre pieces. "I don't dare show these to Mama. The old men don't gossip, you see, when they give you money like the old women do. But I don't dare show them to Mama because I got them from old men. The old women babble always as soon as they give me anything. Take some!"

"No, no." The pile of money scared me. "No, no!" I backed away.

Such a treasure I wouldn't have been able to hide. Mother would have asked question after question. The coins looked so dangerous lying in Hanna's thin hand. Her hands were much smaller than mine, but they were already knotted and calloused from helping Mina make the birch brooms.

"Throw them away, Hanna, throw them away," I begged. "You'll only get whipped," I entreated.

"Take just one," she whispered. "Just one. I got clothes from you."

I took one. Hanna stuffed the others in the thicket again, putting a stone over the place. A dark, green-coated treasure, senile old men's snuff money.

Hanna hooked her jacket, groaning a little for every hook she fastened.

"I'm your friend, Hanna," I whispered. "I'm your friend. Grandma's sister went with her friend, and she was beaten so she drowned herself. Tell our teacher, Hanna."

"Hanna, Hanna," we heard someone call just then.

"*Ja-a*," Hanna answered and then whispered, "I'm coming to school in the morning. Buy something with the money." Then she sprang away.

It was already late. With my hand pressed hard on the five öre I climbed over the fence and came out on the road. I didn't want to say good-bye to any in the poorhouse.

I hid the coin under a stone on the way home. Maybe it's still lying there. Maybe Hanna's treasure also lies in the thicket still, getting greener and greener.

Chapter 5

Even a patient nature can get tired of ditchdigging when dog day heat makes the sides of the ditch hard as flint and the peat in the ditch becomes as sticky as fresh spruce roots. The sun burns your blue shirt white on your back, and the spade handle feels like full grown nettles in your hand. Your throat is dry right after a swig of weak beer; drops of sweat run down your face, make your eyes smart.

Polluted springs lurk nearby, rust mouldy springs that many ditchdiggers and harvesters have drunk death from. Or death has climbed from the soles of your feet up through the stretched veins of your calves, for rust mouldy springs seep day after day through your shoes while the sun burns your head and back.

Thunderclouds roll every day over the plain without giving rain, waking only fear of fire and death in the sultry night, making sleep bring nightmares in the field barracks and tenement shacks. Those malevolent bolts of lightning awaken you every hour, and the work day is exhausting and unbearable.

The most patient can lose patience, and my stepfather had no patience to lose.

After the first day in July he walked away from that steaming hot bottomland where the drain pipes already lay in fixed rows through which the drainage would go. "Today I've quit. I'm damned if I'll work there like a black slave."

"Ja, so what will you do now, then?"

"There'll always be something."

"Ja, well, it's all the same to me, I have to do just as much whether you work or not."

Mother looked indifferent when she said that, but I knew how worried she was.

No answer. The door shut with a bang.
It wasn't the same to me.

Chapter 6

During my school days at Holmstad I had begun to write verse. Mother and Grandma and our neighbors didn't think I wrote them by myself. They were right. The poems were very religious, telling how wonderful it would be for me if I were really kind and told the truth and said my prayers. And how little birds sat and sang for good little children. Nothing but reminiscences from Grandma's book of sermons.

I made myself a guitar from a cigar box (having a guitar was my most fervent childhood wish), put the verses to melodies, and sang to whomever would listen. The strings made from coarse yarn naturally made no musical sound. I strummed so hard on them to make them sing.

One day I had the greatest excitement when I heard something clang from the cigar box. The birds were flying here and there from the trees. I tried to take a lighter touch to get the box to sound like the birds flying over. But I never was that lucky.

At that time I thought that all the flowers grew for my sake. All birds sang for me. Everything strange and beautiful like the sun and moon and stars and flowers and birds were there for my sake. Even the toy-store window and the bakery window in town, although I hardly ever had resources to buy any of these splendors. But you couldn't buy the moon or sun either. So everything was arranged for me, just as the planets shone for me so I could see the path.

Seldom did I find friends who thought like me. They picked flowers hit or miss, carrying the bunches home. Birds they threw stones at. Everything beautiful that they found they tried to possess and destroy, hide, or take home to the grown-ups. Often when I pretended I was a bird and my arms were wings, I was laughed at. No one would play being a bird. What friends played when we weren't in school was mostly papa-mama-children. They never tired of that game. It was played wherever I moved, north or south, in town or in the country. I never found any pleasure in playing that game; it had lost all fantasy, was monotonous, dumb, ordinary. To be spared just standing and looking on, I forced myself to play.

They always wanted me to be the child, too, and that wasn't any fun. God knows what kind of parents most of them had, for I got only violent blows when I played I was their child. If any sweets were to be found and meals were pretended to be eaten, I had to sit in the background in the playhouse and wait until the "big ones" ate.

"Children must learn to wait," said the one who was most often my play-mama, "and you must *stand* at the table when you eat so you'll grow." So I had to stand and pretend that I ate the stones and sand pies while the papa and mama stretched themselves out on the playhouse "floor," saying they were resting after noonday dinner.

Frequently, I had to crawl under the skirt of some big girl and come out on command, and then that family said they'd had a child. Most often of all, the playhouse papa pretended he was drunk, imitating so well the boozers I had seen in the tenement houses, their gabbling, their curses, their imitation so exact that now when I recall it, I believe there were more actors coming from the poor than anyone suspected.

We imitated everything that happened under our eyes. Drunk men, drunk women, fights. Priests in cassocks and collars preaching doomsday and the Salvation Army singing with their guitars. When we played we were fine folks, we pretended that our skirts trailed behind us, lifting our noses high in the air. The boys stuffed grass in the fronts of their pants and then were squires.

To come crawling out from under a skirt to be a newborn child was the craziest of all, I thought.

At that time I most decidedly knew that babies didn't come in that way. How they came I didn't know, but I was positive it wasn't in that crazy way. But most of my friends knew better. I had to bend over, yielding to superior strength, and let myself be "born" time after time or be laughed at as dumb.

The verses that I wrote when I was eight won, as I said, no attention. They were too much like Sunday School and Grandma's sermon book. There were only dreadful sermons in that book. Sometimes they took three hours to read. We never held any Sunday devotions except when Grandma stayed with us at times for

a week, and then I always was the one who had to read those mile-
long sermons with their tiresome, complicated style.

Often I was truly grateful to my stepfather, however bad I
otherwise thought him to be, when he impatiently interrupted me in
the middle of a boring sermon, saying that would be enough. At its
beginning he sat beside Grandma on the settee, his hands piously
folded, and listened for two or three pages. My mother regularly
went to sleep, she was always so tired. Neither did she have any
further religious leanings than respect for "God's word" like
Grandma.

There's so much in the Bible that is written for a working-class
woman's benefit. There you can find support for nearly everything.
God doesn't hold with drunkenness or bullying or mean men or
masters who make folks sweat and slave. Although I often heard
both Mother and Grandma say about the sermon, "Now whatever
in the world does that mean? Can't you find anyone who knows
anything? He should certainly show how and not just talk . . . talk
and promise gold and green fields and prophecy about punishments
that never come." Grandma thought there should be a sermon on
Sunday, for she was accustomed to that as a child. And Mother
thought that a girl was bettered by "sitting devoutly with God's
word and not just running wild with the kids." The teaching you get
as a child often enough works just the opposite, for I have never
later in my life listened to a sermon of my own free will.

Often my stepfather got tired after only two pages, and
sometimes when he'd been at Skull-Jon's tavern on Saturday night,
he'd mutter, "That damned droning. Surely for one day you should
get some peace." Then he'd lie on the settee, and Grandma had to sit
on a hard wooden chair. Then *their* Sunday was disturbed. Grandma
crabbed at him. He stood it for an hour—he was afraid of Grandma,
so old she was now, and then he was off to some fellow boozer. But
my Sunday was saved; I got to go out and play.

I often swiped a hunk of bread and went far enough so I couldn't
hear them calling me for dinner.

The happiness with my beloved teacher and little Hanna didn't
last long. The sun had burned too hot on a ditchdigger, a working
man who lost patience. An eight-year-old and her mother had to get
ready to move.

Never had I grieved as much over a move as I did over this one.
It was often hard with the others, of course. You had somehow

become good friends with schoolmates, got your playhouse set up in some thicket or corner, for naturally it wasn't a miniature villa with furniture and everything there'd be in a gentleman's park or outside a summer cottage for rich kids' happiness. A board laid across two stones, the board often swiped with much difficulty, and some empty anchovy cans and shards of china were our playhouse. With a real miniature house there isn't enough room for a child's fantasy world. An imaginary, shimmering playhouse can never be built by man's hands.

But hardly had you swiped your board for the playhouse and gathered together a few housekeeping bits than it was time to leave it for good.

This time moving away was so hard and sad. At Old Island Road, it was good to be leaving those "educated," and at the paper mill place I never felt I really belonged, what with the stocking needle and other setbacks, but here I had Hanna and the teacher and a lot of kids that I really liked. And I was popular, got to recite "Spring has come on the meadows," got praise, got an audience.

Poor Hanna couldn't learn to read. An old woman at the poorhouse read the lessons with her, repeating the lesson over and over again until Hanna had it by heart but without learning the alphabet. She had to stay after school sometimes, reading a, b, c, d, and writing the letters over and over. If she ever learned to read, I never knew.

Chapter 7

Mother began to go to work grumbling, looking and feeling sick. When she was home, she'd sit for long spells, gabbing with a neighbor who had four kids. Two of them were severely retarded. Someone was to take them soon. "Then maybe I can have things a little more like a human around here," the neighbor said. But no one came to take them, not as long as we lived at Holmstad. One poor child was five, the other eight. Neither of them could talk. They wobbled when they walked like newborn calves. When they ran their heads jerked back and forth. I was very interested in them when we first came to Holmstad, but school took up all my time, and then they became so difficult in the long run.

When we'd be playing house, the two came right in our midst. They *sneaked* out of their house, never getting permission to go out. I never saw their mother go out with them. I only saw her come roaring like thunder to get them and wallop them. Then they yelled in a strange way, staring right up in the sky with their slow eyes, screaming as if they waited for help from above. It was as if they screamed not for the beating but for something wholly different. Then they were suddenly silent. Their mother pulled and pushed them, hollering because they wouldn't move, but they couldn't understand that. All the kids thought she was crazy, and we jeered at her. Never did she come to get them before they'd wrecked our playhouse, broken our things. I kept my distance from them always. They became all the less interesting and all the more to be avoided. As soon as I laid eyes on them, I headed them off and got praise from their mother. Praise that made me sick. I slammed our door so I wouldn't have to hear her. I'm sure if she had handled those poor souls better we children would have, too.

When we had first moved to Holmstad, my mother said that the neighbor was a real slut. Mother never went to her place, and when the neighbor came to us and started talking, Mother was very short with her.

But that was *then*. Only a few months afterwards, as soon as Mother was home from her cleaning work, she sat talking endlessly with "the slut." They talked only about pregnancies. The neighbor had borne nine children. She had always had them in a maternity hospital. "And I had all the kids in agony. They could get only four even to live. You see here how only the youngest have their wits. The other two are idiots."

I thought everything she said was strange. I had a hunch she lied to Mother and felt Mother was silly to listen to such stuff. I had, of course, my teacher and Hanna and "Spring has come, her garland weaves the meadows" to think about. When the neighbor came in, I tried my best to get out.

She was big and coarse as a beer driver, and her eyes bulged out of their sockets. She smelled so bad. How could Mother sit with her? But Mother seriously and attentively listened to everything she said, and sighed, and all the time in the midst of all this she was sick.

When Grandma visited us, the neighbor never dared to come in; she thought Grandma looked so strict. Grandma didn't know that Mother was friends with the neighbor.

One day when the neighbor was with us, I heard Mother say, "If I could try to be at the maternity hospital this next time."

"*Ja,* Hedvig. Think how good you'd have it, and there'd be no need to drag washing home and get food and everything. Though you'd have to have someone looking after things here at home, of course."

I thought that sounded really crazy and didn't attach any importance to anything they said. I never saw the neighbor's husband. He's at the wharf, Mother said when I asked.

One evening after the visits with the neighbor had begun, Mother didn't come home. There was nothing to eat in the house; Mother would buy something on her way home from town, she had said. I waited and waited, went out a while and played, but the kids trooped home, one after the other, and I was alone. It was nearly ten o'clock. Then I dragged myself along home again. Mother hadn't come. The key was outside under the mat where I'd put it. I was anxious and hungry. I hadn't eaten anything since lunch at school, and it had been a scrimpy one that day.

I knocked at the neighbor's, having a weak hope that Mother

might be there. Mother used to shop for the neighbor, since it was hard for her to get away because of her retarded kids and the baby was only six months old.

"Well, what about that! No, she hasn't been here."

I went into our place again and sat on my acorn settee. I heard how they rumbled around and talked in the room above as they dragged out their beds and made them. From the windows that were cracked open, talk could be heard from the houses near us.

Everyone had companionship; everyone talked to someone; all had eaten supper and would soon be going to bed. It was only I who was alone.

I opened the window and leaned out. On a green-painted seesaw by the wall a man and woman sat. The man embraced the woman. They kissed. I must have rattled the window, for the man looked up. But the woman drew her arms more tightly around his neck and kissed him.

"Jenny, the kid sees us," he said, pushing the woman away.

"Pooh, a brat!" She looked up at me. "You, there! You go to bed. Don't stand there spying on folks," the kiss-loving Jenny said.

"Shut up, old woman! I'm not looking at you one bit," I answered sharply, shutting the window with a bang. I heard the man laugh.

"Only gypsy kids out here," the woman said. Then it was quiet again. When I opened the window, they had disappeared. The green seesaw was empty. The owner's manager who lived in the house next door watched that seesaw like a treasure. We had tried to outwit her a hundred ways, slipping near when she went to the shop or rested after lunch, trying to teeter on the board, but always there was someone she had told to watch it, and we were driven off. Among the boys it was a game to tease the woman, banging it hard, as if someone had just been there and teetered.

Maybe a drayman or a horse carriage had driven over Mother. Or had she fallen in the river, or had a tramp murdered her? It was so quiet now. Everyone had gone to bed. Stubbornly, I looked and looked at the street, thinking I saw Mother time after time.

Long before the tollgates of the town, a row of old willows grew. Just there by the willows, I thought over and over again, it was Mother coming. But it was only the shadows of the willows that moved in the wind.

It got darker and darker. The willows looked like tall horsemen against the darkened sky. The riders came nearer and nearer.

I think that I had just fallen asleep on the window ledge when I heard a knock on the door. It was the neighbor. She had a shawl over her shoulders and had on a hat that looked like a hunter's, a little peaked hat. She looked so funny in it. Her big face shone like a china dish under the hat. "I know where Hedvig works. If you'll go with me, we'll see if she's gotten sick at work. She's busy cleaning the cellar in Bergman's brewery and is all by herself."

"Oh, *ja,* I want to go with."

"Have you eaten?"

I held back only a second. "No, I haven't eaten."

She went back for a piece of limpa and a bit of dried herring. "It isn't much, but you've got to have something in your belly."

I trudged with her toward the tall willows, chewing for dear life on the food I'd gotten. The willows stood there rustling. It was very dark under them, and I drew nearer to the big woman when we walked past them. She looked so strange in the night, too, big and wide, in her shawl and hunter's hat. We were on our way to Mother . . . I accepted the neighbor now. Mother was nothing beside the teacher, but she should be home and have a little food ready. It would be dreadful if she were run over or gone away altogether. What would happen to me?

"Your dad is certainly never home," the neighbor said, taking my hand when I drew nearer to her by the willows.

"He's sitting at Skull-Jon's tavern," I said indifferently.

"It would serve him right if we went there and sat, too. All the women should go and sit at the taverns."

I thought she sounded crazy as usual. There weren't many grown-ups who toed the line when I measured them against my new teacher. And for that matter even my own narrow-mindedness couldn't have competed with the shame that all of our little neighborhood heaped on the woman who walked beside me. She looked queer, and her ways were such that people found her odd, crazy. "It's not strange that she has idiots," they said. Tonight, not even that she was helping me find Mother and had given me a bit to eat when my belly groaned with hunger, could soften my heart with sympathy for her. I accepted her only as a necessary helper in my misery. If only she hadn't had that hat on. But the worst was that she had those two idiots that no one came for. The doctor had said they'd be taken as soon as a place could be found for them.

"It doesn't suit me to be married," the neighbor had said to Mother one day. "I'm too big and rough. I won't last long with the kids." That was her usual, strange way of talking that no one understood. Mother only pretended she did. She agreed with the neighbor that she shouldn't have married. Mother sounded as if she were a bit crazy herself as well. Now I walked along, hoping that Mother wouldn't get mad that I came after her like this.

The door to Bergman's big brewery was open. The night watchman made no difficulty, and we got to go in. "Hedvig is still here. She's doing the cellars by piece-rate. She's working herself to death, that's for sure," he said. Like a hunched-up dwarf with a giant's beard, he stood there with his lantern. I thought he wasn't real. I tried to touch him, but while we stood there, Mother came. She looked flushed and excited. She had tidied herself up a little in the beer cellar. She was so beautiful when she had roses in her cheeks. Now she was smiling, too, which wasn't often. Her white teeth glistened, her eyes shone, it was so long since I'd seen her like this.

"It was terribly kind of you to come along with my girl here. I've been so anxious about her. There was nothing at home to eat, but I wanted to finish tonight. I had so little left to do."

How strange, here I thought she'd be mad because I'd come for her. She always used to be. If only she hadn't said that we'd had nothing to eat so folks heard that. Why did that stooped night watchman have to know that? But that's the way she was now. She hadn't been like that in the room at Old Island Road. Then you didn't need to be afraid as soon as she opened her mouth that she'd talk about all her troubles. Mother didn't mind about anything anymore, didn't sweep anything under the rug. It was awfully unpleasant.

"Hedvig, you look so wonderful compared to me. There isn't such a big difference in our age," the neighbor said. Although the arc lamp in the doorway shone, the night watchman lifted his lantern to look at Mother, twisting his crooked back so that he could direct his gaze up at her. I went up to Mother and took her hand.

"*Ja*, she looks like a woman should," the night watchman said. "But now you must go, for I have to lock the door."

The three of us walked away. I had Mother's hand in mine. "Everything's probably closed by now, so we can't even get some coffee. I would have treated you, for I've made good money at the brewery. Cleaning by piece-work is best of all," Mother said cheerfully.

"*Ja*, think, here I'm so big and strong and have to sit at home with those everlasting miserable wretches. And they don't come to take them," the neighbor answered.

"Why was the old man so bent over? Was that a real man?" I couldn't get the night watchman out of my head.

"A real man? I can promise you he is! A good man. He has a little money saved up, too. He's been with the blast furnaces at Lotorp for thirty years and got medals. All the blast furnace workers become stooped like that," Mother said, more for the neighbor than for me.

"Well, well, that's so," she said indifferently.

"Isn't anyplace open? I'm so hungry," Mother said.

"Only the beer cafes," the neighbor said.

"*Ja,* but you could get a sandwich there. We have my girl with us, so no one could say anything about us. If we were dressed better, we'd go to Strömsholm," she continued. (Strömsholm was a fine restaurant on a little island in Motala River where a big band played and where people sat and drank punch.)

"Heavens above! I've never been there," exclaimed the neighbor.

I had been there with Mother and my stepfather before they got married, and I trembled with fear that Mother would take the neighbor there the way she looked in that hat! So splendid it was there! So many elegant people! And waiters! Fine ones who waited on you! We had such a nice one who waited on us. He served me soft drinks and cakes and gave me an orange. "For your bright eyes," he'd said as if I were grown up.

"That's certainly not wise," my stepfather had said, quickly breaking up the party. He hadn't liked it there. The waiter had been too attentive to Mother and me.

"No, we can't go to Strömsholm," Mother said, glancing at the neighbor's hat without her noticing. Mother was bare-headed. The scarf she wore for work had slipped off her head; she was so beautiful now.

The clock struck eleven-thirty in Emanuel Church, and the neighbor said that now we must hurry or else the beer cafes would be closed, too.

We found a cafe just as we approached Saltmeadow.

"It's quiet enough now, but at midnight the night shift comes, so it's best you sit in the kitchen," the cafe hostess said.

"We're so hungry. My work took so long. Can we get some food?" Mother asked.

"Oh, *ja,* there's always plenty for the shift."

67

It became a real party. Fried potatoes, beef and salmon, sandwiches, cheese, soft drinks, prunes, and milk.

The big neighbor ate until she nearly choked. She helped herself to seconds and thirds. "It's best to stuff yourself," she whispered to Mother. "It costs the same."

But Mother didn't answer her. Mother didn't eat much either. She had got pale now and looked so tired. The husband of the cafe hostess who waited on us was plainly used to hungry people, asking if we didn't want more. "Just say the word," he said. "The rule here is that folks can eat as much as they want. Folks at the quay want that. And they don't eat any more because of it." Back went the neighbor. "We don't dish out the helpings. Then it becomes so institutional. You must help yourselves now to everything. Will you have coffee?"

The neighbor wanted coffee but not Mother and me.

The clock struck twelve. We heard a murmuring, then a buzzing, then laughter from the longshoremen in the cafe. "Maybe your man is with them," Mother said to the neighbor.

"Him? Oh, no. He's out of work now. He didn't have a steady job. Those fellows are longshoremen; they always have work. They're organized just like the socialists. My guy says that the gentry don't like it when workers are organized."

Mother looked a bit scornfully at her but didn't answer.

"We'll have the bill now," Mother said to the sweaty waiter as he came into the kitchen with a big bowl for refilling.

"Right away, right away!"

"We can sneak out," the neighbor said. "You've asked for the bill, and they haven't given it. They can't have anything to say if we just up and go now."

I almost thought she was right.

Mother pretended she hadn't heard. The neighbor got up. She belched again and again; she had eaten too much.

Mother picked up her bag. Four ten-kronor notes were in it.

"Lord, have you earned that much? Well, you can sure live like gentry now for a month," exclaimed the neighbor.

"There are debts to pay," Mother said.

"*Ja,* that will be two kronor," the waiter said.

The neighbor shook her head meaningfully. She thought that was too much.

"Thanks so much." Mother gave him a ten kronor. "Seven and fifty öre I'll be wanting."

The neighbor now looked horror-stricken.

"Thank you, thank you, so nice of you," the waiter said as he hurried off to make change.

"Are you nuts? That would have lasted for a whole week," the neighbor said.

The waiter came back with the change. "Come again, and thanks for the tip."

"Thank you, the food was well worth the money."

"Come this way," the man said, holding the kitchen door open. It looked onto a dark yard. "I'll go along and open the gate. We don't have permission to serve stray customers, but since you ate in the kitchen, it will be all right. Where do you live?"

"Out near Holmstad."

"Take along a couple of posters and put them up there." He ran back to get two posters.

"What are they for?" Mother asked.

"*Ja*, Kata Dalström and Fabian Månsson are speaking at Oxvallen on Sunday."

"Of course I'll do that," Mother said, taking the posters.

"Since they didn't have the right to serve us food, you shouldn't have paid," the neighbor grumbled.

"No one gets food free, not even those who steal it, and I don't steal. You may have to beg before you die, but tonight I didn't need to beg," Mother said shortly, and the neighbor heard the anger in her voice.

I pressed Mother's hand hard, hard. She had style.

"Kata Dalström has been in jail; she's a dangerous woman," the neighbor said.

"She isn't dangerous. It's because she's a friend of the poor that she's been in jail."

"Then she's gotten something from them. Does she have money?"

"I don't think she's got money. You don't get that if you're a friend of the poor. She doesn't think that folks become better if they get money. It's something else she wants."

"Do you know her, Mother?" I whispered breathlessly.

"I heard her once. She's a wonderful speaker."

"You can't be an important person without money," the neighbor said stubbornly.

We walked over Saltmeadow bridge. The water smelled so good.

The night was still. If the neighbor hadn't been with us, I would have asked Mother more about Kata Dalström, but the neighbor was against everything and was so strange. Mother and I would have walked leisurely home, talking about all that she would buy now that finally she had a little money again. But there walked that neighbor who was so negative, saying that everything was impossible if you weren't rich.

"Down here at Saltmeadow a fortune-teller lives. Shall we call on her? She takes folks at night. She's away ironing at the mangel house during the day, for her man's sick," the neighbor said, her voice sounded so eager.

Saltmeadow was a part of town that had a bad reputation, storage yards, and a few rickety shops here and there. Mother hesitated.

"She's truly foretold the future for everyone I've known who's gone to her."

"*Ja,* it might be fun to try it. How much does she charge?" Mother asked.

"One krona per person, but I can just listen. You have money, Hedvig, of course, but you mustn't pay for me."

"Of course I will when we're together like this."

In this way I got one of my childhood's most detested memories.

The neighbor turned off the street. We followed her down a narrow path between big junkyards. A lantern shone far down the path.

"Good Lord, don't go any farther! Tramps lie here with their women. They can rob you, it's happened." Mother stopped.

"Naw, I know the way. They don't dare to be here with those lanterns down there." Silently we followed her. I came last, hanging onto Mother's shawl. It was so exciting to be going here. I would really have something to tell Hanna about in the morning.

We walked past a little house. You could hear quarreling, then screaming from within, and Mother speeded up the neighbor who wanted to stop and listen.

Now we came to a big lumberyard. You could smell the water from Bråviken and hear a steamboat tooting. Walking toward us were two women, talking in high, screechy voices. Without saying hello, they asked, "You going to the fortune-teller?"

"*Ja.* Isn't she at home?"

"Oh, well, but *ja,* you'll see when you get there." They walked on without saying good night. They seemed so stirred up.

"They were certainly drunk," Mother said.

We were now in front of a ramshackle place that looked like a woodshed in the darkness. From a window a light flickered, showing that someone was up in the house. The neighbor banged on the door.

"Come in."

We stepped inside. A tall, thin, blonde woman whose age I couldn't place was trying to loosen an unbaked loaf of bread stuck fast to a newspaper. She had a bedstead full of unbaked loaves all stuck to Norrköping's newspapers. When she finally got the loaf free, black print was left on the bottom of the loaf as well as bits of paper. Ads, murders, marriages were burned onto the loaves, and I thought here you could really chew on sensational events with the bread.

The woman with those terrible loaves didn't stir up as much interest even so as a worn, thin, sallow man sitting only in his shirt on a wooden bucket. There was a dreadful stink in the house. The man didn't mind that we came, just sat there and groaned. Sweat ran off him. Holding her nose, Mother opened the door. "You shouldn't have invited us in before that man was in bed," Mother said sharply.

"Shut the door, dear hearts. You shouldn't, of course, be looking at a sick man's dying. He sits there for hours. He's got cancer. There's nothing to be done for it. They won't take him at the hospital." She slung the loaf with the newsprint into the oven and shut the door with a bang. The man hadn't moved, didn't look as if he'd seen us.

"We'll go," Mother said.

But the big neighbor, being acquainted with the woman, gripped Mother by the arm and said, "Let the door stay open. It's still warm out, and when he's incurable, he won't die from a little air." Her green hunting hat wobbled on her head.

"You'll be wanting your fortunes told. That'll cost one krona, payment before, or they won't work. I've had fine ladies and gentlemen, too, I'll have you know and none of them's cared about the smell. You don't when you're getting to know the fate of your future. Even the mayor's been here. You're such a young woman, stylish, too. You'll have a new fiancé, I can see," she said to Mother.

I was completely bewitched by her torrent of words and by the room itself, the filthiest I had ever seen. Dirty dishes and rags, an old blanket at the window. A fat dog lay sleeping, didn't bark even though strangers had come, and then that man who sat on the bucket with his eyes closed. He was leaning over, his head against the edge of the bed. The bed gleamed black. If it had had sheets, they'd have been black, too.

"I have to make some rolls first," the fortune-teller said, shaping rolls with bits of newspaper sticking to them. She heaped a pile of them on the table and got more newspapers to spread on the bed.

"I buy this waste newsprint, it's so cheap. He uses so much paper because he has to sit on the bucket so often." And she made more rolls striped with the black printed paper.

"Put a cloth under them, or you'll have the same problem with them again," Mother said. "Or put a bit of flour under them. You can't just set yeast bread on newspapers. There's so much lumber here at Saltmeadow so you could certainly make a breadboard. It's no wonder you get cancer when you live like this."

Mother was angry, but it had no effect on the fortune-teller.

"We've stolen so much wood here that if I take another piece, I'll have to sit in Trädgard Street [the jail was there]. I don't have enough flour at home to put under the bread. It won't stretch any further so I have to set them just on the mattress." And now she put the bread on the disgustingly dirty mattress.

Clearing off a corner of the table, she pulled out two chairs. I had to stand.

"Look up so I can see your eyes," she said to Mother, who obeyed her reluctantly. The man on the bucket didn't move. Out in the darkness you could hear rustling and then a steamboat whistling.

The woman looked Mother straight in the eyes. Then she spread out some dirty cards on the table. "You're going to suffer a bit of a loss, but you'll also get money. A woman's after your man, but you'll get a fine, new, rich fellow. In a month you'll be in different circumstances altogether. . . . Hell and damnation, now the bread's burnt!"

She yanked two loaves out of the oven and put in two new ones that hadn't risen yet. Then she continued, "Your relatives hate you, but you'll win out. You have loved a man you didn't get, the one you now love you'll get."

The man now began to moan and groan loudly. His cries turned into agonizing screams.

"Dear God, your man's dying," Mother said.

"No, he's not about to die. The worst is over soon."

But Mother got up, putting a krona on the table, and taking me by the hand, we went out. The neighbor stayed on. We were forced to wait, for we weren't sure where we were. Again we heard the man groan and then shriek. It didn't stop the women, who just kept on talking.

"If only we knew the way, we'd go," Mother said. Now the man screamed again even worse. Mother went back in. "Can't you help your man into bed? Are you going to let him sit and die right there? He won't live until morning," I heard Mother say. "Get the bed ready. I won't mess with it, but I'll help you get him to bed."

The man cried now like a little child, as if he hadn't the strength to scream anymore. I heard someone shaking out rags, and I looked in. The woman was making up the bed. It stunk so awfully as she shook out the rags.

"Now spread the newspapers under him and take them away as soon as they're messed. Don't let him sit like that in such torment." I could tell Mother was very moved and ready to cry.

"I'm strong enough to carry him myself," the neighbor said, lifting the dying man to the bed of rags. It looked ghastly—she, big and fat in her hunting cap, and that deathly sick man in her thick uncaring arms.

"Leave at once now; otherwise we'll try to find the way back ourselves. I hear folks talking, and I'll call them if you don't come right now," Mother said to the neighbor.

"Hell and damnation! Now the bread's burnt!" the fortune-teller said.

The neighbor came out with Mother. She had a loaf in a newspaper under her shawl. Bread and newspapers, you could say, almost like a parody of the great Caesar who when he "turned to clay, might stop a hole to the keep the wind away."

"Feel free to come another time," the fortune-teller called from the doorway. "And if you shouldn't come before next year, the wretch in there will still be living. You needn't be so soft-hearted; you go there with your nose in the air, but you'll get yours," she yelled at Mother.

No one answered. We followed the neighbor's hunting hat which looked like something between a scrap heap and a wood pile in the long twilight.

We came to Berg's bridge. The water thundered as usual past the water-washed walls of the weaving mill where the night shift waited for morning, where the machines thudded, and the textiles lengthened. Mother told the neighbor she should throw the loaf she'd got from the fortune-teller into the river. "It will probably make the fish die," Mother said spitefully, "but that can't be helped."

"The bread is good enough for those wretched imbeciles at home," the neighbor said, the hunting hat tilting to each side of her head as she emphasized each word with a nod.

After that, Mother never answered the neighbor's prattle the rest of the way home. When we finally got there, it was nearly morning. The neighbor clumped into her place without saying good-bye or thanks, for Mother had graciously invited her in for coffee. The children's crying could be heard as usual coming from the neighbor's room. Mother looked sad as she made up the beds for us.

"What made us go to that nasty old woman? We never should have gone there." I tried to encourage Mother to talk.

"Life is terrible. Never could I believe it could be like that. And then you were along—that was some fine sight for a child! Try to forget it. Maybe we came when it was a specially bad time for the fortune-teller. But try not to think about the horror. In the morning you can come with me, and then we'll see a funny play called "Jeppe on the Mountain" at the factory union."

I did go along with Mother, but I don't remember the play, maybe because we sat in the highest seats from the stage or maybe because I just don't remember that packed comedy. But the visit to the fortune-teller's is clear even today. (I never had a chance to see the play again.)

I told Hanna only about the watchman with the crooked back at the brewery. The visit to the fortune-teller's was too embarrassing. And I didn't want to say anything about the play, for then Hanna would have been sad. Broom-Mina didn't understand theater, and they had to be in every night at the poorhouse anyway. Hanna didn't get to come home with me more than that one time. She had to make herself useful.

That I went to the theater with Mother would have seemed like I'd betrayed Hanna. I would happily have told the teacher about it.

Mother settled what we owed in the shops, paid a little on the rent, and bought remnants, hiding them in a box and sewing tiny vests out of them. She was still cool toward the neighbor, so she didn't come in to our place very often.

Mother was home now for two weeks. She sewed and got things ready, waiting for my stepfather every night. He didn't come. The

74

money she got at the brewery was soon gone. Then she had to go on cleaning jobs again.

At that same time the owner evicted the neighbor with her children. Not even then did we see her husband. Hanna told me during a recess at school that the neighbor lived at the poorhouse now, and that all the women crabbed at her because her imbeciles broke everything that was not fastened down.

Chapter 8

One night I was awakened by my stepfather's rumbling and talking. Mother had set the table with dill pickles, jam, and a loaf of limpa. Two bottles of beer had been set there, too.

When he saw that I was awake, he told Mother to give me a sandwich with jam and a slug of beer. It was two in the morning. "She's certainly not got so fat," he said, sounding tipsy and generous. A jam and limpa sandwich was not everyday food, and I sat in my acorn settee bed, eating with good appetite and sipping my beer which made my head spin.

At first I didn't pay any attention to what they were talking about. I was thinking that in the morning I'd share a good sandwich with Hanna—limpa, jam, and pickles, and tell her that I'd had beer. I had never been offered it before, though, of course I'd sneaked it, as all the other kids had when it was in the house, without becoming a victim of alcoholism. Just the opposite, it tasted horrible. Now I heard Mother say, "We can get the attic room at Valdemar's. Their house is finished now." And she continued to talk about a farmer's daughter from her home place that she'd been friends with and who was now married to Valdemar and that they had everything so fine. Valdemar worked at a sugar factory. "We can move next week. We can wait with the rent for a month," she added.

"*Ja,* then I can talk to the haulage contractor," my stepfather said.

Just like that, everything was decided upon. As long as they hadn't found a place to live, I had felt myself safe. Now all hope was gone. The piece of bread got so big in my mouth. The limpa and jam wouldn't go down. The beer was bitter and terrible, and suddenly I threw up.

"Such a strange kid," my stepfather said. "She can't even hold down a bit of food."

"She's not used to beer," my mother said.

76

I crept down in my bed, drawing the blanket over my head so I couldn't hear them. I hated them both. I would run away—I could surely live with Hanna in the poorhouse or . . . I gave my imagination free rein, and just as I was about to fall asleep, I was the best of all in school and lived with the school teacher.

But it turned out otherwise. We moved to the molasses-maker's house. My stepfather got a place with the haulage carrier in town. The salary was intended for an unmarried man, and he got his board there and a place to sleep in the stables.

A time of degradation began for me now, though I didn't understand that then. It was a time of uncertain bread. It had always been that, but I had never felt such a sharp knowledge of it, for always there had been *something* for me.

It became a time of lice and dirty aprons and playing hooky from school. Gypsy winds began to blow over the days.

It was far to Grandma's. Those "well-off ones" were conspicuous by their absence. "Here it is heaven to be" had not been heard for a long time. Not once when they were riding about had Mother or I run into them. *Ja,* we didn't do that when we lived at the house on Old Island Road either, but, well, what difference did that make now anyway?

My stepfather drove off with our belongings early in the morning while Mother and I stayed at our old place to scrub before we left. Often Mother had to rest while she scoured that dark little room. She had begun to be so fat. I had to get her the broom and rags. It was hard for her to get up from her knees. She could hardly manage to do anything.

And on that moving day we didn't have anything to eat. No neighbors invited us for anything. Everyone was out drudging to get bread. No one had anything to offer, for it was a Thursday. No one in Norrköping's outskirts ever had a thing to offer the day before payday. *Ja,* some had more than their fill in booze, but we didn't go about in their company. Besides, no one really knew how poor Mother was, Mother who would be moving to her friend's, a farm owner's daughter.

Mother had a package lying on the window sill. I knew what was in it. Two sheets. We'd be walking through the whole town, but we'd be leaving the two sheets at the pawnbroker's on our way in town, and we'd have no food until we did.

I wasn't proud at all anymore. I trudged barefoot beside Mother in a dirty apron and tousled braids. Mother wasn't proud either. She had a big old felt shawl drawn over herself even though it was a hot August day. How I hated that shawl. "Hock hound," as the town's most well-known pawnbroker was called, wouldn't even loan fifty öre for it. I knew Mother had tried. Now it hung down brown and ugly on Mother's shoulders. From her braid, her back hair straggled down her back. She walked along, stooping and staring straight ahead, like an old woman. I scratched my head furiously, for I had now got lice in my thick long hair, and they flourished in the summer heat. My feet were streaked with sweat and dust.

Mother was so tired every night that she forgot to see how dirty I was. I crawled happily into bed with my dirty feet, something that would have been unheard of the summer before in that fine room on Old Island Road.

Getting out of washing my feet, even washing at all, was a glimmer of what was to come. But the lice were troublesome now. Mother, who always before was so careful about that, who had walked that far way when she worked at the factory and I didn't live in the same place as she did, walked that long way a couple of times a week after work to see that the woman I stayed with didn't let lice get started. The story about lice dragging folks into the lake Mother had told so convincingly I firmly and wholly believed it for awhile.

Now I trudged along beside Mother.

We went over Berg's bridge where the iron cables hung loosely between the posts. Motala River roared on both sides of us, foaming and thundering in its everlasting toil, drawing those thousands of wheels round and round to keep hands at work and let the fabric glide over the bars in weaving mill after weaving mill. Furiously itching my head, I carelessly glanced at the white water, no longer believing that anything could now happen, that I could be dragged down into the water by any crawling louse in my hair. The time was over for that foolish tale.

Mother got a krona on loan for the two sheets. She sent me to a bakery to buy a limpa. So we continued through town, each chewing her piece of bread. It was our first meal that day. I had already discovered that Mother didn't have anything much at all to eat when my stepfather wasn't home. When she knew he'd be coming, she scrounged everything she could for dinner, even borrowing potatoes from the neighbors. That's the way it had to be, for if she had nothing to give him, he'd go away again. I was of the opinion that he could gladly go. But Mother thought otherwise.

We came out to a tollgate that I had never seen before. On each side of the road were fences and inside them were farmyards and fields, greenhouses and flower gardens. A strong scent of flowers enveloped us. Thick fir hedges took over where the fences stopped, making me impatient. Because of these dark hedges you couldn't see anything of the splendors within. The apples hung already red on the trees that were so big their crowns stretched over the hedges. It was the greatest temptation to try to knock down a couple.

My mother walked much more slowly. I saw how the sweat dropped in beads down her pale face. Then she had to sit at the edge of the road, and holding her hand against her diaphragm, she began to vomit. Standing there in the dust, scratching my head, I was ashamed of what Mother was doing. It was so humiliating that she was sitting at the side of the road and throwing up. Her face was deathly white. The ugly shawl had slipped off. Her hair straggled on her neck. She looked as if she never ever wanted to get up again. Think, if anyone came.

There the apples hung, peeking over the fir hedge, flowers spread their scent, but Mother just sat by the ditch, looking like a miserable heap of rags.

"You can try at least to swallow," I said. "Try to, so we can be on our way."

Grandma always gave me white pepper and brandy when I had a stomach ache, and she always said like an order, "Now be good and only swallow, and don't throw up that, for then it won't do any good."

"Hurry up, have some sense, someone may come," I crabbed, so that Mother got angry, saying I didn't understand.

"Go on a ways ahead!" No, to walk on ahead I didn't want to do. So I just had to stand and wait, and waiting was the worst thing I knew. Better then to go back a little. Then folks who came wouldn't think that Mother sitting alongside the road was a friend of mine. And then, too, maybe I could knock down an apple.

I backed up a little way, but I couldn't get any apples down. They hung nearest just where Mother sat. *Ja*, it was clear. I got madder and madder. Mother was a real drag. And here you had to stand like a freak. I turned back again. Scuffled in the dust so it was like a

79

cloud, didn't even look at Mother as I walked past her. There she still sat by the ditch in her horrid shawl.

An old man pushed a wheelbarrow past me. He didn't notice me. But, of course, he would catch sight of Mother where she sat. So maddening. Maybe if I ran I would have time to warn her. Springing past the old man as fast as I could, I could see Mother coming round the bend in the road. Finally, we could continue! Mother greeted the old man, and certainly recognizing him, chatted a bit.

So we trudged on again, side by side. We were like two scraggly animals on our way to our hole. Eighty öre were all we owned to face the needs of our new place.

The farmyards ended. The road went on through nothing but an ugly, empty area owned by the factory. It was boiling hot, no shade, all the trees had been cut. The very air was dusty, and from the ditches came a horrid smell. The only flowers were burdock and wild parsley.

In the distance glistened a cluster of houses, and among them was the cottage we'd be living in. It lay on a half-acre of land flat as a pancake without a tree or a bush, and it wasn't finished yet by a long shot. A bit behind it was a little outhouse, its new boards gleaming bright gold. It didn't have a roof and the door wasn't hinged.

I remember how you had to pull the door open and shut as best you could when you had to use the outhouse. The door was almost too heavy for an eight-year-old; sometimes it fell down, and my stomach cramped so hard the door just had to lie there so anyone walking by had a free little show to gaze at. It was about the worst thing that could happen when the door did that. As long as we lived there the outhouse had no door hinges and no roof.

The porch steps were made of two new resinous boards placed on two blocks, and on the top one our landlady stood looking at us. I wished it had been Valdemar instead, whom Mother had talked about, and who worked at the sugar factory.

"You've sure taken a long time. Albert was here with your furniture early this morning. A nice handsome man you've got there, Hedvig. And there's your girl. *Ja, ja,* I knew about her, *ja, ja.* Mine's nine years old now. We had to get married, Valdemar and I, as you remember, but that couldn't have happened unnecessarily. [She pointed at Mother's stomach and slyly grinned.] It looks like it could come anytime, and the midwife's so fat she could never get up our attic stairs here."

So this was a farmer's daughter. I stared as hard as I could but I couldn't find the least hint of a fairy tale or sniff of richness about her. She rattled on and on without stopping. Mother couldn't get a word in edgewise as she prattled again that my stepfather was a fine-looking fellow.

Her hair was reddish. Her face was covered with freckles; her lower lip looked like *two* lips, and her stomach stuck out like a round hill.

I scratched my head thoughtfully, standing first on one foot, then the other, and thinking that to be a farmer's daughter wasn't much after all. I couldn't understand why Mother had talked so much about that. I had thought a farmer's daughter was something altogether different.

My mother had seen many farmers and farm daughters, so she ought to know something, but I hadn't had a chance to see any before this. Mother always talked about how bold those daughters were with the school teachers and the tenant farmers' children, and how they always married rich men and had splendid weddings, and what big gardens they had.

Here you couldn't even find a tree. I had always thought farmers, cherries, apples, and flowers just went together, but here there was nothing, not even a flower, just nothing. I stood there scratching, not noticing that the landlady was looking me over.

"Do they bite all the time?" she asked, grinning with her ugly lips. "We'll cure them with gray salve."

"I haven't felt well for a while and couldn't see to everything," Mother said. Her face was red with anger.

There wasn't any more talk. The landlady went in so we could come up the steps and go in. She pointed at a little winding staircase. "You can't go wrong," she grinned.

Finally we had reached port again.

It was sweltering inside. The window was at the north. Mother tried to open it, but it was nailed shut. There were no hinges on it either. What the loan company had allowed them hadn't stretched for things like that, Valdemar once said.

The room was very small, but everything was new. The walls freshly papered, all the wood unpainted, shining golden and beautiful. The ceiling was sloped on both sides, and so low that my tall Mother's crown of hair brushed against the new, resinous ceiling boards.

They couldn't get the bed up the stairs; it had been stored at the

81

baker's place. But luckily my acorn settee had made it up and into the room. Mother lay down on it. I sat on a chair and looked around. At least it was prettier here than the room at Holmstad, but so narrow. No stove, only a rusty little paraffin heater. And that little, little window. Never here either would long, blue-starched curtains reflect the luster of the high ceiling and clean neatness of the room. But the dresser stood in a corner, and you could surely get a few leaves for the vases, and on that heater you could boil a pan of water for coffee. "Where have you packed the bucket? I'll go and get some water so we can start cooking," I said to Mother sort of commandingly. For now I had decided to take charge of things a little.

Mother pointed to a sack. I saw her lying there crying. But at that time tears sickened me almost as much as when folks threw up. "You shouldn't be crying now either." I wanted so much to pat her comfortingly, but it was as if something held me back. Mother wasn't the same now. She seemed so distant to me, had so many secrets, and was so preoccupied with my stepfather and her own sickness. I felt sorry for her, wanting to help her, but I didn't want to be near her. I felt she belonged to something I didn't understand and couldn't share the least part of.

"She could have invited me for a drop of coffee, the skinflint," Mother muttered.

"I'll make coffee as soon as I get some water. You lie still so you won't be sick again."

"We don't have a bean of coffee, not even a lump of sugar."

"But you got money for the sheets. There's sure to be a little store around here. *I* don't want any of *her* coffee," I said, thinking of the farmer's daughter and of how different she was from Mother, and without the least bit of disgust, I patted Mother's hair.

It was a good half-mile to the pump. The farmer's daughter, our landlady, showed me the way. And when I was nearly there, an old woman came toward me saying I couldn't take any water. "Where are you from?" she asked, putting on her glasses that hung from a cord on her breast.

"We live . . ." *Ja,* where did we live?

"Well, where do you live?"

"We live at the farmer's daughter's." (I had never heard the name of our landlady, but I remembered the most important and the strangest thing which eventually had something of a fairy tale about it in that sad move.) "Her man works at the sugar factory; he's called Valdemar."

The old woman laughed so her stomach jiggled. "Herre gud,* do you live with *Molasses*?" (That was our landlady's nickname in this district of folks who owned their own homes.) "Why didn't your mother come for the water then? You're not strong enough for such a big bucket. But that's what they always do—send their kids here, for they know they're forbidden to take water here in the dry weather now when the well's drying up."

"Mother didn't know that. She's sick, and we've just come and have never been here before. Dear lady, please may I have some water, just enough for some coffee?"

All at once I thought life had become unbearably hard. I knew about a lot of things that weren't for the likes of me. Bright-colored Dalarna bags that held your handkerchief, gaily painted rubber balls, the bigger they were, the more fabulous. Real sandwiches and liver sausage and white bread. Dolls that opened and shut their eyes and had real hair. Fine shoes and short dresses. Princess dresses they were called. Rope swings in an orchard, piles of storybooks that I'd seen in places where Mother scrubbed—all those things I knew were out of my reach.

But they weren't within most of my friends' grasp either. We had so much else that interested us that we really didn't mind much that we didn't have such splendors. I was never class conscious on that account. I was often hungry, but that I had in common with so many that it wouldn't cause any wonder or any special suffering and brooding over.

But water. . . . No one but me in the whole world had been denied water. Jesus got only a little vinegar, of course, but then he died, too. I had heard about folks who thirsted to death in deserts and about bold travellers there who took water from the bellies of their camels. But there certainly weren't any camels here. There wasn't even a desert. Here was a pump, but you couldn't take any water from it. In the desert you could take water from a well when you came to an oasis, but here it was forbidden.

Forbidden. How could you solve that? Nothing helped. How would a bold camel driver be able to get water from his camel if the camel were forbidden to drink?

I thought the woman who stood there with her glasses had

*"Good God."

83

become an evil, dangerous power. I got so scared I trembled. She didn't answer my plea either. She just looked coldly at me through her glasses. The pump handle hung so temptingly near, and Mother lay on the acorn settee at home waiting. Then something startling happened that I never told Mother about.

"Dear lady," I said, curtseying. "Let me take only a liter."

"You can have as much as you're able to carry," she said, taking off her glasses.

As much as I could carry. *Ja,* that she'd get to see. I pumped and pumped, but then I had second thoughts. Better not to take too much, best to take only half a bucket. Suddenly I was so thirsty. After I stopped pumping, I bent over, trying to catch the last drops in my mouth.

It often happens that just those unexpected difficulties always are so much harder than those you have a little hint about. It's those unexpected troubles that make many able to go on living. The only thing that spurs you to get new strength. The other things become so little and light when some new terror turns up like a black thundercloud, then rolls away. The sky becomes all clear again. Sore feet, a sick mother, a troublesome stepfather, dirty aprons, and lice in your head become almost like dear old friends you're glad to have on your side when the new danger comes.

The water bucket was big; I was hardly more than twice its size, but I carried it steadily even though my arms trembled under the weight. The woman followed me a ways. Setting down the bucket, I curtseyed and thanked again. Then I asked in a shaky voice if there was a store nearby, that I needed just about everything. Could you buy coffee or sugar any place around here? Or bread?

"A store, I keep one myself," the woman said, brightening up. "Do you have any money with you?" Now she looked grim again. I showed the modest sum. Mother had sent thirty öre. One hecto of coffee, two hecto of sugar.

"In the mornings you can buy milk here," the woman said, not looking at all surprised at my meager amount of cash.

The people owned their houses and had their money tied up in the bank, a bank where they never got to take any out, and the whole district here was largely made up of these homeowners. In the store, the poorest of all the renters were looked on more favorably than the homeowners. The renters always had cash sometime in the week; the homeowners never had any. God knows what they lived on. Sometimes the landlady didn't have cash for so long a time that she had a renter smuggle a flask of water, for the renters weren't forbidden that by the woman in the store; then the water became the landlady's. The renters were the best customers. The whole district suffered from lack of water. The veins for water were too deep and cost too much to drill. For my ready money of thirty öre I was promised I could get water once a day.

"The pump and well cost me three hundred, I'll have you know, but here they want to take my water for free. If they can build a house, well, they can build a pump, too." The storekeeper had no loan on her house; it was free from debt.

When I came home with the water and bags of coffee and sugar, Mother was up getting things in order. She had done some unpacking and had pushed the sacks back so you could move. From one sack she had taken some sticks of wood that had been left over from our first place (you never left wood behind) and made a fire in the tiny heater. It became uncomfortably warm in the room.

"The pump cost three hundred, but we can get water once a day, the woman we live with is called *molasses,* and we can buy milk at the store in the mornings."

Mother looked as if she didn't know what I was talking about. The trouble I'd had in getting that forbidden water she'd never hear about from me. Mother never would have understood how awful that was and what I'd had to do to get a little water. Grown-ups never understand such adventures. They think it's only for you to go there and take. She didn't ask about it either, just ground the coffee and made it. We drank it black. I dipped my limpa in it, but Mother just drank coffee, several cups, and ate nothing. It was our first meal in that new place.

"You must never call her 'Molasses'; that's a nickname," Mother said, and I saw her mouth twitch a little.

Then Mother began to get our things in order again. The day turned to night. The celebrated August moon streamed through the nailed-down window, casting shadows like crosses over the floor.

"Wonder if *he* will come home tonight," Mother said, making up my acorn bed for two and a bed on the floor for me.

I didn't answer.

I lay on my bed and saw my mother lying there, fingering and counting the acorns. "There are sixty-four," I said sleepily.

"Are there so many?" And I heard her counting them in a whisper.

I was asleep before she had counted all of them.

"He" didn't come home in the night.

Mother became fully enlightened on the question about water the next day.

She had felt so well in the morning that she decided to go into town to get "a place" with someone, as it was called at that time among poor people when every penny was spent.

She told me to sleep another hour for it was only seven. Before lunchtime she came back with a big bundle of washing. She had bitten the sour apple, swallowed her pride, and gone to those "well-off" relations. Well, of course, they certainly wanted to help Hedvig and could give her a little work. She had got the weaving master's dirty work clothes and the women's kitchen aprons, as well as the coarse kitchen hand towels. Fine washing of course you had to be so careful with that you washed it yourself.

Mother had been to the haulage carrier's, too, but since my stepfather had already driven away, she hadn't chanced to see him. So she had gone to a store where she'd shopped when she worked at the factory, and there she'd been given a little on credit. Soap for the washing, two loaves of limpa, some margarine, a bit of American pork, and a little gristly sausage, at that time, the smoked sausage for frying. And a few kilos of potatoes.

Together with the bundle of washing it was a heavy load to carry home. Mother had hardly a month left until she'd have the baby.

It wasn't a year since she'd had a baby in that beautiful room at Old Island Road, and now she'd be having a baby again, that I knew.

Mother cooked a few potatoes and fried the sausage. It tasted so good after two days of watery coffee. It was the first meal, I think, that Mother had made for just the two of us. Believing that life was beginning to brighten again, I prattled on about how fine now we could make the room.

Mother ate quickly, gulping her food—how hungry she must have been. I tried not to notice how she smacked and chewed so frenziedly and ugly. I knew she'd soon be sick and start to throw up, but I wanted to be friends with Mother now that we sat eating such good food alone together.

Then all of a sudden we heard the landlady's high-pitched voice. Mother stopped eating and listened. I did, too.

"I felt sorry for her, I knew her from home. *Ja,* she had a kid before she was twenty with a gentleman's son who wouldn't even look at her again since he'd got what he wanted. Now her next man's left her, not to wonder at, he's such a nice, handsome fellow. She doesn't bother to keep herself or the kid decently clean and doesn't have enough sense to keep from having a kid every year. A guy gets tired of that, you can bet. He's got someone else in town now, and we might as well look for the rent in the stove."

"Won't he be coming home any more?" I asked Mother. I had understood every word that had drifted up through those thin walls.

"Oh, *ja*, he will," Mother said bitterly, and she looked so grim that I dared not show my disappointment that "he" would come home again.

The babbling continued below, but Mother got up. "I'll go now and soak the clothes so we'll get a bit clean. Folks are beginning to be so persnickety about themselves," she said bitterly. Mother, who had been known as the cleanest and neatest of all the factory girls.

Thus, she got informed how things stood at the well pump.

Mother, of course, couldn't wash the clothes.

She came back with the master weaver's dirty shirts and pants. I saw her coming down the road, and I heard how she threw the bundle down in front of the house. I knew that Mother was beside herself with rage. She went in to the landlady's without knocking on the door. She wasn't used to rushing into folks' places like that.

Up where I was I could every word.

Mother didn't say hello. She began without any polite niceties. "You know that we can hear every word you say down here," she began.

The landlady didn't answer. None of her coffee friends was there.

"You're worried about me and my dirty child and my man. When did you wash yourself last? Or do you run there and steal water at night?"

No answer.

"You can't find any water around here for three miles. You should have told me when you rented that hole to us. You offered me a room when I chanced to run into you and happened to tell you I was out looking for a place for us. Braggart that you are, you promised me I could wait with the rent for two weeks. I've been here only one night, and you are ready with your shit talk for the neighbors. Do you think I'm not well enough known that I can't get four kronor together that you're asking for a month? You don't need to spread lies about me for that amount and yell so my child hears every word through the chinks in your 'villa.'" Mother said "villa" so sarcastically. (She who doesn't own anything can allow herself to talk sarcastically about others' possessions.)

"And then you talk about cleanliness." (I heard how Mother still was mad. I can't say I felt sorry for the landlady.) "Do you remember what *my* father said that time to *your* father?" Again I heard Mother's voice. "Do you remember what he said? It became a proverb in the whole parish. Your father stood in our house and was going to drive me out because I had come home and was going to have a child and I wasn't registered in the parish. Your father was so afraid about the parish then. But who was it who signed a note for your father when he was bankrupt because he'd gotten so swelled with self-importance playing the big farmer until his money was gone? Well, *ja*, that was *my* father who did that for yours. And your father's name wasn't ruined thanks to the money that people knew the gentleman's son had left for my 'dirty kid.' You couldn't indeed have done anything else but rent me the room when you knew all this, knew that my father used the money to get yours out of bankruptcy. And then, just then, my father died, and we hardly had enough to bury him after your bankruptcy firm got theirs."

The landlady began to bawl, wailing that Hedvig had embarrassed her so she wouldn't be able to look people in the face after this. And I heard one of her friends loftily tell Mother that she'd have to take the washing into the town's public washhouse. (Mother who had just lugged the dirty clothes from the town.)

"Out here we hardly have enough to wash the dishes after a Sunday meal," she scolded, as if she wanted to show that she was wholly neutral in Mother's quarrel with the landlady.

I heard the door slam again without another word from Mother, and she came in very cheered up.

She warmed up the pan of water. Washed my hair and searched it for lice so that my head burned and ached. Then she looked for a clean outgrown apron for me from a packing sack.

"Now we'll go to Vilbergen to Grandma so I can wash this muck and get enough money for the rent. Did you hear how I gave it to her?"

"*Ja*, you had a right to." I was surprised that Mother hadn't got sick from all the potatoes and sausage she'd eaten.

"Was there a lot of money that Grandpa gave away? How could he give away my money? Was it maybe not my money because I was so little?"

Mother stared straight ahead for a while without answering. I waited, for I was tense with excitement.

"I don't know," she said absently. "I don't know. We certainly won't be staying here very long," she added swiftly, gathering up the dirty shirts and stuff she had been trying to get done the whole morning.

"Can't we unpack and get things in order before we go?"

"No, I have to wash these clothes so I'll have something for the rent."

We had three miles to walk to Grandma's.

Mother washed those oily work clothes and those greasy aprons, ironed them, and took them to the master weaver's, but they didn't have any money just then.

"It was just as I told you," Grandma said when Mother came back. "They've owed me for a rag carpet for twenty years."

Their washing still isn't paid, thirty years later, but those "well-off" relatives had even so helped out by giving Hedvig a little work.

That doctrine was the "well-off" relatives' standing code from that day to this: poor people must have work so they can get along on their own.

Mother got money for the rent from Grandma.

"Otherwise you'll be eaten alive. I know her sort," she said.

The landlady got her rent that same night. She thanked and prattled on as if there'd never been a hard word said. It looked as if she were sincerely glad for the money. It was the first cash she had seen for a long time. Those four kronor gave the first bit of relief from the homeowners' burden. All they had were debts. But here was finally something. Rent. Real cash.

Mother was very reserved. Childhood friends can be very reserved with each other under certain circumstances.

The room was just as we had left it. The water that Mother had washed my hair in was still in the pan on the chair. The acorn settee was turned into a bed for two, rumpled and unmade. My bed lay there in a corner.

O, you, my lovely home at Old Island Road, with white tablecloths, new rag rugs, quiet—and where I was alone with a mother who was so happy. Never, never more was I so alone with her. Now there was so much that was in the way: worries, dirt, debts, my stepfather—everything stood between us, and now Mother was so big and ugly and thought only about my stepfather.

Ever since the first night in the room at Old Island Road, when Mother lay in the same bed with my stepfather, I had never been alone with her again. And never again was anything so clean and neat as in that room. Here, in front of that skimpy, nailed-down window hole, you couldn't put up a cottage curtain. It would just make it darker inside. The roller shade with the girl and the clogs had no room here, wasn't needed either. No sun shone in to take the color from the gaily colored rag rugs.

The acorns were no longer mine; Mother lay and counted them at night. And the only thing there was even a little mystery about, the fellow Valdemar, I hadn't been lucky enough to see once. He worked at a sugar mill. Good heavens, they must be rich. He carried home sugar syrup every night. Out on the attic step was a big four-sided tin can full of sugar syrup.

"They got that from the sugar mill," Mother said. It was unclean sugar that the mill couldn't sell.

Grandma had said you'd get a freckle on your nose every time you stole a lump from the sugar bowl. The landlady had so many freckles! How, I wonder, did Valdemar get the syrup? I must see Valdemar. He probably had as many freckles as his wife, so he must have stolen the syrup.

Stuffy, hot days. Drooping, full of dust the burdock hung and the wild parsley. The days Mother wasn't in town scrubbing or doing washing, she lay on the acorn settee and threw up. Everything she ate, she threw up.

The lice flourished in my head. From the slanted ceiling in the room tar oozed from the paper on the roof. Downstairs the landlady baked bread every day with sugar syrup in it. Sugar syrup that made the bread rise more quickly. It was sweet as molasses. I got a bit one day. But out on the attic step stood the sugar-syrup can, full of secrets, horrifying ones.

The resin ran from the new walls. Resin drops hung everywhere, gold, gleaming. I'd stand a long time out on the attic step looking at the tin can, and one day I put a drop of resin in my mouth. It must be syrup. A house with a big tin can with syrup, so the resin that oozed had to be sugar syrup. But it was tree sap. So bitter that I shivered.

The landlady's girl went to school. I should have, too.

"It isn't worth the trouble; we'll be moving soon," Mother said.

I tried to meet the landlady's girl when she came from school, but she wouldn't look at me. I waited a long time for her to come out again, but she wouldn't come as long as I sat on those resiny porch steps. As soon as I'd go away, she ran quickly out down to road to another house where she had friends.

She wasn't *allowed* to play with me. But I couldn't grasp that. I thought if I could only talk to her we'd soon be gathering together interesting playthings, doll houses, and get sugar syrup for doll parties. I had full confidence in my ability to conquer this new girl. I wasn't used to playmates avoiding me. But I was never lucky enough to get her to stop. One day I grabbed her skirt.

"Let go, you dirty brat!" she yelled. And the farmer's daughter with her big lips came out.

"Ida has to do her lessons now." The freckles glistened black on her face. Little by little I understood.

The ones who owned their own houses mostly rented out their tiny attics if they could spare the room to single men or women. There were so few children in that area; those who were there were too fine for the likes of me.

The only one that stood up for me was the woman in the little store. I got to take as much water as I wanted. Mother never took anything on credit in that store. She had credit in town. The woman in the store "respected" us, and one day Mother and I were invited there for coffee.

I never had any playmates in this place, but I had other friends. I became good friends with the baker.

He lived in the same room as his bakery which was in a cellar next door to the little store. I stayed there often until late at night when Mother came for me, and then she always got a big limpa, freshly baked. We had plenty of bread during our whole time in that place.

Sometimes he was drunk. Then he took off his shoes and socks, climbed up in the big dough trough, and trampled in the dough with his feet, singing and yelling, "Like this you baked bread in my youth!" And he stomped in the dough so that he got dough way up on his legs.

When I told that to Mother, she had to lie down and hold her mouth. Mother began to be really difficult.

One day the baker said to me, "If your Mother would have a little money, I'd marry her, she's a very good-looking woman."

I thought *woman* was the same as fiancée or chick as boys used to

91

say, so I said to my mother that night that the baker wanted to marry her, for she was a good-looking chick. I thought Mother wouldn't understand if I said "woman."

"How dare he!" Mother said.

"I was thinking you maybe should marry him. He sells so much limpa," I said.

"Don't you think I have enough with the one I have?" Mother said.

I hadn't seen my stepfather for a week and had nearly forgotten him.

Chapter 9

The next night, a clear August night, the full moon shone over the sugar-syrup house. I had sat up in the stuffy room waiting for Mother, and had fallen asleep.

When I woke up the room was bright with moonlight; the sloping ceilings cast scary shadows over the floor. Mother still hadn't come. Downstairs at Valdemar's they must all have been sleeping, for it was so quiet. If I hadn't been so hungry, I'd have huddled down in my bed on the floor and gone back to sleep. Mother made up my acorn bed for two every night but woke up alone every morning.

My stomach growled loudly. I had eaten only some bread with my coffee the whole day, and the slices weren't big. Mother had said she'd be home after lunch; in the meantime I had helped the woman in the little store weed her garden. Mother thought I'd get lunch there, but the woman had got suddenly sick, and everything was topsy-turvy. People stood waiting in the store and weren't served. The baker who used to help the storekeeper was on a binge and was either in town at Skull-Jon's or out in Vrinneviss Forest where the drunks hung out, drinking beer and playing cards. I was completely cut off from any friends that day.

After I had finally got it through my head that the landlady's Ida and her friends thought I was too dumb to play with, I no longer worried about it. It was more fun without them, I tried to tell myself. I sat and listened to the baker and the storekeeper when their places were closed for the night and Mother was delayed in town. They would go to each other's place, letting me stay. If I were at the storekeeper's, sometimes she'd give me a sandwich. The baker liked me to stay at his place, for he wanted Mother to come and fetch me.

"Sit here now till your mother comes, and then I'll give her a limpa."

"I can take the limpa," I'd say. No, the baker always wanted to give Mother the loaf himself. One night the storekeeper said that the baker would have been a rich fellow "if he had got a clever girl like Mia's mother."

Today the shopkeeper was sick and the baker away. At the time that hadn't meant much; I was used to managing by myself, only there was very little food up in our room.

Shivering now and a little scared I stole out on the highway which lay chalky in the moonlight. Not a soul was around, and I ran as fast as I could toward town.

I shied like a frightened horse at those dark fir trees' thick shadows on the road and stayed as far as I could on the other side which lay like a trail of flour beside the shadows. When I came nearer the storekeeper's garden, the air was so full of the smell of flowers that I stopped and sniffed eagerly with big gulps as if their scent could be eaten.

I was nearly halfway to town, running the whole distance. Now I stood somewhat out of breath and reflected. I was barefooted and bareheaded, best to wait here. I slumped down in almost the same place that Mother had sat several weeks before in her ugly shawl and been sick. The apples hung far out over the fence now as then, and still wanting one, though I was alone at night with those watching moon shadows around me, I didn't dare to steal a green apple. My stomach still growled for food. I knew from experience how bad green apples tasted. The ground was dewy and a little chilly. I drew my dress around me as best I could, tucking my black sore feet under my skirt and waited. Flower scent and moonlight came in waves over me. Here I'd come some night and sit when I had eaten, I decided. I stared up at the blue moon harbor, and all at once I thought of the highway, the flower smells, and I sailed away. It was like when you stand for a long time staring at the water shallows, and the place where you're standing seems to move under you.

I sat there for an hour or so, shivering, nodding off a few times. I began to feel frozen, and my bones were so stiff I could hardly get up and try to go back home. Perhaps Mother had stayed in town all night. I was so tired I didn't mind about that, and my hunger had gone. I stumbled up from the ditch. Then Mother came. She was sweaty and looked upset.

"Herre gud, Mia . . ." and she threw her shawl around me. We sat

94

down in the ditch, and she got out a slice of wheat bread for me. "We'll warm up a drop of coffee when we get home; I haven't had one cup today, and I've got some coffee beans with me." I crept closer to Mother; I knew her whole body was shivering.

"You'll freeze like this. Come, now we'll go." I had got warm so I gave her the shawl and crawled again from the ditch.

"I won't freeze, no, freeze I won't, freeze, oh, no." Mother sounded as if she didn't know what she said.

"Heavens, how good it smells, doesn't it, Mia!" Mother drew in the flower smells as she walked on the highway. I didn't answer. I thought Mother walked so strangely; she was limping, but she had such a big stomach, that was probably why. But even so—no, it was too crazy. Mother was walking without shoes, was only in her stocking feet.

"Are you crazy, Mother, walking in your stocking feet? Where are your shoes?"

"Shoes, *ja*, I've lost them." I knew by her voice Mother lied. What could have happened to Mother's old scuffed tight shoes that pinched? Grown folks didn't lose their shoes. Both at once. Oh, no, I knew that. I had seen enough. My head got so strangely hot in spite of the cold moonlight when I saw Mother trudge along in her stockings. God, the Father, what had Mother come to?

"Take off your stockings, you'll ruin them," I dared to say.

"I don't care what's ruined." I could tell she was crying.

"Did you hit him with your shoes?"

"*Him*, no, I hit *her* on the nose with my shoe, she knows well enough he's married, and she knows me, too, well enough." Mother was silent.

The flower-filled moonlight seemed to cry out our misery.

Ja, I understood a little, but I couldn't understand Mother even so. She didn't need to take it so hard that he went with another. It was even wonderful, others could gladly have him so we could be through with him.

"Did you hit *him* with the other shoe?" I boldly asked.

"No, I threw it away, I couldn't just go and limp in *one* shoe."

No, that was clear enough. She didn't have the heart to beat him, but I sure enough got whipped sometimes.

We had passed the yards with gardens, and now in the home owners' district with its ugly houses the shadows over the road became straight; the smell of flowers was finished. Mother looked like a beggar woman as she walked in the dew-wet dust that stuck fast to the thick soles of her stockings.

We stole as quietly as we could up the narrow staircase, but Mother's string bag, happening to hit the syrup can that stood right by the stairway, sounded like a church bell I thought, and Mother swore. "What the devil, damn syrup can, just about fell over it!" I hadn't heard Mother swear before.

I was full of wheat bread and just wanted to go to sleep, but Mother couldn't sleep. She had to have a cup of strong coffee, for she had such a headache, she said.

"There isn't a stick of wood, Valdemar's haven't any either," I hastily informed her. I sat on my bed with my clothes on, trying not to fall asleep.

Mother crumpled a few newspapers, set them on fire in the little heater, sloshed water in the tin pan (water that I pumped every day from the storekeeper's well), swept a towel around the coffee mill so it couldn't be heard downstairs when she ground the beans. But the paper burned up with a flame, and the water was hardly lukewarm. I became wide awake when I saw Mother break up a wooden basket that my stepfather had carried his lunch in when he was a ditchdigger. The dry wood flamed up like the newspaper had before the water came to a boil. Now Mother looked grimmer. She had taken off her dress and had on only her cotton vest and underskirt. Its waistband cut into her thick waist; her stomach was big and high.

"I'm going to have a cup of coffee if I have to burn up everything," she bitterly said.

She went out on the staircase, picked up a nearly new scouring brush and stuffed it in the stove. Two wooden spoons and a worn wooden whisk went next. Finally the water boiled. I was fully awake. The coffee smelled so good I asked Mother for a drop, and I got a fresh roll, too, with the coffee.

"I bought a sack of fresh good whole wheat bread, for now anything goes. It's no use to save and starve, you starve if you've got, and you starve if you don't. But I got the coffee made anyway," she said triumphantly.

I was so perked up by the coffee and Mother's recklessness that I was eager for us to go out on the highway again to the fence where the flowers bloomed. "We can probably come across something, maybe some apples, too." I was in the same mood as Mother; there was no use in worrying. But Mother would not.

"Don't talk nonsense . . . at least I got the coffee made," she tiresomely went on.

As many things as she burned up, was that so remarkable? It was as if that victory with a red roasting stove and an empty woodbox had pepped her up more than anything. She was certainly proud that she'd dared destroy things, dared burn up wooden spoons, scouring brush, and lunch basket in order to get a cup of coffee. She had learned a new side of herself that she hadn't known. That side cheered her. Made her sure. It looked that way.

"In the morning you must wear your boots," I said anxiously, afraid she'd maybe think of going barefoot now like some of the gypsy women I'd seen.

"Certainly, I'll wear them. What good does it do to save? No, I'll not do that anymore."

When I tried again to get to sleep, Mother was washing the dirt from her only pair of stockings that she'd walked in all the way from the tollgates. The acorn settee was made into a bed for two; she knew well enough that "he" wouldn't come home, she could have asked me to sleep with her. But she didn't. Finally I slept free from care.

The next night Mother came home with another pair of shoes that pinched that she had bought at Stamp-Kalle's for fifty öre. She carried them in a package. Her rashness hadn't lasted long.

The week after this I had stopped at the baker's one night and got home late. I finally got to see Valdemar. He came from work and had as usual a little flask in his hand that I knew held sugar syrup. He was an awfully tall, heavy fellow with a broad white face and a tiny little mouth that could hardly be seen. He had no freckles. He was sitting on the stoop boards waiting for the landlady, his wife, and daughter, for they had taken the key with them.

I sat down on the stoop beside him, scratched the lice in my head a little, hid my dirty feet under my skirt, and tried to strike up a conversation with him. I liked him as soon as I saw him and wanted to know a little about the sugar mill.

He greeted me heartily at the same time that he took snuff from his mouth, and while he spit and coughed and dried his lips with the backside of his hand, he said, "It's too late for such a little lady as you to be out, best to go up, I know your mother is home."

But I stayed, pretending that I hadn't heard him. The thunder rumbled a little; the clouds clustered over the ugly neighborhood, darkening it. It was stifling hot. Valdemar looked so enormously big out there in the night; it was certain it was he who made the biggest sugar loaves the woman had at her little store. Sugar loaves with a hole in the very topmost peak so you could pull a thread through it and hang it on the Christmas tree. I had three of them in my cupboard. Mother always bought the top of the loaf, for she said that the sugar was the hardest and cheapest, and I got the last bit with the hole. I thought of asking Valdemar to make the hole a little deeper so the top bit for the Christmas tree could be bigger.

"Think that you, uncle, can make sugar loaves," I said encouragingly.

"There are so many of us who do that; I'm not alone," he said in a friendly way. I had been mistaken. I thought he had worked alone in a white room turning out sugar loaves on a lathe and getting to take home all the syrup because of his difficult work. It wasn't worth talking about the holes in the tops now. I moved a little from him, he smelled so bad. All the people out here in this district smelled bad because of the lack of water. And it never rained.

"As soon as we get rain I want your mother to come here and wash," the woman in the store said. But the rain didn't come, and I certainly wasn't clean anymore. I smelled bad, too, but Valdemar smelled far more terrible. I wasn't able to talk more with him. Our dirt and stink got in the way. I didn't want to show him my dirty feet, and to sit near him I couldn't. I sat there curled up like a ball on the very edge of the porch stoop.

He sat there like a big tired clump. Like a round dark stone he looked in the deepening twilight. His head drooped on his chest; he had to be asleep. I was tired, too. I had sat in the warm bakery until the baker had told me to go home, for he wanted to sleep.

The lightning flashed here and there in the sky. No other person was to be seen.

Mother wasn't home even though Valdemar thought she was. She had got a cleaning job at a new building and could work as long as she wanted at night.

Valdemar had dozed off. Neither of us heard Mother coming until she stood there saying, "Good evening." She had a bundle. A big one.

"You've not ever seen how we have it up there," Mother said. "Come on up and I'll cook coffee."

The big fellow could hardly squeeze himself up his new stairway. Mother let the door stay open. She lighted the stove, and now with its warmth Valdemar smelled so bad that Mother got deathly white. I was afraid, too, not because of the smell but that Mother would shame us.

She went down to the yard for a while to get air, telling me to watch the pan. *Ja,* that was good she went out. I filled the tin pan and set out cups. Mother came back now and took out the wheat bread and other things from her bundle so that Valdemar could see all she had. A little herring, pickles, strong crumbly cheese, two aprons, a dress she'd got for me from some woman. I thought it was like a party; tomorrow everything would be fine, too.

"You know how to manage well, Hedvig, even though your man is away," Valdemar said, dipping a big piece of bread in his coffee.

Mother didn't say anything.

"*Ja,* I didn't think when we worked together at Kolsta that you'd be coming here and renting a room from us," he said. Mother didn't look happy.

While they talked a little about this and that, I got sleepier until I heard him say, "If you have a can, you can have some syrup. We have so much here, and I can take home more for sure."

Mother took out a can, and he filled it with that sticky gray-black syrup. Finally. Never more would I be wrong about wood sap and sugar syrup. I slept in my corner of the floor where my bed had been laid since moving.

Suddenly I woke up to an awful scene. The landlady stood in the narrow door, making such a row that her lower lip looked like three. Valdemar still sat in his chair, not saying a word, nor my mother either. Their daughter pushed her head between her mother and the doorjamb, looking curious.

"You're just what I always said, you, but you'll soon be on your way!" she yelled. "You'll pack up and be off tomorrow. What are you doing with guys that belong to others? I know you, I do. Haven't you got enough, you, maybe? You're so big you can't even walk. Go down to your own place, Valdemar. I'll say only this, you didn't have a scrap but I married you anyway. Then you carry on like this, doing this as fast as I'm out of the way. I always thought it'd be like this."

Both Valdemar and Mother said nothing. The girl began to howl, and then the mother screamed "whore" to Mother.

Then Mother got up. I saw how angry she was. She looked for something, then took the knife she cut bread with. Now I began to yell, too.

"Hedvig, put that down. You surely know what she's like," Valdemar said, taking the knife from Mother. At the same time, the landlady sprang in and knocked over the syrup can; a cup also fell on the floor.

"Comb the lice from your brat and take your rights with your own guy," she shrieked.

Then Valdemar seized her by the neck; he couldn't stand up straight in the room, and he dragged her by the skin on her neck so that her face looked awful. One end of her mouth was stretched to her ear, her eye was narrowed to a slit, and her round freckles were pulled into ovals on one side of her face.

"Shut your mouth, you damned hag! I ought to throw you down the stairs," he yelled. "I've worked eighteen hours while you run with your old women and take the key with you so I have to sit like a fool and wait till it suits you to come home. Then you scream at people who haven't done anything. Hedvig had just come, her girl, too. I've worked overtime now for two weeks so I'd have enough for the loan in October, but, you, what the devil do you do? Put me in debt with the stores so I'll never be out of it. I'll end up in jail just like that."

The whole time he held her by the neck, and their daughter forgot to scream, just stared at her mother's grotesque face.

"Let go of her," Mother said. "Let her go, and all of you leave. Albert can come whenever; he said he'd come home tonight."

It became quiet. The man unloosed his hold, and the three pushed their way down the stairs.

I was wide awake. There lay the sugar syrup in a cake on the floor, and *he* would come. All at once everything became so dark. That was, of course, why Mother bought such good food. I began to cry.

Mother didn't say anything. She sat on the acorn settee and looked absently at the syrup and the dented can. Suddenly it began to spatter on the tarpaper roof. The rain had come.

"Don't cry, Mia. I'll manage so we can move," she said, coming over and patting me. I didn't answer.

Mother scraped up the syrup—some of it was usable—scrubbed the floor, for now there was water enough for that, the rain had come. She made up the settee for two, tidied up, undressed and waited, but I slept, getting away from all the dramatic events, though downstairs they quarreled, sometimes mumbling and sometimes Valdemar's voice sounded hateful and terribly loud.

Late that night my stepfather came. He hadn't been here since he'd moved in the furniture.

He came up the narrow stairs stumbling and swearing so that I woke up and saw how pale Mother was. Down at Valdemar's they hadn't slept; they still were quarreling so that every word could be heard.

My stepfather threw down a rain-soaked package on the floor and sat down on a chair, a flood of water running off him. "That's a devil of a fight going on down there."

Mother shushed him. Downstairs they yelled, accusing each other of old sins about farms and poor hired men, about red hair and big lips.

My stepfather swayed on his tilted chair; he was very drunk. Fumbling in his pocket he dug out a fat sack which he threw at me. It was full of fine candy. "Take some from da sack, open up dat package there," he stammered. From his other pocket he pulled out a mouthharp and began to play a lively waltz.

"Are you crazy? It's two in the morning." As Mother untied the package, I saw how her hands shook.

"Who gives a hang—they carry on like the devil down there. Big Valdemar must not be getting what he wants from his old woman or why else are they fighting?"

He continued his playing. Played and looked at Mother and the package.

"Damn it, cut the string!"

Mother had untied the package at last. A new pair of shoes for me and a plaid piece of goods for a dress as well, Scottish plaid it was called and all the fashion just then.

No man is so stupid that he doesn't know the way to a woman's heart. I saw Mother beam, but I wasn't happy. I yawned sleepily. And he didn't ask what I had to say. He didn't care about thanks from me. Mother didn't tell me to thank him either. He looked only at her. The gifts were for her. The best gifts he could give, he knew that well enough.

"Don't play anymore," she said. She had become beautiful again.

"Why're they fighting down there?"

"I don't know," Mother said. "They've just had a falling out."

Crawling down into my bed, I lay and cried. I liked everyone just then except my mother and my stepfather. The baker was much better. Valdemar was best of all. Hanna, Hanna, you who were still left with my god! Even the landlady who had yelled at Mother was all right. My stepfather now began to throw up; probably both of them would. I'd had enough. In the morning I'd run away to Hanna in the poorhouse.

Down below they were still fighting.

"I drank too much beer. I'll clean this up myself," my stepfather said. "You're getting big, Hedvig. When is it coming?" He was soberer now.

I slept a little. Hearing my stepfather shout on the landing for them to shut up down there, I woke up. The landlady yelled that he should go back in to the whore he was married to who slept with other women's men. He came back to Mother looking wild. He was still drunk.

"Is it Valdemar!" he shouted. "Is it Valdemar!"

Mother screamed. I heard Valdemar coming up the stairs. I lay perfectly still. Everything had happened so suddenly. The whole night was like a dark devil dance with the landlady the worst of all the witches I'd ever seen on Easter cards.*

My stepfather had grabbed hold of Mother's long hair. She hit him in the face, but he knocked her down. I began to cry.

Valdemar now burst in. He grabbed my stepfather by the middle, carried him out to the landing and bumped him down the stairs.

"I'm an honest guy though my old woman's crazy, crazy, you understand, but how dare you come here and believe the worst about Hedvig—that she gets kids with just anyone!" (I remember every word as if they were letters of fire.) "Do you think I'm such a scum like you, you who've laid with your whore in town the whole time since you moved here as everyone out here knows? Don't show your mug around here anymore or I'll break every bone in your body!"

They disappeared into the yard.

In a couple of hours they both came back together. Then everything was quiet. The landlady didn't make another peep; neither did Valdemar nor my stepfather. But my mother was very sick. Though it was only five in the morning I had to get dressed and go with Valdemar; on his way to work he would show me the way to the midwife that Mother needed. A nice woman that Mother washed clothes for without payment.

I pulled on my old cast-off beggar's dress and a clean apron

---

*In Swedish folklore at Eastertime, witches rode through the air on broomsticks for a tryst with the devil. Witches were often depicted on Easter cards.

Mother had brought home with her. The plaid goods and the new shoes lay in a corner.

It still rained. When we had walked a ways on the wet highway, Valdemar took my hand. After I had given my message to the midwife, I was to go to Grandma's. We plodded along, the big tired man and I. When we got to the turn-off to the sugar mill, he took out a little black book that had a tiny pencil attached to it and wrote something on a sheet.

"Your father certainly didn't think of this, but if 'Miss' isn't home, put this note in her door." He hunted in his large dirty coin purse and gave me ten öre. Then patting me with his great paw, he told me to be quick.

I thought a lot of Valdemar. I think a lot of him still even though he is dead.

The midwife lived alongside the tollgates in a pretty little house. I read the name on the gate: Miss Fransson, midwife.

Opening the gate, I walked through a little garden of sweet peas and marigolds and knocked on the kitchen door. It was locked. No one came. Then I saw a note. It was written, not printed, so it was hard for me to read; I couldn't understand it, but I spelled out "to Gjuteriet." A suburb. I grasped that she was out with someone in Gjuteriet who would be having a baby, and I put up the note Valdemar had scrawled with the old tack that was on the door.

It had stopped raining, but I was soaked. I wasn't cold, for it was still sultry and the thunder still rumbled. I sat on the steps a while, so tired after that stormy night that I thought I couldn't possibly walk way up to Vilbergen to Grandma's. Creeping down under a bush by the step, I slept until "Miss" woke me up.

"How long have you lain here?

I didn't know.

She held Valdemar's note. "Is your mother Hedvig Stenman?"

"Ja, uh—she's sick now, she's having a baby."

"You live quite a distance from here. How far is it?"

"It's not far; it's in the district where they own their homes."

She muttered something about it should still be a month, that it was too early. "Was your mother lying down when you left? Was she very sick?"

"Ja, Unc . . . Father hit her and she got so sick."

"Will you go back with me and show me the way?" asked "Miss" hastily.

103

"I'm to go to Grandma's. I'm not supposed to be with Mother when she's having the baby."

"Go with me to the crossroad and show me which road I should take. Here, take this." She gave me a big roll. Gathering up some things in a bag, she then rinsed her face, chewed a roll, and after she had written a note where she was to be found, we were on our way.

It was the same woman who had been with Mother when she had the baby in the room at Old Island Road. Now Mother no longer belonged to her district, but she had promised to come anyway. It was just as far to the midwife in our district.

Now there would be no coffee, no fine curtains, no large beautiful room, and no Grandma who knew how it should be when a baby was being born, as all this had been in the room at Old Island Road. But "Miss" certainly must have liked Mother, for she was with her even when her third baby was born, and we lived in another suburb.

I couldn't myself take to "Miss" at all. I put her in the same category as Mother's sickness. Things were always in an uproar when "Miss" came. I was always pushed aside. Some of the women said it was "Miss" herself who brought the babies. I never believed that. I never gave much thought about where babies came from. It was natural that they came; that belonged with all the other neverending hardships like mean teachers, bad men who beat their women, and "aunts" who got big and moaned and groaned about it. For a long time I believed that all women who were fat, no matter how old they were, would soon have a baby. I was scared of women with big stomachs. I was terribly afraid of a policeman who stood on the corner in a suburb that we once lived in because of his saber and uniform and because he had a big stomach. I thought he was twice as dangerous with the stomach because he was a policeman. I was afraid of all fat old men.

That sickness, screaming, and fights always went along with fat stomachs had been my experience. I had seen many newborn babies in the places where we rented, and I thought they were all awful.

Once in my aunt's house, before Mother got married, there was a neighbor who had twins. "The kids look like two monkeys," my aunt said to another woman who nodded in agreement. Both of them hadn't liked her before she had the twins.

"She's going to die," my aunt said. "She lies there, going on about rats running on the bed covers. It's so terrible to die from having two brats."

Aunt talked in an accusing tone, as if it were the mother's fault

104

that she would die from having her new babies that looked like apes. She didn't die. One day I got to see the babies. I was well over six years old. They lay with their mother in a big bed. The family had only one room. I thought the babies were dreadful. I jumbled together all that about the rats that their mother had seen in her delirium and the unfortunate twins and had the worst fantasies. Those rats had brought the babies. The two poor babies were carried out one day in a little casket. I was happy with relief. I had been in terrible fear the whole time they were in the house. No, I couldn't take to the midwives who came and helped to bring babies into the world.

"Now you can turn back and go to your Grandma," the midwife said.

I curtseyed and turned back.

People had begun to come on the road. Drivers of milk carts in lines, butchers, farm foremen. And moving vans of furniture that never lost any time on the road. Twice I tried to hang on at the back but got a lash each time. A milkwoman's cart stopped at last, and I got to ride through the whole town. She had nearly the whole West Street on her milk route. She asked if I wanted to help her. "Oh, *ja*, I'm free, I can certainly do that."

"Don't you go to school?" she asked, looking sharply at me, her big white kerchief bobbing.

"No, Mother is having a baby now, so I don't have time."

"Where are you going?"

"To Grandma's at Vilbergen."

"*Ja*, but we're not going way out there in that direction."

"I'll ride back with you anyway, there's no hurry; Grandma doesn't know I'm coming. I had to get the midwife for Mother."

"*Ja*, but what about your father though?"

"He—he's home. He couldn't go because Valdemar had beaten him."

"Those swine," the milkmaid said.

"Valdemar's nice. My unc . . . my papa was mean so Valdemar beat him."

"*Ja*, scoundrels are what they all are," the old milkmaid said.

I got a lot of sympathy from her. That a new piece of dress goods and a pair of shoes lay in a corner at home in our attic room I had forgotten, or I knew well enough those were his bribes to get Mother back again. Gifts weighted down like that are seldom appreciated. To get something in that way has never appealed to me. Compulsory gifts are the most depressing of all philanthropy.

I helped the milk carrier until after lunch, sharing her lunch sack, even getting some gulps of milk that tasted like cream. She drove me a little ways on the road to Vilbergen although it was out of her way and then gave me ten öre, too. Now I had twenty öre.

I waited until she was out of sight, deciding not to go to Grandma's until it was nearly evening. With twenty öre you could loaf around looking at things. At Grandma's I just had to sit and wind the bobbin spools for her everlasting weaving. And then those difficult questions. I knew that she would ask me about everything by the hour, and she always noticed if I skipped over something or stretched a point. Grown-ups were so troublesome with their questions. Even the nice ones were just the same. They wanted to know everything; what Mother said *then* and *then* what Father said, and what *that* one thought and what the other one thought. It was just impossible to remember. And if you said something that trapped you, then everything got mixed up.

Now I was free. No one knew where I was. No one expected me. But—that was a but: What should I do now?

I had come out on one of the town's longest esplanades. The sun had come out after the rain, drying the benches, and I sat on one of them to think.

The esplanade was empty at this time of day. Now and then an old longshoreman from Saltmeadow hobbled by, but not one of them looked at me. Big Björn, the town's most dangerous longshoreman, came swaying along, his hat dangling on his neck, singing to himself. He sat down on my bench a while but didn't look at me. I tightened my grip on my twenty öre. It was sunny and the middle of the day but you never knew. The big policeman from North Station walked slowly in our direction. Big Björn didn't see him, he was surely asleep. He sat with his head on his breast, his shoulders against the arm of the bench, his legs sprawled out.

The policeman stopped beside the bench. Now I was rigid with fear. Policemen terrified me, especially this one who was big and fat. Big Björn was huge, but he wasn't fat. But the policeman didn't look at me. He put his hand on Björn's shoulder and shook him.

The big fellow only grunted.

"We'd better settle the matter now," the policeman said. Then the giant got up, heading right for the policeman but he was too drunk.

106

"*Ja,* come along now," the policeman said. "Don't fight. It's only about your fine yesterday at Skull-Jon's tavern."

Then Björn went with him. I lost my respect for Big Björn after that. He had been a legendary figure to all the kids in the suburbs. I had heard about terrible fights when the police wanted to take him, that it took ten of them sometimes, and here all the time it had been like this! As if drawn by a magnet, I followed the policeman and Björn. But the policeman must have had eyes in the back of his head, for he half turned and said, "*Ja, ja,* do your errand now or you'll go to jail, too."

My heart stopped in my breast. I just stood there, not daring to move, while Björn and the policeman disappeared out of sight down that long esplanade.

Smoke belched from all the town's factories. Every person who was not at home had something to do. Kids my age were in school. The esplanade lay like an endless path before me. Nothing could I find out about; no one had I to visit. The whole world was deserted. No fun, no games, no kids were to be found. Twenty öre, what could you do with that without friends? I didn't walk in Grandma's direction.

I tramped along, turned off into town, and went up and down the streets. Not a kid did I see. All of them must have died. Here, where there used to be kids in all the yards. I tried standing a while in yards a few times, but then big folks came at once asking questions. One woman scolded me because my feet were dirty. "I have new shoes at home," I said, and my heart weakened a bit toward my stepfather.

"*Ja,* it's always that way; it's never that bad for them. They send their brats out to beg, and then they have new shoes and everything at home," the woman said. She thought I was out begging!

I ran as fast as I could.

It had been a terrible night and the day seemed to be just the same.

I had an enormous longing for my school desk and my teacher, and I cried, knotting my fist at my stepfather who just moved always.

Now I was completely lost, didn't even recognize myself as I walked in the heat and sobbed. An old woman asked what the matter was. I wanted to know the way to Holmstad, my old school. As soon as I asked her, it came to me.

She told me the way, and I saw that she was going to ask me why

107

I was bareheaded and why my hair was all snarled and why my face was dirty and streaked with tears, but I curtseyed and ran off.

It took me an hour to get to Holmstad, and when I got there, school was over. I was hungry and very tired. My head felt so strange. I sat down on the school steps. Maybe the teacher still might come. If she didn't I'd go to Hanna at the poorhouse. I must talk with one of the ones I loved. It was my fate to sleep on steps that day, for again I fell asleep and was awakened by my teacher.

"Why are you lying here, Mia, and what has happened to you?"

"Mother is having a baby; I got so tired and then I thought the police would get me." She looked at me hesitantly. "Here are twenty öre," I said, giving them to her. But she gave them back.

"Come up with me," she said, taking me by the hand.

Now everything seemed calm again; all happiness returned. Here I was with the teacher's hand in mine. I didn't dare to scratch my head; not even if a thousand lice had bitten me would I have scratched my head. I knew how afraid she was of lice, but, oh, how it itched horribly after sleeping.

Up at the teacher's was a tall handsome man. I think he was handsome.

"Where have you got hold of a little street urchin?" he asked, grabbing my teacher around her waist.

My teacher! I took my hand from hers and ran down the stairs and out. I heard her calling me, but I didn't stop. I ran as fast as I could.

Never more would I go to her, never more would I go to anyone. I would go to the forest, go there, only go there. All of them had a guy who grabbed them around the waist. Hanna got a lot of money from drunk old men. Gave me a whole handful. Mother had a man who grabbed her around the waist. No one in the world cared about me. They just had their guys and got money or sat and cried. My beautiful teacher! Now she'd have a baby, too. Sure enough. And Grandma? But her man was so quiet and wanted it to be quiet when he was home. And there I had to read the book of sermons and wind the bobbins and then Grandma asked about Hedvig and then sometimes she said that Albert was handsome and that was his misfortune. I thought he was ugly, the ugliest I had ever seen. But you never dared to say what you thought.

I sat down by the roadside, and then I discovered I had lost my twenty öre.

That sobered me a little. I began to think about Mother and the sugar syrup and the resin that ran from all the cracks of the house, and that Mother used to be slim and beautiful and happy when she had the baby.

That put some backbone in me, but then I remembered how the man had put his arms around my teacher, and the tears came. I sat there, crying and sniffling in my unconscious jealousy, tired and tense after the little sleep I'd had and the whole worrisome day. All the humiliating days in that sugar-syrup house bowed me to the ground. Everything swept over me. I became more and more confused. My sobs became nearly screams. The whole world was against me. No one called for me. Then I heard voices coming along the road and I tried to stop crying. They were kind voices. Hanna and Broom-Mina.

"Heavens, is it you? Come along and you'll get coffee. We're having coffee days in the poorhouse just now."

Hanna looked scared as she always did when she was with her mother, and then I remembered Alvar and began to cry again. When sorrow is great and wants to defeat you, then the dead come from their graves to help.

"What's the matter with you?" Mina asked.

"Mother is—is having a baby, she's sick," I was able to say but that wasn't the only reason I cried.

"That'll pass," the experienced Mina said. "You'll be happy again. Now you'll be living at your grandma's, I heard."

As Mina talked she kept walking, and my tears dried. Hanna and I straggled behind. Hanna was able to whisper to me, "No one sits in the desk with me, and one day teacher said it was empty after you, Mia, left, for there was no one who read poems like you."

My heart began to bloom again, even though as Hanna talked about the teacher, I felt as if I'd been caught by a hook, for I saw again how the man had held her. I didn't think worse of him for that but of the teacher who let something so nauseating as that happen. Like a jade she was, sitting on a seesaw and kissing. Anger against the teacher brightened me up, and I was dry-eyed by the time we got to the poorhouse.

In the kitchen's big fireplace there were at least twenty coffee pots each on its little live coal. Every old woman cooked her own coffee. There were no live coals left for Mina's pot, but she firmly swept up quite a heap of them from the other women's, though they called her all sorts of names. Mina's shiny pot boiled up in a flash.

She had bread from town, and I got to dip as much as I wanted; Hanna, too. The other women looked enviously at us.

"Did you buy some snuff for me?" asked an old women who lay in bed quite a distance away in that huge room.

There were fourteen beds with small tables between them and three large windows with lots of flower pots. The same flowers in all of them. Mina had carried the coffee to the table beside the bed where she and Hanna slept together.

Mina brought a cone of snuff to the old woman who was so sick she couldn't drink coffee. She lived on snuff and a little porridge, Mina said.

I stayed and played with Hanna as long as I dared, getting to Grandma's after eight that night, tired and all in but in good spirits. Grandma thought, of course, that I had come directly from home. She just saw that I got to bed after she knew Mother was having a baby again.

Gloomy days followed at Grandma's. First and foremost she was determined to get my head clean of lice, and she couldn't. Her hands were so crippled with rheumatism that she could hardly hold the fine-toothed comb without dropping it again and again, pulling and combing my hair so that I cried. Worse, I had to go to bed every night at eight, for that was when her old man did, who was so tired, so bent, and so white and thin. He was so quiet also, saying scarcely a word to me, but nearly every day he gave me two öre. I think he forgot from one day to the next that he'd given me anything.

I had to lie there while the sun still shone and listen to the old people's moaning and groaning before they finally settled down in their old bed and began to snore. They were both so old and crippled from work that they groaned in their sleep. I got more and more wide awake and everything seemed unbearable.

Sometimes I crept quietly from bed and got out Grandma's box of clippings. She had lots of newspaper clippings from Ostgöten, of "Lasse in Bravika," and songs of "Jeremiah with the Downtrodden" and other diverting things.

One sorrowful song began: "The laborer's fate is to be a slave from his cradle to his grave." Grandma and the old man were laborers, but slaves should be black, I knew, so I didn't understand the song. Grandma's brother had helped free the slaves and they were soot black. I had seen slaves in Sunday School papers.

My stepfather's schoolbooks were in the box, too, scuffed and dirty. In a nature book a picture of a glass beaker and a description of an experiment interested me a lot. For lack of anything else I tried to shake strong soap water in Grandma's only glass carafe to achieve some kind of result. Nothing happened, only a scolding from Grandma. In *The History of Sweden,* as the book was called, there was a king who "died of a shameful sickness." *Ja,* that was really true. A tall red-haired old woman who often visited Grandma, talked almost never about anything else but the kings. According to her, they were all dreadful. They have every kind of sickness, and one king had died of "lice sickness" she said. "They turned him in the sheet," she said. "Fie upon such a one; they had to do that or get a five öre fine."

Ja, here it was—"He died of a shameful sickness." Lice sickness was naturally the worst of all, and the king had that. Maybe I'd get lice sickness now, too, if Mother didn't get well soon. "Be turned in the sheet." I huddled down and tried to pull the sheet around me, Grandma's coarse, sturdy sheet, but it didn't work to turn yourself; someone else had to do it.

"What are you doing now?" Grandma would say while her man snored and she crawled out of bed on the outer side. She would take the box of clippings and threatened to send me home if I didn't behave. I pretended to be afraid, though I wanted nothing more than that she would send me home. I certainly didn't want her to see that; she would have been so sad. I snuggled down, saying that I would sleep if only she wouldn't be cross and send me home.

It wouldn't have been so tiresome if that red-haired old woman hadn't come so often. She was there almost every day. And she preached to Grandma to give me mouldy bread, for that made you strong, and that kids should get whipped every day for that's what the Bible said. And then she began on the kings. It sounded as if she had known all of them personally. Grandma had a group picture of royalty on the wall and a portrait of a beautiful princess who had a thick fringe. "Victoria fringe." All the truly fine women had those fringes, although the red-haired woman said that only "tarts" who walked in the "virgin park" in Norrköping at night had them.

I didn't like that fringe because it was too smooth. I wanted to have curly hair.

Grandma never gave me mouldy bread. She made me a big sandwich when that red-haired one went home.

"God forbid, child, that you have as rough a time of it as we had," and her hands shook.

111

"Why is that 'aunt' so mean to kids?" I asked.

"She hasn't any children, you see, she's had it hard, and now she thinks she's such a good person because she had it hard. She wants folks to torment children unnecessarily. Hunger makes dogs treacherous. Eat your sandwich now."

On the wall over the sofa where I lay hung photographs of the Captain and the chimney sweeper. The chimney sweeper was the most handsome. Thick, curly hair, curved, fine nose, and large bold eyes that looked right at me.

"He wasn't sober when he did away with himself," Grandma used to say.

The Captain had a full beard and was an old man. The chimney sweeper was dead, I knew, but Grandma hadn't heard if the Captain was dead or alive. Maybe he was alive and would come in his ship someday in Norrköping's harbor. Then the kids in the terrible district where I lived would see that.

I fell asleep thinking of those pleasant prospects. Hanna and I sailed away in a three-master, like the big ship that used to come to Norrköping with cocoa, raisins, cinnamon, and other good things that we didn't know the names of. On Hanna's and the Captain's and my ship there would be big heaps of oranges on the deck.

Chapter 10

We were now well into September. Already the air struck frostily over the hills at Vilbergen. I had read everything in the clipping box. I could recite my stepfather's *History of Sweden.* Of all the books and clippings in the box, I liked it best of all, so dry and silly and full of lies that history was.

It provoked me in some way that the red-haired old woman should be right, that there was a king who died of lice sickness. I had seen it put like this in the book, "a shameful sickness," and children read that in school.

The history with that shameful sickness stayed clearest in my memory. There was another episode about the people being without a king. They chose a handsome prince for their king, and he rode to his death on his horse. Gustaf Vasa and Karl the Twelfth had swept past me without leaving tracks, but this, that the prince never got to be king, dug deep in my memory. I saw all the people in the land standing in a ring in a meadow around the dead prince and his horse. The flowers nodded sorrowfully just like in the song about Hjalmar and Hulda. That bullish Karl Johan who came after that wasn't much to cheer about. He fought and lived a wild life like all the rest. What I retained most clearly when I read that history was a king with "lice sickness," whatever that now could be, and then a prince who lay dead in a meadow in a ring of sorrowing people.

When I later went to a folk school, my own Swedish history was just as dumb, just as deadly dull as my stepfather's; it was like Bible history whose events were blurred. Geography was like Chinese until I left school. I had travelled up and down Sweden several times before I was ten, but my experience of the land and the geography lessons in school didn't go together at all.

Never had I encountered the places that were in the geography

113

books. Norrköping was there, but not the town I knew. Kolmarden, too, but there was nothing about the handsome man in the cottage.

From eager ambition I learned those dull history lessons, listening sympathetically when my schoolmates stumbled in that ruler-straight dust. Later (I was eleven) by chance or luck, I had come across Starbäck's *History*. It was supposedly beyond the reach of children of my circumstances. I shivered as I read about "God's friend and everyone's enemy," the Sture family's distresses of slavery, and the serf's struggle and bravery. Knutsson's long regency, the scarred, mystical Knights Templar, and thousands of other interesting things.

It was the same with Bible history. Until I was twelve I never read my lessons in that dry little schoolbook. I read right from the Bible. The teachers didn't like that. Sometimes I had to sit in the shame corner when I had used the word order in the Bible. Such things weren't for "poor kids." A school teacher said those very words to me. (He's still living. He taught "poor kids" for ten years after me.)

One afternoon when it was even more tiresome than usual at Grandma's, for I had no shoes, and it was too cold to go barefoot outside, my stepfather came. He was somewhat drunk.

"Mia's to go home now," he said, slinging a big bag on the table.

"How is Hedvig and . . .?"

"Hedvig's well again and slim as a string. She wants the girl home."

"*Ja,* but . . .?"

"Uh, it died. It was too early. Everything's okay again. I have a job at the docks for a bit, could be another three weeks. I earn seven kronor a day. There's coffeebread in the bag and Mia's shoes. Hurry up and cook coffee, for my shift starts at seven."

Grandma was too dazed to speak. When her head cleared, she said, "Seven kronor, are you mad? You earned seven kronor a day and didn't come here and see that the girl had a pair of shoes? You didn't come here and talk about the other that happened, we just had to go along here and be anxious? No one would have known the girl when she came here, full of lice and in rags."

"That's over with now. Hedvig is on her feet, and it'll be another tune now. Here, take this, and be happy about things again." And he gave Grandma two kronor. Grandma looked so strange.

"Thank you. This is the first time you've done that," she said in a low voice.

114

I looked at the chimney sweeper's portrait. My stepfather strongly resembled him. I put on my new shoes which had been lying at home almost a month now; otherwise I'd have to walk home barefoot.

"They'll be new now when you're going home," my stepfather said. We drank coffee and dunked the bread hurriedly. Grandma cried when we left, but she wasn't all that sad, I thought.

The day my mother had got sick, my journey to Grandma had taken the whole day. Now it went much faster. The new shoes were pinching my feet a little, but I wasn't thinking about that. My hair was tousled, for Grandma hadn't had time to comb it, and my dress was shabby. I was bareheaded, too, but my stepfather didn't care about such small things. He held my hand firmly, and I followed him, half-running to the tollgates. Then going through town, we took longer, for I had to wait at a cafe while he drank two beers, but he didn't stay long.

At New Square it was market day. A lot of stalls had been put up. At one of them hung a huge bunch of balls in all possible colors. They hung in a large string bag. I could hardly force myself past the stall, and just as we had nearly done so, my stepfather stopped to talk to a maker of plaster of paris figures who had set out his wares on the paving stones. I didn't care for them. I turned my back on them, yearning for a ball in the net.

My stepfather asked the price of every figure, but only one quickened his interest. A big group almost half a meter high: a barefooted boy in blue trousers leaned against a stump. Between his feet sat a frog who looked up at him. The frog was green, the stump grayish-brown. The boy had rosy cheeks and looked thoughtful. The frog was best, I thought, for now I became interested, too.

The piece cost two kronor and fifty öre. My stepfather wanted to give only two kronor. "You make enough, you second-rate organ-grinder."

The Italian spoke such broken Swedish I couldn't understand what he said. But my stepfather got the piece for two kronor. I knew it wasn't even worth thinking about a ball when he had spent so much for Mother. He bought a straw hat with a pair of long, narrow ribbons that hung from its brim for me for seventy-five öre.

He wanted me to put on the hat. But I couldn't. Not with that dress. I knew what went together. I carried the hat home in a bag.

Everything had gone so fast I couldn't sort it out. I was still back in my state of worries and loneliness. It itched and bit in my head, and I couldn't feel really safe about the change in my life, in spite of the new things, before I saw Mother standing before me.

"I should've taken a horse cart so we could've come faster," my stepfather said, who had got tipsier with the beer he'd drunk.

"We don't have enough for that. Mother would be cross," I sullenly said, trudging ahead of him with my hat bag.

He silently followed me.

Chapter 11

The sun drew long dusky paths across the sky, sometimes cutting through, lighting up the frost-brown grass and rustling burdocks. It is me and still isn't me, or have I changed my skin, walking, skipping, dancing along, conscious of my neat appearance. My hair shimmers, clean and brushed in gleaming braids. On my feet new brown leather shoes, new stockings, a Scotch plaid dress, a straw hat with long streamers hanging down my back. In my hand fifty öre. I'm on my way to the storekeeper's garden, and I'm cutting through the hedge.

Finally. And I come to the storekeeper's garden in my childhood's best finery. The gardener must see that I am a lady; otherwise he is blind. Mother has sent me to buy fifty öre of flowers that the storekeeper will have, for she's been so very kind to Mother ever since she lay sick. Mother is up now, walks a little slowly, and is so pale, so frightfully pale, but slender, so slender again. And fine and stylish. On the dresser is a big chocolate grape that my stepfather gave me. It's wrapped in tinfoil, and inside it are soft white candies. I know that. One oblong bit after the other I have eaten.

The chocolate sits beside the boy who leans against a tree and looks at the frog. I've searched for frogs several days now, but I couldn't find any. The plaster frog looks as if he were talking to the boy. Maybe frogs can talk. The plaster frog could for sure.

"The first time I have enough money I'm going to get a bust like that," the landlady said when she came up and looked at the work of art. "It's just as if it's real. So much so you get scared. How much did you, Stenman, pay for the bust?" (The landlady stoutly maintained it was called a "bust.")

My stepfather stood there, twisting his mustache and looking hesitantly. "I got it cheap. I knew the fellow, otherwise I wouldn't have got it so cheap. I gave five kronor."

I saw Mother flush a little but then understand that he was boasting to the landlady.

Valdemar also came up and looked. "It's best to have boys like that. They're not asking for bread," he said, looking meaningfully from the plaster boy on the dresser to my stepfather.

"No, they're not asking for bread," my stepfather said goodnaturedly.

"I'm damned if that frog isn't just like a frog. It's almost not right that they can make something so real," Valdemar said.

"That piece really worried them; they looked almost sick," my stepfather said when Valdemar left.

Now I was on my way to the head gardener and the storekeeper, consciously fine, clean, and beautiful. That made the way so light. The big reward had come. I was not compensated. The landlady's Ida looked like a duck compared to me, and she had humbly bitten a piece of my chocolate in spite of that big tin can with the sugar syrup on the landing. The landlady ran up several times a day when she thought of some old childhood incident that Mother had something to do with. It was as if that hated time with lice and rags had never existed, or the awful night with horrible words.

Now I danced along the road to buy flowers, on the road where I'd cut through the hedge, the same hedge that had terrified me so in the moonlight. I was a completely different person from the one I was when Mother walked on the highway in her stocking feet. Something so terrible had never happened. Such worries had never been. My stepfather earned money, taking it home to Mother, taking good food home, too. He was a little tipsy sometimes at night, but he came home every night, and while Mother walked about quiet and pale in our room, he looked after the wood and also took over carrying the water. The storekeeper was utterly charmed by him, said he could take as much water as he wanted. I often heard him say to Mother: "You're so wonderfully elegant, Hedvig, but you're so devilishly stiff." Mother never replied. She didn't look any happier over his praise.

"Flowers," said the gardener, "that'll be hard now we've had frost, but we'll see what we can scare up." I got a huge bouquet of dahlias that the frost had spared, asparagus plumes, phlox, golden rudbeckia, and a big spray of sweet peas that had bloomed again in the fall rain. I walked inside the high hedge; winter fruit trees were heavy with fruit, heaps of it on the ground, but I didn't waste a minute on that, following the gardener wherever he went, snipping flower after flower, a string in his mouth ready for tying them. Inside the hedge it was so good not to be thinking of apples. With fifty öre and fine clothes and the gardener calling you "little miss," you couldn't stoop to stealing an apple, not even think of it.

"They're still real hard," he said, tying the big bouquet filled with scent, "but take a couple, little miss."

All at once I became shy. Was it just like this then, you only had to bend over and take an apple and bite into it though the gardener looked on? It was too easy. I had imagined something strange, a whole ceremony. I stood there, very straight, then dropped a little curtsey, but didn't bend over and take anything. The gardener gave me two apples.

"Where do you live?"

"In the homeowner's district."

"Do you have a house yourself then?"

"No, we rent from Valdemar."

"Well, I never! So you're Stenman's." He inspected me from top to toe. "Such an uncommon little girl, it's hard to believe it." He went into a toolshed for a bag and filled it with good ripe pears that he picked. "Take these home so you'll have something to share. They're good."

I curtseyed stiffly and politely, but something hopped inside me, hopped like the frog at home on the dresser sure enough did one night. One morning she would be gone. Inside me now little happy frogs throbbed and hopped. I went out through the gate, out on the highway. I had been inside the hedge.

"Well, well," the landlady said when she saw the flowers. "Who's getting those?"

"The storekeeper," I said decidedly and went up the narrow stairs. The sweet peas scented the whole stairs and landing; the door was open to our room. The boy in the blue trousers was on the dresser, the green frog glowed up at him, the chocolate grape cluster lay alongside, the vases were filled with bunches of straw. On the acorn settee Mother rested. Everything was so peaceful and fine, and in the cupboard I knew there'd be plenty to make a sandwich.

"Such pretty flowers! You must take them so they don't wilt. They're really fine, and so many for fifty öre."

"And I got these to boot." I gave Mother the pears.

"To boot? Why was that?"

"The gardener thought I was so fine."

"Hm," Mother only said. "Hm."

"He *said* it. Do you think I took them?" (I remembered that it wasn't so long ago that I had suggested Mother go and steal in the garden, that night when she burned up the wooden basket.)

"No, you haven't taken them. But must you be well dressed in order to have a taste of pears? A barefoot child wants that good taste in his mouth, too."

Mother, she was strange as usual. That didn't bother me. It was clear that folks give good things to fine kids; the others look too shabby.

I took a pear and the flowers and started out again.

"Do you know what you're to say?" Mother called after me.

"I'm bringing greetings from Mother and thanks for all your help when she was sick," I repeated.

Mother nodded. "Don't forget that now, and watch the flowers. . . . If one could just take two," and Mother nipped off a couple of sweet peas and put them in a brandy glass where they looked so pretty. I stood by the syrup can with my flowers, and Mother liked looking at me in all my finery, for she didn't tell me to hurry, just gazed reflectively at me.

There were some kids outside the store. They had seen me many times before and always jeered or else disappeared when they caught sight of me. If the landlady's Ida were along, they always hurried off. She led them. Now they didn't recognize me. Ida was there now, twirling one end of a jump rope; a girl swung the other end while another skipped in and out.

I thought they swung the rope too slowly and the girl skipped clumsily. Without taking any notice of them, I went into the store and gave the woman the flowers. "Mother sends greetings and thanks for all her help . . . your help . . . what she . . . for what you helped with . . . for you went to her when she was sick." I finally got it straight.

"Dear me! Give my greetings and thanks to Mrs. Stenman! I have to admit though that you looked pretty awful that first time, and now so fine you look, child. Why, you probably won't want to help me in my garden anymore?" She cut off a big chunk of yellow hard candy and gave it to me.

"Oh, yes, but I do. I'll run home, put on my everyday clothes, and come back."

"No, I was just joking. Be fine now the whole day. The children want to play today. I see them there waiting for you."

I didn't answer. She looked a bit sharply at me, and I looked a bit defiant.

"I don't want to play," I persisted, then curtseyed and went out. Ida and some of the others were waiting.

"Mia," Ida boldly called, wanting to show the others that she knew my name.

"Haven't time," I said, walking toward the road.

The kids followed. The storekeeper came out.

"You can borrow my rolling hoop."

A girl handed me a splendid plaited barrel hoop with a proper hoop-stick.

"We'll turn the rope so you can skip," Ida said eagerly.

Jump in the dust with my new shoes? Well, I should show them how you should jump, so I should. I could brush off the dust later; Mother didn't need to know about it.

"Can you jump?" a girl asked humbly. "If you can't it doesn't matter. We'll teach you."

"Take this." I gave the hard candy to Ida to hold. Two of the girls began to turn the rope, and I hopped in. Jumped both feet, jumped nonchalantly from one side to the other. "Faster . . . faster," I yelled, beginning to dance around. Now they'd get to see! My new dress flapped, braids bobbed up and down; the girls were red in the face from whirling the rope, but I urged them to go faster. Out of the rope without making a single mistake I hopped.

I didn't show how winded I was, just took my candy from Ida and began sucking on it.

The silence was praise now. The storekeeper stood on her steps laughing. "You can join the circus, Mia. Greet your mother and thank her for the flowers," she called to me.

"They jump like that in town," a girl said in a low voice.

"I learned how in town. We used to bounce a ball, too, when we jumped. I can dance a waltz with a rope, too."

"Are you from town?" they asked surprised, just as if they had never seen me, as often as I had crossed their paths at home.

"Ja, I'm from town." (They didn't know that I had gone to Holmstad school and that my best friend lived in the poorhouse.)

I began to walk slowly home.

"Won't you stay and play with us? Please, do it. Jump a little more and bounce the ball. Do that. I'll run home and get the ball. I have two; you can have one." The girl was so eager that she sidled up, stroking my new dress tenderly with her dirty hand.

"Stop that," I said, shoving her away.

It disgusted me. I wanted to be home with my chocolate cluster of grapes and the boy with the frog, home with my thin, pale mother who still was anxious every night, muttering to herself if my stepfather would be coming home. She thought sure he'd go away again though he assured her every night that he never would again.

This with the kids wasn't right; there was something wrong. My pride had been blasted away. I stood there on the road in their midst and felt utter sadness.

All at once it came to me. They had waited too long. I had been alone too much. I didn't want to be with them. I knew how to jump rope long before, before I had the new dress, too. Did I have to be in my new dress before I got to play with them? They weren't at all fine themselves. I couldn't clear the whole thing up; I just wanted to get away. They looked so dumb, so snotty and envious.

I felt if I had spit on them, they would have pretended I didn't. They had been brought up to respect what was new, rich, and stuck-up. Now when I was fine with a big piece of hard candy in my hand, I could do as I wanted to them. That was mean. It was so uncertain. As soon as clothes and shoes didn't come up to scratch everything was changed. Then I was an outcast. Why were there always kids who were so unlike Hanna? Why was there only one Hanna? What did they want? They had taunted me, had run off as fast as I came near before this. What did they want now?

All my love for Mother returned at once. To our room, to our well-known things there. Alone had we been, Mother and I, and the vases and dresser and the rest. That crowd that stood around me were farther away than my acorn settee. My longing for the security of Mother, who never snubbed me, never smirked at me, came over me. I wanted to get away from this crowd. I didn't want anything from them. Everything that I had so eagerly longed for was nothing. Kids were nothing. Playmates who only talked about "fine" things were nothing. My stepfather tolerated me only for Mother's sake, these kids here for my new dress. Mother was still the only one, for Hanna's image, Hanna's voice lay in my heart. I ached for Mother, maybe she was calling me.

Without answering their questions or their plans to stay and play, I started home. They followed me.

"I'm going home. I don't want to play. Here, you can have my candy." I gave it to the nearest girl and left.

They stopped, breaking off bits from the chunk of candy, just as

122

you get sparrows to stop for some corn. Heavy in my mind without being exactly sad, I went home.

It was the first time I felt that incurable lonesomeness that can seize you when you see both sides of people. Meanness and snobbishness against misfortune—fawning, crawling for favor. Or for what seemed advantageous. A mood that soon changed, became stained with desolation, became bound with chains. Chains whose names were emptiness and insecurity.

It was now October, and it had been decided that we'd move. Not a day went by without Ida coming up, begging me to play. A pack of kids stood below waiting. Ida had told them about our fine "bust" of the frog and the boy, and though I had to wear my old dresses, yet I was the leader in our games the short time we remained.

A child doesn't brood long about fickleness and shallowness, but a little thorn still stuck. I became a tyrant to all those kids. I never condescended to stand and turn the rope when we jumped. I put on the show alone. They must obey me in everything; otherwise I wouldn't go along. I dragged them on adventures that they got whipped for when they got home; even Ida got smacked one night when she'd stayed out too late, but no one dared to tell on me. And mother didn't whip me now. She didn't have the strength.

I had been with the grown-ups so long, hearing their talk, and giving free rein to my imagination. The storekeeper had talked about an old man who ate potatoes with the peels on; he had been a hired man on her parents' farm. I knew where the farm lay, only a little ways out from our district. Several murky evenings in October I led an expedition of kids out there, and we stood on guard outside the kitchen windows to see if we'd get a glimpse of an old hired man eating his unpeeled potatoes. I had gleefully told the kids that this had to be the most curious sight they'd ever see.

There were thin blinds at the windows, and we easily saw shadows in the lamplight within. But we never saw the shadow of the old man. Often we saw two faces draw near to each other. Then we girls stood quietly.

"They're kissing each other," I whispered. "They like each other." And we held our breath.

"She didn't go to her friend, she drowned herself in Åbacka," I said, retelling the story when we walked home in the fall darkness without getting to see the old man. They listened breathlessly, getting whipped when they got home, for they had stayed out too

123

late, but the next night they sneaked out to the storekeeper's again, and we scrambled off to the farm. Shadows were always there, for we came just about the same time each night, and when we had waited a while, and they drank their coffee or ate or whatever they were doing, then the two faces and the two pairs of lips drew together. And always I could tell a story on our way home.

One day I asked the storekeeper where the hired man was who ate potatoes with the peels on. Where was he now?

"Herre gud, girl, how you talk! He's been dead for thirty years." she said.

Ja, that was a shock. I hadn't thought to take anything like that into account, that it was thirty years ago he'd eaten potatoes with the peels on.

I never told that to the kids. Using the excuse that I had to help Mother pack, I never went out anymore at night. It was good we were moving, and nothing need be said about the old man in the daytime.

My stepfather's temporary work was over. He was home the whole day now. I often heard Mother say that the salary was too low at his new place.

"How can we manage on one hundred and fifty kronor for a whole year?"

"*Ja,* but with free room, wood, and flour?"

Mother didn't look convinced.

124

Chapter 12

At the end of October, my stepfather, Mother, and I sat, bumping along in a horse-drawn cart with a foot muff. A cart with a foot muff was impressive looking. The horse was big, fat, and lazy, stopping at the hills, though it was a light load, for none of us was well fed. Mother was slender again, my cheeks were quite thin, and my stepfather had no fat to spare. Mother and my stepfather were close again now; I had been helplessly shoved to the background it seemed to me.

Rumbling after us was the wagon with the acorn settee and everything. It was drawn by a pair of heavy horses who tried to run past our light load every time our lazy horse tried to trot a bit. The sugar-syrup house was two hours behind us. Our leavetaking had been polite.

The night before, Valdemar's had invited us for a good meal with beer and brandy, though not so anyone got drunk. I had on my new Scotch plaid dress and new shoes. Taking me on his knee, Valdemar didn't smell bad at all. It had rained. Before the night ended my stepfather held the landlady on his knee and said she was so fair and round, and Mother just laughed, for the landlady looked so funny on my stepfather's knee, staring at Valdemar with fright and red in the face from my stepfather's flattery. Everything was like a party, pleasant and untroubled.

Mother got a big can of sugar syrup, and she gave the landlady a dress that she'd got from one of the women she'd worked for.

Now today Valdemar had come home at noon, having asked for permission to help us move. The baker had brought a big limpa, but he was so drunk he didn't know what he said, just yelled, "As soon as Mrs. Stenman becomes a widow, I'll come with a priest, and you'd better watch yourself, Stenman, so she isn't widowed too soon."

But my stepfather didn't get mad, just laughed with Valdemar at the baker. I heard Valdemar say to Mother so that no one else could hear, "If things get bad again, Hedvig, the room is here even if it isn't so good."

Two hours there were between me and the sugar-syrup house. As it grew dark, the air was frosty. My eyes got heavy from the swaying rhythm, and I dozed again and again. I was a little chilly, too. But my mother and stepfather talked on. God knows what they had to talk about! Only a couple of times had Mother turned her head to ask how I was doing. And my stepfather looked over and asked if I thought it was fun to travel.

Just then, when he asked, it wasn't fun any longer.

It was pitch dark when we reached our place. The house lay off by itself on a lonely side road that wasn't used much. One other family lived there, and light shone from their window. I noticed one tree outside the driveway, a tall tree with bare branches.

My stepfather had been hired as a driver here for the winter.

We came into an empty room with lime-plastered walls. "It smells like farmhands' quarters here," Mother said, letting the door stay open.

How could she know it smelled like hired men lived here? I sniffed all I could with my snub nose, but couldn't smell anything other than snuff and rats.

"Ja, damn it all. Let the door stay open," my stepfather said, who had been like my mother's echo a long time now.

The room wasn't bad at all otherwise.

I liked it as soon as I had come in.

An enormous thick wall with a baker's oven was at one gabled end, and in the open hearth a little old-fashioned iron stove had been set in. "Ankarsrum No. 4" was on its cover. The floor was made of broad knotty boards, swept but unscrubbed. The large room had three windows and a low ceiling. The plaster was falling off the walls.

Mother got to borrow a lantern and some kindling from the new neighbor. From the horse cart Mother had taken a basket with a lamp, coffee beans and pan, and some bread to dunk, and now she lit the lamp. Without taking off her coat, she began to make a fire in the stove.

The driver of the wagon informed us that the room had last been used as a dance hall for young folks.

I was most interested in how our things would now be arranged. Everything should look fine here. But Mother let the furniture be piled in the middle of the floor. "Such an old house is certainly only for fine ladies," she said in a voice of experience. The driver of the wagon laughed and stroked his mustache, as if stroking underneath what Mother had said.

All the furniture was soon carried in. Mother had coffee ready, and so we drank coffee in our new place.

"*Ja,* one should offer something stronger," my stepfather said, "but the ladies are now all suddenly like this."

The driver looked a little reproachfully at Mother, critically, too, and I got just then a tremendous respect for her. Think that "he" didn't dare to drink even once any longer. What had Mother hit upon?

Wondering about this, I fell asleep at the table without drinking my coffee.

When Mother had found a pillow and sheet, she wakened me, saying it was time for bed. The driver had gone, and my stepfather stood with a poker in his hand, watching a rat hole by the stove. Two rats had already been out and bid us welcome.

I woke up at dawn a little confused. After the unaccustomed journey, the floor seemed to roll and my acorn bed to rock. But it was good to lie in my acorn bed again. It had been a long time since I had. It felt so peaceful not to be lying on the floor. A bed on the floor was like a tramp's. Now I didn't have to do that. The familiar acorns lay reassuringly near. The big oven wall looked like a fortress against the chill of both the North and South Poles.

Mother was standing with a little tallow light. "There are cockroaches in the walls," she said.

This new thing didn't bother me. I had never seen them or heard tales about them.

Through the window I saw two hazy stars fade out; a pair of tree branches stretched up their silhouette, and on the outermost tip of a branch hung the waning moon.

While I watched, I became wide awake and filled with an expectancy of joy. Trees, stars, moon, a big bake oven like the one at Grandma's. I sat up in my bed, which would stay there in the middle of the floor until one found out how things were with "fine ladies."

Then I heard my stepfather clumping on the porch, and a woman calling "Good morning," and his answering greeting. He came in, bringing the smell of the stable and the fresh October morning in his clothes. "The woman next door runs around in only her slip. That's the new way here," he said to Mother.

"She probably woke up late and didn't have time to dress. And don't make fun of *her*, and you don't need to mock her either," Mother said irritably.

"Mock her, what kind of talk's that? Shouldn't be in such a hurry that a woman can't put her skirt on."

"Maybe she doesn't own a skirt." Mother changed the subject. "The walls are full of cockroaches."

"*Ja*, that can be a good thing, then the wall lice won't thrive," my stepfather said, sitting down at the table and eating a breakfast of two pork slices, bread, and porridge. That was the usual breakfast at Vikbolandet at that time, both in the farmers' and the gentry's kitchens. In the hired hands' houses, porridge was the usual breakfast, but today Mother had prepared a breakfast that belonged to the owner of the farm. Perhaps she thought that the time would soon come when we had only porridge.

"There are wall lice here as well," she continued. "Other than that, I think this will be a good room for us. And the horses looked so well fed, and we were driven here in a fine cart and didn't have to sit on the furniture wagon like gypsies."

"The farmer will talk to you. I think he wants a milkmaid. So you can do that, and that way get the repairs done."

"Can I? You can do that since you took this place."

"*Ja*, well, I think it's good here. Just scrub the floor and get the walls whitewashed, and this place'll be fine, at least better than Valdemar's chicken coop. The doors have hinges here anyway. Get up now, Mia, and help your mother get things in order."

I got up at once, thinking that for once my stepfather was right. With blue-starched curtains and vases with birch branches, things would look fine, and Mother's rugs, which there had been room only for two at Holmstad, and no room at the last place, could now be spread out the width and length of the room.

As the dawn brightened into day, Mother blew out the lamp and the room scantily filled with October light, that autumn morning light that is neither bright nor dark, and everything looks gray and impossible. The room that just before had been warm with the smell of coffee and pork gravy became suddenly cold and gray. The furniture was heaped together, looking the worse for wear and cheap. Never had I seen our things look this way before; they were

128

really ugly. The dresser, the bed, my acorn settee, all of them were ugly. The floor, black and dirty, was impossible to walk barefoot on. Mother had the same thought as I, for she grimaced just then at the floor. "The floorboards used to be white when folks danced on them," she said, "but now they must have meant to keep potatoes here until summer."

My stepfather got up, took his cap and whip. From a half-kilo packet, whose tinfoil I greedily noticed, he packed snuff in his box, put a big pinch in his mouth, and talked with a thick voice all the while. "Mmum, mmum, didn't you get a drop of coffee, Mia? You mmum could certainly have had that your first morning mmum, mmum in our new place. Well, mmum, good-bye, now." He brushed some snuff bits from his mustache. Then turning at the door, he went back and grabbed Mother around the waist. "It'll be great here, Hedvig, and in a little while you'll make this rat hole fine. You're so clever." Then he left.

I sat, dangling my bare feet from my acorn settee and feeling completely overpowered. And I imitated him out loud, "Sure, Hedvig, you'll make this rat hole fine, you're so clever." Mother laughed.

My everyday clothes were still unpacked, so I got to wear my Scotch plaid dress and new shoes. I thought that was good. Folks at this new place would get the right impression of me, although I'd have to tell the kids around here that these weren't my everyday things. My next best, I could say.

"There will be no more coffee in the morning for you now. You'll get a cup of sweet milk instead. We get two liters a day and four liters of skim milk so that will work out well."

I tried to resign myself as well that first morning, but I wasn't happy about it. Mother saw I was gloomy.

"You've gone about any which way, living mostly on coffee and bread. You haven't grown a bit all summer. Now you're going to drink milk instead of coffee. You'll get a sugar lump in your milk."

Mother knew where the shoe pinched. When coffee was given to poor kids, they weren't thinking so much of the coffee but the sugar lump that they thought the grown-ups might snatch from them. My mother remembered how that could happen from her own childhood.

"He's become so nice," I said while I ate my bread and milk. "Hmm," Mother only said.

There was a knock on the door. A young woman came in; she was our neighbor. She was probably twenty at the most. She was the one, too, that my stepfather had seen just in her slip when he came from the stable. Mother looked carefully at her. Now anyway she had a skirt on over the slip. But her arms were bare. Her bodice was gray and soiled. Instead of a blouse or a jacket she wore a man's vest; all its buttons were missing. Her breasts were very high, and I saw a rag sticking out between them. The front of her vest and that of her bodice were stiff where something wet had spilled. She had big, full lips, blood-red, and wide, glistening teeth. Her nose was narrow at its top and then became broad with flaring nostrils. Her eyes were large and bulging, her eyebrows thick and black. A long black braid hung down her back.

"I wanted to come in and say hello and tell you my name," she said, shaking Mother's hand. "I'm Olga."

"*Ja,* it will be all right for you to call me Hedvig," Mother said a little stiffly. She was not at all pleased about this carelessly dressed girl whose bodice was wet and whose belly stuck out like a thin old woman's sometimes does, but her face looked so young. She shook my hand, too.

"Get up and curtsey, Mia," my mother said sharply.

When she came in, I had been sitting looking on indifferently before she took my hand in hers, partly from Mother's stiffness toward her and also she looked so shabby and poor. I had never seen any person look that poor. And though I was only eight, I had seen a great many.

"Sit down, Olga," Mother said in a friendlier voice and began making coffee.

"Such a pretty dress Mia has," Olga said, sounding as happy as a child as she talked about my Scotch plaid dress. I boldly stuck my feet out to show my new shoes, too, so she would see how fine I looked there.

Mother poured the coffee and set out store-bought wheat bread and a coffee cake that the landlady in the sugar-syrup house had sent for "welcoming folks" at our new place. Olga tried not to look so much at these sweet things, but her eyes were drawn in spite of her attempt to the bread basket and the sugar bowl.

"Olga should have her hair pinned up," my mother said suddenly.

"*Ja,* I try hard but I have a headache almost constantly ever since I had the little one."

130

Now I paid attention: an "aunt" who had a child and went around with a braid down her back—that didn't seem right.

"How old is the baby?"

"One month."

"*Ja,* it's been a month for me, too," Mother said, looking far, far away.

Olga looked closely at Mother, looked all around the room, and then at Mother again.

"*Ja,* she died."

Olga's bulging eyes were full of tears. She looked at Mother as if she had won the highest prize while she herself hadn't won anything at all. "I wish mine had died, too; he's always sick and I'm always sick and the milk runs from my breasts so I go around wet and he hasn't enough strength to drink."

Now I thought the talk had become dull. Childbirths and such stuff I'd had enough of the last time. I sneaked out.

At least there were steps with a bench on one side here. There wasn't a roof over the steps so the bench was wet and dark and mouldy from the rain and marked with countless rings from water buckets and milk pails.

The house in my opinion was exceptionally fine. It was plastered in a pinkish color with a black-painted door and dark metal window frames. It was wholly different, I meant, from those owner-occupied ramshackle wooden houses. I thought the house was made of stone. But the dividing wall was made of only thin fence boards plastered on both sides. The only real wall was the big one of brick that went the length of the house. The house had once been a bakery and brewery for a large estate that nowadays had been divided up into farms.

The land lay desolate and dark gray from every direction. A dark border could be seen in the distance, Kolmarden. The only tree for miles around was the one that stood before the house, an old apple tree whose three main limbs branched out a meter from the ground.

A red-colored band in the east with a stream of steel-edged clouds promised sun, and when I looked through the bare branches to the sky, I saw two apples hanging from the highest branch. Those were my apples. There wasn't the least doubt about that. As soon as I changed into my everyday clothes, I'd climb up after them. Some pale marigolds still bloomed around the trunk in spite of the October frost. They were mine, too. Finally I had something of my own. I listened a while. Not a sound could I hear other than the cawing of crows and the voices in the house. Mother and Olga were still talking.

I couldn't see the farmyard, the yard where the horses would be who had brought us here. But back of the house there was a winding path that disappeared down a steep slope. Sure enough, there was the farm. I couldn't hear any children but it was still too early, I assured myself. The "youngsters" hadn't gotten out of bed yet, and I felt a peg higher than any farm kids that surely must be here, because I was up before them and also because yesterday I had journeyed here in a light horse cart.

There were no other kids at this place. Not any that could play with me. Three farm laborer families at the farm had kids, but they were still in diapers, Mother said. Two of the other laborer families were so old that their kids were already in America. I was entirely all by myself on the whole farm, a big one with hundreds of acres. A long way to the next farm and still longer to school. Three miles. That was too far.

"It will just have to be," Mother said. For three months now I hadn't gone to school, and these were school winter months. "You must practice your reading and writing so you won't forget," Mother said.

No, I didn't find playmates, but instead I became a mama. Not, of course, that my motherhood made a sensation in the papers. It was Olga's baby I became a mother to.

I wasn't exactly thrilled. It was of bitter necessity. When the threshing machine came, all grown-ups had to be in the fields, Olga, too. The baby in diapers was handed over to me.

After that morning Mother worked a week both day and night fixing our room, and my stepfather helped her in the evenings. It was really a pleasant room we lived in. The walls were gleaming white, and one wall was white with blue flowers that Mother painted with the blueing she used for the curtains. All three windows had curtains. Long curtains for two and looped ones nearest the kitchen stove. "Long curtains aren't suitable in a kitchen," Mother said. My stepfather built a sink out of two packing boxes.

Half the room was a kitchen and half was a parlor. It was almost finer than the room at Old Island Road, but . . . still . . .

When Mother had everything in order she invited Olga in for coffee. I was so excited about what Olga would think that I forgot the apples still swaying against the sky that whole week despite the frost and my attempts to get them down. At long last she came with the baby covered with an old man's jacket over his diapers. Olga had her hair twisted into a giant knot on her neck. She wore a clean, bleached-out man's work shirt with the sleeves rolled up and an old patched apron. Everything was clean but unironed.

She came in timidly and awkwardly, hardly daring to step on Mother's rugs, saying nothing and just looking around.

"Hedvig has certainly worked in fine houses?" she asked after a while.

"Not just those." Why had Olga asked that? I saw very well Mother knew why Olga had asked. I almost trembled with curiosity over what Olga would say next. Here came for once an admiring audience. An uncritical one from the world's unsuspicious, unbiased public. Here not a detail would be lost on she who was used to the most meager furnishings you could think of in a home. For I had never seen such poverty, not even in the south suburb of the town, as I did at Olga's.

It was an easily pleased audience. The blue flowers on the white wall fascinated her most, that and the boy with the frog. Mother hadn't found any alder trees around here—the plain was upland until Twelvemile Forest—so pine twigs were in the vases. Mother liked the alders, for there was a big alder marsh near the tenant cottage where she was born. Often I heard her talk about the marsh and the alders. The elks there were bigger than anywhere else. The snakes were horrifying there, and no other marsh in the world has as many lingonberries. You needed only to go around the corner of the cottage to get baskets full of them in no time. (An alder marsh is still for me today something that offers overwhelming abundance with free access for poor people.)

"No, I haven't worked in fine houses; I've only worked in farmers.' I had the girl beforehand, so I couldn't expect to find a place in any fine houses."

I thought Mother was foolish. What would that have mattered? I saw how Olga now brightened up; she wasn't so humbly impressed any longer. "The girl beforehand"—that was what those "educated" ones always shook their heads over. When here was a person who really saw that we were fine folks, why did Mother have to put that in about "the girl beforehand" and farmers' houses and everything like that?

"Hedvig, you have it as fine as it is up at the farmer's house,"

133

Olga said. "Finer, for they don't have anything like this boy and the frog."

No, I was wrong. Olga was still in the dust, a pariah who humbled herself before the Brahman's shadow. Mother had, of course, only made-over clothes, cast-offs from others, but she looked like a fine woman beside Olga. I was dressed, too, in made-over clothes, patched and mended, darned-over holes in my stockings, and new buttonholes set in my old coat, but, I, too, was dressed in finery compared to Olga's poor baby who lay bundled in that old jacket that smelled of the farmyard and stables. A tiny, blotched, whimpering baby with red-rimmed, festering eyes.

The purest incense can nobles in the end get from the simplest people. Mother and I never were in fine folks' company; Mother saw how they were dressed and made the clothes she got from those where she worked into stylish ones, and so we were as good as anyone.

But as soon as Mother lost her grip and began to vomit and there was talk about the midwife who came with a bag, then we were right down nearly on the same plane as Olga here. No, so shabby, of course, Mother had never looked; a man's old shirt she had never worn, but it was certain that those babies who came were the reason for poverty. Olga said that, too.

"But in town, there you can always get a little something, always get some kind of hand-out," Olga said, looking as if she were about to move to town right there and then.

"Dunk your bread, now," Mother said. And Olga did, trying to put a bit of bread and coffee in her month-old baby.

"He's too little for solid food," Mother said. "And, Olga, don't let him get used to coffee; he'll only fret and won't sleep."

"He can't grow and gain any if he just sucks milk," Olga said. Then the baby choked and got blue in the face, couldn't even yell, just gasped and hiccuped.

Mother took him, put him over her knees, and patted the dirty jacketed baby a little on his back, and right then and there the little bundle shrieked. Suddenly I thought it wasn't so fine any longer. It was strange how a kid's yelling could spoil a fine room.

Olga looked worried and wanted the bundle back again, but Mother sat down by the stove, unwound the jacket, and felt his diaper.

"He's wet," she said.

"*Ja*, I don't have a dry change for him; it's hanging over the stove."

Holding the screaming baby on her arm, Mother went to a box that I never cared to look in, I knew well enough what was in it: a couple of sweaters and shirts and little clean rags enough to put on that doll that was alive and smelled so bad. She took out the things. Everything clean, a whole outfit he got, and a soft shawl from a discarded blanket she bought at the factory.

"It's best one keeps such things; you never know how many babies you'll have," Mother said.

I thought everything was getting far worse. She put warm water in our washbowl. Ugh, was she going to wash that brat's behind in our washbowl? *Ja*, this was some coffee party. But still I was curious. I stood there on pins and needles, ready to run outdoors, while Mother unwrapped one stinking rag after another. A tiny miserable body appeared. The skin on his seat and legs were red and raw. I thought he looked dreadful, as if he'd been scalded and was just skin and bones. I couldn't see how Mother wanted to hold him. Olga didn't look at all happy. It wasn't a mother's pride that shone in her eyes.

"He's like he's been skinned," she said sadly, as if she were ashamed. "I haven't any salve; potato flour makes it worse."

"You don't have enough changes for him," Mother said. "We must help get him healed, or you'll never get any rest at night. That's why he can't eat properly and your milk leaks out. The poor little thing's always smarting with pain."

She turned the pitiful little body over. "No, you know, Olga, this won't do at all," Mother said, taking away a piece of soap that was stuck in his tiny butt cheeks.

"His belly's so hard, and up at the farmer's she told me if I tried with a bit of soap that would help."

I was getting cross now. Mother had totally forgotten me. I saw that she was taking care of the baby tenderly, that she liked him so much though he smelled so bad. It was only two months since Valdemar had helped me get the midwife.

Now here sat Mother with a baby even so, an ugly, dreadful thing that I thought looked like those twins the rats had brought to the neighbor who lived next to my aunt in town.

Mother put the baby in the lukewarm water in our washbowl. I decided then and there to wash myself only in Mother's washtub. I did that, for that matter, often, for my stepfather let hair from shaving himself stick in the washbowl. But this was even worse. To wash that bad-smelling kid in our washbowl. Mother certainly didn't know what she was doing. Meanwhile she took no notice of me but splashed water on the baby so it spilled out on the rug. Then she dried him with my clean hand towel that had just been hung up.

The day wasn't turning out right for me. I was on the sideline. The baby had stopped crying and was lying still, staring up at the ceiling with his hazy eyes.

"He's so sweet," Mother said.

Then I crept in between Mother and the woodbox so she'd really see that I was still there.

"Go away, Mia, you're in the way," Mother said.

I had to crawl out. Resignedly I went over to my acorn settee and sat down but began kicking the wood with my shoes.

"Shame on you acting like that when you're so big," Mother said, putting a shirt trimmed with lace on the wrists on the baby. Over that she drew on a flannel vest. Everything new, the same clothes her own baby would have had. Grandma had sewn the flannel outer vest. She should find out what Mother was doing with it now.

"Now we'll see if we have something that will heal his bottom," Mother said. "You can gather these in the fall; at home we picked them by the bushelful, *ja* sometimes sold it. It's club moss powder.*"

"*Ja,* I've heard of that, but there's none to be found around here."

"It grows everywhere," Mother said in a convincing tone.

Mother had got the club moss from Grandma, I knew, but she was acting as if she'd picked club moss gold powder herself when she was little to have ready for her kids. *Ja,* the grown-ups weren't so accurate themselves, that's for sure. They could stretch things. Even Mother. She'd probably have that brat here everyday now.

But even so Mother handed a fine, sweet-smelling bundle to Olga. And Olga got up and curtseyed to Mother, *curtseyed,* took Mother's hand and thanked her, curtseyed and thanked. All my hatefulness disappeared.

"He's never been so fine," she said. "Goodness me, so fine he is!"

"See now if he won't take a drop of milk," Mother said. "You must have a farmer get a little garlic syrup when he goes to town.

---

*A European herb of the mint family used to make lycopodium powder.

And if you don't give him anything else but breast milk, he'll be a strong little boy. Nurse him at least three months."

After that both mothers sat talking about such things, and Olga drew away a ragged wet towel from her breast under the blue shirt and put the baby to suck. Then I stole quietly out.

Garlic syrup, bought in town, that kid should have! Wouldn't the syrup Mother got from the landlady do? The farmer had to buy syrup at the pharmacy!

Up there hung the two apples, swaying and looking as if they were smirking. I couldn't throw a stone, for the windows were too near. There wasn't a long enough pole that could be found to reach them. Everything was out of my reach, not even two frozen apples could I get hold of. Loneliness and silence were everywhere. What would happen to me in the end?

Mother was then so . . .

I roamed about the flat countryside an hour. Then I remembered that I hadn't got any coffee, and that was what the party had been for—for us to drink coffee with Olga. I set off for home at once, a little cheered up. On the steps was Mother with a basket in her hands; she had been calling for me, and Olga stood beside her with the baby on her way to her own room.

"You're so impossible when you run off like that. See here now, hurry with coffee to Albert!"

That's what I got. Not even so much as a roll this time.

I trudged off with the basket.

"Don't rattle on so much to him," Mother said.

I didn't answer. I ought to tell him that Mother had a coffee party in the morning, then there'd be trouble.

But I didn't.

My stepfather drove the straw from one stack on the steam thresher, and I rode with him on the load until lunch time. When we came home together, we were on good terms. Mother looked a little cross when we came. "You hadn't permission to stay," she said.

"I let her," my stepfather said. "She hasn't any kids to play with here."

That's what Mother got.

But otherwise I had never seen Mother and my stepfather get on so well as they did that late fall, not even in the room at Old Island Road.

And with me he was so awfully nice that I called him "Papa," not "Uncle" even once. What had caused the change I didn't know if it

137

was Grandma or the police. For the police had looked for him in the sugar-syrup house. I heard, too, that he'd got a real beating from my uncle because he, as my aunt said, had scandalized all Mother's relatives in town. Whatever had happened it had been for the benefit of Mother and me. And everything seemed as if it would be really good after Mother began earning money again for milking.

On the evening of the same day that Mother dressed up Olga's baby, there was a knock on the door, and Olga's man stepped in.

He was a dark little man, much like Olga; they could have been brother and sister. The same wide, full mouth. His teeth couldn't be seen, for he had such a big mustache. He had snuff in his mouth so that it made a ball behind his bottom lip.

"Come in and sit down," my stepfather said, looking somewhat surprised. He was sitting by the table spreading unsalted butter on a big cut on his thumb.

My stepfather had ugly hands, broad and full of cuts here and there that never healed. Not even when he was without work and only drank did his hands heal.

"*Ja,* I shouldn't stay," the man said, but he sat down and Mother got the coffee ready.

He looked around just as Olga had, but he didn't look as impressed.

"You've made it nice here," he said.

"*Ja,* we've got off the worst of the dirt. We have a devil of a time with the cockroaches. You have to knock your pipe on the coffee pot in the evenings; otherwise you'll get stronger coffee than you want," my stepfather joked. And Olga's man smiled dutifully.

"*Ja,* you have to be glad if you can earn enough food for a day," he said. "Course some can get enough and more for fine things." Karlsberg stared enviously at the boy and the frog.

"We don't have any fine things," Mother shortly said.

"*Ja,* God knows that well enough, we haven't," my stepfather said. "Come on now and have a drop."

The coffee would be strong and good; Mother had brought a kilo of coffee beans from town. "Steam roasted" it was called, and folks in the country never bought it; they roasted their own coffee.

So the men drank coffee again and chewed snuff although it was late in the evening. I heard Olga tiptoeing outside on the porch. Then Karlberg got up, stopping at the door. "I wanted to come in and thank you for Hedvig's taking our boy in hand and helping

Olga with him. She doesn't know much about babies. I thought she wasn't taking care of the boy right, for he screamed night and day."

Karlberg took Mother's hand and bowed, just as Olga had curtseyed to her. "Thank you, Albert, too," he said, shaking my stepfather's hand. "You have a capable housewife. Olga will become a good one if she can just learn how a little and we can scrape enough together to get some things."

He thanked again and left.

Two grown-ups had stood, bowing and curtseying because their boy had got a dry diaper and shirts. I felt suddenly a strong longing to be that boy.

But my stepfather looked like a thundercloud. He didn't say a word the rest of the evening, not even asking for help when he tied the bandage on his cut. He just glared at Mother.

"You're glaring so it makes a shine on the walls," Mother said hotly.

He didn't answer. Took off his clothes and got into bed, turning his back to us. He stretched himself out so that I wondered how Mother would find any room in the bed.

When he left in the morning, I heard him say, "You can get something else done today than just sit with Karlberg's brat on your knee."

Mother's tone wasn't a bit better. "That doesn't concern you," she said, just as the door closed.

But nothing came of their stormy weather. That night my stepfather was bright and cheerful again.

A few days later the farmer's wife visited us.

Olga rushed in to Mother that afternoon and whispered, not daring to talk out loud, "Jesus, Hedvig, here comes the farmer's wife! She's coming to see you." And Olga ran back to her room.

Mother took this news more calmly, but I hurried to my stepfather's shaving mirror and tried to smooth my hair back from my forehead and tighten the knot of the ribbon on my braid. Olga's nervousness had rubbed off on me.

"Is she a 'farmer's daughter'?" I asked.

"Don't muss up your hair anymore. Here, put on this clean apron and then go out and play afterwards."

Now Mother looked a little excited, too. As if she thought it might be so. Well! Now I'd get to see a real farmer's daughter.

"Is she a real proper farmer's daughter?"

"She's a land surveyor's daughter. Behave yourself now," Mother ordered.

Daughter of a land surveyor—that was something I'd never heard talked about. Here was the farmer's wife, a little, plump, prim woman with a round, rosy face who didn't look at all like the only picture I'd had of a farm woman—Valdemar's wife. No freckles, no double underlip. Dressed for town she was, without an apron. That was because she was a surveyor's daughter, I decided. I had the notion that all farm women should look alike in some way. All factory women did; all of them wore fringed shawls and were pale. You could recognize a factory worker at once.

"I wanted to come down and welcome you," the farm wife said at the door.

"Thank you, please sit down. Come, Mia, and say hello."

I curtseyed and greeted her and then stayed near the door, ready to run out if it became dull.

"It's so pleasant here. And so clean you could strain milk in every corner," the farm wife said.

"Oh, clean, *ja,* but I've really just got the worst of the dirt off."

I could see how flattered Mother was.

"I've been wanting to thank you for your kindness in sending the horse cart so we didn't have to ride in the wagon," Mother said, who knew what to say all right.

"Oh, that was nothing. The horse and cart were free." The farm wife also looked flattered. Everything was so agreeable when people knew what they should say and do.

"Maybe I could just put the coffee on," Mother said. (That morning she had said there was enough for only one pot more, and I waited with excitement that the farmer's wife would say, "No thanks.")

"*Ja,* thanks, I'd like some," she said, and Mother put on the pot, using the last of the "steam roasted."

"*Ja,* the neighbors probably already have made themselves acquainted."

"Oh, *ja,*" Mother said.

The woman was about to say something more, opening her mouth but closing it again.

Mother got out napkins and cups and saucers. "I think I'll ask Olga, too," Mother said, not wanting Olga to be left out, knowing we'd be having coffee.

"*Ja,* ha, *ja,* of course. Do that. Olga worked for us and married our

140

hired man, Karlberg. She was expecting a baby, so it was best, certainly, that she got married."

Mother didn't answer but went into Olga's, saying to me, "You can be in with Olga's boy while she drinks her coffee."

Olga came in dressed in a skirt and jacket that Mother had got from a woman in town. The clothes were of the same cut and age as Hanna's old thirty-hooked jacket, but the material was softer. The clothes had been meant to be made over for me. Olga was really beautiful in those old-fashioned clothes. She had the boy with her, dressed in the lace-trimmed shirt with a clean diaper and blanket. Olga must have got ready as soon as she caught sight of the farmer's wife rounding the bend. Her back was so straight as she walked that she looked more stately than the farmer's wife herself when she showed her boy and asked if he hadn't grown.

"*Ja*, that I can promise you he does. I didn't think he'd live through the night when I saw him new-born." But the woman stared more at Olga that at the baby. She looked mean, staring like that at Olga.

"Olga, you look as if you thought you were a bride all over again. It's almost exasperating how well you look; you'll probably be along for the threshing," she said, with needles in her voice.

"She has difficulty with her milk; she's not ready to work like that with the threshing," Mother said, for Olga couldn't seem to speak.

"*Ja*, but maybe we should ask, hm, ask her herself, though?"

"Please call me Hedvig. I had, for that matter, a baby, too, a month ago. The baby died. I'm not so strong; I don't think I'll be helping with the threshing." Mother sounded short and decided.

The farm wife changed her tone a little, gave Mother her sympathy, and trying to get the tongue-tied Olga to talk, praised her boy. Then she started in about a childbirth she'd had, though the baby had died, just like Mother's. Now I left. Talk about childbirths! Never anything else!

The fog was so thick outside that the two apples looked as if they hung from the clouds.

Both Mother and Olga had to help with the threshing; coffee and sugar were gone, and it would be two weeks until payday.

There was so much talk about the steam thresher that I came to think of the machine as a terrible dark beast that dragged folks to work, dusty, thundering, roaring, going from one terrible journey to another.

One morning Mother woke me up at six. Heavens, how she looked! Would she become as Olga had been? An old, leached-out, patched shirt of my stepfather's, a shawl around her waist, an old scrubbing skirt, and an apron made of sacks, her hair wrapped in a big scarf, knotted at the neck. "How you look!" I said, starting to cry.

"What's the matter with her? What's she crying about?" asked my stepfather.

"*Ja*, it's because I'm dressed like this. But get up now, Mia, you have to take care of the boy."

Then the tears ran even more.

"What a devil of a cry-baby!" my stepfather said. Then I got scared and put on my clothes.

"There's food in the cupboard. We'll be eating at the farmer's today, but I'll run home at noon. Olga will come home, too, so you can keep the fire going in the stove. No, it's not worth it, it'll take too much wood. Hurry up now. Here's your milk."

"*Ja*, look after the young one properly now. You're so big, you can surely do something useful," my stepfather said.

Mother didn't say anything. She never used to keep quiet when my stepfather scolded me like that. It was a sad morning. Would they both be against me, the two of them? Would I always be alone now? Would they go away and work and come home and crab at me, both of them? I couldn't drink my milk, just sat and hiccuped.

"You've spoiled that one properly," my stepfather said, slamming the door.

Mother stayed behind, took me in her arms, and told me to behave myself. "I had to go work for a farmer when I was as old as you."

"You didn't either, for you were eleven, you told me so, and Olga isn't a farmer," I said.

"What if I was eleven then. Shame on you. Watch yourself."

"You told me you were eleven when you went to work for farmers," I sniffed, "but I'm only eight, and I have to clean up the boy. I just can't do it. Think if the boy dies; then it'll be my fault."

"The boy won't die. You need only rock him when he cries. See now, what a clever girl you can be."

Then Mother, all bundled up in her rags, patted me and held me, but I thought everything was awful; the way she looked, she didn't

142

need to hold me. And then she had lied that she was eight years old when she went out to work. She was eleven, she had said that, and so had her sister, my aunt.

"I *will* look after the boy. Best you go, otherwise 'he' will come back and scold," I said, drinking my milk with a gulp.

"You must not say 'he,' you must call him Papa. You're beginning to be spiteful. Now you look after the boy, you understand? Or I'll give you a hard beating," Mother said, sensing that I hadn't appreciated her earlier friendliness. Then she left.

Olga put her nose in the door, looking as bundled up as Mother. "His pacifier is under his pillow. I've turned down the lamp. You don't need to go in for a while, he'll sleep a long time now. I've just changed him. Good-bye now. I'll pay you when I'm paid after the threshing."

Then *she* left. I heard her man clump off. And now I was alone in the whole house.

But it wasn't so awful and tiresome as I had imagined. A calm peace fell over the house, a peace filled with memories of folks, kids, and things that had happened that I hadn't thought about at all in this new place. Thoughts about Hanna, Grandma, and my teacher came back to me. I hurried to wash my face and hands and comb my hair as best I could. I couldn't braid my long hair so that the braid was beautiful. I let it be as it had been yesterday.

I warmed my slate pencil on the stove and tried to curl my hair in front as I had seen my aunt do, but I only burned my fingers. Then I set about making beds as well as I could with the heavy blankets. It felt as if I were waiting for someone; it was as if I were freed from the grown-ups who had gone away. It was a feeling that I had never before experienced.

I tiptoed across the porch, still dark in the early morning, to Olga's; always before I had been afraid to cross it in the dark. It smelled bad inside, and I hurried to blow out the lamp so I could get outside again. I thought the baby would sleep longer if it were dark in there. It was not seven. When the baby woke up, I'd carry him across the porch and into our place; the grown-ups wouldn't need to know about that. I couldn't stay at Olga's. One afternoon I had stayed with the baby while she went to the little store near us, and I had cried the whole time. I didn't know why I cried. But it was so empty, so desolate in there that I felt I had to cry. There was hardly anything there. A table without a cloth, a chair, a bed, nothing more. Nothing. At the windows hung scallops Olga had cut from paper. The floor was bare, rough, and dirty. Near the door lay a sack. There was no litter. Olga swept often, three times a day just like at farmers' houses where they swept the kitchen after every meal. But it was so dirty here anyway.

The bricks on the hearth were black and splotched with spilled milk and porridge. There were no other dishes besides the two plates and two cups that Olga washed after every meal. Nothing else. The walls were peeling. No other decoration except some marigolds. Olga had dug them up and potted them in a jar. They were only frostbitten dried heads, but the leaves were a beautiful light green. How green those leaves looked in Olga's bare room. Two sheets and three towels were all the linens she owned; one of the sheets was on the bed. It was dirty, for "Karlberg is so careless," Olga had said. He took his midday nap on the bed in his barn clothes and boots.

"My linen cupboard," Olga had called a margarine box where she kept the baby's rags.

They had no close relatives to give them anything. All of their friends were as poor as themselves. The farmer had given them the bed and table. Karlberg had got the sheets from his half-brother who lived at Kolmården. When I had sat in the twilight, rocking the clothes basket set on two hunks of wood, it looked so dumb—an old clothes basket, so rickety on those round chunks of wood in that ugly room, I cried, hardly knowing why I cried except that I realized Olga and her man, Karlberg, had it so poor, so ugly.

I was angry at them. I had heard old women's gossip in other places. "You must try to have things at least tolerable," those old witches said when a poor young couple married. Gossip has more influence than sermons, and I had no patience for Olga's and Karlberg's poverty. I was afraid of their place just as I was afraid of Mother when she didn't try to keep our place clean.

Just as the sun began to stream in, paling the rays of the turned-down lamp, I heard the thunder of the threshing machine. Now my aloneness seemed emphasized. Everyone was busy, held fast by that thundering beast; now it snarled at me to do something useful, as my stepfather had said.

I blew out the lamp, kindled the fire in the stove, and began to do the dishes, listening sometimes out on the porch to check if the baby were awake. I tried all over again to get the white spread on the big Gustavian bed to lie as even as Mother did, but it still hung crookedly no matter how I tugged and smoothed. My acorn settee I hadn't got right either. The leaf that opened out was jammed; the blankets were bunched up, keeping the leaf from closing tight. I worked so the sweat ran, but it didn't help; the covers on both beds looked sloppy, and I began to feel respect for Mother's bed-making skills. After this I'd really watch how she did it. I sneaked a little of the forbidden coffee, drinking it from a cup and holding the handle with my little finger elegantly outspread. And so Hanna was with me again. I felt her presence so strongly beside me that I talked out loud. Sitting by the dresser where my doll and cards and shells were stuffed in a drawer, I rearranged the things, then took off all the doll's ragged clothes and put them to soak in the washbowl.

"You can wash them, Hanna, and hang them up so they'll be dry by noon," I said. No one answered, of course, but that didn't matter. The doll had a china head and her hair was china, but I had covered that unreal hair with a thick wig of blue and white mudwort. I had really thought about taking a hunk of my own hair, but when it came down to it, I couldn't.

"Spring has come, her garland weaves the meadows . . ."

"So beautiful," Hanna says.

"I have finished school now. I'm taking care of a boy, and I get two kronor a month for it."

Hanna looked happy.

"You can tell that to the teacher."

Two kronor was the highest wealth I knew. A two-kronor piece was something so impressive that when Mother said, "I have two kronor," I thought that all our troubles were over. If she had only a fiver, I thought that unlucky clouds were sweeping near me in the form of hunger and unwashed clothes. A five-crown piece with its dirty yellow color looked so cheap that I couldn't understand how it could be worth anything at all.

The steam thresher thundered down there. Time went by, but now I had my teacher here. While she sat on the acorn settee, I read aloud from a book:

Little Hans runs down to the shore
To gather sea shells small,
On the hot, deep sandy floor
Barefoot he must walk or crawl.

I read on and on, at least half the book aloud. The room drifted away more and more. I was standing at the teacher's desk reading to the children. The teacher listened and had tears in her eyes when I read about Pikku Matti. I thought he was affected, but Mother thought he was wonderful: "He didn't care about sweets and gaudy things, did he; he loved his grandmother and grandfather, he did." That sounded like a reproach. But I hadn't, of course, any grandmother or grandfather. My grandma wasn't really mine. Pikku could have followed the general to Stockholm to the king and eaten those sweet cakes, and then taken a few of them home to his grandfather and grandmother, and he didn't have to be so contrary that other kids hungry for sweets had to be tripped up. I thought he was dumb, but the teacher liked Pikku Matti just as much as Mother did. And now I read that whole long story two times.

The six-week-old baby who lay in a clothes basket on the other side of the porch I had forgotten entirely. My world had suddenly become so interesting, so populated, so full of mystery and possibility, for it was the first time I had been all alone in a house. Alone. No one could hear me, spy on me, or call for me. Now was the first time I could really look at the plaster boy and show it to Hanna.

I had discovered a new world, a world that many before me had found, and without such a discovery could hardly have managed to live life to the end. The world we carry within us. Fantasy's world. The one that is woven with sun, moon, and stars, trees, voices, and images. A world where we can be with those we've loved the most, those old friends that you never show to everyday people who find it so easy to criticize those you've loved.

The thunder of the threshing machine was silenced, and I heard a cry that cut directly through my dream world, a cry that made me throw the doll and books every which way as I ran into Olga's place.

There the boy lay screaming, screaming in a hoarse, terrible voice. He was blue in the face. He had surely been crying for a long time. I ran back to look at our wall clock we had got from Grandma. It was ten-thirty. They were having a coffee break from threshing; thanks be to God, it wasn't noon.

I went back to the boy.

It was so gray-cold there. It smelled of the barn, sour milk, and babies. The room was like a trash room where someone by mistake had thrown a clothes basket with a baby in it. A room like one folks put spades, crowbars, water buckets, and some chickens or anything else.

I rocked the basket as much as I could but the boy wouldn't stop crying. I took hold of him, turning him a little on his side. I was

146

forbidden to lift him. When I turned the baby, I saw two big wall lice creep from the nape of his neck. His little neck was red streaked. He quieted as soon as he got in another position and the lice had gone. He hiccuped now and then, but I rocked the basket and hummed without stopping until at last he probably got so dizzy he dropped off.

In Olga's stove there was no dry wood. I had to go to our place for some kindling. My stepfather was very careful about seeing to the wood. Mother never had to worry about wood when he was home. He cut and carried in piles of it, driving into the woods on Sundays for drier logs. Our neighbors thought that Hedvig had a really thoughtful man. Olga's Karlberg almost never cut wood. Olga, herself, stood at the wood block, chopping and splitting the wood. It was "women's work" to chop wood in that district.

I got a fire going in the old stove, another Ankarsrum: No. 4. The baby slept, and I tiptoed out.

I stood for a long time on the porch steps and listened, cupping one hand above my eyes and the other behind my ears, to hear if the threshing machine had started up. I think I stood so my stomach stuck out a little, too. That was the custom of the housewives when they stood on their porches on big farms. I was the wife of the house now, playing my role of farm wife just as I'd seen them when they came out on the steps, always with their hands cupped over their eyes, as if the daylight bothered them, as if they crawled from an ancient cave, hands over their eyes because of the sun, or if it rained, too, and their stomachs, big or little, always stuck out.

I was so much in my role that I didn't notice an old man walking on the road before I saw his back. Then I got scared and hurried in. I was afraid of old men. My experiences of them had been snuff, brandy, swearing, and meanness. Other worse things you had to keep secret. Old women were better; they, at least, had a clean apron and a newly ironed scarf on sometimes, and they didn't have snuff in their mouths. I bolted the door and stood a while listening. Then I heard the threshing machine start up again and felt calmer. It was safe again, no one would come for two hours yet. I forgot that I had orders to stay the whole time with the baby. The sun shone a little in the November haze, and a beam lit on the boy and the frog. Then I saw that the plaster boy had no eyes. He was a humbug. He was nothing. I began to wash the doll clothes. I remembered the foreman's Anna and began to bawl her out, "You slut, you, think what dirty dolls you have! You'll never amount to anything; you can't even keep your kids clean."

Then I thought of a song I'd heard; the words were dirty. I never would have dared to sing them if Mother had heard them.

Stringing up a line in front of the stove for my doll clothes, I sang in a loud voice, "Don't be sad, my little Lotta, you will sleep with me tonight . . ." Standing on a chair so I could reach to hang up my washing, I had fired up the stove so it was red hot, and I sang the whole song while I stood there. I felt as if I were a circus lady or an actress at the Workers' Union in Norrköping. Still standing on the chair, I sang more verses. A guardsman's song that I knew only one verse of, I sang several times.

Suddenly there was a loud knock on the door.

"Open up, you impossible brat," I heard Mother say.

I got so scared that I couldn't get off the chair. I just stood there while Mother pounded and scolded.

"Hedvig, you scared her," I heard Olga say. "The baby is sleeping, and the stove is burning so nice at my place. She's certainly taken care of things right. It doesn't matter what she's singing; she doesn't understand those words. She's just heard some hired men yelling them; she learns things so easy."

"She's big enough so she knows what's decent. She's eight years old," Mother angrily said. "Open this door now!"

I got down and opened the door.

"Ugh, so warm. I told you not to make any fire. And what's that for a song you were singing? It's really something when a person has to stand here and be shamed before folks. Never would I have believed you could be so nasty. Why did you learn such terrible stuff? Who taught you that? Answer or I'll whip you!"

I didn't know who had taught me the songs even if Mother had beaten me to pieces. Some of them my stepfather and his friends had sung when they were drunk. My uncle didn't drink, but he often sang bad songs. Some of them I had heard on the street; I liked their melodies. I knew that the words were dirty and that the grown-ups wouldn't like to hear them, but no one in particular had taught them to me.

"Will you answer?"

"They used to sing them."

"Who's they? Don't lie!"

"Uncle and my step—he—papa."

Mother dropped the subject.

148

"Heavens, you've used most of the soap. Well, you certainly were the right one to leave here and look after things! Never would I have thought you could be so naughty."

I didn't say anything. Now I saw how crazy I'd been. I wasn't supposed to play. I was to work, look after the boy, and "behave myself." I shouldn't have been with Hanna. Aw, Hanna hadn't been here or the teacher, and I couldn't tell Mother that I'd believed Hanna had been with me. Mother certainly ought to scold; she would soon be on her way again.

"The machine broke down, so we won't go out anymore today. You can bring in some wood now."

I put on an apron sack, wound a wool scarf on my head, and went slowly to the door. Mother had always been nice at the same time she'd scolded me—patted me on the cheek or something, but she didn't show any intention of doing that now. Instead she unbuttoned that ugly man's shirt and looked far off, serious and sad. I went out downhearted. On the porch I heard Olga humming. Carefully I opened the door.

She sat with the baby at her breast. She hummed and looked so sweet. It wasn't so awful in there any longer I thought. No, much better and happier than at my place just now.

"He cried a bit, for there were two wall lice that bit him; otherwise he was good," I whispered. Olga nodded.

Then she winked for me to come nearer. "Did you get whipped?" she whispered. I shook my head. She drew me to her, stroking my cheek. She smelled awful of sour milk, but I tried not to think of that. I was so sad that I'd take a pat from anyone just now. You can be thankful for the warm tongue of a dog on your face when the world is gray and hard and against you.

"Those songs weren't so bad, but don't sing them anymore. Go now and get the wood."

I went to the woodshed, my heart a little lighter.

That was my first day to work for someone. It ended shamefully. The next day the threshing machine had been fixed, and now Mother decided that Olga's boy should stay with us.

Mother stayed for a long time after the others had gone in the morning to hunt for wall lice in the clothes basket. She undressed the baby, taking off each piece as if she thought Olga hadn't looked after him properly, but he was dry and fine and powdered and smeared, and you could smell the garlic syrup on him a long way off. That flattered Mother certainly, for she sat some time with the baby on her lap without dressing him again. She pinched his little toes, said he'd become as fat as a sausage. Just at that moment she got a warm little stream right in her face, and she began to laugh. *"Ja,* that was really good," she said, drying herself with her apron. "Now you'll be nice and dry the rest of the morning." Then she dressed him and laid him in the basket.

Ja, just like that, she'd gotten peed on, right in the face. Then she'd laughed and dried herself off without even washing herself with soap, but when I had sung those songs! Was it like that when you were big?

I was big now, not as big as Mother, but still big enough so I got whipped for everything. The big ones sang dirty songs and didn't get whipped; the little ones, they got to pee on folks. *Ja,* he was just a little baby, the boy, but still, Mother didn't need to be so mad at me, a *little* mad she certainly could have been at the boy. Now she left, too, saying only good-bye, didn't pat me, bowed over the clothes basket instead. "Good-bye, little pig, sleep now," she said, tucking the blanket a bit better on him.

Jealousy made me speechless. I didn't answer when Mother said good-bye to me. I felt sick; I didn't want to look at the baby or at Mother either. I wanted to tattle to Olga that Mother had looked to see if she'd taken care of her boy properly.

But when the daylight came, and the lamp was blown out, the sun rose clearly over the frosty November day. The sun shone right in our room on the white wall painted with blue flowers, making it so fine that everything became so bright and beautiful I forgot all my anger. My play of yesterday began anew. I had plenty of playmates, talked out loud to myself, was out in the yard a long time, tried to get down those stubborn apples, and called to an imaginary Hanna not to fall when she tried to reach them.

The boy slept the whole forenoon, and when Olga and Mother came running home during the short time the threshers had for dinner, I got much praise. Olga had smuggled two slices of wheat bread from the mid-morning coffee break and gave them to me. They were dry and crumbled, but they were welcome, for it began to be almost empty in Mother's cupboard.

Mother looked a bit disapprovingly at the bread but didn't say anything.

My motherhood lasted for two weeks, and I became very used to having a little one to think about. The days went; the grown-ups came back at night, dirty, dead tired, their voices hoarse from the dust. They swore about the planks that were too low for the food table and over the threshing machine's owner who drove them like a slave driver. He had more farms he'd have to finish before Christmas.

In the farm wife's kitchen two babies lay in their baskets while their mothers worked with the threshing. The farm wife and a maid had to make meals for the whole farm's people those days and also feed the cattle. The women who had milking to do did it before they went to the fields and after the day's work at night. But since the farmer provided the meals during threshing time, everyone was willing to help. It was so good for these women to get out of the everlasting cooking of porridge and to sit down at a plentiful table. It reminded them of the worry-free days when they'd been hired girls. For however tedious life as a hired girl had been, being a farm worker's wife brought sadness and poverty so terrible that it became a sunny glint on life when the threshing came, even with its dust and drudgery, but also with a well-spread table at the farmer's house.

Olga sang when she came in the evenings with the milk running from her breasts and her head throbbing and aching.

For me the last days of the harvest were very slow. The only thing left to eat was a little bread and milk. And I got a little molasses on the bread. Mother still had some left that she'd got from Valdemar though she'd given Olga a full cup.

I began to fantasize about limpa and herring and dill pickles and sharp, crumbly cheese that the storekeepers sold in town for twenty-five öre a kilo. Those were things my stepfather used to have with him when he stumbled home from Skull-Jon's tavern and wanted to stay with us. Mother had also bought such treats sometimes when she'd had good places to clean. I often invited my invisible playmates to eat invisible herring and dill pickles the last days of the harvesting on the farm. There weren't such things in the little store that was so far away, almost to the train station. It was over three miles to the store.

In the store were only American pork and sometimes some sausage. But it was so old that it was hard as rock and couldn't be cut for frying. Olga had bought sausage when she'd been to the little store and had given me a little, but I couldn't chew it. There wasn't any limpa at all in the store; no one *bought* bread in this district.

Now and then our last place began to look pleasanter than it had been. There the baker had watched for Mother with a loaf of limpa and wanted to marry her. I liked it that a baker wanted to marry Mother. Life would have been more certain if she had. There was just my stepfather who was in favor or not in favor. But Mother wouldn't even look at the baker. Ever since she'd found out that he kneaded the dough with his feet when he was drunk, she'd talked about notifying the police.

Then I had the storekeeper woman there who found out my weakness for hard candy, giving me a chunk sometimes when she wanted something done.

Here were people waiting for their pay, and when they got it, there was nothing to find to buy. I had clean aprons nowadays and no lice in my head, for Mother had become so terribly careful again, but here there were no kids to play with so it was pretty much the same. Nothing seemed to go the way I thought it should. Everything in life went the wrong way. In the sugar-syrup house, where it would have meant so much to be fine and clean, for then I could have been with the kids right from the start, and the landlady's girl, Ida, would have played with me before I got the new dress. But there Mother wasn't able to do anything, and the new dress wasn't sewn until the last days before we had to move here to this coal-black farm land. I said all this out loud. I had heard my stepfather say to Karlberg, "Go around here on coal-black farm land."

The same morning the threshing machine left, Mother didn't wake me. She still lay dozing, although my stepfather had gone to the barn. He had fired up the stove and warmed something that was to be coffee. It was rye Mother had roasted, but today was payday both for Mother's work at threshing and for my stepfather's wages. And in the evening Mother and my stepfather would go to the little store. Mother still lay in bed. When she saw that I was awake, she told me to get up and kindle the fire. She was so hoarse she whispered.

Now I heard my stepfather tramping up the porch steps. He had milk with him; we got it at seven-thirty every morning. "You needn't get up, Hedvig, I'll eat a little bread and milk," he said.

He hadn't, of course, anything else to eat.

"Help Mother now all you can; she caught a cold at the threshing work. You're so big you can do something useful."

Mother was silent. I dressed quietly. The tears would come in spite of myself. "Olga is going to give me something for looking after the boy," I said, trying to remind him that I had also worked the last two weeks even if I hadn't caught a cold.

"Those poor wretches. They'll need everything they'll get. They don't have enough to give you anything. It's not good to take money for what you did either," my stepfather said.

So that was what my work was worth. But I knew Olga would give me something. Why should I take care of their boy and not get anything when Olga and Mother were paid for threshing?

"*Ja,* I know that well enough," Mother wheezed from her bed. "I always have paid for the least thing I had other folks' children do for me, and their mothers have come and wanted to pay for their youngsters' work sometimes. Mia has good reason to get a tip. You shouldn't be unjust."

See, there had my fair-minded mother come back again. She was on my side though she was so taken up with Olga's boy.

"When you can hardly get a word out, I think you should be quiet, but that's like women," my stepfather said.

"Shut up," Mother whispered, looking as if she were thinking of getting up.

"Now you lie still! And don't spoil the girl like that all the time. She can certainly learn to do something useful," my stepfather said.

"Don't concern yourself with her, Albert," Mother whispered, and then my stepfather left, slamming the door.

I began to bloom again: Mother had come nearer.

"You'll get everything I get from Olga," I said.

"Olga is so good-hearted, but she's so poor, so you mustn't take more than twenty-five öre at the most from her," Mother said.

"I'll take only ten öre," I said.

"No, twenty-five öre you can take, that'll be enough for a new hair ribbon."

But Olga's Karlberg gave me a whole krona that night. And when Olga got back from the store the next day, and came to us to get her boy who had stayed with us, she gave me a little package. There lay a wide blue hair ribbon a whole meter long.

Such a fine present and such good pay I had never got before. The blue hair ribbon was the first real present I had got from a friend, even counting the "well-off" relatives. So it was an Olga who had cut papers to curtain her windows who had given me that!

When I unwrapped the package and saw the ribbon, I began to cry. The tears came then, though I was often dry-eyed when things went against me, even when I was whipped with a birch branch.

Mother became enraged sometimes that I didn't cry when she whipped me; she whipped harder, saying I'd end up in jail when I got big since a whipping didn't faze me. But I was too angry to cry though the branch hurt; I wanted only to fight again.

When Olga saw my tears, her thick red lips trembled a little. She patted my cheek, took her boy and left. It wasn't so long since she herself had worn a ribbon in her braid. Maybe she'd never got a hair ribbon from anyone.

"You didn't thank her. I can't understand what's happened to you," Mother whispered, for she was just as hoarse that day, too.

"*Ja*, well, I thanked," I said in a low voice.

My stepfather also thought I had been well paid. "I'll have to borrow from you when I'm out of snuff," he joked.

I thought he was hateful. And Mother stood there and laughed so hard I thought she was mean, too. Them with their snuff and their tricks and laughs at another's expense! Didn't even get along and sometimes fought, but always they stood together against me. But I could soon take care of myself.

Chapter 13

One day in the beginning of December the two apples were gone from the tree. It had been very cold but we'd had no snow. I searched everywhere, quite far from the tree where they might have dropped. I couldn't find them. My nose, blue with cold, dripped.

"Have you lost something?" Olga asked. Her nose, too, was blue, and she had on the old jacket.

"No, no."

"What are you looking for? Have you lost something?" Mother asked, who wanted me to cut rags for rugs.

"No, no."

"Carry in a little wood now, and then help with the rags. You must read and write, too, so you won't forget what you've learned. In the spring, you'll begin school again."

I carried in the wood. "My stomach hurts," I said when I had carried in an armful and hurried out again. I crawled on the ground, combing the frosty grass with my fingers, though I had seen both my stepfather and Olga's Karlberg spit out snuff there by the steps. I couldn't find the apples.

I didn't dare to be out any longer. I had to go in. Someone had found the apples and taken them. Maybe the crows had. I had been so sure that they'd be mine, they had hung so free on the tree. No fence, no shopkeeper's window on the road.

I sat on my acorn settee and tried to cut rags for the rugs. Mother had given me a flimsy worn-out apron that was easy to cut, but the scissors went so slowly, so slowly.

It was early in the day. The potatoes for noon dinner boiled on the stove. Outside it was gray cold, desolate. Completely desolate since the apples had disappeared. Inside it was potatoes cooking and desolate. Mother cut and snipped like an old stubborn woman, like the one who cut oats with her finger until her old man drowned her.

155

"Say, old woman, that your fingers are cutting the oats."— "No, they're clipping them," the old woman said. The old man grabbed her, giving her some hard blows. "They're clipping, they're clipping," she still shrieked. Then the old man dragged her to the lake and shoved her in the water up to her waist. "Will you say that they cut the oats?"—"They're clipping it, they're clipping."—Then he pushed her in up to her neck. That didn't help. "They're clipping," the old woman said. Then the old man held her completely under, the water was now over her head (ugh, I'd often tried that in the washbowl to see how it would feel), but the old woman held up two fingers above the water and clipped with them. Then the old man got so mad he drowned her.

I always admired the stubborn old woman more and more every time I heard the old tale told. It's hardly just anyone who lets herself be drowned rather than given in. That much I had found out myself.

Mother sat across from me and clipped and clipped. The potatoes smelled awful; something rotten must have been put in the casserole. The herring had already been put out on the plate. Outside it was cold and forlorn.

"How can one manage to get anything at all for Christmas . . . Now he wants to buy new driving gloves again and a new whip. He's chewed snuff like a horse since we've come here, and his boots are worn out," Mother said while she clipped. She expected no answer I knew, and I didn't care about how things would be for Christmas.

We could hear Olga singing to her baby at her place.

Ja, my stepfather certainly did have snuff all the time. A half-kilo a week. I already had five big tinfoil wrappers from the snuff. I had hidden them to have for the Christmas tree.

"Twenty kronor a month I get with my milking, and one has to buy potatoes here, and there's no pig here; it just won't do." Mother stopped clipping and went over to drain the potatoes. "He wants three liters of brandy here for Christmas. That'll cost three kronor and fifty öre just for that, so we'll no doubt eat herring and potatoes for Christmas, too." Then she began to clip again.

"To be dumped here in the country is the worst that can happen to one. Food is high, and there's no money for it."

"And there's not any kids here," I put in.

"No, there aren't . . . you clip so slowly it's terrible. We have to hurry, for Grandma will be here for Christmas, and we must have the rags ready so I'll be sure to get some kronor."

"When will it be Christmas?"

"In three weeks."

That was so far away I lost interest. It'd be just as cold and gray out, just as potato-poor inside.

"These rags for curtains won't take another washing. I'll have to do like Olga, cut papers to put in the windows. But not even a little scrap of paper's to be found here. I don't have any boots so I could go to town either. Nine miles isn't exactly like a walk to the next farm."

Everything seemed to get harder. Out there swayed my empty branches; here sat Mother who snipped and clipped and found everything impossible.

I dragged the scissors noisily over the row of acorns on my settee, and then threw them on the pile of rags and began to cry.

"What's the matter now, for heaven's sake? Don't take things so hard. You don't need to cut rags; play with your doll for a while." Mother sounded cross.

"They've taken my two apples," I bawled, throwing the apron over my head.

"Your two apples, what in the name of Jesus are you talking about, child? Have you gone here and become foolish? *Ja,* I wonder if it isn't that. Farm workers usually have children, though poverty brings trouble even to children, but that no one can help. You must try to tolerate things until spring; then you'll have to start school again. But I regret that I moved here, I do. What is it about the apples you were talking about? You must have dreamed that."

"They hung on the tree," I sobbed under my apron, "and they took them in the night."

Not any of the grown-ups had noticed those two apples, not even Mother.

Olga came in at that moment wanting to borrow a teaspoon of salt. "Are you sad, Mia?"

Mother told her why I cried.

"Apples on that tree won't do to eat; they're green fruit, and those that hung on like that fell because they were rotten. If you look, you'll see their cores. They fell now because it's so cold. But at the farmer's there's a whole barrel of apples they share at Christmas at the farm party, so you'll get an apple at Christmas. It's only three weeks away."

"She's too much alone; she gets these ideas," Mother said.

"If Hedvig [it was hard for Olga to say "you" to Mother] will permit it, I'd like for Mia to go with me on Sunday. We're going to borrow the farmer's horse and ride to Karlberg's brother who lives up at Kolmården. They have a lot of kids, so she'll have more than enough playmates that day."

I had stopped crying. I thought Olga was the sun itself just now, although she was having one of her messy days when she had neither combed her hair nor washed, and her bodice was nearly black with dirt. She had on a skirt, but above it she was almost naked, for the dirty bodice was cut low and had ragged short sleeves. It was a wonder she wasn't frozen. She had no stockings on, going slipshod just in clogs. Her long braids hung on her back just like the first time I saw her. Her face was pale yellow, for the baby had really grown, sucking at her breasts night and day. But her big lips shone blood red. She looked as if she had a sickness of the lips; they looked swollen and raw. It was as if all the blood in her thin body had risen to her lips. Full, sensitive lips that shone red and sore from dreadful, secret questions.

Mother and Olga talked, their voices lowered.

"You mustn't run around so much in your underclothes, Olga. You'll regret it when you're older. Running here on the cold porch in the mornings is just crazy."

"I always wake up too late and Karlberg won't get up until he's had his coffee."

Now Mother lowered her voice even more and leaned closer to Olga. "It isn't good, Olga, as newly married as you are to go about like that in your underclothes. You'll spoil your man. He'll become too free with you. Hold yourself back a little."

"Karlberg doesn't mind about that," Olga said, blushing.

"He certainly does; don't believe otherwise. He sees you almost always with bare legs and bare arms. He'll be hanging after fancy women if you don't watch yourself."

"When you have just these awful rags . . . and Karlberg goes around only in his shirt, and he doesn't wear even that at night." Olga straightened her slumped shoulders.

"*Ja*, but don't let your man get used to your bare skin. I've seen a couple of times how that turns out when newly wed women don't hold themselves a little distant."

"It doesn't mean a thing to him, not a bit; he doesn't see if I have anything on or nothing. He goes to sleep as soon as he gets into bed and he sleeps when he's on his feet, too. *Ja*, well, if I try to wear

158

anything new, he glares and crabs," Olga said bitterly, taking her salt and leaving.

I thought Mother was being uppity when she talked like that to Olga. I wished I could have got out of putting clothes on in the mornings; it was so tiresome.

A barrel of apples, and it is three weeks before the barrel would be opened. Such waiting it always was for everything. Only Jesus is it who's certain about the time. I wonder where they have that barrel. I snip and snip around and around the ragged apron that will be dyed flax blue and become a strip for a rug. Mother snips and snips; the twilight falls outside. Olga slams her stove, the farmyard bell rings, and right after that, the men come tramping up the steps.

It has become almost ordinary that we eat in peace.

My stepfather's good humor is lasting again for a long time. He comes in, throws his work cap on the settee, and sits at the table. We sit down, too, Mother and I. Mother peels the potatoes, first a big pile for my stepfather. I peel my own. I detested herring and potatoes, but I didn't dare not to eat, for then my stepfather crabbed at Mother. It had happened many times when I tried not to eat. I thought the herring smelled awful. I got beads of sweat on my nose every time I had to take a bite of that red salted stuff. But herring was the cheapest of meat stuffs. We had to eat it. All salted food was hard for me. When I had an egg one Easter and didn't want to put salt on it, there was an uproar at the table.

"Let her eat it the way she wants to," Mother said.

"*Ja*, but that's so damn foolish. I've never heard of anything like that. That's ruining good food. You've got to teach the brat to eat like other folks."

"There's a lot that's happened that you haven't heard about," Mother said angrily.

"The brat will put salt on her egg or she'll leave the table," he yelled.

Then Mother was really furious as she could be sometimes. "You're like a childish old woman," she yelled. "You're like your fine Aunt." And she took my egg and threw it in my stepfather's face.

He got up half-way, looking wild.

"Don't you get up before you've picked up the shells on the table. I've eaten an egg before I saw you and have had one to give my girl, too," Mother screamed.

159

It became a terrible row. Mother gave me a sandwich and told me to leave, and I heard my stepfather say when Mother shuffled me out the door, "Take your baggage, you, and go to hell!"

Baggage, that was what I was.

Ever since I had made myself say nothing about the food. The few times Mother could give each of us an egg, I got to eat mine in peace. But I had a sinking feeling the whole time I sat and carefully ate the egg. It was such good food that I didn't want to just gulp it down like an ordinary bit of bread, but I sat the whole time on pins and needles.

My stepfather never hit me or ever pulled my hair through our whole stormy relationship. He expressed anger toward me in rows or coming to blows with Mother.

That injustice was my childhood torture. I didn't react so hard to physical pain but to injustice that I couldn't do anything about. I believe I would have got along better with him if he had hit me. When my mother boasted that my stepfather had never "touched" me, I got very angry at her.

"Is something wrong?" Mother asked my stepfather all of a sudden. She was still out of sorts and *he* still looked provoked.

"No, what's the matter with you? Am I in the way maybe? Don't I have a place at the table?"

"Idiot."

Quiet for awhile. My stepfather had eaten a big pile of potatoes and drunk milk. He had margarine on his bread. I didn't want anything on bread. That didn't go over either.

"Those who work must have the best and the most." That was what Mother was always trying to imprint on me. That lesson took so well and was imprinted so one-sidedly I thought it meant that *only men worked and they should have the best.*

A lesson that later in life almost made me starve to death. But a lesson with blows isn't easy to get rid of.

My grandfather had been a very strict father and husband. Mother often talked about it. If the children dared to begin eating before he came to the table, they had to leave. If they took a bite of herring from its back instead of starting with its belly, they got whipped for their gluttony. Luther haunted poor cottages and manor houses, Luther who brought brutality's capriciousness through domestic punishment, allowing God's will to be carried out by farmers in place of the priests. What souls could be cured or saved through those means, which were darker and harder than those of the priests?

When my mother talked about her father's strictness, she always added that so strict you didn't have to be, even if you believed in God. She wouldn't be so mean to her children, she said, looking assuringly at me. Mother had, for all that, taken much after her strict father. Poor people have a hard time with authority.

In my childhood, grown-ups talking about bringing up children always said that you should be a proper person. No one ever gave a clear definition of what it meant to be proper. According to one, you were proper if you washed yourself and combed your hair; another held that you kept yourself in good order; and another, that you didn't drink. All of the "educated" were proper people.

Now I sat there chewing my salted herring and sweating. Mother and my stepfather chewed theirs in silence, "keeping their eyes glued elsewhere," it was called.

"Karlberg's want to take Mia with them on Sunday to their relatives," Mother said.

"Why would they do that for?"

"*Ja*, I don't know," Mother said indifferently.

Mother was so unpredictable. She nearly always was on Olga's side, helping and everything. I stopped eating. If I'd been sitting at my grandfather's table, I'd have got a whipping for sure, for red, rancid bits of herring belly still lay on my plate.

"Was it *Karlberg* who arranged this with you?"

"Arranged?"

"*Ja*, arranged. You can play the milkmaid, of course, but the master drives away and the mistress rides along."

"God in heaven, so nasty you are! I haven't seen Karlberg for weeks. Olga asked me today, and they'll be taking their baby so they can show him to their relatives."

"Hmm, as if that was anything to show." (My stepfather didn't like little children.)

"Mia can go with them. She needs to be with children. We won't say another word about it," Mother said decisively.

"I don't care, but if you want her to get lice as well as a cold, it takes two hours to get there, it's all right with me. You can surely tell what kind of relatives they'd have, only gypsies in some shack up there at Kolmar'n."

161

"Gypsies aren't always the worst," Mother said meaningfully.

I took my cap and scurried out. The trip was going to take place, Mother had said so; they could quarrel as much as they wanted.

But Mother and my stepfather had made up again.

It was harder for Mother to get Olga and her baby properly ready than me. I had my Scotch plaid dress, of course, which had begun to get tight; my shoes were a little tight, too, and the worse for wear. But it was worse with Olga and even still worse with Karlberg. With tightened lips, Mother sewed the whole week, and when my stepfather sometimes grumbled, she said that Olga couldn't very well go to her in-laws in her coal-black slip nor could you let on that you lived with neighbors who didn't have a rag to wear.

Mother's pride showed itself in these funny expressions. I thought Mother's pride was good. You couldn't for your own honor have neighbors that looked just any old way. You had to have at least something decent on.

"Karlberg looks just like a trashbag, but I don't care about that," Mother said diplomatically. "But Olga must be clean and dressed right, her boy, too."

"Karlberg will freeze his ears off if he sits on the wagon with that thin squashed hat of his," my stepfather said. "He can borrow my cap."

"You do as you please. I'm not asking for anything," Mother guardedly said.

"Does he expect to go in clogs, too? You can't send the girl with them if he goes like that," my stepfather said.

"He certainly expects to, he hasn't any others. Ever since he's been a hired man he's taken no care of himself, hasn't any clothes, and then he's just newly married," Mother said disapprovingly. I understood very well that she criticized Karlberg so she wouldn't make my stepfather jealous.

On Sunday Karlberg had on my stepfather's cap, jacket, and Sunday shoes. Olga had a made-over dress from Mother's ragbag as well as a pair of shoes that Mother had broken in wrongly, for these both had the same straight soles; only rich people had left and right shoes. Olga tried them, taking the one Mother had worn for the left on her right foot, and the right one for her left foot, so she had them the right way, but they hurt her feet.

"Better a blister on the foot than a wrinkle in the shoe," Mother said.

And Olga laughingly agreed with that, though it was a jibe at ladies who wore shoes too small so their feet would look small. The shoes Olga got were wrinkled, big, and coarse. Both Mother and Olga understood gallows humor just as most did who lived life in such gray quarters.

The baby was bedecked in the best Mother had in her dresser drawer, and there was a change for him that was clean and ironed. Olga's hair was in a shining giant bun on her neck, and she held her back straight the whole time. We waited in the December darkness at five o'clock on Sunday morning for Karlberg to come with the horse cart that he was to borrow for the journey. Olga had a limpa and a sugared wreath of bread in a bundle. Mother had helped her bake.

"They'll be thinking we have a farm," Olga said. "They're very fine themselves. Karlberg's brother is as handsome as a count."

Mother looked quite proudly at us, and my stepfather thoughtfully stroked his mustache.

"Hedvig's not such ugly neighbor trash herself, would you say?" he said.

"My own mother hasn't been as kind," Olga said, holding her baby tighter. I heard her voice break.

I had a sudden longing to stay home. Mother was so awfully kind.

Would she be lonesome here with my stepfather now while I journeyed out in the world?

I was so bundled up that I couldn't move. I had no coat, but Mother had wrapped me in my stepfather's wool vest, the brown shawl over that, and a thick wool shawl on my head. I wanted to go stand by Mother while she waited on the steps listening for the cart, but I couldn't because of all my wraps. I wanted to tell her that I would stay home, that I'd never wished to leave here, that I'd be sweet and obedient and do everything she asked me to.

When I heard the cart rattling up the hill, my good intentions were forgotten. My heart leaped up, beating fast. Mother's goodness and everything were forgotten for the journey.

The horse trotted along. It was the same horse and cart that had taken us from the sugar-syrup house. Again I sat alone in the back seat, wishing that Hanna were beside me. So fast is a mother forgotten.

Chapter 14

It was dark, without stars, but morning's darkness is never so black as evening's. A little light lay over the hard frozen road as we jogged along. Fine folks were out travelling.

"It's a terrible road, the horse'll get sore feet," Karlberg said.

"He's been just newly shod," Olga answered.

That was all the young couple said during the nearly three hours the journey took.

I think that Olga was overwhelmingly pleased by the trip. Otherwise so slump shouldered, she sat as straight as a ramrod the whole time in front of me on the seat. She had pulled her head scarf back, holding her face a little to the side against the wind. Sometimes she nodded. Karlberg took some snuff now and then, spitting the wad out and clucking to the fat horse.

It got lighter and lighter. The dark rim of the forest I had glimpsed for two months in the distance was coming nearer. Folks were up at the farms, looking curiously first at us, then at the horse. After they'd looked at the horse, they greeted us.

Gypsies don't greet farmers from the bay part of the country, but our horse was no gypsy horse. Olga's hair was very black, and Karlberg was a little too dark to be taken for farmers from our countryside. Both Olga and Karlberg nodded stiffly and distantly to the heavy-set farmers, to their younger, leaner sort, to bent, old tenant farmers, and some other early risers. The land lay gray and hard; the people we met looked grayer and harder. Even the yards with their bare-branched fruit trees looked gnarled and dead in the frosty December morning. Dark and soft the forest towered above us still some distance away. We would be going right into the forest.

I dozed now and then. The horse's hooves' clip-clopping makes you as sleepy as the train's mechanical clickety-clack.

The little cottages and big farm houses became scarcer. Clumps of pines soughed, signalling the nearness of the great forest, and soon we were hemmed in on both sides by giant fire and pines. We were no longer caught in the day's gray fastness. The cold wind seemed cut off in this peace, and I saw that Olga's back relaxed and slouched a little. It was as if she had held herself so straight only for the gray land's wind and cold and its people's long curious glances.

All of a sudden Karlberg turned off the highway and drove on a rugged, bumpy forest trail where we hung on for dear life at every step the horse took. Olga and Karlberg were still silent. Maybe both were too excited at the coming visit to speak. This was the first journey they'd made together. They came with a horse, they were well-dressed according to their lights, limpa and a bread wreath were in the bundle, and the neighbor's little girl in her plaid "modern" dress and fine shoes had come with them.

There is excitement in a journey and in a first journey.

The cart stopped in a glade before a Sunday-quiet hovel. It was a little shed, its corners nailed to four giant fir trees, forming its corner posts. The trees didn't stand in a perfect square, so the house was a little crooked, but I thought it was wonderful just as it stood. I decided to build a house just like it. Building would be quickly over and done with; the roof of fir branches and some rough boards for walls. The little house stood all by itself; there were no sheds or barns or outhouses.

A pale, thin woman with large eyes that seemed to stare a little came out on the steps, looking with such surprise at the fat horse, the cart with its footboard, my stepfather's cap on Karlberg's head, and Olga's coat that she couldn't say a word of greeting. She stared at the fat horse again, and then, catching up her apron to her eyes, she began to cry. Olga winked meaningfully at Karlberg just as if this was what they had expected. The woman hadn't discovered me. Her apron still over her face, she went into the house.

A bare-headed man came out on the steps.

Olga was right. He looked wonderful. He was the handsomest I ever saw in my whole childhood. Maybe he wasn't for others, but he was for me. A long string of children followed him out.

Olga hurried to get me unbundled from all the shawls Mother had wrapped around me so that I could stand there in all the splendor of my Scotch plaid dress and my fairly new shoes. I was duly admired by six pairs of children's eyes. I had eyes only for their father. Karlberg, my stepfather, Valdemar, my uncle, all the "well-off, educated" relatives, the foremen of the factories, the beer drivers—all the men I had ever seen paled into shrunken, twisted, ugly brutes who at night in the darkness took the shapes of juniper bushes or scrub pines standing ready to overthrow you as you came trembling and shivering from the woodshed or the store.

A tall man with wavy hair brushed back. (All the men I had seen had a forelock plastered on their foreheads, or maybe I just thought they all did because my stepfather had one.) Shining brown eyes that perhaps looked darker than they were because of his blonde hair. His white teeth flashed with every word he laughingly said, and when he smilingly bid us welcome, his eyes crinkled and beamed with laughter. Every movement he made was different from other men's. The striped homespun shirt he wore looked finer and different on him than on other men. I still see the picture of him standing there bare-headed that December morning with Kolmården's giant pines behind him, the simple gray house, just a shed that had four huge pines for its corner posts, looking even more roughly made than an ordinary woodshed; he stood as proudly as the great crowns of the trees swaying high over the roof of fir branches.

But all of this became splendid just as it *should* because the man stood there. Taking me by the hand and holding Olga's baby, who screamed to high heaven, on his arm, he kicked the door open, and invited Olga and Karlberg to step inside.

Again Olga was right. They were gentry.

It was an enormous room with three windows. On the floor lay a carpet made of gunny sacks sewn together, sacks that had come at a time of hard necessity filled with rye from the Russian steppes.

I knew the story of these Russian rugs, for Grandma had one over her rag rug for everyday. And Grandma had told me about the Russian rye flour and how all of Norrköping had cheered when the Russian ships had come with their precious load, the time when no one had seen bread for months in town.

A bookshelf hung between two of the windows. Only fine folks had bookshelves; I knew that for sure. Mother had a few old books—"Braviken's Pearls," "Laurie Duncan's Fate," and "A Sailor's Wondrous Strange Stories from Barbary," but they lay in the bottom of a box. The Bible and a psalm book lay on the dresser. They lay there always, gray-brown and notched like old pieces of wood. I never wanted to look into them. Grandma had books in a box. But no one at our last place or Holmstad or in the southern suburbs of Norrköping had a bookshelf. Only in some of the fine houses where Mother cleaned were there bookshelves. Even a couple of the "educated" houses that I'd visited a few times didn't have bookshelves, and they didn't even have a Bible on the bureau. They had a rack for newspapers with *Ostgöten* and *Hemmet* in it. *Hemmet* had a series of articles called "Legends of Country and Court." But one time I was at the "educateds" and took the paper from the rack without asking permission, just to get a peek while they gabbed with Mother, and I got such a scolding that ever afterwards I was afraid of *Hemmet.*

Here there was a bookshelf. For me their social position was clear.

A cupboard that hung from the ceiling and wasn't nailed to the wall gave the impression of people of rank. At the windows were narrow strips of white cloth bordered with lace. A big square table with a cloth, a pinchback sofa and chairs, a clock, and two pictures of God on the walls. Both pictures were alike. God with a shepherd's crook, a lamb, and a long white beard.

In the big fireplace a crackling fire glowed. The housewife stood by it, looking down at the floor. Her eyelids were red. The man led me to her, and taking her hand, I curtseyed. She seemed to be interested. I thought her eyes were strange, her face so narrow. Her gray hair straggled thick and bushy around her pale, narrow face, as if it had been full of flour dust. She had a big stomach. The midwife will be coming here soon, I thought. Olga told her who I was, and the woman became more interested.

"You have lived in town," she said, sounding as if she were envious. "You have been in town," she repeated, and she looked at her children so penetratingly and reproachfully that they stared at me, too, who had lived in town.

"There's no fun in town," I said loudly and clearly, "not a bit." I felt I should say that, and I had hit the right note.

"No, if you believe what Hedvig, her mother, says, the town isn't any place to live," Olga said.

"Only topers live there," I said, as if I had been married to three such fellows.

Everyone laughed, but the handsome man looked almost stern.

"Toper is not a pretty word; there are many unlucky ones who drink," he said, looking seriously at me with his shining eyes.

That was something altogether new. Never had I heard such a thing. To be unlucky, that was breaking a bone or dying or going blind. Folks drank because they were bad, I'd learned. I'd seen men who drank fight their own wives, driving them out at night, and

167

sometimes the wives had gone for the police. And these men weren't unlucky. I had heard many of these topers say that they could drink as much as they wanted because they had a right to drink.

It was a strange Sunday.

Of the many children I found myself attached to two girls, one my age, and the other was probably around twelve.

The girl my age had her father's brown eyes and her mother's light, nearly gray hair. Her hair hung loose, curling in ringlets, and I thought I was going about with a princess. It was so different from Hanna's rattail and my own tight, long braid. My hair wanted to curl at the temples, but Mother brushed and combed it, wetting and pulling it so that not a wisp hung loose. On high and mighty occasions I got to have my hair hang loose but not in front; that had to lie flat.

Both the girls were dressed in bloused dresses of the same material as their father's shirt. Homely, coarse cotton stuff, but even so, they looked so splendid I thought.

Here they didn't need any Dalarna bags. There was an individuality here that outweighed everything else. In this house there was something of a fairy tale. The man with his easy graces and slender well-knit figure, the girls with their glorious curly hair.

Karlberg sat on the sofa looking like a bearded troll beside them. And my stepfather, who Grandma said was so handsome that it was his bad luck—pooh! He with his stubby mustache, his thick forelock, his hard gray eyes that rolled and got white when he was angry. Coarse and stocky he was, nothing else.

"Father has sewn our dresses," the girl informed me. "We get to wear them because it's Sunday."

Her words made me radiant. In the middle of the forest folks celebrated Sunday. They dressed up not because guests were coming but that it was Sunday.

"Does your father sew?" I breathed.

"*Ja,* Mother is always sick and she's so sad."

"*Ja,* I saw that she cried when we came. Was she angry that we came?"

"No, oh no. She cried because of the horse; she has had a horse. Our Grandfather had many horses, but Grandfather is angry at Mother, and Father is angry at Grandfather, but Father is much nicer than Grandfather."

I thought about this. Somewhere back of all this grandfather talk lay the story about the horses. But if the grandfather had owned twenty thousand horses, he wouldn't, not for a second, have been my choice. I was skeptical about grandfathers after I'd heard that my own grandfather had given my money to a farmer's daughter—Valdemar's wife.

All grandfathers were dumbbells even if they had horses or only money.

My princess with that gray-white curly hair and brown eyes turned the subject of her family to me. Pinching a bit of my plaid dress, she asked if it had cost one hundred kronor. I knew, of course, that it didn't, and I thought her blue and white striped dress that her father had sewed was something that in my heart I'd now be longing for. Grandma had had many weaving patterns just like it was the homeliest in the world. Old men and other really poor folks had it for everyday clothes. I have never seen fine people wearing it. Not even the weaving master's foreman's greasy clothes were of that simple material; they were plain blue, which was something new among the higher-class workers who had means enough to get it.

I would ask Mother to write to Grandma for a piece for a dress. It was the same sort of weave I'd made hair of for my doll. Blue and white. I had a wild sort of hope that the father of the princess maybe would sew it for me.

The man was moving about the whole time, he and the twelve-year-old girl. They were like a team. I didn't see the housewife do anything about the house the whole Sunday. She mostly sat with Olga's baby on her knee. She and Olga had so much to talk about. Olga's big mouth, which had been nearly blue with cold after the long journey, glistened red and raw again; the heavy braid of her hair bun seemed to draw her face up, and the wings of her broad nose shivered as she eagerly, feverishly whispered to her sister-in-law, sometimes stroking the little lace border on the wrists of the baby's shirt.

The father and daughter took care of the meal. Though I didn't look at the girl openly, I tried to watch her. A narrow face like her mother's and nearly as white. Her hair was like Karlberg's. Something in her face was also like his. He could easily have been her father if she hadn't had those brown eyes. He was, of course, her uncle, but not a real one, for Olga had said that Karlberg's brother was just a "side branch" of the family. Side branch was often used as an expression about myself, but no one tried to explain what a side branch was when it concerned people. When I lived with my aunt, I had often played at Ostra station in Norrköping; old freight cars stood on tracks that the trainmen called side branches. "You can play on the side branch," they said to us, "but don't you dare go on the main line." One of my mother's brothers also worked on a side branch that went from the southern line out through Vikbolandet. When I heard that people were born on the side branch, I always got a confused picture of old rusty freight cars and railroad tracks here and there.

With the smallest child, about two years old, on his arm, the man strode through the room, out to the kitchen, in and out, until the table was all set for coffee. Every time his wife offered to help, he forbade her, laughing with his brown eyes. "Sit, Elin, sit and talk with Olga; it isn't often you have company."

Now I no longer wanted to be the shining princess; I wanted to be the gangly, dark-haired, pale girl who helped that happy, handsome man. I got up and went out to the kitchen, which was little and dark. I said what I'd heard Mother say when she and I were invited out and were hungry and wanted the folks to hurry up and get the food ready they'd invited us to eat: "Is there anything I can help you with?" Then I curtseyed. No, I shouldn't help; I had journeyed a long way and should have coffee now. Olga's cake was sliced, and the rye rusks, the house's own food was heaped up, and though the coffee was certainly not "steam roasted," it wasn't even coffee but plain rye, I had never before been where it was so truly festive and dignified.

Each of the children had a chair, higher and higher, according to their size at the table. That wasn't customary in tenant farmhouses. When guests came there, the tenant children stood in a group with their fingers in their mouths and looked on while the guests were invited to help themselves.

The man served the whole time, and when he filled my cup and stroked my braid, I got so confused that I said I didn't use sugar in coffee. Why I did that I don't know. Sugar was a delicacy. Maybe that's why. I wanted perhaps to make a sacrifice in some way to my new god, and that happened to be two sugar lumps. The man gave me three lumps anyway that I put in my cup at once, a big slice of Olga's sugared wreath, and two rye husks. Olga looked on with interest; I felt ashamed. She knew for sure that I used sugar at home, that when Mother was low on sugar, she went without for my sake. People who know shouldn't be along the first time you're with guests that you want to please. They know all your faults and weaknesses. You're so bound up with all that and can't throw off its chains, just have to go on with your sinful life so you won't be laughed at.

Karlberg had quietly slipped out. I knew he wanted to spit out his snuff. So he did. He went *out* to get rid of his snuff here at his own brother's. At home he spit it on the hearth. I had heard Olga crab at him for that. I wasn't the only one who wanted to change a custom, without crabbing, without a sermon. Only because this simple, original place was so clean, so austere in style, a crowd of children brown-eyed and blue-eyed, in the homeliest clothes, coarse, cheap clothes, and a man who laughed with love at his wife, a heavy, pale sorrow that fate had given her who dared to break with rich parents. She cried when saw a horse. She grieved at the poverty that hung threateningly over her hovel and children, her children, who'd never get to ride a horse, and a poverty whose deep hole would swallow them all if the man didn't hold them up, the man whose strange power over her senses she had never ceased to wonder over with her inborn provincial understanding. A wonder that split her in two. It was an atmosphere filled with anxiety, love, and trust.

It was new for Olga to see a man openly show his love for his wife, and it was new for me. Olga was nineteen, and I was eight, but both of us knew that this love was only in books; marriage was rows, kids, trouble, meanness, or at the best, a dreary toil and moil that custom had made for two sullen or quarreling people to hold together as a couple.

"In Jesus' name we go to the table," prayed the older girl before we began to drink the rye coffee.

I never said the table prayer at home unless Grandma was with us; she thought it was beautiful that children blessed the food because food was, for children, a double gift, she explained. First, the grown-ups got the food from God, then the children got it from the grown-ups.

Grandma's hands were knobby and twisted from hard work and unyielding earth and old shacks and the factory's oil. Her knees were stiff with big knots and lumps, for rheumatoid arthritis had taken hold with the help of drafty, cold rooms.

I was convinced that she was offering only a way of speaking words when she thanked God for the meal. For she often wished she was dead. I already knew well enough at my age that an old person like my beloved Grandma tried to trick death, tried to win his approval by thanking God for food, for gifts, for life which was only hard because death was the only thing left that might offer hope. Maybe . . . maybe . . . peace was to be found behind it. Maybe if you were careful not to anger death, if you begged, if you were solemn, if you trembled as before a powerful guest when he came . . .

At the table here there was no fear of death or any desire to win anything from that harsh master. Everyone was young. On the walls God hung among golden clouds with a staff in His hand and a lamb on His arm. Two identical pictures.

My mother never said table prayers.

My stepfather sometimes thought manners required it. "The girl should pray before meals; that surely isn't asking too much. It's what kids should do."

A discussion always followed about it that made the prayer forgotten. I remember one especially that ended like this:

"It would really be hell if kids didn't say a prayer; I had to do it when I grew up."

"And look how you turned out."

When Grandma was with us Mother always folded her hands when I said the prayer.

It was with Grandma as with the man here. In their company you wanted to be a little different than usual.

Nearly that whole day I was the center of attention in the house. With the exception of the man himself, not one of the others had lived in as many places as I, travelled as much, seen as much. Only the man and Karlberg and I had been on a train, and Karlberg only one time on a little branch line. None of them had been in a factory. None of the grown-ups treated me like a silly little girl. They listened breathlessly to both my real stories and my fantasies.

That it was a child who told the stories didn't diminish the impression.

They held the idea that a child didn't lie.

In this house there wasn't a question about lies or truth. The point was to tell about something that had happened out in the world. And it was an eight-year-old illegitimate child circumstances had thrown here and there who provided the entertainment.

172

I told about the bridge by the paper mill over the Motala River that was so rickety and battered that a long section hung down into the river. How you had to hang on tight to the railing and nearly lift yourself over that dangerous place. The factory workers on the night shift had to take lanterns with them so they wouldn't fall in there when they crossed the bridge.

"Did you walk over it though?"

"Oh, *ja*, I went on it every day to school." (This was when I had the stocking needle teacher.)

"There were angels who walked beside you and held on to you," the twelve-year-old girl said.

I didn't want to protest.

"Two tar boilermen were drunk one night, and they went over the bridge without hanging on to anything, and they didn't fall in. My uncle went over it, too, and he was drunk, but he just fell down and crawled over that rickety place, but the tar boilermen walked upright the whole time."

I got up and demonstrated how upright the tar men walked, weaving a little to show how strange it was that drunks came over a bridge that had parts of it hanging right down in the river.

The older girl looked hesitantly at her father.

"Would angels protect drunk men?"

Olga looked delighted; she was proud that she had brought such an interesting person with her. Shifting the baby a little nearer to her breast, she straightened her back and waited for someone to comment on this wonder of wonders.

"Drunk men are like children," the man said and smiled. "Drunk men don't worry very much about how they will walk, exactly like children. That's why they are so often protected." He smiled at me with his shining eyes, but I couldn't give in. I didn't want angels to protect drunk rascals.

"The train ran over Tin-Johan," I said, relenting a little. "He was drunk, too, they said. He died."

"*Ja*, his time was up," Olga quickly said. The others nodded.

The children, six in a row on their homemade chairs, had finished their coffee. The father and mother got up first, though. I hadn't seen this before either, that grown-ups took children into such consideration. That father and mother stayed at the table and waited until their children had finished without nagging them. But maybe that was because it was Sunday.

In the workers' homes where I'd been, you didn't have time to teach children table manners in the right way, that's to say, by showing them table manners. It isn't good to teach what you don't know anything about.

I wanted so much to stay inside, but the children pulled me away. Olga wrapped me up in Mother's old shawl, tying the wool scarf on my head, and out we went.

"It's been so long since you've been with kids your own age. Go and play now," Olga said.

Children were all the same to me just then. Grown-ups had such one-track minds. I didn't have any desire to play right then. I longed to sit and listen to the brown-eyed handsome man with the quiet voice and see what books there were in the shelf.

Outside, Kolmården looked uninteresting, and the kids irritated me, but I had to try. The house with the roof of fir branches and the four giant pines for cornerposts were still worth that. Such a house would I build the first chance I got, my own corner nook, as soon as I got someplace where there was a forest. Now we lived on a plain with hardly anything even for cover, not even a juniper bush.

"Your father's so fine," I said to the older girl.

"Ja-a," she drawled. She looked long and doubtfully at me. "Mother's folks are rich; Grandfather is a magistrate. He has six horses. Two horses never do farm work, only draw fine carriages," she said, almost whispering.

It was clear I had made a mistake. In this house it was the mother who represented fineness.

"That's why Mama cries when horses come here."

"Ugh, horses," I sniffed.

For a while there was silence. The girl hesitated.

"Father is so sweet," she said softly.

I believe that she didn't think that being fine was anything. She loved her father for other reasons. People who were fine were difficult, they cried when they saw a well-fed horse, and couldn't go on journeys or ride it. Or were reminded of their lost happiness.

Instinctively, I understood that.

"Your father is so handsome," I said.

"Olga says that your father looks so wonderful."

"I haven't any father; he's my stepfather," I said stubbornly.

Nothing seemed possible to play. We walked around and talked a little. I tried to draw a hopscotch, but the ground was so frozen and covered with yellow grass that my squares couldn't be seen. We looked for a rope, and I showed them how to jump rope. It was too

174

cold, and they had too much on for this to be any fun, but they were highly interested in my demonstration. I didn't know what I could find to do anymore. But they showed they had resources themselves. After I had showed all my arts, they asked me to follow them a ways so we could hit the ball. Now I was surprised. Ball? Did they have balls here, and outside, too? Didn't they care about them more than that?

The balls they showed me were hard ones, cut out of growths on curly grained birches, and six clubs. The man who made the balls and clubs for the children had certainly heard tales of golf.

A flat smooth place, a big circle with holes here and there, simple drawn-up rules. The children were very clever.

I was far behind long afterwards. And long afterwards still, for I never had an opportunity to practice that poor home's primitive beginnings of an ancient sport that according to many novels is the gentry's pastime on England's heaths.

The wind through Kolmården's tall pines and spruces soughed peacefully over us, dropping frosty needles in the December sun.

Five children played an old lordly game, a game found anew in all simplicity by a shoemaker who loved his wife and children.

The grown-ups came out after an hour or so. Not the wife, who was reading, but Olga, Karlberg, and the man. He was bareheaded and was about to go back in, but instead took the club from his older daughter and showed me how I should swing it toward the ball.

Karlberg also joined in the game, and with his powerful arm hit the ball far into the forest. Olga then got a club. She was very quick, getting two balls in the holes. She sprang as lightly as a new calf and her cheeks were like roses. The man praised her game.

I was so jealous that I got tears in my eyes. Here I had taken care of Olga's boy, sat in her ugly room with the newspapers for curtains, and now she came and was so clever, played though she was big, and caught on so fast. The grown-ups shouldn't have come here. Not Olga and not Karlberg, not any of them except the children's father. With him it was different. The other grown-ups could have kept to themselves.

"Now let's go in and eat, so we can talk a little. We have just a few hours before you must go."

Dinner consisted of potato pancakes with lingonberries and

syrup. Thick pancakes, made the day before. They were good and satisfying. I decided then and there to convince my mother to bake potato pancakes every Saturday and heat them for Sunday dinner. Then it would be Sunday, a restful Sunday. That would be different than when those "well-off" came to see us. Mother had to rush about the whole Sunday, stand at the stove and fry meatballs, cook potatoes with cream, and use up all our money on only that big meal that wasn't nearly as good as this one.

Olga looked meditative, too, as she chewed her pancakes and syrup.

"You are used to better food, of course," the wife said, who had joined us, no longer looking so tired.

"No," I said almost angrily. "No, I think potato pancakes are the best food in the world."

"It's already two o'clock; we're eating like fine folks," the man joked.

"Two o'clock? Fine folks don't eat dinner before four, my dear," the wife said.

The man just laughed.

"Then we're really fine, for we don't eat dinner at all sometimes," Karlberg said, but Olga nudged him saying, "That's not happened so many times."

Olga's words made me think of my mother and stepfather who sat alone back there in the house on the plain. It was good they weren't here. Although Mother would have liked it here, my stepfather, oh, never in his life. He would have glared and been silent, thinking that coffee made from rye was dishwater and that there were too many kids in the house; he called potato pancakes filler food if they didn't have pork, too. It was good they were where they were.

Mother would have talked about the alders at her old home where she was a child, telling about the other end of Kolmarden where she grew up and where everything was so remarkable. And if my stepfather had not been along, she would have told about me, that I was "on her side" or "on a side branch," and that she wouldn't have married if she hadn't had me and wanted to have a home for me.

It was good they were where they were.

The older girl and her father cleared the table while we sat there, the children expectantly waiting for something more. They all looked serious, and I tried to look as serious as they did, too.

The man came in from the kitchen and took down a heavy book from the shelf.

The Bible, I thought? Sermon book? Lectures? In spite of those beautiful eyes, the blonde, wavy hair, the white teeth, and the handsome figure, my idol sank just a little bit.

But it wasn't the Bible. Nor the book of sermons either. I saw that as soon as he opened the book. There were illustrations and big new print. It wasn't that flourishing old one that I had to plod on with in Grandma's sermon book. He held the book open before him. It was *Pilgrim's Progress.*

I had never heard the book talked about.

I understood afterwards when I was older, because of the impression the book had made on me, that this book was the reason for many more heretics and backsliders from the church than from Martin Luther and the big philosophical free thinkers.

He read wonderfully well. He read better than anyone I had ever heard, better than my idol in Holmstad school. And what things he read about! Giants and trolls. Wrath, lies, robberies: everything was about trolls and dragons and temptations that were inflicted on that poor Christian. At last it was explained. There lay giants and trolls breathing out poison in all corners of the earth and confusing people. For over an hour we sat quietly listening. The older girl who sat beside me whispered what would happen next every time her father turned the page. She knew the whole book by heart.

A big book, as big as the Bible at home on Mother's dresser.

"We have a big Bible at home," I whispered to the girl.

"Everything in there is in the Bible, although not as wonderful as in here," she whispered back.

I was completely overwhelmed. At once the Bible came alive. As soon as I got home I would begin reading the Bible. Of course, I'd find something about what we'd heard here. When you take things from the Bible, it certainly had to be in the Bible, too. Or had someone picked the best from the Bible so it was only a dead piece of wood on the dresser?

Christian had found a safe harbor in some desperate place, and now the man laid the book down.

"We'll sing a song now, too," he said smiling as if he were assured that everything would come out all right for the poor Christian.

I was so eager that I shivered. They would sing. Sometimes Mother sang at home, but not so my stepfather could hear her. He couldn't stand any "droning" unless he was drunk. Then he sang in an awful voice the song about the prophet Jonas, ". . . then there came a whale hungry and starved so Jonas he swallowed boots and all." Now as I thought of that old drinking song here, I was almost afraid I had said some of it aloud.

"While all things smile and bloom," the man started up with a good voice, and the children and the wife and Olga, too. They all knew the song except the two-year-old and me. That felt so lonely. No, now I saw that Karlberg didn't know it either.

Outside the ground was frozen hard in the snowless winter. The December sun had gone down after its short round, the twilight drew nearer the windows.

"While all things smile and bloom
in life's fleeting spring,
think of him who so true
holds his heart's door ajar.
Open, open before autumn
Sweeps every flower afar . . ."

Now Karlberg sang, too. I could tell he didn't know the words. I hummed the melody and didn't feel left out any longer. Then it was quiet until the two-year-old on Karlberg's knee yelled, "Cake!" He wanted to have more of the wreath cake Olga had brought. The father obediently went to the kitchen for a slice, and when that hungry little fellow was quiet, Olga said, "Mia reads so beautifully; she reads by heart."

Everyone looked at me. Now it was my turn. I knew nothing that seemed right here. I thought that among religious people you couldn't say, "Spring is coming," or "Alone on a bench on a path . . ." "No, I can't, I can't remember anything," I said, blushing furiously.

"I can see you do," the brown eyes laughed at me. "Elsa," he called to the older girl, "You read a little first. Mia is a guest and shy, but maybe she'll think of something while you're reading."

Elsa was in the kitchen. She came in drying her hands from doing the dishes or whatever she'd been doing, looking puzzled.

"Recite something, Elsa, you first, then Mia will." Embarrassed, Elsa looked at me. "I don't know anything proper."

What did she mean by "proper"?

She recited something about birch trees, woods, cabins, and children. She recited in a monotone, but even so it was captivatingly beautiful. The simple words seemed just right for her to be saying.

The cabin she was telling about could have been this one. When she had finished, she said, "Father wrote the verses." (Maybe that was why she'd said that she didn't know anything proper, meaning something from a book.)

So he wrote poems, too, just like me. It was the first time I had come across anyone who wrote poetry. I searched my memory—should I recite one of my poems? No, that would be too silly. The one I was thinking of was about Jesus, but still . . . I could do the one about a bird, maybe, but I had muddled it so badly that I couldn't even remember all of it. "Sometimes the bird sometimes sings in the woodland, once I held a bird in my hand," I repeated to myself, but couldn't think of the rest. Now everyone waited for me to begin; I had to say something. "Alone on a bench the old beggar sat," I began tremblingly. When I was through, they all said it was good and beautiful. "Spring has come, her garland weaves," I began at once. I said it with emotion, thinking of my teacher in Holmstad, and Karlberg, who knew the poem, clapped his hands. I looked shyly at the man. His eyes were very bright and serious. "That was as beautiful as a prayer, and you said it as if it were a prayer."

"She should be in the theater," Olga said.

The man frowned at Olga.

"Mia has a whole bunch of poems she's written herself," Olga said, and at this, I thought they all looked dumbstruck.

"No, no, I can't write; I never remember what I've written; it's nothing, it's so stupid," I said almost crying.

"No, you don't need to give us any," the man smiled. "But now Elsa, Mia, and I have read and recited. More of you must sing for your supper. You, Olga."

"No, I don't remember anything. It was hard for me in school. I was a dumbbell," she laughed.

Solemnly, the wife blinked and looked down; no one asked her to recite.

"Well, listen to this now," and Karlberg rattled off:

"The old hag sat in the ashes, a sip left in her flask,
I'll take seventeen geezers for a drop.
The old man lay in the kiln, feeling real sick
Cause there was no brandy for him to sop."

I was embarrassed at Karlberg's manners. What would those fine, learned people think? But they laughed, saying that Karlberg didn't need to go on. It was a street song that everyone, including me, knew.

As far back as I can remember, that was my only literary experience with grown-ups until I was twelve, the only time anyone asked a guest to read or recite a poem and wanted to listen.

The man had liked "Spring has come." The teacher at Holmstad had liked it, too, and that poem I had all by myself chosen as the most beautiful of all the ones I had read in school. No one had told me it was beautiful, but I knew it was. There is a secret bond between people, a bond that reaches far out in the world, an unseen bond. Maybe there was something written about it in *Pilgrim's Progress.*

"You said the poem like a prayer," the man said.

The journey there had been quiet but going back it was an endless chatter. Karlberg, who could go the whole day without saying a word to Olga, talked without stopping while we drove through Kolmården. And we had got only rye coffee and rye rusks before we left.

When we came out on the plain, and the moon climbed up over the hoarfrost, Karlberg hummed a song. Olga sang along; she knew the words. It was a very sad song about falsehoods, a shipwreck, and death. Before we had learned the words we were home again.

I was too tired to talk. All I could say when Mother asked me was, "You can't believe what fine folks they were, a bookshelf, and everything, and a big cupboard, and the man wrote poems."

"*Ja,* that can't bring much to a Lapp shoemaker up at Kolmår'n," I heard my stepfather say. But I fell asleep as I sat on the chair.

Chapter 15

On Monday afternoon Olga came in with all of the clothes she had borrowed, including the ones Mother had sewn for her.

"Not those, keep those until after Christmas when my mother-in-law comes; you need them. It's not too much. I hear Mia had such a good time; she's quite gone on your brother-in-law."

I blushed with shame as I sat with the thick Bible, skimming the pages to find something about Christian on his journey. "Gone on him"—you said that about a young woman and her fiancé: "She's so gone on him, and he's so gone on her."

Olga threw herself on the acorn settee. Mother took the clothes and went out to air them. Olga looked a little astonished and nearly offended. When Mother came in again, Olga said, "I have brushed the clothes so you wouldn't need to take the trouble."

I thought Mother was fussy. It was a touchy question. You aired out clothes after tramps when you thought they had lice. Mother knew when she had overdone something, for she said everyone knew she always aired clothes when others had used them.

"So don't think, Olga, that I believe you are careless in any way, either about lice or anything else. I learned to air my Sunday clothes when I worked, and it's now a habit with me."

That sweet Olga brightened up at once, saying that it was a good idea to air Sunday clothes and that she'd do it when she got some. She was in a teasing mood today.

I was mad at Mother. "So gone on him," she had said. Not a word would I ever tell her again after she'd blown what I'd said into this. Never more. It was she who was "gone on somebody." She was "gone" on my stepfather. I'd tell her so when I was big enough to dare tell her that.

"The magistrate of Langlid's daughter," I heard Olga say.

"What in the name of God, that's the worst thing I've ever heard," Mother said.

"They sent her away, but it didn't help. She grieved and was nearly crazy, and when she came home they met the whole summer, nearly every night. And then she got with child, and folks said that the magistrate whipped her. The magistrate went to my brother-in-law, who was in the harness room at a farm nearby repairing saddles and said, "You can fetch the whore, not a thread will she get from me, you'll take her naked, your wretch, your whore." The hired men heard everything. And that same night, my brother-in-law took her to his shack. He brought clothes. She had to take off everything she had on. He waited in the magistrate's yard while she did that. It was late at night; everyone was asleep. So she became just like a runaway from her home district and not a thread had she taken, just like the magistrate had said. But then she got strange, the poor thing. You have to be used to poverty from your childhood to be able to take it. She cries when she sees a horse."

Mother looked thoughtful. It was just like a real novel. Though in novels the poor people married rich ones; here in this one it was just the opposite.

"It's no wonder she cries when she sees a horse," Mother said after a while. "It would make you strange to live up in Kolmården with a shoemaker and have a lot of kids after you'd been the daughter of a magistrate."

"You haven't seen my brother-in-law," Olga said, looking in the distance. "You'd think differently if you saw him."

"All fellows are alike," Mother said.

But Olga shook her head. "No, no, not all. There are for sure . . . ja, well, but probably you have to be a magistrate's daughter to get anywhere with them even if they are only harness-makers," she said somewhat bitterly. "If there's a handsome fellow among poor folks, he usually turns up his nose at a poor girl. They always want those fancy pieces who never are satisfied, crying like babies when they see a horse."

How much I liked Olga just then. I thought she was right. Mother thought so, too.

"You're not dumb, Olga, and I want to thank you again for taking Mia along, but she's gotten too many ideas—now she's going to read the whole Bible and that can't be good. Will you have some of this old rye coffee with me?"

Like a heretic of the Catholic Church I felt persecuted just because I was determined to read the Bible. Both my mother and my stepfather got irritated as soon as they saw me with that heavy book in my lap.

"That's not for children. It demands more wisdom to read the Bible," Mother said.

"She's big now and should do something useful," my stepfather said.

The short December days went fast. I had only to carry in the wood and water, look after Olga's baby sometimes, and snip rags. Mother now had milking to do for the farmer and between times the everlasting cooking and cleaning. Our only lamp was eight years old, and kerosene was expensive. Seven o'clock at night the lamp was blown out, and I had to try to sleep. If I didn't try to take down the Bible, I could use the barn lantern for an hour after our lamp was put out, for it used the farm's kerosene. At Olga's they burned the lantern all night. These weren't like the modern ones they have in the country nowadays, but a light in a little box with four glass panes and a weak wick that smoked and smelled and flickered. But young eyes put up with a lot, and I read many hours in that smoky light that winter. One of the panes had broken and had only paper in it.

One night when my stepfather was out getting a haircut at one of the tenant farmer's, and Mother was at Olga's, I tried to read a while in the big Bible, searching in it more eagerly than boys looking for water beetles in a ditch. I was right in the middle of the chapter on Judith and Holofernes and leaned a little too much against the lantern so the flame caught the paper pane. It burned up, making an ash and a dreadful smell in the room. I was already undressed and ready for bed, but I had to go out in my barefeet on the dreaded darkness of the porch where the snow lay heaped to set down the lantern, which still smoked. It was cold in the room and the smell was awful, so Mother was really cross when she came in. "What have you done now, Mia, and why aren't you asleep?"

"I read a while."

"You've been reading in that old Bible again." Mother didn't exactly say the word "old" in the tone of an antique dealer. "I think you've become silly over reading those old stories all the time. It'll just make you wicked and disobedient. I'm going to carry the Bible to the attic. And you've had the lamp burning. We haven't a drop more kerosene than what's in it to spare." She looked at the door.

"Now there'll be hell to pay when he comes. Where is the lantern?" She lit a match and peered around the room.

"*I* used the lantern. I didn't light the lamp; the paper burned up. It's on the porch. Dear Mother, please paste something in the lantern or he'll be so mad."

Mother didn't say anything, nor did she fuss at me anymore. She got the lantern and put in a new paper pane, making a paste of flour and water. Just as she was finishing, my stepfather came in. She said that she'd knocked the lantern over when she used it for bringing in wood.

"Mia can surely bring in wood when it's light. Something useful she can do." He threw his cap angrily on the floor. The tenant farmer had given him a terrible haircut, clipping his hair too short.

"You're always harping about Mia, always after her about something. I used the lantern when I went to the privy, if you have to know, and as long as I was out, I brought in some wood, and happened to tip over this old piece of junk. You could try and get us a good lantern. I'm just glad it didn't set the woodshed on fire."

She paused. "Now you know what happened. Can't you sleep peacefully now?" she mumbled.

"Hell and damnation! I look like a convict." my stepfather said. He held the lamp in front of his shaving mirror. His head looked like a turnip covered with bristles.

If my stepfather slept peacefully I don't know, but at least I did, for now I knew he'd never find out about the lantern.

Chapter 16

For his salary, my stepfather got a hundred and fifty kronor a year; my mother earned eight kronor a month for milking twice a day. That wasn't many kronor a month to manage with. It wasn't, of course, back in the gray distant past. Here and there was a telephone at the big farms, and up in Stockholm streetcars rattled down the streets. Trains crisscrossed the country. The anarchists' newspaper *Brand* found its way to Norrköping. It had stories about the big strike. And it wrote that women should refuse to have children for starvation and war. Hinke Bergegren encouraged all young women to refuse to go out with soldiers.

My stepfather had been a night guard at the paper. My mother had saved two copies of it she had bought when we lived at the sugar-syrup house, and now read these with Olga.

"I've never gone with any soldier," Olga said triumphantly, "but how can we keep from having kids?" she whispered to Mother.

"*Ja,* talk's always easy, but preventive ways are to be found."

I heard both Olga's whispered question and Mother's answer. My ears pricked up every time children were mentioned. For myself, I wondered like Olga why people had kids if they didn't want them. Why should Mother have one every year? I was curious where babies really came from. My school friends had said from the stomach. *Ja,* but that didn't seem right. For Mother was so thin now. So I was alert and eager when Mother and Olga talked about children. But I didn't dare ask Mother where babies came from, God help me.

The wife of the farmer who owned the big farm hadn't any kids, but she was a proper person—she'd said that herself. She'd said Olga hadn't behaved properly. When you didn't behave properly, you had a kid.

I couldn't get the thing straight at all. Grown-ups talked every which way. "Children are God's gift and man's torment," Grandma said; and when Mother had me baptized at the priest's he had said a prayer for her that she should repent her sin. I had heard Mother tell that to Grandma.

It was a sin to have children.

Then children were sinful, too. I couldn't make head or tails of this no matter how I twisted and turned it.

The wife on the big farm was thinking of taking foster children, for otherwise the relatives that she couldn't stand would inherit the farm. Olga told us about that.

"She could take my boy," Olga used to say; "he needs to own a little something."

Two of the tenant farmers on the big farm had pigs which they butchered for Christmas. Mother got a piece of pork from them for a "taste" as they said. Olga didn't get any. I think that Mother's long curtains and the blue-painted flowers on the wall and maybe my Scotch plaid dress were what made them give Mother the pork. Fine folks choose fine folk. They knew Olga just as well, knew every stitch she owned, knew, too, that there was hardly ever a cup of coffee to spare. I remember that Mother shared the pork with Olga. But she didn't tell my stepfather about it. From the big farm itself we got some fresh pork, and Olga got just as big a piece. The tenant farmers who owned pigs didn't get any pork from the big farm, and that caused muttering from them and the hired hands.

Mother salted and stored the pork she got so we could celebrate properly at Christmas. We'd buy the "lutfisk"* from the big farm where they'd soaked a barrelful. The day before Christmas Eve the farmer himself would go to town for the holiday brandy. Everything was planned out carefully.

Mother did as much Christmas cleaning at Olga's as at our place. In return Olga scrubbed the porch and got two bunches of pine branches. Both of our homes shared and shared alike whole days together, that is until at night when the men came home. Then the doors were slammed tight shut, and sometimes you could hear a crabby low mumbling that it'd be better to take care of your own place by yourself. But Olga shut her man up by saying that *he* could just take care of the place, that if it weren't for Hedvig's Mia, she,

*Dried codfish soaked in lye.

Olga, wouldn't get free to milk once a day and earn five kronor a month. My mother's response to my stepfather's grumblings was about on the same lines. "Shut up about what you know nothing about."

Both men, Karlberg and my stepfather, didn't get on well together, and it was just as well. They crabbed at their wives, afraid they'd just lie around the house gossiping and having too good a time together. I knew Mother was putting off my stepfather when I heard her say to him one day after he'd come home and Olga had just left, "Have to watch that she's not in here all the time; she's not exactly nice."

Olga had told Karlberg that she didn't like Mother all that much, that Mother was too picky and always putting her nose into things. I heard both women tell each other they'd said that about each other.

These women had to put up with a lot. They had to be so careful about everything. In order to keep going they had to hide their own pleasure, even lie a little sometimes. Otherwise they'd make their men jealous.

It was the afternoon of Christmas Eve. Six hard green apples lay on a plate. Just as many lay on Olga's plate, too. They were the Christmas apples from the barrel at the big farm.

The curtains were freshly done; even at Olga's, Mother had seen to it there were curtains. I think she had used a worn out sheet, blue-starched it, and put a lace border on it. Two of our old rag rugs lay on Olga's floor. Karlberg had repainted the bed, table, and chair.

Olga's fireplace wall was whitewashed now, too, and had blue flowers on it, and on her table were two hollowed-out potatoes wrapped in fluted paper, each holding a candle. *At Olga's it was fine.* Karlberg had grumbled plenty about painting, for they had to lie on the floor while the bed dried, but Olga wouldn't give in, saying that the wall lice would disappear if their junk were painted. She hadn't dared to say that now they'd have things fine. Karlberg wouldn't have stood for that; he had no patience for such things. "You should be glad if you can scrape enough together to put food in your mouth," was his everlasting refrain.

But Olga had things fine now, so fine that on the morning of Christmas Eve, Mother had found her sitting bolt upright on a chair while the baby screamed in his basket. Olga just sat gazing at her room, seeing a vision, a dream come true. "I can't believe it's my room" she said to Mother.

"*Ja,* you put your dress on now, and don't run around in your slip at Christmas time."

Olga sat in her spruced-up room, wearing only her old slip and cotton bodice, which was gray and dirty; her face was dirty, too. Her braid was still down her back. Her chapped lips glistened red.

"I don't want Grandma to think you are sloppy, for you aren't," Mother said seriously.

"I'll always have a dress on now," Olga said, "although Karlberg doesn't like me to. He thinks you shouldn't 'dress up' when you're home. It's Christmas so he'll probably let me put on a dress."

"He can only try to say you can't. I'd tell him off."

But Olga shook her head as if to say Karlberg wasn't anyone to fight with. I was standing beside Mother, listening to their debate and thinking that Mother boasted. She was afraid of my stepfather; instead she could "tell him off."

It was Christmas Eve. The day had grayed and darkened although it was still only three o'clock. My stepfather's shaving was now over with.

That was always a whole ceremony in itself. He should have had the room all to himself. You couldn't even move. First, the table had to be cleared and then the mirror taken from the wall and set up on it. Warm and cold water and towels. And then he sat there, sharpening the razor, puffing and blowing and shaving. Clipping the hair in his nostrils, ears, and eyebrows. When he was in the army, as he had told us so often, he had done all this for the captain. *Ja,* he had to make the captain spic and span in all possible and impossible places, describing the captain's toilet in detail and laughing and carrying on in such a crazy way that both Mother and I had to laugh, though my stepfather thought that the captain had gone too far in his "spit and polish"; it was enough to clip the hair from the nose and ears.

Every Sunday he played the captain. Shaving always took two hours. All the while Mother was furious. If it was summer, she went outside to get away from "the fuss" as she said. But I thought it was interesting to watch my stepfather while he shaved. He blew out his cheeks, putting his tongue like a big wad of snuff in his cheek to stretch the skin. Why he puffed and blew like that I couldn't understand. It was a bad habit, I thought.

Just for his stub of a mustache he could sit for an hour in front of the mirror, and pull and clip so that all that was left was a little brush under his nose, like Charlie Chaplin's in miniature (although, of course, Chaplin hadn't begun shaving at that time, being just a fourteen-year-old beggar running around London). I thought with all my heart and soul that my stepfather's stubby mustache was the ugliest in the world.

As he sat there shaving and gazing at himself in the mirror, he didn't hear anything. You could have stolen everything around him, packed it up, and fled. He just stared steadily at himself, wholly absorbed.

Now this Christmas Eve the "fuss" at last was over. Shaved and dressed up, he had driven to the station to get Grandma. I was all dressed up, too, and ready. Mother still had the milking to do, so she hadn't put on her best dress, but she'd be ready before Grandma came, for on Christmas Eve the cows were milked two hours earlier. Putting on her shawl to go to the barn, she said, "You may light one of the tree candles if it gets too dark; otherwise go into Olga's." Then she patted my clean hair which nowadays never had any lice in it.

"You'll see, Mia, this could be a pretty good Christmas." I thought so, too. (But how Mother could be so optimistic when she knew the farmer had laid in three liters of brandy waiting to be drunk, I couldn't understand. But then I didn't think much about that.) "Be careful with the fire now," she said as she left.

It got darker and darker. I had the tree that Olga had given me all decorated. Four small tops from the sugar cones, a bit dusty, dangled on their white threads. Only with a superhuman effort had I managed to save them. Twice when we'd run out of sugar, Mother had shaved some from my cones. I had strung up two green apples. The plate still looked plentiful with only the four apples on it. My doll with her blue-green braids for hair and red cheeks sat clean and brushed in the commode. Although now that Grandma would be here I'd had to squash my things in the middle shelf, for the washbowl was on the top shelf, and the chamber pot on the bottom. I could use only the middle shelf during the holidays. One had to use, of course, the commode when night guests came. Otherwise Mother kept the washbowl and soap on a little bench beside the stove. Guests could stand at the commode and wash and dry themselves on a guest towel with the word "Memories" on it. The guest towel was one that Grandma had woven; it had a thick fringe.

It hung under a mirror that Mother had got from a sister; the glass always fell out as soon as you touched it. You could never see your image in that mirror, only something that flashed here and there when you tried to look at yourself.

It was so quiet in the house. Olga's baby slept and she was getting herself ready. Karlberg was out. Olga had sounded anxious when she told Mother she didn't know where he was.

"He should just go up there and fetch the Christmas brandy for himself and Stenman," she said.

"I think there's a good chance he'll be drinking with all of them up there before he comes home," Mother had answered.

It was not quite dark, and Karlberg still hadn't come. I lit one of the little candles and sat on the floor by the tree to read. I read just the New Testament these days. It told about Christ. Still, it was something that reminded me of Christian. Christ journeyed here and there like Christian, but he wasn't like Christian. There was really nothing here like Christian. She was wrong, the girl up there in the forest house.

In one place I thought it seemed to brighten, and I read the chapter over and over again to find a real similarity. It was about the three disciples on their way to Emmaus and how Christ appeared to them in a vision. But it came to nothing. Jesus got busy with something else. He always was in such a hurry. He just gave some hasty orders, and then he disappeared again in his heaven. The story had a tremendous hold on me, even so, though I didn't find the Valley of Despair. I read on. The candle got low, and hearing Mother come, I hurriedly shoved the Bible in its place. Mother went in to Olga.

I lighted another tree candle, and after awhile Mother came in.

"It will really be a happy Christmas now. Karlberg is drunk and has threatened to beat up the farmer himself. He's acted like a crazy man up at the big house; now he's on his way here. Poor Olga, it'll be a fine Christmas Eve she'll get. Never would I have thought Karlberg was a fellow who'd make such an ass of himself." Mother stopped talking, no doubt thinking I was too young for such talk.

The brightness fell from our room. It was only a poor hired man's place. Christmas made its entrance as usual in farm workers' houses with women frightened out of their wits and children sitting in the corner, wondering about *Christmas.*

190

"It's a shame for Grandma's sake; they should be coming any time now."

Mother rattled in the stove, ground the coffee, set it on to boil, and hurried to change her clothes. The coffee began to smell so good. The table was set with bread and hard gingersnaps. The dough hadn't turned out right. Mother thought she had thrown in too much spice in the dough and had put in more milk and flour. The gingersnaps got hard as rocks.

"They'll get softer if they sit a bit," Mother had said.

But such a luxury that cookies will "sit a bit" doesn't fit in a farm worker's house. The cookies can be *too* good; they disappear too fast. These cookies were wonderful; they didn't melt in your mouth.

Now we heard the first Christmas greeting.

A bellowing as if someone was being murdered. When we could disentangle the words, we knew what Olga had to expect.

"I told the farmer to claim his kid. I'll tear out the farmer's guts. I should go and slave for his kid? But now I'll send his goods back. Now she's going up there where she belongs."

I understood only too well. I had heard this song in the same tone of voice on many porches. It was one for a holiday.

"Open up, you damn old hags. Are you sitting there and gossiping again? Come out here, Hedvig, you're so devilishly fine. I want to talk to you."

"It would be best to take something and knock him over the head with it," Mother said, who always got furious and wanted to fight head-on.

"No, no, he'll kill you," I anxiously whispered.

Standing on the porch he yelled the worst names at Olga, and rattled his key in the door lock.

It was quiet at Olga's. Getting the door unlocked, he went in. Mother opened our door.

"I have to see what the drunken wretch is going to do," she said aloud.

At Olga's the lamp burned, but neither she nor the boy were there. He stood on the threshold, weaving and staring. "*Ja,* so she's left. That's always her way when you take a drink; she won't stand for it. But wear myself out for her kid that she had with the farmer, you bet that's all right. What for damned rags has she put on the windows?" he hollered, spitting out his wad of snuff on the blue-starched curtains.

Mother lost all control, giving him a blow on his neck so he fell across the threshold and sprawled there.

"What are you doing, you damned wretch, spitting snuff on the curtains, for God's sake! I ought to beat you black and blue." And Mother gave him a kick in his pants.

"No, you, damned devil . . ." He tried to get to his knees.

"Don't try," Mother said, "a gypsy like you I've seen before!"

"Gypsy? No, now!" And getting up, he got another blow from Mother.

"Now you've driven out your wife and boy on Christmas, you drunk, and spit snuff on the only curtains Olga will ever get if she's thinking of staying with you, and you're lying about her, saying that you're not the boy's father. Everyone can see you're his father. Jesus, what a beating you deserve, and you'll get one, too. If only it weren't Christmas Eve."

Now Mother cried.

"Take your bastard, you, and get in your own place. You and Olga stick together cause you have a bastard brat yourself, but now you'll have hell to pay!"

He tried to get up again, but Mother beat him so I felt sorry for him in spite of his terrible words. He had been nice to me. "Folks who drink are unhappy," the man up in the forest house had said. His own brother had said that. But then I looked at the curtain, spotted, dirtied. Mother should beat him as much as she could, if only she'd do the same with my stepfather, though he was nice sometimes.

"Get in with you, you can't lie here!" Tugging and pulling on Karlberg, Mother tried to get him over the threshold.

"Albert will be coming anytime now with my mother-in-law. You'll get another beating when Albert comes home if you sprawl here like this," Mother lied.

My stepfather wouldn't have hit Karlberg; he would have helped him yell at Mother.

Poor Karlberg. He hadn't eaten all day. He'd drunk a lot and had been up since four in the morning so he would be finished early on Christmas Eve. He couldn't put up any more of a struggle. After one last attempt to hit Mother, he crumpled up across the doorway. He slept where he lay. Mother and I helped to get him inside, pulling and shoving on him like a dead pig, and hardly had we succeeded than we heard the jingle of sleighbells. A sleigh stopped outside.

It was cold in our place, for the door had been left open. Mother was sweaty, wisps of hair clung to her face, her braid had fallen down her back, her dress was unbuttoned at the neck, and her eyes were red from crying.

It was Grandma who had come.

Mother smoothed her hair as best she could, whispered to me to get the coffee ready again as fast as I could, and then went out to welcome Grandma.

"Blessed be this house," I heard Grandma say.

"Aren't you freezing cold?" I heard Mother ask.

"He who loves God doesn't need to freeze," Grandma answered. I thought that didn't sound right.

I felt like a fool. Was this Grandma? I felt shy, not wanting to go out on the porch. I always felt shy when folks talked like that about God. I thought it sounded too bold when every other word they said was about God and how much they loved Jesus. I felt ashamed, I'm not sure why, maybe because it sounded so personal. Jesus was dragged into everything—my stepfather, the bed, the sheets, all the sins folks talked about. "Jesus has forgiven me." All such expressions had the same effect on me as the forbidden subjects kids talk about when they're afraid the grown-ups will hear them.

This Christmas Eve was getting even stranger. The best would have been if Mother and I had got to be alone together. Grandma could surely have been like her old self. That Karlberg who was nice otherwise had gone crazy because of the brandy.

Olga with the baby! Had she run away in the snow, maybe?

Now Grandma stomped in on her knobbly legs, stiff with cold. Mother was helping her take off her shawls. On her head she had on a black curly fur hat, new and warm. Grandma would have looked like a fine old woman in that hat, but for a horrible red band on it, a big, wide band with "The Lord Is Near" printed across it. It was even worse than the Salvation Army. One had got used to that. This was something crazy.

"The Lord is near, God bless you, child," she said to me.

I felt more and more lost. The tears weren't far off when I went to her, and curtseying, welcomed her. I had written a little verse that I'd meant to say as my greeting to her. It had rhymed with Grandma and was about her being a wonderful one, but it wouldn't do to say my poem now.

Mother had gone out to my stepfather who was still with the horse.

"Has Karlberg come home?" I heard my stepfather ask.

"No," Mother said firmly.

"He should be getting some swigs. Where the devil can he be?"
The sleighbells jingled. He was off to put the horse in the stable.

Mother came in emptyhanded. Not a package had Grandma
brought with her, though she'd come from town. That wasn't like
her. She always brought something, even when she came every
week.

It didn't seem to me that Grandma's arrival was any better than
Karlberg's had been a while before. There was no difference.
Everything was a disappointment. My body ached just as it had
when I had sat and clipped rags. Mother saw my sad face and
frowned furiously at me not to show my disappointment. I
understood I was not to show my feelings, but she didn't look very
happy herself. Perhaps she wasn't aware of that, but I, I, of course,
had to look happy however awful things were. Just like that stuff
with Karlberg: If Mother hadn't jabbered at the farm that I was
illegitimate, Karlberg wouldn't have had anything to accuse her for,
but Mother never kept that hushed up. "It's in the priest's records,"
she said.

But Karlberg didn't read any priest's records. Everything had got
all mixed up. What was Grandma doing here anyway? Now her nice
old man would have to be alone for Christmas. I hadn't even
thought of that before, not until I'd seen that Grandma didn't have a
package for me. Only then had I thought there might be others who
weren't treated fairly. He was always so quiet and humble, had
slaved all his life, and I had never thought about him until just now.
And I asked something I never had before, "How is Grandpa?" I had
never called him that either.

Mother looked pleased. There was a twinkle in her eyes. She
looked as if just now we were really close, she and I. I had heard, of
course, a little gossip that Grandma didn't treat her old husband
kindly enough; but I had also heard Mother defend Grandma.
"Grandma is a strong and responsible woman, and he is so quiet
that he just wants to be left in peace."

Now Grandma said, "Grandpa? *Ja,* well, God bless you, child, he
feels so good, *ja,* he's sent some Christmas candy with me. But I
know now that you should celebrate Jesus' birthday in your heart
and not with candy. You'll get something else from me instead."
She drew out a little package from her pocketbook and gave it to

me. It was a new songbook, her strange sect's songbook. "Our battalion's glorious war book, blessed be Jesus," Grandma said.

Mother had helped Grandma off with her coat and wool lappets, and she stood there so fine and neat in her dark wool dress with its lace collar. In spite of everything it was dear old beautiful Grandma with her black wavy hair, and as Mother came close to me, she whispered under her breath, "Don't mind about all that; the old woman's gotten a little foolish; those damned pietists have got ahold of her. It's because we haven't been close by, and she's not had anyone to talk to. It'll pass."

"So fine you are, Grandma." And I took her hand, stroking all the tender bumps on the twisted joints of her fingers.

But then Grandma said nothing, no blessing, nothing. I saw her shrunken throat tremble a little, and I led her to the acorn settee. Maybe I would get to say my verse for her after all?

The hope that flickered up was put out as soon as Grandma sat down. She folded her hands and said a long prayer in her own words for our "home." And a lot about Albert that he'd stay sober and that Hedvig would keep her health.

When she finished, Mother said very evenly, "Albert hasn't touched strong liquor since we moved from our last place, and there's nothing wrong with me. It's gone well here, though the pay's so little that we're nearly threadbare, but that . . ." I think Mother thought of adding that Jesus couldn't remedy that. But she stopped herself and said, "Now we'll have coffee, for Albert's been invited up to the farmer's where he'll get . . ." Christmas brandy, she was about to say, but again she paused. "He had an errand," she said, pouring the coffee.

"*Ja,* well, Albert hasn't been drinking, *ja,* we've been saying prayers for him in the battalion, also for you and Mia, Hedvig. You see that it helps."

I saw Mother swallowing and swallowing. She was trying not to be angry, but she was.

"It would have made more sense to begin the prayers a little before; then you and I would have been spared a lot," she said bitterly.

"You are still in sin's net, Hedvig."

"*Ja,* what can one do. Drink while it's hot, Grandma, you need to, it's fifteen degrees out."

Mother got up and lighted the Christmas tree. Then Grandma folded her hands again and prayed, letting her coffee get cold.

195

She didn't look at the Christmas tree, although gleaming stars made of the tinfoil from packets of snuff hung from the branches, as well as the tops of the sugar cones, and ten candles fastened with yarn.

"Let that be, now. The holiday is long. Drink now; we'll read and pray when Albert comes," Mother firmly said, and Grandma did as she was told.

Nothing ever goes the way you think it will.

It had been dreadful when that awful Karlberg had bellowed and acted like the devil himself, but this wasn't any better. Karlberg would be nice again in the morning, but here the prayers and all the rest of the craziness would continue. Whatever had happened to Grandma?

"She's getting childish," Mother said.

"Children certainly aren't silly like that," I snorted. We stood out on the porch, listening for my stepfather. He didn't come.

He never came home that whole Christmas Eve. Grandma waited, saying prayers, and Mother got the beds ready. We ate a little, and then Grandma went to bed. My mother and stepfather would use the acorn settee, and my bed would be on the floor.

Grandma said long prayers in bed, and Mother and I sat quietly listening. No sound could be heard from Karlbergs'. Olga hadn't come home either. Were folks completely crazy here on the plain on Christmas Eve?

Grandma slept at last.

Then Mother got us both wrapped up, and we headed up to the big farm in the snow. It was eleven o'clock on Christmas Eve.

Everyone at the farm was up. The little round wife of the farmer was all smiles. "Ja, Stenman has been here. He drank cognac and ate a sandwich and invited all of us to try his own brandy. That's been quite some time ago. He's probably at someone else's place now."

Had she seen Olga?

"Ja. The wife of the farmer rolled her eyes to the ceiling. "Olga's in bed here. She always does that when Karlberg gets drunk. Olga was a little too free and easy as a girl, and Karlberg thinks about that when he's had too much. Ja, he just got so crazy that he blamed the farmer for both that and the other, but when he sobers up, everything will be all right again. Though it really was a show to watch. If Olga ever happens to be home when Karlberg comes there drunk, there will be murder as sure as I'm standing here," the farmer's wife said.

"*Ja,* this has been a happy Christmas Eve," Mother said.

"*Ja,* but it's always like this. Once a year they should have their fun. Won't you have some glögg?"*

"No, thanks, I have to get home. My mother-in-law is here with us for Christmas."

Mother and I walked down to the stables. Although the sky was clouded over, there was enough light from the snow so we could see the cleared path. Mother listened in the cow barn; it was very quiet, just a little panting and sighing as usual from the cows lying there sleeping. In the stable she stood for a long time listening. I couldn't hear anything other than the thumping of hooves, but Mother softly closed the stable door saying, "He's lying in there. He must have helped himself to a lot to get so soused. Well, he can stay there. He won't freeze to death. We can't drag him home, drunk and mean, in the middle of the night to Grandma." Then Mother mumbled something that I couldn't get.

"What did you say?" I called, plodding through the snow, eager to get home, for it was cold.

"*Ja,* it really helps to pray to Jesus, I'll tell you."

We walked home quietly, each in her own thoughts.

"We must try to keep this from the old one," Mother said. "And you, Mia, say the prayers now when she asks you to and sing songs with her. It isn't worth saying anything about her fads. The worst will be with Albert. If he comes home drunk in the morning on Christmas Day, and she starts praying to God, it'll be holy hell."

I was already so let down from Christmas Eve's unusual events that what she was saying about more misery to come didn't disturb me. I was in a hurry to get home. It was warm and fine there, and my stepfather wouldn't be coming home, and maybe, just maybe, I'd get to lie with Mother in my acorn settee.

The lamp had been turned down. We saw it gleam in the window. We listened for a bit on the porch, but it was still quiet at Karlbergs'.

"He won't find it too warm on the floor," Mother said.

We stole softly in. Over in the bed Grandma slept. She gently snored. It was so peaceful. Everything looked so spruced up. Clean sheets in the beds, the food still left on the table, red beets, pickled herring, some cheese, lutfisk, pudding, delicious white pudding.

Four big green apples. All at once I was overwhelmed with

*Mulled wine.

happiness. It was Christmas at last. Mother threw herself in the chair at the table. "Sit down and eat as much as you want."

I wasn't that hungry, but still, it was nearly midnight, a forbidden time otherwise. Mother and I sat at a festive table. Grandma slept there in the bed, and Grandma was still Grandma. Though she had become a little foolish, it was still fun to have her in the house.

Mother ate heartily. It was as if she got an appetite after she was sure we wouldn't be disturbed. She stirred up the fire under the coffee pot, too. Then she went to the box where she used to keep the shirts and vests for the babies she'd expected. She took out a little package.

"This is from Albert and me," she whispered. "You're going to have it now. It will be a Christmas present."

I unwrapped the package. It was a knitted green cardigan with brown borders. A new thing, store-bought. I think it was the first time I got something that was store-bought, not counting shoes and hats.

"I meant for you to have a cap, too, a woolen cap, but there wasn't enough money," Mother whispered.

I was completely stumped. How had Mother and my stepfather kept such a secret?

"Who bought it?" I asked.

"Albert."

"But you have, too . . ."

"*Ja*, I paid half."

I didn't quite believe her. I thought she had bought the cardigan herself and wanted to give Albert credit so I'd like him. I think so still.

I crept quietly to the commode for the songbook Grandma had given me. It had fine new covers. It looked so splendid lying on the folded cardigan. I was lucky.

"Olga and Karlberg have also bought something for you," Mother said.

"What next! Oh, be nice and tell me!"

"No, then Olga will be sad."

It was the same here, too; it was Olga who bought the thing, but all grown women wanted you to think their men were nice.

"You can sleep here with me in the settee," Mother said.

Chapter 17

We had a couple of muddled days until the brandy was finished. Sometimes Grandma forgot that she was saved and quarreled with my stepfather just as before. And spit three times to the left.

Karlberg was in and drank coffee as well as brandy, but he didn't get as drunk as he'd been on Christmas Eve. What had happened then he didn't jabber about. Olga went about red-eyed from crying the whole time, and one of the curtains had been taken down.

"When the boozing is finished, and he's sober, I'll show him what he did," she whispered hoarsely to Mother on the porch the day after Christmas. "Can you believe that they're human? They're like animals, worse, animals don't spit out snuff! For five öre you could just poison them."

On the third day after Christmas Olga gave me a package. I had been waiting for it so much I could hardly answer all the times she'd greeted us the past two days. I knew she had it somewhere in her place, and I felt she wanted to give it to me by herself.

"I should have given you this on Christmas Eve," she said. "It's from Karlberg and me."

It was a store-bought apron in the brightest colors.

It was so bright it almost hurt my eyes. It had cost seventy-five öre. I clasped it to me, feeling almost dizzy from its splendor. Mother helped me put it on with the new green cardigan.

"Now you go in and thank Olga and Karlberg. Today Karlberg isn't going to make a fuss about spending the money."

I understood. The house was quiet again. The brandy was finished. Karlberg sat on the chair, pale and washed-out. Olga walked around stiff and straight, and one window gaped dark and blank without the curtain. I became a little bashful again over what had happened on Christmas Eve, he'd been so awful.

"Heavens, how fine you're dressed, and so good you look with a little color!" Olga said, and I blushed and felt my heart beat faster.

I curtseyed and thanked them both. But Karlberg threw up his hands.

"Don't thank me, I'm not worth it. You're right in thinking I'm a real son of a . . ."

I didn't know just what I should say, for I thought that he was a "real son of a" and even so just now was nice again. My stepfather never felt a bit sorry, never asked to be forgiven no matter how terrible he'd behaved. He only crabbed if Mother reminded him, asking what good did it do to rake up all that old stuff even if the "old stuff" had happened yesterday.

"I think 'uncle' is nice and 'aunt,' too.* I'll look after your boy whenever 'aunt' wants," I said politely, although I was really afraid she'd ask me to take care of the baby while Grandma was with us.

The Sunday after Christmas we had a prayer meeting at our place. It was Grandma's idea. The strange thing was that both the farmer and his wife, and their maids, and most of the farm workers came and crowded into our room.

There were more than a dozen, probably fifteen at the most. My stepfather had made two benches by laying boards across the chairs, and he was hypocritically sanctimonious, practicing songs with Grandma, for they were to lead the singing at the meeting. My mother had a clear and beautiful voice, but she wouldn't be joining the singing here.

"I'll cook coffee as far as it'll go, for you've got to give them something when it's Christmas-time, but for all the rest of it, you'll have to take care of as best you can. Who'll give the sermon I don't know, for I don't think Albert's up to it," she said somewhat spitefully.

But "Albert" cleared his throat, grunted, and stroked his stubby mustache, looking as if he could preach more than well enough.

I had a tremendous respect for Grandma.

She stood in front of one of the windows behind a table that had been shoved almost into the long curtains. Her knotted hands pressed against the sides of the table. She had on a black dress with a lace frill and was truly a Grandma I had never seen before. She

_____

*Children were brought up to call adult friends "uncle" and "aunt"; they would not address them directly with "you."

200

stood there half an hour, and after all the farm workers' wives with their bundled up babies had come in, she invited them to sit down, showing them places to sit. Two Windsor chairs were set out for the farmer and his wife. I felt as if I were someone else; Mother looked as if she, too, didn't live here any more. When everyone had sat down, Grandma began to make a speech.

"I am just a simple old woman here on a visit with my son and his wife and their daughter." (She said exactly that: "on a visit." Never had I heard Grandma talk so fine. "Their daughter," *ja*, that was me.)

"I am only a simple, poor old woman on a visit here, and I cannot talk with any grand words; our meeting place is also simple compared to the splendor you are accustomed to in church [she said "splendor"] but I don't want to leave here before I have told you how gloriously we, some of us people down there in Norrköping, have found Jesus. We are nearly a hundred now in the battalion of Jesus, his battle battalion, and 'the Lord is near' is our war cry. And now [Grandma continued in her trembling old voice, which she tried to make strong and steady; I saw how tired she was and how sweat beaded her wrinkled forehead], now I ask you to think, you who live here so isolated and have not noticed the signs that have taken place and that the Lord promised would take place right before His coming. You must think of the Lord's coming; He will soon be here. He will come anytime. Be prepared. I ask you to join with me humbly in prayer before Christ's coming."

Grandma began to pray loudly.

The little round wife of the farmer, dressed in her town-sewn dress, sat devoutly with her eyes closed, the farmer, too. Olga sat, slowly rocking her baby in her arms. Olga and Mother were the only ones who didn't look devout. Mother looked anxiously at Grandma, drops of sweat ran from her temples and her gnarled hands shook with tiredness. Mother wasn't listening to her prayer. Nor was I either. I was astonished. Where had they all come from? I hadn't been sent with any invitations. Not to any of them.

My stepfather had put up a note on the stable door, Mother said. "Prayer meeting at Stenmans. Everyone on the farm welcome."

And everyone had come, even the farmer himself and his wife. After all the eating and boozing! There sat a young farm worker's wife sighing "Jesus" now and then. Karlberg and a young farm worker sat side by side with piously folded hands. I compliantly folded mine, too.

"Those who drink are unhappy," he had said, the handsome man, who maybe was that Christian who in his journeys had seen the valley of despair. He should be here with us now, just now, when Grandma was so remarkable and looked so fine, and everyone sat here with us and was humble and devout. There had to be something to us after all. We weren't then like ordinary folks. I began to like the prayer meeting; we were just like the family up there who had the bookshelf.

Grandma finished her prayer with these words: "Bless us, Jesus, that we in your name can confess and testify here this afternoon to your glory."

Then she sat down at the table, leaning her tired head on the tablecloth. I saw how she trembled and shivered. Mother took a glass of water to her. *Ja,* that was right; the priest drank water when he was in the pulpit. I had seen that myself. Grandma took out her fine white handkerchief and wiped the sweat, for it was unpleasantly warm in here, though Mother had cooked the coffee at Olga's. We didn't dare to open the door either. It was so cold out, and there were three babies in the room.

Among the farm hands there was a tenant couple, the Ekströms, whom I hadn't seen before. They were very well dressed with new squeaky shoes, and the old woman had a black silk shawl. Mrs. Ekström got up and rattled off a prayer with great speed and sat down again.

Then Mr. Ekström got up, a little bent man with a white beard. He shuffled to the table where Grandma sat, stood in front of her so she couldn't be seen, put one leg in front of the other, and laying one hand on the table, began, "Thank you sister for coming from the city to give us for a while the peace of Jesus." (He called Grandma "du"* and sister, and then he had hidden her so we couldn't see her. Demonstratively, although Mother looked threateningly at me, I got up, pushing myself past mothers and their babies, and stood by Grandma.

The old man, irritated by my bothersome interruption, lost the thread but began again, "Sister has talked about signs and wonders. *Ja,* that is true. Prophets don't lie. No horses tread the highway now. *Ja,* thanks, dear Jesus, I have not got mixed up with anti-Christ, I have never ridden a train."

I felt how disturbed Grandma was; she straightened up and was

*He used the familiar form of "you"—"du" instead of "ni."

about to say something, but the old man continued, "I have never sacrificed to anti-Christ, and you, sisters and brothers, our sister from the big city knows what she is saying, for there the monsters go loose [I began to get interested; this sounded really wonderful] but Jesus can come whatever day He wants. God will come from the clouds when we least expect. Be ready, wash yourselves, leave your work, think not upon Mamon [he said "Mammon" with one "m"]. Watch out for the big beast and for Babylon's harlots. Let us pray and wait for God."

Mother went out, shutting the door hard.

But the old man wouldn't stop. He began to pray, using the craziest words, they sounded like forbidden ones about sex.

"Now I think we'll sing a song," my stepfather said as soon as the old man finished, and Grandma had her songbook already open. I had my new book, too, which she'd given me.

"No one attains everlasting peace
Who does not pass life's fiery way.
The soul must suffer battle for faith,
Salvation wins its victorious day."

It was a simple march melody, and we raised the roof as we sang. Mother's blue flowers on the oven wall just fluttered, *ja,* I thought they fluttered.

So the meeting ended. No one else wanted to pray.

The farmer and his wife didn't stay for coffee; the farmer looked pale and sick. He certainly had a hangover after all the drinking at Christmas. But all the others stayed, and I remember Grandma and that old man Ekström getting together long enough for Grandma to tell him she didn't think it was sinful to travel by train.

Grandma stayed over the next Sunday, too, but Mother was firmly against any more prayer meetings. Remorse over what had gone on at the farm was also over. As soon as the farmer and his workers got over their hangovers from the Christmas brandy, their wish to save themselves vanished. As Mother had said, "As soon as their brandy runs out, so will their devotional spirits be finished."

That was so, too. Not many days after the prayer meeting, my stepfather made fun of how folks had sat at the meeting, how they had sighed and prayed, but Mother said, "You weren't one bit better, sitting there, rolling your eyes to heaven." She imitated him.

Grandma was angry, and spitting three times to the left, said that they were doomed to destruction, all of them.

"*Ja*, Grandma, as if you know. Things must go how they will. We can't change that, but when you know how some carry on, then it makes you madder to see them sit here, rolling their eyes to heaven, than when they're up to their usual devilry," Mother said. "It's different with you, Grandma, you mean it sincerely, and are tired and old. You become different then. My mother is very religious, too. Well, she just about has to be, for she's in the poorhouse," my mother added bitterly.

The days began to be all alike again. The Christmas food was finished. Just herring and porridge were on the table. There wasn't even a pat of butter on Sunday now, for Grandma, like me, got sweet milk in the morning. Mother was getting worried. The pay was fixed here; you couldn't take on more work for extra cash, and it was over three miles to the store, too. But you couldn't give Grandma just anything to eat.

Now it was just gray every day again. The ragbag for the handwoven rugs was brought out. Grandma praised the work but didn't say a word about paying for the balls of rags, cut out of the stuff Mother had begged from the places where she'd cleaned, and then wound into balls. My stepfather had sometimes even helped. Grandma either was thinking like the "well-off, educated ones" or she thought *we* were well-off, for it looked that way at Christmas. The real coffee was gone now, and she crabbed about the rye meal coffee.

"*Ja*," Mother said, "The coffee would have lasted another two weeks if I hadn't made it for the prayer meeting."

Grandma didn't answer.

"Why is it that the children you have with Albert die?" Grandma asked the next day when we were cutting rags.

Mother looked warningly at her, giving a nod in my direction. But the old woman pretended she didn't see Mother's look.

"Can't understand why the babies die; you've had the girl here, so you've had one who lived. It's so strange, I think."

"Are you afraid the family's going to die out, or what kind of talk is this? Can I help that the babies die? You've been married three times and haven't had any kids. Think about that. Starvation can happen to one as well as to another. It's not certain Albert would make a good father either. Mia ought not to be hearing all this, but since I've been with Albert—and Grandma, you know well enough what's right for a youngster to hear."

Throwing the scissors on the settee, Mother got up and walked back and forth. I was afraid. Grandma was afraid, too. Mother had sorrowed so much over the meaninglessness of having babies who died, that she couldn't stand for anyone to talk about it, and then here was Grandma doing it.

"I will say I'm glad the babies died. Coming from Albert's stock, they could have taken after him. A father who sleeps with others the whole time I'm carrying his child and doesn't take care of anything," Mother went on mercilessly.

Grandma had folded her hands. But Mother went to the door.

"I have no wish to hear any prayers. If you think I'm sinful, then it's best to stay away from my company. Broom-Mina and Hanna, Albert's daughter, still live in Vilbergen," Mother said bitterly. The door shut.

I sat on my settee and cried. Grandma, too. We both cried.

"Why did I have to say that for?" Grandma sobbed.

"*Ja*, Mother has cried so much, why did you, Grandma, have to say that? Mother isn't sinful, Grandma. Mother's so nice, just ask Olga if she isn't, Grandma," I bawled.

"*Ja*, of course she's nice, one knows that well enough. There's no one like Hedvig. Why did I have to talk like that? Dear Jesus, forgive my sin," Grandma prayed. But I walked back and forth just as Mother had, and kicked the big rag balls so they rolled in front of my feet.

"Don't pray, Grandma, it's so terrible. It sounds so awful. Pray to yourself at night, I do that. Sweet Grandma, don't pray out loud. It's so awful."

Mother had mentioned Hanna, and I felt an aching longing for her. I couldn't stand Grandma's prayers. That Hanna was my stepfather's child I could never believe, not as sweet as Hanna was.

Grandma sat silently on the settee. The tears rolled down her old cheeks. But I didn't try to stop them. I thought it was awful when folks prayed out loud.

I went out to look for Mother. She was in at Olga's. They both looked serious. Olga had washed the curtain, and it hung again at the window. The place was neat and scrubbed, and she obediently wore the dress Mother had given her for as long as Grandma stayed, though the dress began to look a little the worse for wear from taking care of the boy.

"Think that she's become religious. *Ja*, that's like the old, they get strange . . . I could go to the store if Mia looks after the boy. Maybe I could try to get a little coffee and sugar on credit. I'll say it's for you. I can't get anything, but they think you have money because Stenman is always so neat and trim."

Mother made a face.

"*Ja,* they're welcome to think that. I have two kronor, but I don't dare to spend them. If all else fails, I'll still have something put by."

I wondered how Mother meant to get along on two kronor. The doctor maybe? But he took five kronor.

"I'll be on my way when Karlberg comes. You'll see, you'll be smelling real coffee from the porch steps in no time. And then your mother-in-law won't be nagging you any longer."

"Come in now, Mother! Grandma is so sad. She's sitting in there crying."

Mother looked indifferent, but got up and came back in.

"Forgive me for Christ's sake, Hedvig. It was bad of me to talk like that."

"I forgive you without Christ, if there's anything to forgive, but just understand that it isn't my fault that the babies die. I won't let anyone die from starvation or filth as long as I can help it. I *take care of what's mine,*" Mother said emphatically.

I thought she was hard on Grandma.

Mother was quiet awhile. Grandma still looked just as sad.

"Now I'm going to ask you, Grandma, if you'll buy these balls of rags from me. We've worked on them all winter and I need to earn some money. You know how it is out here in the country. Albert doesn't save the least bit; he'll have his no matter how we have it. If you don't need the rags, there's an old woman here who'll buy them. For myself, I can't afford to weave rugs though I need them," Mother said, without caring to console Grandma.

"An old woman?" Grandma's chin trembled when she looked up at Mother. "An old woman who will buy? Dear Hedda . . ."

Grandma always said "Hedda" when she was upset. My stepfather said "Hedda", too, when there was another woman nearby that he wanted to strut for. Then he had no Hedvig, only an ordinary Hedda. Hedda was a little slave, a pig maid, someone who went out and scrubbed and sometimes had a kid. Grandma, though, meant that Hedda sounded much closer than Hedvig, but she usually said Hedvig unless she forgot herself, for Mother didn't like to be called Hedda.

"Dear Hedda, an old woman . . . but you told me I could have the rags."

"*Ja,* if you *buy* them," Mother said stubbornly.

Grandma went for her leather pocketbook, which looked like a little knapsack, and took out a ten-kronor note.

"Take this, Hedda." Her gnarled hands shook as if she was sickened by the note. "Take this, Hedda. May Jesus' kingdom come soon, so we don't need to have sinful money any longer but help each other like sisters. . . . But take it."

"It's too much, Grandma, but I'll do some good with it. But don't 'Hedda' me for it. You've got to have money, Grandma, even if it should become a little better on earth, you must in any case take care of folks while you wait for it to get better. In the store it doesn't help to just go there and say God's name. They want more than that."

Mother had certainly changed; never had I heard her talk so sternly to Grandma before.

When Olga went to the store, she had a new ten-kronor note with her. She got to buy on credit for herself because of Mother's ten kronor, and you could smell the coffee in no time as she had promised. But Mother still didn't look happy. She didn't like the way she'd gotten the money. I understood that.

Grandma sat quietly on the settee, clipping and clipping with a big scissors we got to borrow from the big house. Her swollen gnarled thumb wouldn't go through the loop finger of an ordinary scissors. We had drunk good coffee from beans that Mother had roasted in the oven, and I had taken a quart bottle of it down to the barn to my stepfather and Karlberg who were winnowing seed grain.

Grandma stayed a week after New Year's. Every night she sang a song and said a prayer.

She wanted to kneel when she prayed, but it was hard to get down and up again. My stepfather had to help her when she knelt and when she got up again. She never tried to kneel unless my stepfather was there, and he never dared not to help her.

"Bend your knees for God, Albert," she often said. She never asked Mother and me to since the day I begged her not to pray out loud, and Mother said that Grandma didn't need to "Hedda" her.

My stepfather never obeyed her request. I felt that Grandma was irritated with Mother and me, wishing we'd go out, that then my stepfather might kneel if we weren't in the way. Mother thought the same, for she said to me one day in the woodshed, "It were best we weren't in the way, I think."

But when Mother was milking in the barn and my stepfather was in the stable, then I told Grandma about all the folks up in the shoemaker's forest house in Kolmården, and about Christian's journeys. "The man in the forest house was so handsome, Grandma. He was like . . . Aladdin."

"Who is Aladdin?"

"A person who had a lamp that he rubbed and then a spirit would come and give him everything he wanted."

"That's a troll. A man who read about Christ is no troll."

"He didn't read about Christ; he read about Christian; the man who was out travelling was called Christian, and he journeyed to the valley of despair. It's in the Bible, but I can't find it."

Grandma sat and brooded about this a long time.

"Have you read the whole Bible?"

"Not really, Unc . . . I mean Papa and Mother get so angry when I read the Bible."

"Do they get angry, you poor child? Why haven't you said something about this? Poor child, didn't the man tell you where it told about Christian's travels in the Bible? Is it probably Paul?

"No, it isn't Paul. I've read about him, he's so tiresome."

"God forgive you, child. He's God's holiest man."

"How do you know that? Where does it say he's God's holiest man?"

'Well, ja, he was a heathen and then was saved."

"I gave five öre to the heathen once."

"Paul wasn't a heathen like that. He was much harder to save because he had other gods."

"Heathens have them, too; they have wooden images, the teacher said, and they live in China and Africa and all over."

"Ja, they live all over," Grandma sighed and pondered quietly again. "Have you read John's Revelations?"

"No, are they in the Bible?"

"Ja, bring me the Bible and I'll show you. In Revelations it's sure to have something on Christian's journey, for that book is so hard to understand."

I took down the Bible. As long as Grandma was with us, the old lamp was lighted while Mother was out milking. Grandma moved over to the lamp and opened the Bible.

I showed her what books I'd read. "I couldn't get through the books of Chronicles," I said.

"*Ja*, but then you won't know the story of Jesus' relatives' roots," Grandma said.

I didn't answer. The story of Jesus' relatives didn't interest me. I wanted to know more about Christian's journey.

"Have you read the Book of Job yet?"

"*Ja*, but it was dull, and the prophets are so angry all of them and Nebuchadnezzar ate grass and Daniel ate vegetables and got big and fat; those men in the oven had greased themselves with something so the fire wouldn't hurt them," I babbled on, for Mother believed that.

"You have to think that it's God you are seeking in the Bible. I'm beginning to agree with your mother that you shouldn't read the Bible."

"Sweet Grandma, I *will* think about God. Show me the book about John; dear Grandma, don't tell Mother that I shouldn't read the Bible. She'll take it up to the attic. I say my prayers every night, Grandma.

Around the house an angel brings
Three golden lights on outstretched wings,
Bearing in hand a book, and Jesus on his arm,
In Jesus' name we sleep, now safe from any harm."

I said the prayer solemnly to impress her.

"Will you kneel and say it out loud tonight?"

"Mother will get mad. She says you're just showing off when you say your prayers so others can hear them. If you're sad and can't pray silently, you should go somewhere by yourself and call to God, that's what she says."

Grandma looked perplexed. Suddenly we heard steps on the porch, and she hurried as much as I to get the Bible back in its place. My mother and stepfather came in.

We ate rye meal porridge and milk which was Grandma's favorite and then my stepfather helped Grandma kneel, his face looking as if he'd laid a heavy board on the floor. Mother also looked downcast. I thought they both looked *too* cross, and I got stubborn. I felt sorry for Grandma. I went to the chair that she rested her folded hands on, and kneeling beside her, I said my night prayer in a clear loud voice without a thought about its meaning or about God, only with a longing to show my solidarity with Grandma. She looked frightened and forgot to pray.

Neither my mother nor my stepfather said anything. They sat there like wooden figures, not minding about me or Grandma. They looked so strange.

When Grandma was undressed, she said in a trembling voice, "The girl did that by herself, I didn't ask her to."

My stepfather looked as if he were going to say something, but Mother gave him a threatening glance. I thought they were acting so strangely. I was almost scared. Was it so terrible what I'd done? I knew well enough that Mother prayed to God sometimes and had heard her mumbling prayers, but afterwards she'd always looked grim, as if she were angry she'd prayed, as if she'd lowered herself or wasted her time. But to me she often said that I *should* say my night prayer, "so your thoughts will be on something *else,*" she said. I wondered what she meant by that, for she never explained what she thought my thoughts were on.

"You'll be a beggar, for sure, the way you're teaching yourself to beg, you'd better watch out; it's a weakness in the family. Your grandfather's mother, my grandma, went around begging in her parish, although she was married to a well-off farmer; she was a 'mother of the farm.'* But she couldn't stop herself; she was accustomed to it, for she came from gypsy stock. Stop your begging. You have no need to do it. Least of all should you beg God for something."

I thought Mother was interesting when she talked like that. I would have sat forever and listened but she never talked for long.

"You listen to what I'm saying," she said, "and remember it." It was when she was thin and quick that she talked so interestingly.

Now they stood there both of them and didn't say a word.

I certainly hadn't begged. I had just said my night prayer.

Grandma was in bed. My stepfather had undressed and had put his socks out on the porch, for they smelled so bad. Still not speaking, he lay curled up on the acorn settee. Mother seemed uneasy as she walked about the room. I felt something wasn't right, something had happened. I couldn't undress. I shivered and felt dizzy. It was something; it wasn't because I'd knelt beside Grandma. It was something else.

*The name given to the wife of the farmer who owned the most land in the parish.

Mother sat down now by Grandma's bed.

"How do you feel, Grandma? Do you have a lot of pain at night?" Mother asked in a friendly way.

"*Ja,* pain I have enough of, but I think God has brought good help."

Mother sat there quietly for a while. I sat up, wide awake on my bed on the floor. It'd come soon. What would come? A thunderclap, something terrible, I felt it.

"Who do you have to take care of things there at home, Grandma?"

"Broom-Mina promised to go there once a day. I gave her money for that. I want to be at peace with people, Hedvig. I'm not angry at Broom-Mina anymore."

"No, what reason would you have to be angry at her? She's the one who's had it hard."

I heard how Mother's voice hardened again. But I was so eager to hear about Hanna's mother that I didn't pay much attention to her tone.

"Is Hanna with her, Grandma? How does Hanna look now? Has she grown? Has her hair grown? Does she have a new dress?"

"No, Hanna isn't with her. She's been hired out to a farmer there in Vikbolandet."

Grandma sounded tired and Mother looked worried. She sat there by the bed, looking at Grandma, brooding about something. All at once I felt dejected; Hanna at a farmer's place. I thought of Alvar.

"We had a telephone call today," Mother said.

Grandma was quiet. Mother waited for her to ask about it, but she didn't.

"We had a telephone call that Father-in-law is very sick. They want you to come home, Grandma."

Grandma took several deep breaths. They sounded so awful in the quiet room. My stepfather lay there, completely still as if he were holding his breath.

"Is it his kidneys, his old pain?" asked Grandma in a low voice.

"They didn't say, but they wanted you to come as soon as possible."

"Who rang?"

"The gentleman who owns the farm; he rang from Norrköping."

Grandma said nothing more. She didn't pray either, didn't sigh to God. She was completely quiet.

"We'd best sleep now so you can go home in the morning. Albert

211

has asked for time off so he can go with you. I don't have any shoes; otherwise I'd go, too, for you need help at home."

The old woman said nothing.

"Don't be sad, Grandma. We'll do what we can, and he is so old."

"*Ja,* Hedvig, go to bed now. You've had to do so much." And Grandma turned to the wall.

My mother and stepfather looked meaningfully at each other, shook their heads, gave a whole pantomime. Mother undressed. I began to, little by little. I didn't have high-topped shoes though it was winter, so I couldn't be outside so much, but Mother had pulled a pair of my stepfather's most darned stockings on over my low shoes, and they were damp at night and hard to get off. I sat there tugging and pulling while Mother impatiently stood in her slip waiting to blow out the lamp.

She came over and helped me, tucked me up in my floor bed, and stroking my hair, she said good night and blew out the lamp. Then she crawled into the acorn bed beside my stepfather. They were quiet, but even so I could hear they were awake. I lay awake, too, couldn't get to sleep. I knew some change would soon take place. I saw that in Mother's face. She looked so belligerent. Always she looked like that when she began to feel the ground rock under her.

"Be honest with me, Hedvig. Is my man dead?" From the bed came Grandma's voice.

Mother didn't answer at once.

"*Ja,* you don't need to say. I know he's dead."

"*Ja,* Grandma, he is dead, but I didn't want to tell you until morning, for you need to sleep tonight."

I heard Mother get out of bed.

"Lie still, Hedvig. Don't light the lamp," Grandma said.

Mother lay down again. Silence once more. It was as though the room were charged with thoughts, anguish, unrest. The darkness was thick. Here we had the roller shade at the window; the girl with her nice wooden clogs perpetually went over the footbridge with her filled water buckets, although this couldn't be seen in the January darkness.

"Isn't it too cold for Mia on the floor? Can't she lie here in the bed with me?" came Grandma's voice.

Getting up, Mother lit the lamp, drawing a shawl around herself.

Grandma sat up, thin and shrunken, now that she wasn't dressed. Her little black braid hung over one side of her wrinkled neck, but there were no tears in her eyes. Only her nose looked more tapered than usual and she was so pale.

Mother pulled the bed out a little and put on the blankets from my bed. I stood there, almost freezing while I waited. Then I saw Mother holding Grandma. Without a word, she had taken Grandma in her arms, and Grandma leaned her old head against Mother. Neither of them said anything. My stepfather didn't say anything where he lay on the low settee that the table hid. I shivered with cold as I stood but I tried to keep my teeth from chattering. I didn't want to disturb them, I felt I should not disturb them. Mother was so sparing with any display of affection. I saw Grandma's gnarled hand on Mother's shoulder. It looked so terribly old against Mother's young white arm. I felt so sorry for that old hand. I thought it was something that could never be cured or made amends for when I saw that crippled hand against Mother's white flesh, and the black, thin hair against Mother's thick golden braid that hung over her shoulder.

Mother whispered something and Grandma lay back on the bed. Crawling in beside her, I threw my arms around her as I had seen Mother do. Then Mother blew out the lamp.

"Try to sleep a little, Grandma."

"*Ja,* try now, Mother, to get a few winks," my stepfather said in as friendly a voice as he could with his bass growl. I crept nearer Grandma, holding on to her, hard, hard.

"Thank you," she said in a low voice. "Thanks. But now the hens will be cackling at Vilbergen."

"We don't care about them," Mother said.

"Let them try," my stepfather said.

The old Grandma had come back again. She certainly wasn't any beggar woman. She didn't beg when sorrow came. She was afraid of gossip; she knew well enough that prayers won't stop gossip. I didn't hear her say another prayer out loud. But she was awake the whole night. I woke up often from her restlessness.

When my stepfather and Grandma left the next day, she had ripped the band from her hat.

"I can't go with a red band on my hat when I lost the nicest man I ever had. He was the best of my three husbands," she said in her old plucky tone.

Karlberg brought around the horse and cart. His ears looked frozen, for now my stepfather had to wear the cap himself.

"I'll send a new pair of boots back with Albert, so you can come

213

to the burial, for both of you can't very well take off from work now," Grandma said to Mother. That was the last she said as they drove away from the white-plastered house on the plain.

Chapter 18

For two days I read the Revelations of John, and Mother said nothing. Didn't forbid me to, either. She went between Olga's and our place like a restless ghost. It snowed and was cold. Scanty snow and twenty degrees cold. My stepfather would be gone only two days. Late at night on the second day he was supposed to come home.

"We'll see. I'll believe it when I see him," Mother said to Olga.

"Now don't you believe the worst. He'll be sure to come, he has the horses to take care of, you know; he must work, he's got a steady job," Olga said.

Mother shook her head doubtfully. "What does he care about that if he gets something else in his head. No, I feel in my bones we've come to the end of peace for this time. Now it'll be to move again."

"Oh, see now. I don't think so," Olga said, but she didn't look so certain either.

"What are you reading?" Olga asked.

"Here it tells about a beast with ten heads that's going to come, and lambs and eagles will fly in the heavens," I said.

"Let me see," Mother said. Silently she read a page. "Confounded fairy tales! You'll just get afraid at night, Mia; it's not worth reading anymore of this."

"What does it say? Let me see," Olga said, taking the Bible. She read silently for a while, too. "I never would have believed that such stuff was in the Bible. It's too awful." Olga looked as if she'd seen a ghost.

"Those are prophecies. They're truly going to happen," I enlightened them.

"Those things will never happen; neither lambs nor lions are able to fly. Do you think it's fun to read things like that?"

215

"No, I don't think it's fun; it's boring."

That was so. When the prophet finished one revelation, he went on about the next which was just like it. All the noise and commotion in heaven—it made my head go in circles. All the monsters and harlots with strange heads who sailed in the sky. The monsters seemed like roaring threshing machines. That gave a little more sense to all the warring going on in heaven. These days it was only at night when I dared to look up in the sky. Lambs and eagles and lions could come down through the snow clouds. It wasn't like Christian's journey. I didn't really know what harlots were. Women who did something crazy. Grandma's sister who had drowned herself in the river because her back had been whipped to pieces, her mean uncle had called her a harlot and whore. I'd been to Åbacka with Mother one Sunday before she'd married and we'd picked lilies of the valley. It didn't seem likely at all that whores would drown themselves there in that water. . . . The magistrate had told the handsome man in the forest house to "take the whore," that he should take her naked. The stable hands had heard him. But when I tried to get a picture of the housewife in Kolmården sitting up there in heaven with all those strange heads, I just got all confused. She was so dull and teary-eyed, she was nothing to be afraid of. I was tired of the Bible. There were so many curses and quarrels. Nearly as it was on a porch in town. A peaceful, pleasant world with flowers and quiet people I wanted to have just then. The prophet's heaven of glory was as troublesome as all of his curses and visions.

Everything was in an uproar. Mother just walked back and forth, out and in, night and day. Three days had gone by, and my stepfather hadn't come. Outside the snow whirled and thickened. The road was snowed in as far as you could see. No one tried to get to us.

On the third day in the late afternoon the farmer came to our place. He had a pipe in his mouth, and his clothes smelled of tobacco. I thought it smelled good. He was a short, clean-shaven man with a little head that he turned and twisted like a magpie. He didn't look one bit like a farmer. He talked fast, stumbling on his words to Mother while he turned and twisted his head.

"Do you think, Hedvig, that he'll come tonight? Otherwise then . . . well, *ja,* do you read the Bible then? [He saw the Bible.] *Ja,* it's probably best to begin in time. . . . If Stenman doesn't come, I don't really know. . . . Are you going to the burial, Hedvig? The road's so bad now. It won't be good getting to the train station."

He sat for a while and was silent, but then he came right to the point of his errand.

"*Ja,* well, do you think he'll come tonight, Hedvig?"

"No, I don't think so," Mother said decidedly.

"What, you don't think so?"

"No, I don't. I think he's on a binge now again; otherwise, he would have called you. He has his weakness. It won't do any good to sweep that under the rug."

"*Ja,* well, *ja,* I thought as much, but you see he's on salary. This won't do, we have our laws and rights."

"*Ja,* I can't help that. I'm telling you what I think. I'm nearly out of wood, and I can't just go out in the woods and get him like a cord of wood. I don't know what I'll do. I should have gone to town and helped my mother-in-law, she's so old, and Albert should have come back yesterday and brought boots for me, for I haven't any, but it's like everything else. He loses his head as soon as he gets to town and falls in with his boozing friends. I knew it would be like this when he went."

The farmer didn't say anything. He wasn't angry as I thought he'd be. He looked thoughtfully at Mother, drawing up his light eyebrows right up to his hair line, and moving nearer to Mother, he talked in a low voice as if he were afraid. "*Ja,* I've had ones like that before, but I haven't had such nice folks as you [I felt a tingle of happiness], and I gladly will take Stenman back, and I don't want to lose you, Hedvig. The place here looks like a gentleman's house. And you'll get boots. You just get to the station, and there you can buy a pair of boots. I'll give you ten kronor in advance and will rely on you to come back and to have Stenman with you. I think that's the best thing to do, to go in, Hedvig, and get him to rights, and help your mother-in-law with the burial. Her husband must have been a dependable man; there will probably be a little something to inherit," he said, sounding more and more friendly to Mother, as if he and Mother were on the same footing. "So we'll take care of things here as best we can now. It's a pity this happened so soon after the holidays. The fellows are always a little boozed up, so to speak, after a holiday, and want to have more. But if you want to, Hedvig, Karlberg will drive you to the station early in the morning. So you telephone now and let them know. I won't bother with the

217

police about this now, but scare Stenman with that. And if he doesn't take care of his job, there'll be a summons."

I began to like the farmer as he sat there waiting for an answer.

"That's very friendly," Mother said. "Thank you so much. That's very nice, and I'll do what I can. But I feel he's gone on a binge and then he's impossible."

"They'll always back down to the police. Scare him good. *Ja,* you go in the morning, Hedvig, like I tell you."

I think I liked the farmer most for what he said about the police, that you could scare my stepfather with the police. I had a good suspicion that Mother couldn't scare him enough.

"The law would put both of you in jail," she had yelled several times when my stepfather had been summoned for the factory woman's baby, but Mother never was serious about her threats to my stepfather. That's why she couldn't scare him any longer.

The farmer took Mother's hand and mine when he said good-bye. We heard him go in to Olga. He was there for a long time.

Just before Karlberg was expected home, Olga came and asked to talk to Mother.

Mother went out on the porch. When she came back in, her face was red and she looked angry. "If Karlberg asks you if the farmer was in to Olga's, say that you don't know," she said to me. (I looked somewhat astonished.) "*Ja,* it's nothing really, Karlberg is just so foolish. Olga asked that we shouldn't say anything."

I remembered Christmas Eve and how Karlberg had spit snuff on the first curtain that had ever hung in his home, and I decided to keep quiet. But they weren't fair, those grown-ups. When you lied to get yourself off, then you got whipped, but when it was a matter of getting *them* off, you sometimes got candy if you lied. But here you *had* to lie, for the farmer's wife thought that Karlberg would murder Olga one fine day.

Chapter 19

Nearly the whole night Mother was getting things ready and packing. Warmed the flatirons and pressed. She didn't own a black dress. The one she'd worn when she got married she'd borrowed. She settled on a dark blouse and a black skirt. "That'll have to do for the funeral finery," she said. My Scottish dress, which was red plaid, I couldn't wear to the funeral, but I'd get to wear it for the trip, although it wasn't suitable even for that when you're "in mourning," Mother said. (That the old man was dead I didn't think about at all, for I had very little grasp of what death meant.)

"When I get to town, I'll try to do some scrubbing someplace so you'll have a dark dress and a pair of boots," Mother said.

I was really happy about the trip. It sounded wonderful. There would be a funeral and everybody would wear fine, dark clothes and eat good food. Evergreen branches trimmed the doors when people died. But Mother just sighed and puttered, and right in the midst of everything, she took out a psalm book.

"You'll read this psalm. Learn it now," she said.

It was late and I was tired, but I set to work on the psalm. It was a psalm to read when an old man had died.

Mother knew how everything should be.

The train didn't leave the station until seven thirty, but already at four thirty in the morning we were on our way. The snow was deep and the horse could hardly make any headway. Karlberg blustered and swore. He had a wooden shovel in the sled to get us out of the worst drifts.

Mother had sixteen kronor in her purse—six kronor left from selling the balls of rags and ten that the farmer had sent with Karlberg to give her as an advance so she could buy boots someplace down at the station. The two kronor Mother had hidden just before

Christmas "in case anything should happen," she had used to pay one of the farm workers' wives for doing her milking.

It was a hard trip. The snow kept on swirling down.

"It'll be dark before you get home again," Mother said. Karlberg had to get out many times and shovel ahead of the horse. He scooped and scooped so the sweat ran, and the horse then pulled us out of the drift. It would be a smooth path for a ways and then there'd be another drift.

Mother and Karlberg talked some, but I couldn't hear much because of the sleighbells, but when the horse stopped, Karlberg leaned over Mother, for he sat behind us on the sled and drove, and I heard him say, "Can you swear, Hedvig, that the farmer didn't go in to see Olga yesterday? Myself, I'm sure as the devil that he did. I could smell he'd been there when I came in, he smokes all the time."

I stiffened. *Would* Mother swear? It was so dangerous. But she had promised Olga.

"I can't swear to it. I didn't follow the farmer, but we didn't hear him go in, or how was it, Mia, did you hear the farmer go in to Olga when he left us?"

Karlberg looked suspiciously at Mother when she turned to me. The sled was tilted in the drift, and the horse had twisted his head around as if to see if the driver wouldn't help him.

"No-o, I did *not* hear him. He went straight home."

Karlberg didn't say anything more. Mother stared straight ahead while he shovelled us out and led the horse over the drift. It began to get daylight, and the snow didn't swirl as much. Karlberg got back in the sled.

"Was he with her *before* he came in to you? Did you hear him then, Mia?" he asked, lashing the horse.

"No-o, he wasn't. He came in to us; he had snow on himself. Mother helped him brush it off," I said quickly.

Karlberg looked calm. Children don't lie. Mother stared straight ahead, not looking at me.

When we finally got to the station, we had a half an hour before the train left.

"The farmer wanted me to buy boots at the store here, but I'll wait until I get to town. I can get them cheaper from Stamp-Kalle. If the farmer asks, tell him that," Mother said to Karlberg. She gave him a krona. "Buy something to bring home," she said.

"You need the money, Hedvig. I can't take a krona."

"Take the krona now, and buy something good. I can always lay my hands on a krona, and don't think bad things about Olga. She is the nicest neighbor I've ever had."

Karlberg turned and drove home again, and we went in to the waiting room. Mother's shoes were worn down so crookedly she almost limped as she walked, and I had stockings pulled on over my low shoes. I looked as if I had bear's feet.

When we came to the station in Norrköping, Mother tugged off my stockings. I remember that people had looked pityingly at me when I had walked in the snow in my low shoes, but both Mother and I thought they were dumb to feel sorry for us without needing to.

"Busybodies, they can look after themselves," Mother said. I had on my new green cardigan and was surely fine enough for their old town.

The trip had cheered Mother up. Her eyes glistened. Throwing her head back, she walked springily, not bothering about her crooked shoes. Our feet got wet, for the slushy snow was deep on the long promenade, but we weren't used to walking with warm feet. Working folks were used to shoes that leaked. We weren't the only ones walking with wet feet.

I knew when Mother was in such spirits, something fun would happen.

"We'll have a drop of coffee before we go to Grandma's," Mother said, turning off on a side street.

"At a cafe?"

"*Ja,* sure, where else? We need a little something in us."

Mother found a little dim-lighted cafe that had dark fringed curtains. I thought it was splendid, but Mother said it was a workers' cafe. "A temperance cafe," she said.

The woman who managed it looked a little inquisitively at us, but Mother took my hand, and we went into an inner room where we had big cups of coffee and buttered bread. Oh, it was so good!

The buttered bread had another name than our usual one for it, and the name was not far-fetched: the good fat slices looked like the well-fed behind of a three-month-old baby. You got completely full with just that bread.

"This will be expensive," I said to Mother.

"You'll see that Albert hasn't skimped, and we had to get something in us. Eat now."

Mother wasn't acting as if she were going to a funeral. And she had such broken down shoes she could scarcely walk right. I thought Mother was glad to get away from the lonely farm for a bit. She was most like herself in town. She had shoved aside all worries, and she was so *thin* still. It had been a long time since Mother and I had been out together, and she was so cheerful and had no need to stand in doorways and vomit.

I felt so cheered up, too. The coffee was so good. I had eaten all the bread. But just then I felt a pang. The room at home was empty. Karlberg would be home by now, making a row. He dared to when we weren't there.

"Olga should be with us," I said, my eyes smarting a little.

"Olga, *ja*," Mother said, drawing out the words. "Olga, she's stuck like a tree there. Poor Olga, she'll never get to town."

"Why though, Mother? What has she done?"

"Such a fool for a man she's got." Mother beckoned to the woman for the bill. She gave her a ten öre tip. The woman thanked her so politely.

"We've travelled a long way," Mother said to the woman, "and we didn't want to buy shoes out there in the country but waited until we got to town."

Mother shuffled things a bit in her purse so the woman could see the banknote she'd got as advance on her salary. The woman said good-bye and to come again. That you didn't want to buy shoes out in the country she could see well enough; they wouldn't have anything suitable there for a person like you.

Mother went straight through town to the western limits where Stamp-Kalle had his store.

"After the apple tree blossoms, comes the fruit . . . so, *ja*, good day! Mrs. Stenman's in town! Stenman was here yesterday."

An old man, round as a ball with a big, fiery red long nose took Mother's hand and then patted me on my cheeks. "Heavens, what a braid of hair she's got! Will you take a tenner for the girl's braid, Mrs. Stenman?"

I froze, wanting to get to the door, but Mother just laughed. "He's only joking, don't you see?"

The round old man laughed but continued to look seriously at my hair. People did buy braids, I knew. But nobody was going to buy mine. Not just yet anyway.

"Well, so Albert's been here already then," Mother laughed, but I saw that well-known bitter look on her face.

"*Ja,* he was here, *ja.* Should we be buying something?" he asked, turning the subject.

"*Ja,* I need a pair of boots. I don't have enough to buy new ones. My father-in-law is dead, as you've heard no doubt from Stenman. Mr. Karlsson."

"No, he didn't say a word about that."

"Was he sober?"

"Not exactly." The round man looked thoughtful.

"*Ja,* if you have a pair of second-hand ones for my girl, here, too, it would be good."

He got out a big pile of used boots. I tried on pair after pair. At last we found a pair of buttoned ones that had been half-soled only once. They would do. A little tight in the toes, of course, but I didn't say anything about that. I was so tired of trying them on. The thick boots pinched and pinched in the toes, every pair I tried on, so they hurt.

"They cost three kronor." Mother beat the price down to two.

"I'm going to be buying more."

"So then, Mrs. Stenman, you'll be getting a pair. *Ja,* I have to tell you how it is. Yesterday Stenman came here with a really good pair of lady's boots, and I loaned him three kronor for them. I understood that you had sent him."

"May I see them?"

The pawnbroker took down a pair of heavy, homemade boots. They were a pair of Grandma's that had got too small after her chillblains had made her feet swollen and sore. Grandma wore cloth boots now; she couldn't tolerate leather ones.

"I'll buy them."

"I can't sell them, you know that, Mrs. Stenman. I don't have permission to sell them for three months."

"Stenman won't come back to get them."

"*Ja,* but maybe he's sold the pawn slip and then I'd be out."

"I'll pay that. I'll give you five kronor for the boots." Mother looked as if she were thinking of playing a joke on someone.

"*Ja,* but a little more than five kronor I was thinking of."

"Oh, don't be impossible. I'm going to buy an old black skirt, too, for more kronor, so I have something to sew for my girl. We can't go in bright colors to the old man's funeral." Mother used a tone I had never heard before. It was careless, as if nothing made any difference because that was just the way things were.

We put on our boots, Mother and I, at the pawnbroker's, and in another package Mother had a skirt that had so much material in it, she'd get two dresses for me out of it, she said. Both the pawnbroker and Mother said that the skirt was black, but to me it looked more like green. It was a hard slick goods that was called moire. I remember that later on I got sores on my neck from that awful stuff. Mother gave one krona and fifty öre for the skirt.

The pawnbroker opened the door politely for us when we left.

Out on the street Mother had another look on her face. She walked without saying anything, her head down. People that we met got out of her way. Her face all at once was so old and sad. I knew it was because my stepfather had been to the pawnbroker with the boots Grandma had given him to bring home to Mother.

It went round and round in my head. Mother had paid five kronor for a pair of boots my Grandma had given her, and my stepfather had got three kronor for them, and there was still a pawnbroker's note he could sell that the pawnbroker would have to pay in addition—that a gift could stretch into something like this!

"Where are we going?" I asked Mother after awhile as we rounded one street corner after another.

"To my sister's. I'll borrow her machine and sew your dress. Grandma has no sewing machine."

I was dejected. My nagging aunt with those mean boys, the room like a pigpen, and my loud-mouthed uncle with his long thin mustaches that hung down in the soup and coffee and everything he ate, and which he took between his teeth, sucking the juice out with a hissing sound. I shivered all over when he sat there sucking juice and soup through his long mustaches like tails. He swore every other word, and then he whipped Aunt on her back with his suspenders if she didn't have things ready in the mornings. He'd often get up in the middle of the night to drive to the markets or to the forests, because the haulage contractor he worked for took on every job he could. The contractor had eleven drivers, and my aunt boarded four of them in that one room. Six of her own children she had, all of them boys. Thick-headed boys who didn't even get a bump on their heads when they fell down the steps. I had lived there different times before Mother got married, and I remember that we kids who were so little that we just sat and played on the floor, often got tramped on by big boots. When we yelled, then some driver with a beard would lift us up to the sky so we thought—in any case, to the ceiling, and would say, "It's over now till you get married, I didn't see you. Did you get hurt?" But more often they swore "damn brats" if we yelled when they tramped on us.

I wasn't happy about going to Aunt's. She was mean. That wasn't to be wondered at. She was mean because Uncle was so mean to her and she never got to sleep properly. But mean is mean, and children can't distinguish between reason and reality. Now long afterwards I could understand that Aunt wasn't mean. She had to be as she was because of the way she had it. It's a wonder she didn't go crazy. I never saw her sit for any length of time. As soon as she did sit down, she fell asleep. Her head fell forward, and often she tumbled to the floor. The last time I was with her, it was for three months. It was at the time Mother was going to get married, and I had to sit day after day in a corner of the room and rock her youngest in a rocking chair.

Aunt was Mother's real sister. They were both brought up on that strange marsh in west Kolmården and could talk half the night about their childhood. They sat there and talked about things that I didn't think were the least bit interesting, though I tried to keep awake and listen anyway. I knew how tired Aunt was in the mornings, that she never wanted to get up, and already at four o'clock the thudding and rumbling of the carts had begun on the cobblestone streets as their drivers drove away. Mother had to get up early for the factory, at six o'clock to be on time, and even so they sat there and talked about their tenant cottage. Sometimes they talked about Uncle, and I heard Mother call him a swine. That time they quarreled, for Aunt said Mother had nothing to say, that she also had got mixed up with a swine; my real father had been a swine, Aunt had said.

One morning Aunt was trying to roll up the bedding that lay on the floor; there were three beds on the floor. Uncle crabbed the whole time for they had overslept. All of a sudden he took his suspenders and whipped Aunt's back with them, lash after lash. She had on only her vest and half slip. Her hair wasn't braided but streamed down her back. She was heavy, too, for soon she'd have a baby. The brass buckles on the suspenders took the skin off her back and blood was on her vest. When Aunt was aware of that, she fainted. All the kids began to scream, and I ran in only my short vest right up to that tall Uncle, yelling to his face with those hanging mustaches, "You're a swine, Uncle, you're a swine, Mother said so!"

His face was white; I was sure he was afraid, too. "Shush, shush," he only said, going after water and splashing it on Aunt's face. But the kids kept screaming so much a neighbor rushed in, and she ran down and woke up the contractor's wife who came up in her dressing gown. It was very fine to have a dressing gown; the contractor's wife went around like that in a loose, pink dressing gown the whole day long. She bathed Aunt's face with vinegar and said it often happened that you fainted when you were going to have a baby.

"Uncle hit her. Look at the blood there," I said, pointing to Aunt's back.

But Uncle just pulled at his mustaches, looking happy and interested at the dressing gown, and she looked happy and interested at him with the mustaches and said, "You're talking through your hat. Some talker you are, aren't you, child? Hedvig's kid talks so much. I don't think you're mean like that, Jansson."

Aunt trembled and sat up. "What does Mrs. want here?" she briskly asked Mrs. in her dressing gown.

"*Ja,* I was sent for. You got sick and fainted. I'm going now."

"Faint, *ja,* when you're married to such a swine."

That stopped them. Aunt couldn't stand the contractor's wife.

"I told her that Uncle hit you, but she said I lied," I put in as I tried to button my vest in the back.

My cousins, slow-witted all of them, just stood there, hiccuping and not understanding anything; one of them was nearly two years older than I. They goggled admiringly at the dressing gown just like Uncle.

"*Ja,* go now, Mrs., Janne hasn't had his coffee yet. Mrs. can probably give him a little," Aunt said venomously to the contractor's wife.

Both the contractor's wife in her fine dressing gown and Uncle didn't say a word, for the neighbor woman was still there, so curious that her wrinkled face trembled.

The contractor's wife left, and Uncle put on his shirt and went to the stables.

Aunt was nice to me that whole day. "The kids that I look after have got more to them than the batch I've had myself," she said when she related the episode to Mother that night. Mother didn't live with Aunt, only I did. Uncle was on his way to Söderköping on a trip to the market and wasn't expected home for three days, so they had plenty of time.

"I think she could stick to the unmarried drivers and not lie with the married ones," Aunt said to Mother.

She was talking about Mrs. in the dressing gown, I knew well enough. I was then six years old.

Mother washed the cuts from the suspenders with banana oil, which was an aid to everything just then, according to the newspapers, and then she bandaged them.

"They're like wild animals," Mother said. "God knows if one dares to marry." My stepfather then was Mother's fiancé.

Now we were on our way there, Mother with a pair of boots she had got from the pawnshop, Stamp-Kalle's pawnshop, where Aunt had also been many times. She used to get twenty-five öre every time she pawned her boarders' holiday clothes on Monday, and then after the boarders paid her, she'd redeem their clothes on Saturday.

Everything was still the same on Aunt's street. The cobblestones were as uneven as always in the slushy snow. The ugly hoarding around the entrance was still there, and in the big yard rubbish was piled up as usual. A thin black cow stood bellowing beside a wagon in the cold. The yard served as farmers' quarters, too. The farmers paid the hauling contractor to let them store their things there when they were in town. Their wives often sat in the wagons and waited for their husbands, who usually were in Skull-Jon's tavern. The farm wives were part of the farmers' things. They didn't pay extra for them to wait there. My uncle said that once.

"Those farm devils should have to pay extra for their wives to sit there, they look so damn smug."

But often I saw one of the farm wives sitting there crying. Today no wives were there, only wagons and rubbish and just the black cow, its back wet from the snow.

Mother stood in the yard, staring up at the second story of the big rough-plastered house. "I don't recognize the curtains. She must have got herself new ones," Mother said, turning to go up Aunt's staircase. Up in Aunt's entrance hall we didn't hear any yelling of children. Aunt's old dropleaf table wasn't out in the entrance hall either. A different rug lay there. Mother looked puzzled. She knocked on the door.

A strange woman opened it. Janssons had moved.

"Jesus, didn't Mrs. Jansson's own sister know that! *Ja,* I tell you! Well, now, let's see. Jansson has leased a place at Hagby. Called himself an estate owner, Jansson did."

"Estate owner, what in hell does that mean?" Mother swore though we had a death in the family and were getting our clothes ready for the funeral.

"*Ja,* I don't know. He called himself that. It isn't so far to Hagby."

"No, I know well enough where that ramshackle dump is. What would he be doing there? No one can live there."

"Well, they've got an apartment fixed up and bought new furniture and he's got a pair of horses, drives as his own boss now."

Well, this was news. We were tired, and it was a long way to Vilbergen to Grandma's.

"Good-bye then. And thanks so much."

"No trouble. Good-bye, good-bye."

We stood a little hesitantly out on the street. Our feet were warm and nice, but it had been a long time since the buttered bread and the stomach gnawed. We had been at the pawnbroker's so long, and it had taken nearly an hour to get from there to Aunt's. Now we had at least three miles to Grandma's, and we didn't know if the road had been cleared or if the snow lay in drifts.

"*Ja,*" Mother said, "it's best we go up there, so we can know how things are going. Maybe they've had the old man's funeral and everything, though they wouldn't have had time enough for all that."

Again I thought Mother's voice had that strange tone, as if it meant nothing that Grandpa had died, that nothing made any difference. She had sat in her underclothes and had held Grandma in her arms. I remembered how Grandma's knobby old hand lay like a piece of grainy wood against Mother's white shoulder. I thought that was so beautiful. I loved her so much then. Why was she like this sometimes? The dead old man couldn't help that my stepfather had pawned Mother's boots or that Uncle had moved; nor could Grandma help it. I felt sorry for Grandma still.

I hadn't experienced what *disgust* makes one say.

Walking there in the slushy snow, Mother felt disgust for everything at times.

"Are you hungry?" she asked.

"No, not very. I can wait till we get to Grandma's."

So we trudged out through the tollgate.

It was a well-known way we walked through the snow that now hid so much of the land. It was hardly two years ago that Mother had walked here almost every night to Grandma's to weave her new rugs that now lay on the floor in the house on the plain. Olga was left there alone now. She had the key to our room, for she was to keep a little fire going every day. For doing that, she got to have Mother's share of the farm milk.

Someone had been out with a snowplow so the road was cleared, and that helped a little. "We have an hour to walk," Mother said, increasing her stride. I kept up as best I could. I was good at walking.

"I needed another pair of stocking on over mine for these boots, they're so big, so I'll get blisters for sure on my heels," Mother said, slowing down after awhile.

That wasn't what was wrong with my boots. They pinched for they were too small. I wished I could take off my stockings.

Suddenly we heard sleighbells behind us. A pair of horses were pulling a wagonload. We moved out of the way so they could get by. The wagon stopped where we stood.

"What in the devil, is it Hedvig?" a rough voice hailed. It was one of the contractor's drivers that Aunt boarded. "Are you going to Vilbergen? I met Albert yesterday. He was in mourning. There'll be beer after the funeral so I've heard. Get in and ride now."

The wagon was loaded with sacks of grain that he'd be hauling to a store far out at Vikbolandet. The driver helped us climb up on the soft sacks. He was far from sober. He willingly wanted to hold on to Mother. She pushed him aside, but tried to look pleased only because we'd be getting to ride. "Hey now, Frans, behave yourself."

"Behave like Albert then! Don't you know he's got himself a new one already? So leave him, Hedvig. Albert's a damn stud!"

So now it's this again.

"You're talking nonsense. Drive now! You can just as well turn off at Vilbergen; we've walked so long. You'll have time to do that," Mother said.

"*Ja,* that depends on what you offer me."

"My mother-in-law will give you a brandy," Mother said.

The horses started up so fast the bells sounded as if a fire brigade were coming. It didn't take long before we swung up in front of Grandma's house. There it lay as it always had since my world's beginning, between two big hills with the lilac bush in the front yard now hidden in snow, and a big cow barn a little ways off to the side.

It was the cow barn the dead old man had taken care of the past twenty years for "a gentleman in town," as he used to say.

Many said that Grandma's last husband was a bit foolish. He couldn't write, could hardly read, seldom talked. They maintained that Grandma took advantage of his simpleness, "worried him," gave him terrible food.

I had never heard an angry word between them. Grandma always talked in a friendly way to him. It's true she didn't get up in the mornings early to help him when he went to do the chores in the cow barn. But she was half-crippled with rheumatoid arthritis and had a painful time just getting out of bed. The old folks didn't have a stove. Grandma didn't want one, for all of her cooking pots since she was first married were for fireplaces. The old man lit an enormous log fire in the hearth every morning in the winter. He had already been out and fed the cows. Grandma had always been along milking, but ever since she turned seventy, she'd had to quit. She couldn't bend her knees to sit on the milking stool, and if she had, she couldn't get up. Now she weaved instead, web after web, for the handloom's seat was high and comfortable. The neighbors gossiped about Grandma because she had such a nice man. For three years now in a row, Grandma had "drunk the waters" for two months in Söderköping for her pain.

"The poor old wretch has to shift for himself," the neighbors said.

"Her ailment isn't dangerous. The old man needs rest more than she does."

But, as Grandma said, "To lie there and gulp down a lot of water in the warm summer you could do just as well at home; it was in winter you needed to go someplace where it was warm."

"You have, in any case, got better, Sofi, and you need to get away a bit," the nice old cow man had said.

Now he was dead. Who would get the fire going in the mornings? Someone had to help the old woman, tie her skirts and things, for she couldn't do that with her crippled fingers. How would things go? My mother talked about all this while we rode at a breakneck speed through the snow. The driver kept on turning to Mother, fawning on her.

We stopped right in front of the lilac bush. Out in the yard smoke steamed from a three-footed kettle. A tub with clothes stood beside it.

"She has help with the washing," Mother said. "You can go now and don't waste time. Here's twenty-five öre for the ride," Mother told the driver.

"I'll go in with you and say hello; maybe the old woman'll invite me for a snort," he said.

230

Mother didn't look pleased. She knocked on the door and we stepped inside.

At the room's only table Broom-Mina sat, big and broad, with her sleeves rolled up, drinking coffee. My stepfather sat across from her, grinning, bloated, half-drunk. Grandma, looking serious, sat in front of the fireplace. I saw how angry Mother got. She was angry before when she heard from Frans about my stepfather and about the boots, too. "Good day," she said harshly. Grandma just stared, and my stepfather sat there, gaping with his mouth open. It was only Broom-Mina who answered, "Good day."

"There's already a daughter-in-law here ahead of me, I see." Mother's voice was steady.

Now Frans stumped forward. He had also stopped in his tracks, a little nonplussed when he caught sight of my stepfather. "What the devil, are you here! I saw you in town this morning."

Grandma was pale. She tried to get up.

"Sit, Grandma. Everything is as it will be," Mother said bitterly. Then she walked over to my stepfather.

He had on a gold and red plaid silk neck scarf that I had never seen before. It was tied as sailors used to have them with the tails hanging down on the chest.

Mother got hold of the scarf and pulled. It was no doubt her intention she could get it off him, but it was a slip knot on the scarf, and my stepfather was beginning to choke. He groped for Mother's hands. She just kept pulling and dragging. At last the scarf ripped in two, and Mother hit him in the face with it.

"You swine," she said, striking him with the flat of her hand. He didn't move, didn't hit her, just sat and stared.

"Hedvig," Grandma said, the tears running down her cheeks.

"*Ja,*" Mother said. "Should I stay or should I go again?"

"What in hell are you doing, Albert? You haven't got that one here to keep the peace," Frans, the driver, said.

Broom-Mina had hurried out to her kettle and tub in the yard. It was cold, not more than ten degrees, but Mina wasn't used to anything very comfortable in the washhouses on farms.

My stepfather got up, thinking to sneak out, but Mother pushed him back in the chair. "You stay until I've talked to Grandma, or have you buried the old man maybe?" Mother asked brutally.

Now Grandma sobbed. I felt sorry for her. Frans did, too, for he began to scold Mother.

Broom-Mina came in and was all worked up now, too. Big and

231

wide she was, and though her hair was streaked with gray, her face was smooth, her skin blooming. She stammered when she talked, and now she stammered even worse, for she was angry. She turned to Mother. "What does she m-m-mean, c-c-calling me a daughter-in-law? She h-h-has a b-b-bastard, she, h-h-herself, t-t-too. Oh, she's been with Frans on the f-f-feedsacks."

"*Ja*, so that's it!" Getting up, my stepfather looked wild. "Is that why you're so cocky?" He went for Mother.

"Get out, you sky-larking slut!" Frans yelled to Mina. "And you, Albert, don't be crazy! Go off to town and take care of the hussy you've got there!"

Now the two drunks began to slug it out. Mother and Mina helped to separate them, pulling at them with all their might. It was lucky no neighbor lived in the house. I had crept close to Grandma, and we didn't say a word, just looked at the mean show. It was true about there being an end to peace, as Mother had rightly foretold.

Mina pushed out the driver, and Mother shoved my stepfather into a chair. "Stay put there, or I don't know what I'll do," she screamed.

"*Ja*, sit there, Albert," Grandma said. "You should know better! Your foster father's corpse lies in the woodshed . . ." She turned to Mother, "He should have gone back home to you yesterday, and then he came today and had used up the money for that trip. He says he sent you a pair of boots I gave him. But you would have been on the way here, Hedvig, before they'd had time to reach you. He didn't send them until last night, he said, and that he'd telephoned the farmer."

"I have those boots on; I bought them back from Stamp-Kalle for five kronor," Mother said, holding out her foot.

My stepfather's head sank on his chest. His jaw hung down. He turned his big protruding eyes up to Mother, looking scared out of his wits. The torn scarf lay on the floor.

Grandma had got color in her cheeks. She looked so strange, so different, as if she were about to laugh; her sunken mouth twitched and trembled. Her fine straight nose quivered. Then she laughed, quietly and low. "Oh, that Hedvig, that Hedvig," she said, shaking her head.

It seemed as if Mother wanted to laugh, too, for my stepfather looked so foolish. Just stared at the big, coarse boots on Mother's feet as if they were blood-thirsty black panthers.

From outside we could hear Frans and Broom-Mina parting. The bells on the horses sometimes jingling, the voices sounding farther off, but the wagon was still in front of the steps.

Suddenly my stepfather leaned over to the floor, grabbed hold of the ruined silk scarf, and ripped it to bits. "Damn rag!" he yelled, clenching his jaws so his cheeks bulged. While he tore up the scarf, we just stared at him, not speaking. He didn't look at us, just kept ripping the poor scarf. Then he got up and left without saying goodbye. No one asked him to stay.

"Now Mina will be off with that half-drunk Frans," Grandma said.

"*Ja*, no child will come of it, so they might just as well," Mother said. "But the washwater will be cold. I'll take care of it, if you'll let me get us something to eat. We haven't had anything."

Plates of herring fried with potatoes on the coals, butter, and milk were on the table. It tasted so good. No one talked. Grandma didn't ask about anything, just laughed quietly now and then.

Suddenly we heard the sleighbells jingling outside, and when we looked out, my stepfather was sitting on the wagonload with Frans. As they drove off, he and Frans were laughing loudly. Mina stood by the tub, rubbing clothes so that she was up to her elbows in soapsuds, as if nothing had happened. Grandma and Mother looked at each other and smiled bitterly.

Out in the woodshed an old slave lay dead and waited now to be buried.

Maybe I was the only one who thought about him. No, Grandma, too. She thought about him.

"Your foster father's corpse lies in the woodshed" churned and churned in my head while I carefully ate little bits of the salty fried herring with big piles of potatoes.

"That was well done, Hedvig," I heard Grandma say to Mother. "You caught him red-handed. He had filled me with lies about those boots."

"Your foster father's corpse lies in the woodshed. Your foster father's corpse lies in the woodshed."

"Has Albert slept here at night?" I heard Mother's voice tremble.

"No," Grandma said quietly.

Silently they sat there. It was always like this with Mother. When she didn't know where my stepfather was at night, she was beside herself, as if it should mean something.

"Your foster father lies dead in the woodshed."

233

I curtseyed to Grandma, thanking her for the food. The whole time it buzzed in my head: "corpse in the woodshed."

Suddenly I was sick, had to vomit.

"The train trip was unfamiliar," Mother said.

Chapter 20

It is the evening of that disturbing day.

Quiet and frightened out of my wits, I sat huddled near Grandma in the corner of the fireplace. I was so tired, so tired of all the fighting and so scared. In the late afternoon I had been with Grandma to see the old one in the woodshed. The coffin hadn't come. He lay on a bench with a sheet over him. It looked ghastly. In that old woodshed alongside the barn, it smelled of manure.

Every contour of the old man could be seen under the sheet. A little old man. When he was alive, he was bent. Now he lay very straight and stiff. Bone after bone stood out all the way up to the nose which made a scary elevation in the sheet.

"He looks so like himself," Grandma said, lifting a corner of the sheet from the old man's face.

No, no, he didn't. This wasn't the old man I'd seen, who sometimes gave me several öre, lying there. This was *no one* who lay there. Nothing I had seen or dreamed about. This blue face with gray stubby beard, the terrifying skin, these bones on a bench. I shook. It was like an omen of all pain.

It became an omen. Twenty years later the light of my understanding was almost put out by a bed of that kind.* A platform of makeshift boards and on it two unmoving figures. Everything as unexpected, unprepared for as twenty years before when Grandma lifted the edge of the sheet from the dead one's face.

Two young little figures who only an hour before had sat full of life talking to me. Talked. But then, twenty years later I knew something about death.

Here I stood beside Grandma who calmly stroked her hand over that terrifying, stiff face, and I was afraid, gripped with horror to the

*Moa's two little sons had drowned in the river near her home.

235

marrow of my bones. How could she touch this thing? Why did they hide this thing here? Why did they say that this was an old man whom I'd seen give the cows hay, who made the fire kindle up on the hearth on cold winter mornings?

Only the stink of manure that I thought made the old man smell bad when he lived was still here.

"He had it hard before he died, but I think he is happy," Grandma said.

She didn't call on God, she didn't cry, she didn't say that the old one was in heaven. I had heard that the dead went to heaven.

This won't go to heaven.

The pile of manure stank. The new hired man for the cow barn rattled his wheelbarrow of manure. He came up to the open door of the woodshed, looking a little shyly at us. It got dark inside; he shaded the door. His shadow fell on the dead one, made him ghastlier, the eye sockets looked like deep black holes, although the eyelids were closed.

"One didn't need to put anything on his eyes," Grandma said. It sounded as if she thought that was a merit for the dead one.

"He gets to rest now," the new hired man said, lifting his old hat as he stepped into the woodshed.

In a blue striped shirt and dirty trousers he stood beside Grandma and looked at the figure on the bench. He folded his hands and bowed his head. Grandma did the same. Neither of them moved their lips. In the barn the cows clanked their chains; otherwise it was still, still as the dead one on the bench.

Earlier in the day I had seen the new hired man put snuff in his mouth and had heard him swear; now that he stood here so strangely with his hat in his hand made me even more afraid. Grandma didn't look as if she were thinking of spreading the sheet back on the dead one, and I felt that I could never move my feet if she didn't draw the sheet over the dead one's face again.

It had been a distressing day; it became too much for me. The house on the plain had been peaceful in spite of everything. My brain was not used to so many impressions at once. I swayed and swayed, trying to hold myself up, but I could no longer keep from fainting. As I tumbled over in front of the dead one, I pulled the sheet with me, screaming shrilly, screaming in horror.

"She was not used to a train trip," Grandma said to the hired man who lifted me up and carried me out, rubbing snow on my head,

236

while waves of nausea rolled over me. The hired man carried me to the house.

"We were down looking at Father," said Grandma.

"What's the use of that?" Mother said and began to unbutton my Scotch plaid dress; spreading her shawl over me, she told me to try to sleep.

I dream sometimes still about the first dead person I saw.

Now I had slept, sat there in the corner of the fireplace, and was gripped with terror. Everything was bad. Everything around me looked bad. They *were* bad. Mother went around mistrustfully, suffering, anguished. Grandma was upset. No one said anything friendly. Everyone was absorbed in herself. Hot-tempered, biting, they all went around.

Mother and Broom-Mina sat drinking coffee now. Grandma sat near the fireplace with her cup as usual, she was so cold.

The conversation was teetering on the edge of a quarrel. Mother had no need of Mina. The washing was done, and now she wanted Mina to go home and not come anymore, for she could manage by herself whatever was left to do for the funeral. At least she was trying to persuade Mina that this was so.

Mina protested. Grandma said that Mina could come and help after the funeral when Hedvig would have to go home.

It was quiet for awhile.

"How about it, is Albert the father of your last girl?" Mother asked.

"What? Which Albert? Oh, Stenman. *Ja, ja,* if *you* got to know *that. Ja!* But no thanks, there'll be no blab about that, one can never know," said that grinning, dumb Mina.

I saw that Mother's eyes were black with hate.

No one said anything more. Mina did not come as long as we stayed there.

Chapter 21

I don't remember much about the funeral.

I do remember there was an awful hurrying on that day, and it was bitterly cold. Mother didn't have enough to get me a coat so I couldn't go along to the churchyard.

I remember the potatoes hadn't been put on when the first funeral guests came, and that Mother cooked them with the peels on, then peeled them in a terrible rush when they were half-done and put them over the fire again so they'd look as if they had been peeled from the start. It went faster to half-cook them first; the peels came off better.

Mother and I stood off in a corner in the fifty-degree chill, peeling the half-cooked, steaming potatoes while people crowded in Grandma's only room, waiting to be fed before they left for the funeral.

The battle battalion band was there, and Grandma told Mother to give them food, too, though she certainly hadn't asked them to come. She was angry about that. Grandma wasn't religious any longer.

I had on my newly sewn green-black moire dress. It chafed my neck. Mother had to tack a band of soft material inside the collar. She had taken her clean ironed handkerchief and cut it in strips. I remember that I thought that was terrible, regretting that I had complained about the sores on my neck. I thought Mother had become dangerous in some way. Cutting up whole things. . . . People had become dangerous. They died, too, so you couldn't even recognize them. And not one of those left alive grieved. I thought that no one mourned the old man.

Grandma fussed about the cold and over all the hurrying about. She was cross that the battle battalion band came with guitars and zithers, and she really spit to the left when she talked about "the

238

gentleman," who hadn't even sent a wreath though her man had taken care of his cow barn for over twenty years.

"He could have paid for the funeral," Grandma said.

Everyone talked about the funeral, no one talked about the dead man. It was as plain as day that he should be dead. He was old and worn-out; naturally he should die. So the talk was about the funeral. To pay one's last respects wasn't done as a last favor. One was *forced* to bury him. Everyone said that the funeral was a difficulty.

"It was lucky for Albert that he had the funeral to blame for taking off from work," Mother said the morning of the funeral.

We hadn't seen much of my stepfather, but at least he was there the day of the funeral. He looked self-important, the sorrowing son who'd be a pallbearer. One of the "well-off" relatives was there, too.

"It would serve him right to ask him to pay for the washing," Mother said. I remembered so well the weaving master's laundry that Mother had drudged over, lugging it back and forth.

"You can't bring that up today," Grandma said.

The "well-off" relative wore a black frock coat with two buttons on the back. He was dressed better than anyone else. He had a top hat, too. None of the others had one. Grandma was pleased that he was there and dressed so fine. She said to Mother, "A top hat makes it a proper ceremony, don't you think?"

Mother just snorted. Grandma wasn't herself.

My stepfather had on a worsted wool suit, so coarsely woven that the material looked like rough homespun. Grandma had bought it for him.

Mother didn't go to the churchyard either. Grandma and one from the battle battalion band and the "well-off" relative rode in the wagon. The battle battalion woman reproached Grandma for taking the band with "The Lord Is Near" off her hat. "Are you afraid to acknowledge God?" she asked in front of all the people when Grandma was getting into the wagon, which they rode in although the road was snow-packed, for a sleigh wasn't provided.

Grandma didn't answer, but she looked as if she thought of spitting to the left.

First came the hearse wagon with the coffin. Some wreaths lay on the coffin. The flowers were frozen. The driver and my stepfather sat on the coach box of the hearse wagon. Then came Grandma, one from the battle battalion, and the "well-off" relative. After that was a wagon with four men in it who were pallbearers.

Mother and I stood on the house steps long after the three wagons could no longer be seen.

We were home alone. We'd clean up while they were gone. Only Grandma and my stepfather would be coming back.

"Now we'll go in and really get enough to eat," Mother said.

Inside it was an indescribable mess. Dirty dishes and crumbs all over, and the rugs wrinkled and wet from all the snow that had been tracked in. The big hearthstone full of three-footed kettles with the remains of meat and gravy and beans and fish.

The tablecloth, Grandma's finest, which was only cotton, was full of spots from the herring and red beets. The plates were partly scraped.

Mother stirred up the fire in the big fireplace, put two of the kettles on to warm, cleared away a corner of the table, and so we sat having our own funeral feast.

"It's empty without the old man," Mother murmured as if to herself.

"Won't he ever come anymore?"

"Are you so dumb, Mia, you who've read so much? Don't you know what it is to die? Death is the end, never does anyone or anything come back again from death."

"Where do they go then?" I stubbornly asked, heartily digging into a big helping of meatballs and brown beans Mother had dished up for me.

"*Ja,* only they know that," Mother said, buttering a slice of bread. She looked as if she would have tried death if she'd been sure where you'd go.

Ja, well, so they didn't know where the dead went! Mother ate and was silent. I ate, too, but I soon got full. Didn't they know anything? Was it like that then? But you certainly went to heaven when you died, didn't you? I looked at Mother to see if I dared ask her that.

She sat there, chewing, staring straight ahead. She had become so different in just a few days. She wasn't at all like the person she'd been several days ago when we left the train station and she'd taken me to the cafe.

"You go to heaven when you die," I said a little indistinctly in a low voice.

"Do you? No, Mia, know this: *you don't do that.* You don't go *anywhere.* A little like when you're dead as when you're alive. You are where you are and must be where you are forever in eternity."

Mother looked worked-up. I didn't dare say anything more.

Reliable people, teachers, Sunday School teachers had said, however, that you went to heaven, but I didn't dare tell that to Mother. And I hadn't any proof, of course, that anyone went there. I couldn't describe how the journey went. and so I had to discard all that and believe as Mother that no one went to heaven. You lay in a woodshed where it smelled of manure.

"Can't we go home, Mother?"

"I promised the farmer I'd have 'him' with me, and it looks as if that won't be soon," Mother said.

Suddenly she got up and went out. I could hear her throwing up.

When she came back in, she saw how anxious I was and soothingly said, "I have a cold, but it isn't anything to worry about."

I had my own idea about that. It was painfully clear to me that now the pleasant, slender Mother had quickly gone and a dull, crying, sick woman whom I could hardly tolerate had taken that slender, good one's place. So it had been nearly the whole time since Mother had got married.

I began to scrape and stack the dishes to help Mother, and she *let* me. She walked around as if she didn't know where she was. Something inside her twisted and twisted. Anguish, fear, bitterness, hate.

I dried the dishes so hard the sweat dripped from me, took out the dishwater, swept, and helped all I could.

"Maybe you'll have time to rest before they come," I said.

"You are sweet, Mia," Mother said. "Come here!"

She held me in her lap, and I put my arms tightly around her neck, and then we cried, both of us, and forgot the time.

But out in the cold churchyard they buried an old man whose duty it was to die, and no one mourned him.

For Mother wasn't crying for the dead man. She cried for the anguish of life. And I? I cried because Mother cried.

We sat like that long, long, and I whispered, "We'll go home alone, Mother. We'll go without 'him.'"

"*Ja,* we'll do that," Mother said. "He's already fixed himself up."

Mother cried herself out, then washed her face, combed her hair, and mine, too. When she had done this, she put the coffee pot on the iron hook that hung in the fire. Then we sat quietly looking at the smouldering coals in the hot ashes until Grandma came from the burial. She was alone. My stepfather wasn't with her. But Mother, having had her low time already, bravely told Grandma that it was just as well.

Grandma took off her coat and shawl and sat down on the sofa.

"Such a week, Hedvig, such a week," she cried out. "That one can't just die. I thought I'd not have to be a widow for the third time, and that good-for-nothing wretch that I brought up didn't even have time enough to take me home from the churchyard, even though I've taken care of him since he was a month old."

She began to cry. It was the first time I'd seen her really cry since the old man had died.

"You know, Hedvig," she sobbed, and her old hands shook, "if I hadn't joined the battle battalion, my man wouldn't have died that soon. I was away too much; he had to be here and take care of things himself. I can never forget that I wasn't home when he died, but I was going around saving others, for goodness sake. As if God wanted one like that Albert. If there is a god he could have let two poor old ones like us die at the same time."

Mother comforted her as best she could, and I patted her gnarled hands, holding them so I wouldn't see them tremble.

Outside it was cold and star bright and the snow glistened. Everything was still. It was as if a storm had gone over the house and then calmed down for all time. Later on that night Mother talked to Grandma about my real father, and I listened breathlessly, and Grandma talked about a good man she had wanted when she was young and couldn't have.

"Now I'll sit here alone after a long life."

"Grandpa went to God and you will go there, Grandma, when you die," I boldly said.

"God bless you, child," Grandma whispered softly. It seemed so long ago now that she hadn't believed in God and had been irreverent.

Mother must have been thinking the same thing, for she took down the psalm book, and handing it to me, pointed to the place. I read the psalm, "When an old man is dead."

"I don't think it's been a real funeral until now," Grandma said.

The long winter night slipped away. The fire on the hearth went out. My stepfather didn't come, and at last we all fell asleep.

So tears had finally fallen for the dead man.

Chapter 22

The blue flowers on the stove wall looked a little blurred in the February sun. Mother had rubbed them with a washrag. She had done the worst of the cleaning, at least, before the move. Olga would scrub the floor after we'd left. All the furniture was ready in a pile in the middle of the room. Uncle, the "estate owner," stood there, his Mongol face looming amidst the heap, as he twisted the long tails of his mustaches and pushed the wad of snuff under his lower lip. His high cheekbones still showed traces of sunburn from last summer, and his fierce narrow eyes glittered as he listened to the conversation. The farmer was talking to Mother.

Out in the yard Uncle's horses, sway-backed and impatient, in front of a hay cart. Their ears were laid back even though each had his feed sack and chewed straw. Elin in her Kolmården cottage wouldn't have cried with longing if she'd seen these horses. Uncle now owned them.

It isn't so good for those who want to go up in the world. Uncle had got tired of the awful wages he'd made for his haulage work that often went on around the clock. The trips without sleep, the bad food, the poor horses, sometimes held up only by their chains. The haulage contractor was an educated man, had taken exams, and when he had poor horses, why shouldn't then a worker who had watched the rich to know how they behaved to earn money, why then shouldn't he buy himself a pair of old gypsy hacks and a cart and a good long whip and make some money himself? An old farm was vacant. No one wanted it. It had got a bad reputation for murder and suicide and was a hiding place for robbers. No one wanted to live there. The gentleman who owned it drove there sometimes with some of his farmhands to plow the swampy land and sow a little wheat. If he didn't have time, the weeds grew undisturbed. Uncle leased the farm. The lease was cheap, fifty work days.

"What the devil, the kids are soon big," Uncle said. My oldest cousin was ten years old and had been along on market trips as a gate boy since he was seven. Had slept on big packing cases from the clothing stores in Norrköping on the roads between Kolmården and Vikbolandet. Slept behind the struggling, flailed horses on the yearly journeys to markets in Linköping, Söderköping, Finspang, Reijmyre, while Uncle and the wife of the clothing store manager had sat in front and talked in strange words on those dark fall nights, for the markets were held mostly in the fall when the workers got their wages. Or else the clothing store manager himself or his head clerk sat there with a flask in his hand beside Uncle. Nearly all the stores in Norrköping sent their wares to the bigger market places.

Uncle didn't drink. That was why he was so sought after to go to the market towns. Uncle didn't have any need to drink. Something burned and seethed in him more than any drink could have done. Life held him in its grip. He hit people and animals when he wanted to get his way.

One time he kicked a drunk driver, yelling, "You scum, try getting out of this now!" Another time he happened to be giving a ride between Norrköping and Söderköping to a rich clothing store owner. She had had too much to drink. "It's best you walk the rest of the way, so you'll be sober when you get home, you baggage," he had said, and just before he had been laughing and joking with her. She had to walk six miles. She probably was sober when she got home to her children and housemaid. Her husband was with another driver going to some other market town.

Uncle was well known for his taste for fighting and his cruelty to horses. But he got things done; he did his work and got to places on time, the storekeepers said, and all of them wanted Uncle to drive. "He's sly. He fights without warning. You don't know where you have him." So went the general opinion about Uncle. But still you could depend on his work, although he lied and you never knew what word would set off his anger.

Now he stood in our room on the plain, twisting his mustaches, and listening. I didn't care about taking in Mother's talk with the farmer. I was fascinated by the changes in Uncle's facial expressions. He was so alive, so completely alive that his presence filled the room, the rest of us were bystanders.

"Ten kronor more, then—you're getting the rest as a gift," the farmer said.

"Take what you want of the junk here," Mother said tiredly. Uncle's eyes gleamed.

"*Ja*, but you've taken some as an advance, the flour and peas."

"They're in the sacks on the porch. I'm not going to steal them."

"They're half-empty."

"*Ja*, what am I to do? I haven't any money. I can't stay here and take over a man's job. I was afraid you wouldn't let me stay. Do what you want. I can't do anything."

"Hedvig, you would have had Stenman with you if you'd really tried," the farmer persisted.

"Go in yourself and try; you'll see. I'll give you the address."

"What the devil, Hedvig can't take a job in your stables. And you heard that she hasn't any money to pay you with." Uncle had stepped forward.

"Be quiet, Janne. This doesn't concern you. It's a good place here, and the gentleman has been kind."

"The gentleman" lighted up, ready to say something nice, I could tell, but Uncle ruined everything.

"You're so damn dumb, Hedvig. Why are you standing here licking his boots for? Are you moving or aren't you? Get out of the way, farmer, or lend a hand so we can get on our way!"

"I know you well enough," the farmer said angrily.

"Do you? You're not lying? If you knew me, you wouldn't stand there talking shit."

"Both your horses are galled. You should be arrested for that. I should report you when I report Stenman. Damned gypsies, the whole pack of you! Cheat all you want, but I'll show you!" The farmer stood unafraid, unleashing his anger on drifters, on those who live hand-to-mouth.

Uncle stood quietly, pulling fiercely on his mustaches.

"Janne!" Mother said warningly. "Janne! Don't try anything here. The farmer is right; he's been kind to me. But I'm begging you to go now," she said, turning to the farmer, "before something happens."

I saw how Uncle's tall thin frame shook. His long, thin fingers twisted his mustaches even more fiercely. He moved slightly.

"Janne, watch yourself! I'll knock your skull in if you start anything! Watch out!" Mother said hotly. "Go, for God's sake, go!" Mother said to the farmer. "Don't you see how dumb you're acting? Go to the police, do what you want, but get out of here!"

Now Uncle had had enough of mustache twisting. He went to the door and opened it. We were relieved. The farmer looked a bit proudly at Mother, thinking maybe to sit down and talk some more, for the acorn settee was right in front of him.

But Uncle came over, took hold of the farmer and carried him out in the snow, and set him down beside the horses.

"You can't say that I've hit you, but you can stand here and blab all you want, you who have the time and aren't moving."

Mother stood there taken aback. I was, too. Uncle lugged out our things. There was no sign of Olga.

The farmer waited a minute, and then went back up the steps and on the porch. Mother heard him come and opened her door. But he was at Olga's, planning to go in.

"Today you can let her alone. Karlberg will soon be here for lunch. Olga will be beaten for your sake," Mother said bitterly.

"Ho, ho! So that's it! What the hell, Hedvig! And he shouldn't get a beating even if he gave you only ten kronor?" Uncle yelled so that Olga was sure to have heard every word.

"I don't know if he's like that, but Olga has a jealous, crazy man, and he knows that and ought to watch himself," Mother said.

The farmer left without a word.

When Karlberg came at noon, he helped with the heaviest things. Uncle blustered and swore and used so many racy expressions that Karlberg roared with laughter. Mother and Olga laughed, too. Although I didn't understand the expressions he used, I laughed with the others. It had been so long since anyone had laughed. My laughter could just as soon have been tears.

When Mother and I walked to the sugar-syrup house, I didn't know then that a time of degradation was coming near, but now I was wholly aware. I saw the future in a mist of dirt, starvation, fights, lice, sickness, and in that mist my stepfather drunk and mean to Mother.

We'd be moving to the "estate owner's" farm, to that place of terrible repute, Hagby. Mother would help a little at Uncle's in return for house room.

We would never get to be alone anymore. My aunt and cousins would be running in and out all the time, and I saw myself bound to the care of a baby in a rocking chair.

"Some of the tramps still live in the brewing house. It's nearly in better shape than our own shack," Uncle had said.

"Are you crazy?" Mother had asked. "Are you going to have drifters like that among the children?"

"They're used to being there. They help now and then with the ditch draining without pay. You have to understand, Hedvig, they can burn you down if you drive them away with the help of the police. They're good guys otherwise, all of them; you don't need to be afraid."

In my mind's eye, I saw the tramps as Uncle saw them, with a little stubby mustache, bristly hair, big shining eyes, the shoulders carelessly slouched. My stepfather's portrait.

The future spread itself in naked misery before me. I don't think Mother saw it as clearly as I.

It was the end of the month so Olga had neither coffee nor sugar, but Mother gave her some beans to make coffee for us.

We were through now with loading the cart and sat at Olga's drinking coffee. Olga's curtains were smoke-laden now, hanging limply these snowy days. At her place it began to be a grimy, everyday gray again. Olga herself had one of her gray days. She went with her braid down her back, her shirt dirty, and that indescribable skirt fastened together with a nail.

Every night we could hear in our place the noise of Karlberg quarreling. Some days Olga seemed completely withdrawn. She just shuffled along, didn't dress, and her mouth shone red and sore.

The baby lay in his basket. He had got so round and big. He had just been changed, was fine and clean, and Mother lifted him up. "You little pig," she said, "you little pig. Now I'll probably never see you again." Olga gave a sob. Uncle, just the opposite of my stepfather, was utterly crazy about babies, but became a tyrant as soon as they had grown a little and could work. Now he took the baby from Mother.

"A fine boy you've got here," he said, lifting the baby high. His long mustache tails flapped. The boy grabbed one of them, and Uncle, pulling back, let him tug with all his might. Olga brightened up, laughing a little.

"A devil of a slut to look at," Uncle said as soon as we were out the door.

"She's married to a fool who begrudges her the clothes on her back."

Uncle shut up but looked sharply at Mother.

Now we were ready. Uncle unbuckled the feed sacks from the horses, and we sat up on the bundles as well as we could.

On the steps Olga stood and cried, half-naked in the winter cold. Her slip looked gray against the snow; her skirt hung crookedly over her hips. Her thick red mouth trembled, tears falling down her cheeks. She was so miserable I cried, and Mother did, too. But Uncle, pulling at his mustaches, sat with his whip ready.

"Write a line, Hedvig! Don't forget me, Mia! Thanks for everything, for everything!" The tears ran and she had nothing to dry them with. Mother promised again and again to write, to come and visit her.

Just as Uncle raised the whip over the bony backs of the horses, two men came on the path down to the house. The farmer and the district constable.

"What the devil's the matter now?" Uncle yelled, reining in the horses.

"I just wanted to check that you didn't take the farm flour with you," the farmer said.

"It's on the porch. I didn't want to put it in the room, for Olga's going to scrub there," Mother said politely.

"This is an unlawful move," the constable said.

"Go to hell!" Uncle shouted and snorted to the horses who trotted off with the heavy load.

The drive was wonderful. The load didn't seem heavy. The bells jingled. But Mother was worried that something might tumble off. "Don't drive like a gypsy," she said angrily.

"I'll drive as I please, remember that." And Mother and Uncle quarreled dreadfully the whole way to the town's tollgates.

But in at Olga's was the boy with the frog. Mother wouldn't keep it any longer. "He can give presents to someone else," she had said and had been ready to break the statue, but she had given it to Olga. Karlberg had promised to make a shelf to put it on. They had neither a dresser nor a cupboard.

"Although as soon as he gets drunk, he'll smash the statue; he can't stand anything that is beautiful," Olga had said bitterly, looking sadly at the plaster boy and frog after her first joy of receiving the gift. But Karlberg had thanked Mother several times, assuring her he'd build a shelf, a fine one.

Chapter 23

As long as we lived at Hagby not a day went by without Mother and Uncle quarreling. Sometimes he came home late at night, and we heard how he tore into Aunt and the children, getting them all stirred up. They hadn't done as he'd told them. Then Mother got out of bed, swept something around herself, and went in and bawled him out, calling him "estate owner" every other word. Mother wrangled mostly about the animals having nothing to eat.

Aunt said these were the best times she'd had since she was married, for now Janne finally had someone to quarrel with whom he didn't dare to hit.

My mother and Uncle yammered almost every day about what they thought of each other. They went over the ground from top to bottom, yelling and threatening each other wherever they happened to be, even in the stable or in the miserable cow barn where the one lone thin cow stood tied up. And always their quarreling finished with Uncle saying that an idiot who could marry Albert Stenman you could believe whatever you wanted to about.

"*Ja,* my sister and I were just about as smart, for it's certainly no better being married to an 'estate owner,'" Mother said.

Mother carried on like one possessed.

Sometimes Aunt took sides against Mother, maintaining that my stepfather couldn't be as bad as her man.

"*Ja,* you should try him. You wouldn't be treated any better," Mother said.

"They would have got on well together, my old woman and Albert, they're just as lazy, both of them!" Uncle thundered.

"I can't put up with this kind of life," Mother complained. "I have to get another place. I can't get work this far from town. I'll soon be naked. Pretty soon my girl and I won't be able to go out the door."

But then Uncle would talk calmly and agreeably. "Things will work out, Hedvig. I'll have money one of these days. Just say when you need some."

Mother worked hard at Aunt's. She fixed the children's clothes and took care of the cow barn and chickens. Aunt couldn't do anything with her hands. She was completely apathetic, and then, too, she was not used to the country. She had lived in town for ten years and had grown accustomed to its ways. To save, to keep supplies on hand she had forgotten about. Sometimes she'd sneak away to Stamp-Kalle's, which was well over two miles, and pawn a pair of sheets for a couple of kronor, buying prepared food to bring home.

"In town you could eat herring every day without any trouble; out here herring wouldn't be fit to eat," she'd say.

How we ever managed somehow to get along, eleven of us, those two months I don't know. I remember that some days we kids had only the horses' oat cakes to munch on. They were baked with the husks on and everything. Mother baked big loaves of this horse-bread. A driver couldn't take much hay with him, for it took up too much room on the wagon, and he couldn't spare the space for just oats.

Mother got up early in the mornings and slaved. When I wondered why she worked like that without ever getting paid, she answered, "I won't sponge off relatives."

Hagby was certainly the ricketiest rookery that had ever been built. Someone said that a factory owner had built it for his mistress. After she had died at a young age from t.b., he had let it fall into disrepair. But not even decay can make a house so wretched. Maybe the mistress had got t.b. from her lover's newly built rookery.

We all lived on the second floor. Uncle's family in three rooms that had been meagerly fixed up; Mother and I were in one room, but there was no fireplace, only a stove. We never dared to open its damper even if there had been wood to burn. One of the dilapidated outhouses served to give Uncle wood for the winter.

On the first floor were two large rooms where the bats and rats lived. Aunt had taken over what used to be a big kitchen for a washhouse and rubbish room.

Sometimes on Saturdays the three tramps who lived in the real washhouse brought friends in. Then a strange collection gathered early in the evenings. Half-drunk men and women. Old women in shawls, young women in hats. They snapped their fingers, whistled, and sang, couldn't keep still a minute. They wanted to "rent" the "salons" on the first floor to dance in. They had got to rent them before from the farm's caretaker who more or less looked after the farm. Five kronor they were used to giving for the rooms.

Then the whole night it was fighting and yelling so none of us could sleep. We could often plainly hear them fight. Sometimes we heard a coarse voice shriek, "How many inches of steel can you take, you devil!" Then Uncle would run down, his suspenders dragging after him, and separate them.

We never heard anyone talk back to him. They never invited him to have a brandy; they knew he didn't drink. But sheath knives and clasp knives they handed over to be left with him.

"It's lucky with this mess that Janne doesn't drink," Mother used to say.

"It'd be better if he drank. Then I'd know at least why he acts like such a devil to the children and me," Aunt answered.

There would always be a long argument between the sisters over which was better, a man who drank and was mean, or a man who was mean and didn't drink.

"It would at least be some explanation," said Aunt who wanted clear reasons for everything except the children's behavior or housekeeping.

"The best would be a nice man who did *not* drink," Mother said.

"Where would you find one? You might as well throw in the sponge before you try," Aunt said spitefully.

"Oh, *ja,* they're to be found. I've come across many, but you never marry them. You pick in the clover and land in the weeds."

Now Uncle came up, sweaty and feverish. His long mustache tails seemed to lift him. He was barefoot and had knotted his suspenders round his waist to keep his trousers up. It was past midnight, and we were in bed, but we couldn't sleep on such a night. He threw a sheath knife and two clasp knives on a chair.

"They were ready, those damn hussies, to use knives," he said, pulling off his pants and getting into bed. "Now we'll put out the lights and go to sleep!"

But you could hear from downstairs the accordion and mouth harp. It wasn't easy to obey that order.

One Sunday morning when it had got quiet downstairs and we could finally sleep, four policemen on horses came from town and banged on the door. Uncle hastily pulled on his trousers and went down to open the door. We all stood terrified in the upper hallway and listened.

"What in hell?" Uncle greeted the police. Someone spoke to Uncle in a low voice. The conversation continued while Uncle stayed down there, and one of the policemen came up.

"May I talk with the older children?" he asked.

My ten-year-old cousin and I, who was eight, were the oldest. Mother dressed me in a hurry.

"Don't be afraid, Mia, say only what you know; don't make up stuff." Mother sounded calm, but I saw how she trembled.

As soon as I was dressed Mother went down with me to Aunt's kitchen where the police were. No one slept there, for it was too cold. Aunt carried on like a crazy person, screaming and howling.

"Calm her down," the policeman said, taking off his helmet. He had a young, smooth-shaven face.

"Tell the man here what he wants to know. I'll go in and help my sister get the children dressed," Mother said.

The policeman took Mother's hand. "Your name," he said. She told him what she was called, and my aunt and my cousins.

"And the girl here?"

"She can give you that information herself. I haven't brought up an idiot, although I've ended up in this nest."

Mother left, and I saw the policeman's mouth turn up. That made me completely unafraid. He asked me about the men who rented the washhouse and about the dances on the first floor.

I told him everything I knew, and I said with a certain pride that they were all afraid of Uncle and gave him their knives so they wouldn't kill each other when they fought. The policeman asked if we didn't go to the dances, too.

"Uncle won't let us."

"Wasn't Jansson usually with them, I mean, your uncle?

"No, he doesn't have time, he doesn't want to, he goes only when they fight."

"Doesn't your uncle usually drink with them?"

"No, no. He doesn't drink. Aunt thinks it would be good if he did drink, but Mother says that she isn't smart."

"Are you going to stay on here? Does your father live here?"

"We're going to be moving soon. I have no father; my stepfather's in town drinking with Park-Frida. He doesn't dare to come here because of Uncle."

The young policeman looked at me, pursing his lips thoughtfully.

"Poor child, you can go now. Tell your mother to come here."

I took the policeman's hand, curtseyed, and said good-bye.

The policeman questioned my mother and my oldest cousin. They couldn't get a word that made sense from my aunt.

The three tramps had disappeared from the farm, and after a while the policemen rode away.

Uncle had stayed with the police downstairs while we were being questioned upstairs. When Uncle came up, he was unusually quiet. Aunt lay on the bed, exhausted from crying.

"Janne," Mother called from our room where I was sitting with her. She looked very disturbed. "What is it, Janne? What does all this *mean? What do the police want?*"

Uncle talked softly to Mother. I saw Mother's face get white.

"Is she dead?" Mother's voice rose.

"*Ja,* that's what they said. They're being held, the whole batch, but we're all right. You were clever, Mia," Uncle said, turning to me. "You were clever and clear. And you, too, Hedvig. I got fined because I rented out the rooms for dancing without getting permission from the constable, but there'll be nothing more than that."

"Was it one of the younger ones?" Mother asked.

"She was twenty-five. They found her just a little ways from here. I had taken all their knives. Someone new must have come during the night."

Someone was dead. They had found a dead woman, a woman who had been dancing here last night. That was why the policeman had questioned me. Those drunk guys had killed a woman.

It was a gloomy Sunday. Uncle was so quiet. Now and then he brought coffee to Aunt who lay in bed and cried. His unusual friendliness made the feeling of depression even worse.

When Uncle went to the stable, Mother silently dressed, and then she bundled me up in what she could find. She locked the door and put the key in her pocket.

We left Uncle's without saying good-bye.

"We'll go to Grandma's," Mother said when we luckily got on our way. "She has an old woman living with her now, but *one* night she can put us up, then I'll try to find something."

It was six and a half miles from Hagby to Vilbergen.

At that time country people were nearly in a panic over the number of murders by poison that had taken place. In the newspapers and whenever people got together they talked about nothing else. Bondesson's realistic accounts, which could be found in nearly every farm home in Ostergötland, played their own part in increasing the agitation, and then, of course, the Broxvik's murder, which according to public opinion, never was cleared up. The verdict had been given, but songs were written about Helga Fägersköld, and were sung and accompanied with guitars, simple songs where her innocence was proved and her fate was mourned.

"He was bumped off for five öre of white," they said when someone died suddenly.

I heard many stories about how this old man or that old woman had run to the police with the coffee pot grounds, demanding that they be examined, for "white" was sure to be found in the grounds. A farm wife, furious when she was forced to be inside and cook meals in the heat of July while her husband and the maids and hired men frolicked in the field, went so far as to grind glass to a fine powder which she put in the porridge; she would have killed all of them on the farm if she hadn't carelessly left the mortar out, and an old milkmaid, who had left the field before the others, happened to see the bits of glass in the mortar.

Sometimes I heard women and old men say that they ought to buy "five öre of white" for him or her, but I had never understood what it meant. The saying had become too ordinary; its true meaning had disappeared. People didn't mean what they said when they used that dreadful threat.

But when the explanation comes, as a rule it comes for both children and the grown-ups. Today for the first time I had come in contact with policemen on horses and a murder. I never saw the victim, and so I didn't have to carry that dark image. Not even the place where she'd been found did I happen to see. I mostly thought about Grandma's story about her sister who had taken her own life because she had been whipped naked. That cropped up in connection with the murder. I interwove the two women, though there were sixty years between their deaths. "She didn't go to her friend." That turned into a law for me. You *should* go to a friend when things get so bad you would rather die. If you went to your friend, you wouldn't need to jump in the currents of Åbacka.

Today I would know what it meant to buy five öre of white. With what easy thoughtlessness one dealt with the concept of life and death, though everyone held death in boundless terror.

It was Sunday, Mother didn't have an öre, and even if it had been a weekday, she didn't have anything to pawn at Stamp-Kalle's. We were completely free people as we trudged along in the dirty March snow. No possessions weighed us down; we didn't own a thing other than the furniture in the room at Uncle's, and he'd probably take it for rent.

Mother was sweating and felt sick, and I had to wait as usual when she vomited. Everything was as it always was. I was now accustomed to it. It didn't bother me anymore when Mother stood there vomiting while people walked past us.

The room at Old Island Road and even the house on the plain were pushed in the background again. The sugar-syrup house, the stocking needle, the paper mill, and Valdemar popped up more and more. Even Mother seemed to be remembering some of those very things, for as we walked along, she suddenly stopped and said, "I could maybe get the room at Valdemar's again."

"There are no hinges on the privy door," I protested.

"*Ja*, I won't ask them; even if they would, it'd just be bullying. It wouldn't work out."

We walked along without talking again, each of us wondering where we'd find a place to stay after Grandma's.

"Won't 'he' be coming back anymore?"

"Oh *ja*, well I don't know, but I'm not sure that I'll take him back." Mother looked terribly angry, and I didn't dare to ask anything else.

At last we got to Grandma's.

The red-haired old woman who stayed with Grandma had got a little grayer since last year. She sat in the dead old man's place with the book of sermons opened before her. Here Sunday was kept. Mother and I hadn't done that for such a long time. At Uncle's you couldn't tell if it were Sunday or Monday. You noticed only what days were market days.

Ja, the book of sermons was sure enough open, and everything was sure enough polished, but the old women didn't act like it was Sunday. They hardly answered our greetings. Grandma looked pale and worn. "Sit down," she said, "take off your things, and sit down."

"We were just going to read a sermon," the red-haired one said in a tone of dismissal.

"*Ja*, please go ahead; we won't disturb you," Mother said in the same tone. She looked keenly at Grandma.

"*Ja*, we're used to reading the sermon at this time on Sunday," the red-haired one said venomously.

"Not I," Mother said.

The red-haired old woman's gnarled cheeks turned a dark brown. "Has Sofi sent for you? I can understand it." She slammed the old book shut.

"What's the matter with you? Can't we come here unless Grandma sends for us? Shouldn't that be her right anyway? As a matter of fact, she hasn't sent for us," Mother added ready for battle.

"You can see how pleasant it is for me, Hedvig. If I were married to old Satan himself, it couldn't be worse. It's good you've come."

It became a real quarrel instead of a sermon. We had come in the nick of time. Living together for two months, the two old women had come to hate each other so much that Grandma vehemently maintained that the red-haired one had emptied "white" in her cup of milk.

"Dear Grandma, that can't be true, think what you're saying," Mother said looking frightened.

I remember how that red-haired one had prescribed mouldy bread for me when Mother was having the baby in the sugar-syrup house, and I was bent upon believing Grandma's assertion.

"*Ja*, Sofi talks like that," the red-haired woman inserted with rage and despair. "The 'white' was English salt, and I needed it as much as she did. She's always been mean. If she hadn't been she wouldn't have been a widow three times. She judges others by her own character. She's no doubt used a little 'vitt' herself at times. Her last poor wretch certainly didn't die just from starvation."

"Wretch," that was the dead old man in the woodshed.

Mother stood there speechless. Grandma sat in her usual place by the fire. The coals glowed. Her hands trembled.

"Red hair and red juniper berries . . ." Mother said meaningfully.

"*Ja*, just as I've said," Grandma sobbed, "but believe me, I want her to go. It doesn't help what one says. She says she's going to stay here a whole year. If I only had a son who was a man, then I wouldn't have to endure such rabble."

"There's no need of a son to take care of this. You pack up and get out. I'm staying here until Grandma can find someone else, someone who isn't so mean as you," Mother said to the red-haired one.

"Was she going to poison you to death, Grandma?" I was terrified.

256

"*Ja,* she was thinking of doing that. God knows if she hasn't succeeded, for I've felt so strange for a long time, I can't eat."

"*Ja,* you haven't been eating right, just been quarreling. That's poison enough, so it is," Mother said as she began to pick things up around the room, and taking the sermon book from the red-haired one.

"Am I to go now on Sunday? Can you mean that?"she asked, drawing herself up to her full height which was considerable. Then she pounded her clenched fist on the table and yelling that if she hadn't bought "white" before, she'd do it now, and she wouldn't give it to Grandma, she'd take it herself and write a note for the newspaper that Grandma had driven her to it.

"Do that, take poison, but don't do it here, for we'd have the trouble of the funeral," Mother said hatefully.

With a furious speed, the old woman bundled up her things and slammed the door without saying good-bye, just as my stepfather used to do.

"What did you have her here for? She has her own house."

"I couldn't stay here alone," Grandma said. "She was so sweet and nice when we worked at Kopparhammarn thirty years ago, but since she's got a little to go on with her own house and some money after her brother died, she's become a real witch. God help me, it's been terrible for me here. Constant nagging about my will. Think of it, Hedvig, making a will for an old woman who's older than I am. The little I've got isn't anything to make a will for. But she just made list after list and talked about the old days, how she'd helped me with the yarn boxes at the factory and that people said that I had a savings account book and that I should make my will to her so that Albert, that wastrel, wouldn't get it. She made me so crazy that I said she would share whatever I had if she stayed with me till death. I meant *her* death, for I'm sure to live longer than her, but she thought I meant till *I* died. She insisted that I got thinner every day. It was a neighbor woman who heard about it, that she'd get whatever I had, and since then I haven't dared to sleep at night. I'm sure she was up to some devilry with the food. . . . She had proof of what I'd promised her."

So that's the way the grown-ups were. They took one another's life if there were something they wanted. I was understanding grown-ups more and more.

When Mother told about the police finding a murdered woman out at Hagby, Grandma was ashen.

"There you see, Hedvig!" Grandma trembled and couldn't get another word out.

"Oh, that red-haired old woman wouldn't have dared to do anything to you, Grandma. The poor thing who got murdered was altogether different. She was murdered because of jealousy. They were all drunk. Now you mustn't think about such things anymore, Grandma."

I saw that the red-haired old woman's being dismissed had cheered Mother up (and I was, too; I *knew* how mean she was); now there'd be more room for us. Mother had been having worries enough of her own, as if she shared something with those who were murdered. She sounded as if she envied the dead, as if she wanted to be murdered herself the way she sometimes carried on against Uncle.

"In the morning I'll go to town and see what jobs there are at the factories. At the worst, I could get something at the cotton mill. I still have my recommendation."

"Then buy both *Ostgöten* and the local paper [the local newspaper was *Norrköping News*] so we can know who it was who was murdered where you were; think of those hoodlums."

Grandma stared unseeingly at the opened book of sermons as if she were looking far away in her long dark life.

"Are you seriously thinking of leaving Albert?" she asked after a while.

"He has left *me*. I haven't had an öre from him for two months, and now I'm in that way again. I don't think he's given it a thought. Though if he does, he always used to run off if there were any question about it. Now I've got to get a little work before it shows too much."

Mother had certainly forgotten that I was in the room listening. "In that way," *ja,* I knew what that meant. Then "Miss" with her satchel came again.

"Don't you know where he is?"

"Folks say he's shacked up with Park-Frida. My brother-in-law has seen them. I don't know. I haven't asked where he is," Mother said tiredly and dismissively.

I had heard stories about Park-Frida. The police used to nab her.

I saw those twisted hands tremble on Grandma's knee. Grandma who was so tired, things should now at the last be good.

I started to cry bitterly, but couldn't say why.

"It's been a terribly upsetting day," Mother firmly said and let me cry myself out.

I always got disturbed about the trembling in Grandma's gnarled hands. Tears and sobs came without my willing them. A strange sorrow came over me when I looked at her hands. It wasn't the terror that made me cry when my mother and stepfather fought for life and death, or when Uncle threatened to kill Mother when she, not at all afraid, talked back to him; nor did the tears come like those from ordinary anger when I couldn't have my way with my cousins. Or when I got whipped. Nor the fright that seized me when the police wanted to talk to me alone.

My sorrow over Grandma's trembling old hands, gnarled hands that shook from grief, and old eyes dry from bitterness and life's suffering was something infinitely more. It was beyond time, like a wave that lifted me over all everyday impressions. That sorrow was like a big harbor where I was alone, where I sank in murky, dark water without dying. The sorrow and tears that came when Grandma's old hands began to tremble, because she wanted to control her eyes, her facial expression, for she was ashamed to show her sorrow over a shiftless man, a drifter whom she loved in spite of all the hard words she said. It was, I thought, a flood from a secret well that made me different from other children. The same well that flooded over and whose secret strong power came over me, filling me with anguish and making me cry that gray winter day in Olga's poor, indescribably poor room with old newspapers for curtains.

(It still happens when I'm on a train or trolley car, that I hide my face behind a newspaper when a pair of gnarled, trembling hands lie on a knee.)

For three days my mother stayed in town to find work. When she came the evening of the third day, Grandma and I saw that she'd been lucky. It was a Friday. Grandma had been so nice to us, had given Mother a loan so she could stay in town, and I got to sleep as long as I wanted in the mornings.

It was so peaceful after all the noise at Uncle's. I split big piles of sticks, and brought in dry wood that the new cow barn man chopped during his noon hour break. I was forbidden to make the fire in the fireplace, but one morning I showed Grandma that I could. Could both shove out the big damper and stack the wood. It was so nice when it burned in the big fireplace; we were still only in March.

"There is nothing worth more than a nice man, Mia. I didn't understand that—to appreciate the old one; you never learn anything about life until it's too late," Grandma would say as she gazed at the leaping flames. She sat in bed until the wood burned down. Then she crawled out of bed and put the coffee pot on the coals.

"Next week I get to start at Brück's only because I've been there before," Mother told us. "But I'll have an old-fashioned machine, so I won't be earning much. I went to Drag's and Waren's and Bruket Holmen, but to get any work there was impossible. I'm not happy about working at Brück's, for Alma, that *he* had a baby with, has started there again. There's a spinner's place free at Kopparhammarn, but there, of course, is the 'well-off' foreman of the cotton mill, so I don't want to go there. I haven't done any harm to Alma; he wouldn't let me keep her baby at my place. So I think I'll begin at Brück's on Monday."

Chapter 24

The March sun melted the drifts at Vilbergen, and April came in
with wild bloodroot and hepatica.

I should have begun school, but every time Mother came home
from work she said, "We'll wait a bit. Maybe I can get enough
together for a dress and a pair of shoes." Or, "Maybe I can find a
place for us. It's a trouble here for Grandma. You need to help her
now as long as we live here; she shouldn't be getting you ready for
school every morning."

Then Grandma used to look at me in a special way. I knew well
enough what she thought, that I didn't help at all. I was out the
whole day with the kids from the town's outskirts, but Grandma
never told on me though I was well on my way to becoming wild. I
knew the complicated slang that was used in the factory quarters,
and I used it with Grandma, but I didn't dare to when I talked to
Mother. My apron was often torn and dirty. My head began to itch
again.

Mother came home one night a week on Saturday. The other
nights she stayed in town with a friend. As soon as she came in the
door, she lay on Grandma's sofa and only complained. She was so
pale, her body always so cold; I felt that was awful, for we slept
together the nights she was home.

One night she got up, lighted the lamp, and hauled me out of bed.
It had crawled onto her, she said. She pulled off my linen; there
were clothing lice in it. It had been a long time since I'd got clean
underwear. Grandma couldn't manage the wash, and then sometimes I was in strange homes.

In places outside the tollgates not far from Old Island Road,
whole families slept on the floor. Not a bed, a table, or a chair were
to be found in their shacks which were roofed with tin. You saw the
tin from inside the room, there was no inner ceiling. The people ate

261

their food from tin plates made from old cans of candy. The potatoes were cooked in a hole in the ground just outside the house; there was no stove inside. They ate potatoes with the peels on, but it had been a long time since small things like that had been a sensation for me.

"They're gypsies," Grandma said; when the children came one day asking for me, she recognized them.

"God help us, were you planning to take that package with you to their place? Understand now, you're not to play with them." She drove the kids away.

But I still played with them. They were fun to be with, and their home life was of highest interest to me. If only they didn't have so many lice. An old man, their grandfather, could play the fiddle. I never saw the kids' father; he was said to be in jail.

Now Mother began her fight with the lice. I knew, of course, nothing, and didn't care about this fuss any longer. I had such interesting days. While Mother searched for a clean undershirt, I stood there, sleepy and shivering. Nothing could be found. She pulled one of the old dead man's shirts over me.

"What are you doing?" Grandma called sleepily.

"The kid's got lice in her clothes."

"*Ja,* then we'll wash and get rid of them. A few lice aren't surely so dangerous," Grandma said crossly. She took that as a criticism of herself when Mother started taking me over like this. It was Grandma who should be looking after me.

"I didn't mean to disturb you, Grandma," Mother said tactfully.

The next day I wore no vest. Grandma didn't know that. I just put the underbodice* on my bare body, pulled on my dress, slipped on my shoes without stockings, for it was the end of April, and ran off without drinking coffee. Grandma wasn't afraid to give children a drop of coffee in the mornings. It was only Mother who had been brought up that way, but why she still thought so I couldn't make out, sick as she always was.

This day I would be going on an entirely special adventure. I had become friends with a girl from the Masonic Lodge's Children's Home. There the children were dressed like those in the forest cottage at Kolmården. They had come in a line one day, two by two, in blue-striped dresses, on their way from school right where some

---

*A half-vest with buttons for underpants, underskirts, and stockings.

other wild kids and I got together and played. I thought one of the girls in the procession was the light-haired one from the cottage.

I ran to the line and greeted her, but she didn't know me. I was mistaken. I trailed after them anyway right to the gate of the children's home, and the girl was attracted to me, for she asked me to wait a bit at the gate.

I waited for a long time, and finally she came sneaking along, looking scared. She showed me a hole in the fence, and I crawled into the children's home garden. It was early in the spring, so nothing was green, but in a plot were some rows of tall plants with sharp, pointed leaves that rustled in the wind, plants I had never seen before.

"What are they?" I asked.

"Those are raisin trees," the girl said without the least hesitation.

"Where are the raisins though?"

"They're in the ground; they grow like potatoes."

I blindly believed her. "Let's pull up some," I said.

"Are you crazy? They won't be ready for many years, and if anyone saw us, we'd go to jail."

I believed everything she said except that it would take so long before the raisins became ready. You could at least look at them. But she ran off and said that she'd tell the teacher if I tried to dig for raisins. I didn't dare to stay but crawled out again. I waited again a long time outside the gate but at last had to go. The girl didn't show up any more.

Now two other kids, who used the tin can tops for plates, and I were going to try and get hold of the raisins. I was to go home with them first. I trotted along. The way was long, but I knew a shortcut, so I didn't need to go through town but had only to follow the promenade to the tollgates where the kids lived in their ramshackle house with no stove.

I came to the circus grounds and Old Island Road. The calf-weighing station had been there for two years. The circus grounds looked desolate. Something began to stir in me. I forgot the raisins in the Freemason's garden, forgot the kids. I sat on the bridge that went over the stream to the circus. When I had sat there a while, I crawled under the bridge. I didn't find any money this time. But the desire to steal raisins from Jerusalem artichokes' winter-sharp, rustling stalks had fled. For of course it was artichokes that grew there in the Freemason's garden.

Now a farmer came who for two years had stopped to weigh his calf; he opened the gate, let down the gangplank, pulled the calf by the tail, dragged it back again by the ears, locked up, and drove away. The calf bawled with fear now as then.

I sat there on the bridge, dirty, irresolute, free as a bird, freer than anyone, but still so apprehensive. It was something, something heavy and dangerous, although it had been two years since I'd bought the hard candies for Mother's only five öre. I sat there without underclothes, lice crawled in my head, no one knew where I was, no one much cared.

Suddenly I remembered Olga's baby and began to cry. Remembered more—the dead old man, the beautiful room at Old Island Road. I cried so much I got hiccups. My doll sat there by herself in the commode at Hagby. An old man played the fiddle among rubbish and lice, they ate on tops of tin cans, and Mother found the lice at night. Everything was hopeless. Never again would things be right. Grandma was alone at home, never tattled on me to Mother but neither was she nice to me as she'd been before.

And Mother, who was only sick. No money did she earn either. My stepfather earned money now, but would never give Mother any. Guys in town never wanted to give their wives any money. We should have stayed on the plain with Olga; there Mother got all the money from my stepfather. I began to cry afresh.

I wasn't going to school either. All the kids except the gypsies' went to school. I cried loudly. Memories had tumbled around me just as they can with a grown-up, and when I was through crying, I trailed along home, sorrowful and angry, without a thought of visiting the shack where they cooked food in a hole in the ground. They ought to take care of things so they were clean, those kids there.

For myself I decided to begin a new life now. I picked some coltsfoot on the way. I should have something for Grandma. Now at the end of April there wasn't even as much as a nettle by the privy to be found at Vilbergen. The old flower women had stripped away everything. Some of Grandma's lilac buds just ready to burst open had already been stolen. That made Grandma sad.

"Now that they've broken the leafy stems, there will be no clusters of blooms," Grandma said.

The store of memories that the bridge stirred up had softened me so that I was ready to steal some hothouse plants set in the borders of the promenade. They would really blaze among the coltsfoot and cheer Grandma up. It isn't so seldom that anger drives you to new crimes. But I never got the opportunity to raid the bright flowers. People hastened along in front of me.

Suddenly I heard a shrill, penetrating music coming from a yard beside the promenade. I stopped, enchanted. It sounded like a mating call from a strange land. Never had I heard anything like it. I trotted into the splendid yard. Only rich people lived in houses on the promenade.

On the stone path stood a man in a top hat, carrying a big sack on his back. He looked like a strolling player. He blew a long drawn-out sorrowful melody, walking back and forth in the yard while he played. A tin cup was next to him, and people came and put money in the cup, but he pretended not to notice, just walked to and fro playing his enticing melody that made my legs weak. I stayed until he finished. Then I followed him from yard to yard. He played the same haunting melody in all the yards. At last I could sing it.

Although he didn't say a word to me, I trudged persistently beside him as he played. He didn't look at me, but people who put money in his cup saw me. That was what I longed for. I wanted them to see what a strange person I was, that I was a friend of this man who could play so beautifully from an old sack.

When I had got nearer I had discovered that the long mouthpiece he blew in was fastened to a sack. There was a row of fringe around the bottom of the balloon-like sack.

I had forgotten Grandma. The coltsfoot had wilted and I had thrown them away. From yard to yard all along the long promenade, I followed the man with his curious sack. At last he noticed me but he didn't look happy. He said nothing at all, but didn't forbid me either to follow him. Every time he played the melody, I was overcome all over again. I was so hungry that I felt faint, but I couldn't tear myself from the strange music. In one yard someone threw money from a window. The man didn't look but I went after the coin and put it in the cup.

"Is that your girl?" asked a trim young woman in that yard. The man didn't understand. Then the woman pointed to me and to him. He shook his head and looked angry. He was ashamed of me. I was so dirty and shabbily dressed.

"Are you a foreigner?" the young woman asked.

The man muttered something in a strange language. He was a foreigner, but the young woman who hadn't understood his answer stood there wanting him to say in Norrköping dialect if he was foreign.

When we left that yard, the man shook his fist at me, saying a long string of words and looking dangerous.

Now a streak of the cunning of children or maybe a tendency for the dramatic incited me. I put my hands before my eyes and curtseyed, curtseyed as humbly as I could, looked at him through my outspread fingers, and curtseyed again. I had to get him to understand me in some way since he didn't know our language.

He looked very puzzled, but I didn't take my hands from my eyes. It was fun to stand there and make a foreign music man puzzled.

He looked at my thin bare legs, blue with cold, in coarse boots. (Stamp-Kalle didn't exactly have kid leather shoes for sale.) A ragged braid, dirt-streaked face, a dress full of stains and rips, an eight-year-old kid, a bit short and very shabby, who stood with her hands over her eyes and just curtseyed. He couldn't understand it.

He turned his back on me. The fringe on the bagpipes swayed. I followed him to the next yard.

Just as he played that fascinating melody again, and I began to walk back and forth beside him, someone put her head out a window and yelled, "Aren't you Hedvig's girl? Aren't you Mia?" I recognized the voice though I hardly heard the words, for the melody overpowered them. It was the worst of the "well-off" ones. It was the seamstress who thought it was terrible that Albert had to take care of another man's child.

I fled from the yard. The sun was high in the sky; it must be noon already. I felt it, for I was so hungry.

Grandma was washing vests and an apron for me. But Mother had forbidden Grandma to wash! She rubbed the piece so clumsily with her crippled hands. She had on her glasses.

She was standing by the lilac bush. I saw her nose run, drop after drop. I stood a long time, looking at her.

She moved a little, muttering to herself. Then she caught sight of me. She had been crying. It was for my sake she cried.

"I have to tell Hedvig about this. I can't be responsible any longer. You've run away every day for nearly a month now. You can become a thief doing like that."

Grandma didn't tell about me to Mother. We had a serious talk, Grandma and I, and I promised never to run away again. I had already promised myself that when I was at the bridge..

But the bagpipe's melody I put words to, and Grandma hummed it.

"Where did you learn that?" she asked.

"From a foreign musician who blew in a sack," I said.

"A Scotsman," Grandma said. "A bagpipe player. *Ja,* that is beautiful. Was he an old man?"

I couldn't tell her, for I hadn't noticed. Grandma had known such a musician once, and with her trembling voice, she hummed the old melody that he had played.

One night when Mother had been sick earlier in the evening, someone banged at the door. It was April and still cold at night.

"Who is it?" Mother asked.

From the porch came a voice, "May I talk with you, Hedvig?" It was my stepfather.

At once I was wide awake. Grandma, too.

"Don't let the cad in," Grandma said aloud.

Mother was silent. He banged again.

No one answered.

"I have to talk to you, Hedvig."

Mother said nothing.

Then we heard a curious sound. It sounded like someone who has a sour stomach and keeps on belching.

Tensely we lay and listened.

Then all three of us sat up and listened.

The curious sound became more and more continuous. Sometimes it sounded as if something were stuck in his throat and then he gasped for breath. Low hissing, groaning, rustling.

"What is he doing do you think, Grandma?" Mother whispered from our bed across the room to Grandma's.

"He's crying. Let him cry. We have cried, both you and I, because of him," Grandma whispered.

He cried. My stepfather was crying.

That it should be so dark. . . . How did he look when he cried? I got so eager to see that I couldn't sit still in the bed, but Mother whispered that I should lie down. I never asked why I should lie down when Mother and Grandma sat straight as rods in their sleeveless slips and kept on listening.

The sobs became plainer. Sometimes he talked quietly to himself; sometimes he nearly howled, then muffled caws like a raven's in the winter.

Unconsciously I made a crying face in the darkness. I followed every shift in his crying from where I sat. I got more and more excited. Shouldn't they go and open?

A man crying outside a closed door in the dark. Outside in the dark. I began to sniffle, too. Finally I cried out loud, high, really loud.

"*Ja*, what a life, in the middle of the night," Mother said.

"Light the lamp, Mama," I begged.

"*Ja*, do that," Grandma said.

Outside the howling and grunting continued.

Then Mother got up, lit the lamp, and opened the door. A cold burst of wind blew in, and the flame of the light fluttered.

"Come in! And don't sit here acting crazy," Mother said harshly.

I heard him blow his nose and clear his throat and give a sob.

"Hurry up, it's cold. Come in if you're going to!"

Not for dear life would I have come in if Mother had talked to me like that when I was so sad. No thanks! I expected him to go, say something hateful. I didn't feel like myself in some way. I didn't like that he had come, but when he sat outside in the dark and cried, he who had surely never cried, well, that was something else. Then Mother shouldn't be like she was when he was mean and swore and brawled. She would see that he'd leave for sure now. Probably hit her first.

He didn't go.

"Hedvig," he said only; then he sobbed again.

"Come in, I tell you, so I can shut the door," Mother yelled.

Now I could hear that she had just pretended that she was so mad. But why should she pretend? I was so curious that I shivered.

"Come in! We'll be nice to you," I called. "Come in! It's getting so cold in here."

Then he came, stumbling on the rag rugs, taking off his cap. Mother shut the door with a bang and crawled back in bed with me. She shivered with cold so much her teeth chattered. I knew how excited she was.

My stepfather went over and sat in the corner of the fireplace. He tipped over the coffee that he hadn't seen in the dark. The light from the lamp didn't reach very far. Now he banged into the three-footed kettles. It was a terrible clanking.

"A person can hear you're home again!" Grandma's voice sounded hard and hateful.

My stepfather remained silent. His face was black as coal. His tears had made his cheeks streaky; his stubby mustache couldn't be seen for soot.

"Think that you came here," Mother said, still shaking with cold so it was hard for her to talk. She ought to have warmed up by now; our bed was so warm that I thought my cheeks were on fire.

"I've been working at the wharf for two weeks. I have a little money with me, Hedvig." He talked in such a low voice.

"*Ja*, I've been working, too. I don't think I need your money anymore."

He sighed, twisting his hands.

Mother was strange then as well; she earned such a little bit that we didn't have any money at all.

"Where is the suit you got for the funeral?" Grandma sounded completely heartless.

He didn't say anything.

This was unbearable. I had to do something. I got up. The long shirt that had belonged to the dead man trailed after me.

Mother didn't stop me from getting up. She didn't seem to notice.

"You could certainly behave yourself," I said, standing in front of my stepfather. I had Mother and others say that many times to me.

Still he didn't say anything.

"We've had it awful because of you. The farmer is going to sue you, and Uncle is going to beat you up as soon as he gets ahold of you. We were in the newspaper; did you see that? It was about how they murdered a woman at a dance at Uncle's."

"Did they dance at Janne's?" He sounded almost like himself now.

"*Ja*, but we didn't have to go to jail, for we weren't in on it. Did you read about us in the paper? It said that I'd been well brought up. The policeman said that; didn't you see that?"

"No-o," he mumbled, giving a long deep sigh.

I stepped nearer to him, getting soot on the dead one's shirt from my stepfather's trousers; I was going to put my hand in front of my mouth and whisper to him, but I couldn't because the shirt sleeves hung far down over my hands. The cuffs I'd made had rolled down. "Why did you leave us when Grandpa died?" I asked, putting my stub nose nearer his sooty, tear-stained face.

Grandma was sitting bolt upright in her bed. Mother, too, in hers. They were listening.

"I-I will never leave again, Mia." His voice broke. His sooty face was twisted.

My heart became heavy; I had nothing more to say. I went back to bed and crawled in, turning my back to Mother, who sat there not saying anything.

He would never leave again. Was that what I wanted? No, it was not. But what I wanted, I didn't know. A mean man had sat and cried in the night; one had to say something, do something. It wasn't so hard when a nice woman cried. She became happy again because she was nice, but a mean man, one that you couldn't stand, one who disgraced you, and one you'd never seen cry, that was something terrible. Then you had to do something, something you didn't want. A hard, mean face twisted with crying and anguish was just as terrible as a gentle face twisted with meanness and hate. Something had to be done.

Mother got up, but I didn't care about that. For it was clear he would be staying now.

On Grandma's old sofa bed there were no acorns. The back was smooth, nothing to count to get your head cleared or to go numb. It felt like sand in my eyes.

Mother and my stepfather talked low, the same things over and over. Grandma put in a word now and then. I didn't care about listening. Stubbornly I kept my back turned on them, tried to edge nearer the back of the sofa, tried to become as quiet as a back, a strong back, something without eyes and ears.

Why were grown-ups like this? Why did they torture themselves and others? Why did they say they loved each other, gave each other gifts, hugged each other after they'd hit each other and quarreled and fought? They were just like us children. We fought and quarreled and were the same to each other. Would it be like that all your life? Would you be friends and then fight and quarrel?

Why did you love someone? Mother loved my stepfather, but not a friendly word did he get when he sat there crying in the night. The grown-ups certainly didn't love each other at the same time. When one of them loved, the other one hated, and when the other one's hate had gone, then the other one was ready for the dark times.

Mother came over and pulled away a pillow from our sofa bed. "Sleep a little now, Mia."

Ja, well, she'd be sleeping with him. I sat up still with my back to Mother. Lay back down without looking at her. And she took no notice of me.

Then I heard water splashing. He was washing himself.

270

"Heavens, have you shaved off your mustache?" I heard Mother say. She seemed to be mocking him a little.

Then I turned around in spite of myself. *Ja*, he was smooth-shaven, and I thought he looked meaner without the mustache. After he'd washed off the soot, it could be seen how thin and yellow he looked.

"Don't take good quilts. I'm still not free of lice; it was so full of lice in the barracks where I've been," he said.

That gave me a start. Who dragged home lice if it wasn't me? I had been in the company of bad folks as well. *Liked* bad folks, though Grandma had warned me. And my stepfather was careful, mentioning the lice right out; I hadn't done that. It made it so bitter. To be like him in that. To be worse now and then.

I was no more forgivingly disposed. He who already has fallen knows nothing more reassuring than when saints begin to fall down to his level. Then there are fewer to judge. But the saints! Even down in hell they try to blame the one who sinned first. I wasn't a bit different from other saints.

Then I saw five ten-kronor notes lying on the table. I could count them, for each lay by itself.

So, now everything was settled. He had cried, had given Mother big money, and now at the end, had been afraid for the bedding's sake, just lying down on the floor in front of the fireplace without undressing with only a pillow for his head.

He had hopelessly got the better of me.

Then Mother blew out the lamp and got in bed with me.

I brooded no longer and slept. But my back was turned away from Mother.

Next morning when I woke up, both Mother and my stepfather were gone. Mother was at the factory. At night she came home, tired and sick, just as before. I didn't see my stepfather for a long time.

Mother and Grandma talked endlessly about it.

"It's best just to say he's sitting in jail, best you say that, Grandma, if they ask, for I've told them that at the factory," Mother said one night when she forgot to see if I was still awake.

"*Ja*, that had better do. That'll work since the farmer had him summoned."

"That will be an eight-day fine, and he can take those days in the winter time; that won't concern anyone," Mother said.

I got the impression that my stepfather was at a hospital and that it should be kept secret. I understood then what it was. I had heard talk about such things. But Mother and Grandma talked so solemnly about the jail, that he was sitting there because he'd left his work place, that I forgot myself one day and said to Grandma that he'd have to sit out his fine in jail in the winter; now he was in the hospital.

Children often wander on the edge of a precipice without thinking about it. In those "educated" circles such a careless child was called a terrible child. Then it is frequently an observation the child happens to make in a stranger's presence about her father kissing a young girl or her mother who let herself be kissed by a "strange uncle." Now I had become a terrible child in an uneducated circle, and for the first time since I knew Grandma was she angry with me.

"Are you going there listening and black-listing?" she asked, her hands trembling. "I thought better of you, Mia. I thought you had sense, and if you understood how something was, then you shouldn't have said it. You knew well enough that Hedvig and I didn't want that to get out. Are you a squealer, Mia? I wouldn't have thought it of you. You should learn to keep your mouth shut if you're to get on in the world. I learned that *before* I was as old as you."

I was utterly crushed. I knew every word Grandma said was right. And I learned to keep things to myself, I think, for my whole life after that day when Grandma blistered me with her tongue for my loose talk.

"Sickness is sickness, but folks are one and all wretches. They've all been sick, but they don't talk about that. Albert is in the hospital; he has to be there to get well, but folks don't need to meddle in that. Now that you know, see that you watch yourself after this."

I had heard tales about there being a "shameful" sickness. In the old history book my stepfather had kept after his schooldays, it had told about a king who died from "a shameful sickness."

Any clearer understanding of this secret sickness I wouldn't get. I though it was shameful in the same way that it was shameful to be poor, dirty, and full of lice. "He died from lice sickness," the red-haired woman had said.

Now my stepfather had got a king's sickness. That I understood and I would certainly shut up about it; Grandma could calm herself about that.

Grandma was serious and reserved with me for several days.

Grandma was more at home with town ways than Mother. She put an ad in *Norrköping News:* "A big single room." I read the ad over and over and cut it out. Think, we wrote for the newspaper.

When my stepfather got well, we would rent a room, for he had been promised he could begin work at Vulcan's junkyard in September.

"That's a piece of luck," Grandma said. "I don't know how the fellow had such luck."

A new word was going around. A word that awakened the same uncertainty and fear as the words "out of work." The new word was "strike."

It hadn't been used much before. Now this summer there would be a strike at the paper mill.

Grandma read in *Norrköping Newspaper,* which Mother bought and took home, how shameful the workers were. What tramps they followed who got paid to stir them up. At a paper mill outside town the factory houses were so bad that the mill hands wouldn't work until they were repaired. They had jammed the big machines with blocks and logs. Right away the newspaper wrote that the workers wanted to get more pay than engineers. But there was manpower still to be found. Boil tar and shoot and mutilate anyone could learn to do. A district judge wrote that. Grandma knew him; she had done weaving for his wife.

"He can hardly put his clothes on by himself. I'd like to see him in a tar boiler," Grandma laughed.

"If anyone needs to strike, we should at Brück's. This week I've earned six kronor; I get such bad yarn I've had to stand and fix it day after day," Mother said in a serious tone.

"Dear Hedvig, don't think of such a thing," Grandma said.

One Saturday at the end of July, my mother, my stepfather, and I went along Broad Street in Norrköping. We had bought a whole lot of things at Stamp-Kalle's and were on our way to our new room that we had got from the ad Grandma had sent in. Grandma herself was going to try the mineral waters in Söderköping once more. She'd be away for two months.

"It's my money that she got from the Captain; the old lady's confused about that," my stepfather said.

"Oh, that's long been used up; don't talk foolishly," Mother said.

The papers were full of the strike at the paper mill.

"I have my book," my stepfather said, and right in the road he took out a little red book and showed it to Mother.

I knew that was a very important book.

"I have my book. They can't do anything to me."

A book, an important book that could protect people. My stepfather was getting more and more different, I thought. He wasn't at all like the person I'd thought so meanly about. He was more free and easy than Mother. And here he was walking with a curious book.

"*Ja,* don't you hang out just anyplace now where they're on strike. That won't do, at least not until you've started at Vulcan's," Mother said threateningly.

"Do you think I'm crazy? I have my book."

It was a member's book of the longshoremen's union. The first union book I ever saw.

Outside the gate there was a small gathering of people. An older couple had got into a squabble.

We had to hurry, for we had to go to Uncle's and pack. Mother had quit the factory; my stepfather was also free. He had come the night before.

It was a warm day. Mother had begun to be fat again. It was the first time I'd seen my stepfather walk with Mother in town when she looked that way.

We were really spiffed up. Mother and I had new cotton dresses and blue canvas shoes. At that time they were the cheapest shoes. My stepfather had new moleskin trousers and a new striped shirt. He had bought a big hat that made him look different. All the dock workers wore these modern wide-brimmed hats.

We walked nearer the group of people. As we drew closer, they became more distinct. A man broke out of the group and went toward a woman, yelling, "You bought only five öre of soap for my shirts, you bitch!" He was drunk. His hat was on the back of his head and was ready to fall off as he danced around the woman and spit.

"That's Accordion Sven," my stepfather said. Mother recognized the enraged man, too; he used to play his accordion at cafes on Saturdays and Sundays.

"She got ten öre for soap to wash my shirts and she bought only five öre," he said, appealing to the curious group who stood there with gaping mouths. "She bought a newspaper instead. Is that the kind of old woman to have? Such a lying devil. Can shirts get clean with just five öre of soap? She doesn't give a damn."

He talked sometimes to the people around him and then to his wife who stood there looking ashamed and angry with a newspaper folded over some packages in her basket.

"One like that tricks you in everything, begs for ten öre for soap and then buys only five öre." He was now at the stage of being ready to cry over anything that happened.

The woman suddenly left without him seeing her.

He was still standing there trying to win over the grinning onlookers after we were on our way.

Nearly the whole way to our new room that I still hadn't seen Mother and my stepfather argued whether or not the housewife was right to squander five öre for a newspaper. My stepfather held that it was not right to buy less soap for the shirts than she'd said she'd need, that she'd lied, and had thrown away good money on a newspaper. "If they get away with that, they'll get away with something else," my stepfather said firmly.

"Ja, that's it exactly, that's it," Mother said scornfully, looking stubborn and ominous.

I felt that they were on dangerous ground. I thought that my stepfather was talking idiotically to Mother, for here he was jabbering about falsehood and it concerned only five öre. Shouldn't a woman have the right to buy a newspaper for five öre? Couldn't they stop talking about Accordion Sven's everlasting soap?

At last they were silent, both thinking their own thoughts until we finally got to our place.

"A clean room," my stepfather said.

"It costs six kronor a month," Mother said.

"Ja, it will work out now when I'll get such good pay."

"Ja, if only you get that work."

Mother sounded doubtful; it was probably that quarrel about the soap that still rankled her.

"Hey, I've been promised it. Otherwise I've got the book here, and can work at the docks as soon as there's an opening."

Mother brightened a little and began inspecting the place.

For the first time a bit of modern luxury came into my life. By the stove there was a sink of polished zinc, a blue painted cupboard made from particle board under it. None of the people we knew had anything so nice, not Aunt, nor Grandma, not even the "well-off" had such a thing. Only in the houses Mother had worked in had I seen a sink in the kitchen. The walls were also panelled and painted blue. We had rented a kitchen. A stove had been put in the room that belonged to the kitchen, and had been rented as a single room. In that part of town, you didn't have a room plus a kitchen. Folks wouldn't have had enough for rent.

Here would be my home for the rest of my life I decided. A sink and everything.

I had learned nothing, forgotten nothing. The ones who decided things were the grown-ups and the sensible.

The moving was set for the following day.

"Next week we'll enroll you in school again; it's about time," Mother said.

"*Ja,* it won't do for her to go on like this; she has to go to school," my stepfather said.

We were on our way to Uncle's to pack.

Hanna! Olga! Never did envy rise against you in my mind. If you had come with the world's finest Dalarna bag and a diadem on your head, my eyes would only have rejoiced had I been dressed in a tattered sack.

My first love, my teacher, I never saw again. And never again the man in Kolmården's cottage.

Hanna and Olga. In life's gray shadows they went away.

Olga—a young woman with red raw lips, that poverty's grayness made immeasurably humble, who stood there and curtseyed for the diapers she got for her baby—Hanna—Olga.

Next week I'd be enrolled in school. For the third time.

I was nine years old on All Saints' Day.

Afterword

In her 1956 Foreword to a new edition of her fourth novel, *My Mother Gets Married,* published in 1936, Moa Martinson, out of love and deference for her mother, writes that the main character in the book is her mother. Strong as Martinson makes the characterization of Hedvig, her mother, it is clearly Martinson's own self-portrait, Mia, who is the central character in this first volume of her autobiographical trilogy. All of the experiences in the novel are described through Mia's eyes, and only she reflects upon these experiences that occur in two years of her life. She is nearly seven when the novel begins and nine when it ends. The action takes place in Norrköping, an industrial city in Sweden, and in factory suburbs and on farms surrounding it, just before the turn of the century. *Church Wedding,* the second novel of the trilogy, chronicles Mia's next five years in the same setting. The novel ends with Mia's letter to a former schoolmate who has emigrated to America; Mia turns down Lasse's offer of marriage. The last novel, *The King's Roses,* like the first, covers two years in Mia's life. From fifteen to seventeen, Mia has been a children's maid in a neighboring parish, a waitress in a large restaurant in Norrköping, and for a brief time, a student waitress in Stockholm. At the end of the trilogy, Martinson provides a tantalizing glimpse of Mia ten years later. Twenty-seven years old, Mia is married to a shiftless drunkard; she is striving to take care of her children; and in her home south of Stockholm, she is holding meetings for farm workers to better their living and working conditions.[1]

My Mother Gets Married, like *Church Wedding* and *The King's Roses,* encompasses a narrow world, but it is one that gives the illusion of roominess because it is shaped by an oral tradition that blends fairy tale and folklore with realistic events and detail. The stories that Martinson relates through her persona (Mia) grow out of the child's quest for adventure, and for knowledge that will enable her to understand a harsh reality, one filled with all the dreadful adjuncts of poverty: hunger, cruelty, disease, dirt, ignorance, superstition, violence, often early death. These are like the mythical monsters of the fairy tale that the child must deal with in order to bring some kind of order out of confusion, to rejoice over small victories, and to keep dignity with a plucky response.

My Mother Gets Married is artistically Moa Martinson's best book. Because it is told solely from Mia's point of view, the novel not only has a consistent psychological position, but also a tightly knit structure that admits little of the didactic interpolation that jars the modern reader in Martinson's first novel, *Women and Appletrees.* Except for the leading characters, the rest are emblematic. Martinson skillfully uses this device of folklore to widen her perspective. Thus, characterizations of people, such as "the red-haired woman," "the neighbor with her peaked cap," "the landlady" of the "sugar-syrup house," "the farmer," and "Aunt" universalize them and their experiences.

The day after Mia's mother, Hedvig, has married and has rescued Mia from "Aunt's" wretched, noisy home, the mother and the child are alone together for the first time since Mia was born. The blissful, peaceful time lasts only for an afternoon. They are in their first home on Old Island Road, a clean room with new rag rugs and blue-starched curtains. Mia sees her mother as a lovely, slender woman who can magically make a room reflect her beauty, but who also has a mysterious, incomprehensible attachment, now seemingly forever fixed, to a shiftless, vain, reputedly handsome philanderer, Albert Stenman, Hedvig's new husband and stepfather to Mia. "I could never stand my stepfather, mainly because he felt he owned my mother, and so he was mean to her, beat her, and then she had other kids that he was the rightful father of so I couldn't stand them either. When they died, for none of them lived a year, I cried in despair, because I didn't like them" (p. 4).

Stenman is "he," a dragon spewing anger, brandy, and snuff, emblematic of everything Mia detests and is powerless against. "He" brings degradation—airless, dirty rooms infested with rats and lice. His shiftlessness causes loss of friends—Mia's curly-haired teacher, her cherished Hanna and Olga. His fecklessness nourishes the insidious separateness and cruelty that the haves inflict on the have-nots. Worst of all, the sexually innocent Mia dimly perceives that he makes her beautiful, slender mother fat, ugly, and sick;

278

when her mother is pregnant, she changes into a coarse, indifferent woman who vomits by the side of the road, lets herself and Mia become shabby, and Mia's thick blonde hair get dirty, tousled, infected with lice. Mia is ashamed of her mother at those times, but she clearly perceives Hedvig's torment. "I had seen her cry many times, but just this one time came to me now. She had sat at the table, her head on her arms, the little hairs on her neck straggled down, her bun of hair had fallen to the side, and when she lifted up her face to me, for she had heard me come in, it was so strangely twisted with anguish that I screamed" (p. 29). Mia feels despair for her mother's anguish and her own jealous betrayal of love.

Central to Mia's story are the tales that she hears. Lying in her acorn-trimmed bed, supposedly asleep, Mia overhears her grandma tell of the grandma's older sister's beating long ago which led to the girl's suicide. As Mia listens, she whispers details of the beating to her doll, weaving the strands of her horror and fascination with those of the old woman's tale showing the vicious ignorance, false piety, and relentless power of male authority. Martinson makes the episode symbolize the shocking brutality against women.

Some of the stories that Mia relates hold for her and her readers the spell of a fairy tale. One is a winter journey that Mia makes from the treeless plain where she is then living, to the forest home of a shoemaker and his large family. The shoemaker's house is a crooked shed whose corner posts are four flourishing fir trees; it is roofed with branches of fir. The shoemaker is like a benevolent king, handsome and tall, whose fortune is love of life, family, and books. Mia is enchanted. As she listens to him read *Pilgrim's Progress,* her imagination is caught by Bunyan's magical web of words as she, herself, spins one of her own. A recent Martinson critic has written that "Mia's account of her day in the shoemaker's croft has the haunting quality of a good fairy tale, realistic detail combining with an overall tone of mystery as she depicts people who for all their physical poverty, appear as mighty as the living forest from which they spring."[2]

In *My Mother Gets Married,* the force of the women characters "burns" like a fire: "it burns so clear, it burns in a thousand rings" (p. viii). The metaphor serves to illustrate the energy of the relationships between women in the novel. Central to the story is the one, of course, between Mia and her mother, Hedvig. In the close attachment that Mia has for Grandma, each protects the other from censure or ridicule. One compelling way that Martinson conveys without sentimentality Mia's love for her grandma is through the child's sensitive perception of the old woman's crippled hands which tremble when she is distressed. Martinson poignantly uses the image of Grandma's hands again to stress the caring relationship Hedvig, as well as Mia, has with Grandma when Hedvig tells Grandma of her husband's—"the old one's" death. Mia sees "Grandma's gnarled hand on Mother's shoulder. It looked so terribly old against Mother's young white arm. I felt so sorry for that old hand. I thought it was something that could never be cured or made amends for when I saw that crippled hand against Mother's white flesh, and the black, thin hair against Mother's thick golden braid that hung over her shoulder" (p. 213). Fully and vigorously realized are the relationships between Hedvig and "Aunt," her sister, between Hedvig and her neighbor, Olga, and between Mia and her friend, Hanna.

Ten years older than Hedvig, her sister, called only "Moster," (Swedish for Mia's maternal aunt), is married to Janne, a teamster. They have seven sons. Though both sisters have faithless husbands who beat them, they seldom talk about their hard lives when they are together; they reminisce about their childhood on the marsh in west Kolmården and their other sisters, Charlotte and Hilda. Cherry trees in full bloom surrounding old gray cottages on green hills make an Easter the sisters never forget; the family has sent them to the funeral of a young cousin in Ulricka parish.[3] Just as Hedvig and "Aunt" seek respite in memories together, so do they share their bits of bread and horse's oat cakes with each other and their children when both sisters are pregnant and neither has any money nor hardly any hope.

An even closer bond that that of family is the one between Hedvig and Olga. Living in separate rooms in desolate quarters for hired men on the flat, treeless land they and their husbands work, Hedvig and Olga break the cruel, hard ring of isolation each feels. Hedvig, newly bereaved of her infant, helps eighteen-year-old Olga with her baby son. Gently she teaches Olga how to make herself and her dirty room clean and pretty. Each woman has a husband who drinks and is insanely jealous. Hedvig loves Olga as a friend who needs her as much as she needs Olga. And Olga respects and adores her older, wiser friend. Knowing Karlberg, Olga's husband, will kill Olga if he finds out that "the farmer," the owner of the farm, has been in to see her several days after Christmas, Hedvig has

Mia lie. Karlberg believes Mia when she tells him the farmer did not go in to Olga's.

Mia loves Olga as a sympathetic, jolly older sister who understands Mia's isolation on the farm. She comforts her when Mia's two apples—symbol of Mia's loneliness on that bare wintry plain—fall in the night, and she can't find them: "Apples on that tree won't do to eat; they're green fruit, and those that hung on like that fell because they were rotten. If you look, you'll see their cores. They fell now because it's so cold. But at the farmer's there's a whole barrel of apples they share at Christmas at the farm party, so you'll get an apple at Christmas. . . . I'd like for Mia to go with me on Sunday . . . to Karlberg's brother who lives up at Kolmården. They have a lot of kids, so she'll have more than enough playmates that day" (p. 157–158). Mia describes her friend and her joy:

I had stopped crying. I thought Olga was the sun itself just now, although she was having one of her messy days when she had neither combed her hair nor washed, and her bodice was nearly black with dirt. She had on a skirt, but above it she was almost naked, for the dirty bodice was cut low and had ragged short sleeves. It was a wonder she wasn't frozen. She had no stockings on, going slipshod just in clogs. Her long braid hung on her back just like the first time I saw her. Her face was pale yellow, for the baby had really grown, sucking at her breasts night and day. But her big lips shone blood red. She looked as if she had a sickness of the lips; they looked swollen and raw. It was as if all the blood in her thin body had risen to her lips. Full, sensitive lips that shone red and sore from dreadful, secret questions (p. 158).[4]

For Mia, Hanna, her first friend, is circumscribed by mystery. What is the love that Mia has for Hanna, the tiny, frail child dressed in old women's outmoded, cast-off clothing, who lives in the poorhouse where she is sexually abused, whose mother is Broom-Mina (who has children by several men), and whose father is Mia's stepfather? Mia is Hanna's avenging angel. To Mia, Hanna is a "beautiful little old troll without wrinkles." "Little Hanna. Never had I forgotten you. You came into my heart, which was blooming with unselfish love . . . [Hanna's] hair was nearly white and so tightly braided that a little tail stuck straight out from her neck. Her face gleamed white as a flower the sun shines on, a flower that soon will be cut. Her face shone with light, a thin little face" (p. 30). The friendship between Mia and Hanna reveals Moa Martinson's range in developing unforgettable characters in *My Mother Gets Married* and in her other novels. Beginning with *Women and Appletrees,* Martinson went on to write fourteen more novels, three volumes of short stories, one of essays, and one of poems. In all of her writing, she tried to show with realistic detail, evocative imagery, wry understatement, and sometimes bitter irony the desperate struggles of the working class, especially those of women. She never left her working-class roots.

Moa Martinson was born Helga Maria Swartz to an unmarried factory worker on November 2, 1890, in Norrköping, Sweden. Her father was a soldier, and it was then unthinkable that a member of the upper class would marry beneath him.[5] Moa lived in foster homes near the textile factory where her mother worked. After her mother's marriage, Moa, like Mia, lived in a number of places. In 1910, having worked as a maid, a waitress, and a buffet manager, Moa married Karl Johansson, a farm worker, who owned a little house between Ösmo and Sorunda, small towns south of Stockholm. Moa lived here the rest of her life. Johansson, a drunkard, made life hard and lonely for Moa. In 1928, he committed suicide. Of the five sons they had, the two youngest drowned in a lake near the cottage. In an interpolated comment growing out of Mia's experience of her grandfather's death in *My Mother Gets Married,* Moa refers to her terrible grief:

> Every contour of the old man could be seen under the sheet. A little old man. When he was alive, he was bent. Now he lay very straight and stiff. Bone after bone stood out all the way up to the nose which made a scary elevation in the sheet.
>
> "He looks so like himself," Grandma said, lifting a corner of the sheet from the old man's face.
>
> No, no, he didn't. This wasn't the old man I'd seen, who sometimes gave me several öre, lying there. This was *no one* who lay there. Nothing I had seen or dreamed about. This blue face with gray stubby beard, the terrifying skin, these bones on a bench. I shook. It was like an omen of all pain.
>
> It became an omen. Twenty years later the light of my understanding was almost put out by a bed of that kind. A platform of makeshift boards and on it two unmoving figures. Everything as unexpected, unprepared for as twenty

years before when Grandma lifted the edge of the sheet
from the dead one's face (p. 235).

To make a living, Moa began writing articles for socialist
newspapers and for the radical feminist weekly, *Tidevarvet* (*The Epoch*),
urging better salaries and housing. Because of these articles and the
help of leading feminists, such as the novelist Elin Wägner, Moa
attended a woman's school at Fogelstad where she began work on
her novel, *Women and Appletrees*. Besides her writing, Moa organized
the farm workers to improve their living and working conditions,
holding the meetings in her cottage. In addition to forming study
circles, Moa helped to establish a library for her parish neighborhood. Like Mia, she was almost wholly self-educated.

In 1927, Moa changed her pen name from "Helga" to Moa after
Johannes V. Jensen's heroine in *Jökeln, (The Glacier)*, a woman who
"gives birth, plants seeds, gathers crops, holds everything together."[6]

Moa married the novelist and poet Harry Martinson in 1929,
supporting and helping him in his writing. While he and other well-
known Swedish writers left their working-class background, Moa
Martinson never left hers, "the domain where I felt at home. Poor
people's still not mapped-out domain."[7] Harry Martinson divorced
Moa in 1940.

From this time until her death in 1964, Moa became well known
to a much larger public in Sweden, continuing to write and to give
controversial radio talks and speeches. She became Sweden's
"public person, an institution, loved and hated—and always only
Moa."[8] In her anthology *Everyday Chores and the Language of Dreams
(Vardagsslit och drommars språk)*, Ebba Witt-Brattström writes, "It is not
difficult to imagine what impression Moa made as she threw one
controversial opinion after the other to the crowd from the podium.
They echoed through the press for a long time: on mental hygiene
(women should get out into the labor market), on spanking children
("you don't smack lilies and roses to make them smell better") . . . "[9]
She directed her anger with biting wit toward a society that
permitted or seemed to ignore poverty, child abuse, and the danger
of atomic war. Although Moa said herself that she had "nothing to
do with the official communism in Sweden," she praised Russia
during the Cold War as the "ideal" society, insisting after the Soviet
takeover of Hungary in 1956, there was a "difference between
Russia's power politics and the communist ideology," but firmly

283

believing that she belonged to the "world's proletariat class, the gifts that I have I will always put to its service."[10]

Moa charmed most of her large audience. To her cottage, which she ironically called "Moa's castle" ("Moas slott"), came writers, artists, actors, opera singers, farm and factory workers, and political figures. She wrote and received many letters, among them ones from the distinguished Danish writer, Martin Anderson Nexö, who admired her work; Elise Ottensen-Jensen, the feminist journalist who first helped Moa to publish in *Fire;* Marika Stiernstedt, writer and chair of Sweden's Writers Union, whose favorable study of Moa's novels appeared in the prestigious *Bonniers Literary Magazine* in 1946; the actor, Karl Gerhard; Prince Wilhelm of Sweden; and Tage Erlander, Sweden's Prime Minister and Chairman of the Social Democratic Party from 1946 to 1968.[11]

Sweden's literary critics, however, mainly dismissed her novels as limited and undisciplined. Even those who grudgingly admitted that her novels were interestingly realistic felt that they were relatively unimportant. This attitude has changed considerably. "She will become one of the classics," predicts Ebba Witt-Brattström"[12] She and other leading Swedish critics, such as Maria Bergom-Larsson, Barbro Backberger, Eva Swedenmark, and Helena Forsas-Scott have written perceptively and admiringly of her work. Forsas-Scott believes that the "serious exploration of her fiction has only just begun."[13] Her response to Moa Martinson's work is picked up and reinforced by Witt-Brattström: "I read everything by Moa and I thought it was so incredibly good. All of women's history was there. . . . And Moa always saw life from the perspective of the little people. She showed real life, everyday chores. I think women wouldn't have survived if they hadn't read Moa—read what miseries women went through and had gone through yet still made it. When you read Moa, you feel that you're *there,* in her environment. You get a picture of life in all its complexity which is well-rooted in everyday existence."[14]

Moa Martinson's role as a novelist of woman's enduring strength is secure. Despite its harsh theme, *My Mother Gets Married* can be drolly humorous. Mia's resourcefulness engages readers at once and continues to charm them. She is feisty, quick, and imaginative. Like her mother and her grandma, Mia never gives up any battle even when she knows she cannot win. Sometimes dishonest with others, Mia is always honest with herself. She is often baffled by the contradictory behavior of "the grown-ups," but she never loses her sense of wonder and hope. Moa does not sentimentalize Mia; she is a consistently believable child. In creating the character of Mia, Martinson draws upon memories, always colorful, often harrowing, of her own childhood, and filters them through her adult sensibility. It is the autobiographical character of Mia that will make Moa Martinson's novel, *My Mother Gets Married*, endure.

Margaret S. Lacy
University of Wisconsin at Madison

NOTES

1. *Church Wedding* (*Kyrkbröllop,* 1938); *The King's Roses* (*Kungens Rosor,* 1939).
2. Helena Forsås-Scott, "Moa Martinson," *Swedish Book Review,* Gothenburg, November 1984, p. 2.
3. Moa Martinson, *Church Wedding.*
4. In *The King's Roses,* Hedvig and Mia read in the newspaper that in a drunken, jealous rage, Karlberg has murdered his wife, Olga, and their six-year-old son.
5. See Franklin D. Scott's discussion of social classes in *Sweden: The Nation's History,* Minneapolis, University of Minnesota Press, 1977, pp. 334–51.
6. Ebba Witt-Brattström, "'Life's Own Runestone'—Moa Martinson and Realism's Dead End" ("'Livets egen runsten'—Moa Martinson och realismens döda vinkel"), *Periodical for Literary Scholarship (Tidskrift för Litteratur Vetenskap),* ed. Urpu-Liisa Karahka and Magnus Röhl, Stockholm, 1983, p. 277. The Danish novelist Johannes V. Jensen won the Nobel Prize for Literature in 1944.
7. Moa Martinson, *I Meet a Poet (Jag möter en diktare)* Folket I Bilds Förlag, 1950. Harry Martinson and Eyvind Johnson shared the Nobel Prize for Literature in 1974.
8. Maria Bergom-Larsson, "Moa Martinson—Her Work and Her Love," ("Moa Martinson—arbetet och kärleken"), in *Women's Consciousness (Kvinnomedvetande),* Stockholm, Raben & Sjögren, 1976, p. 74.
9. Witt-Brattström, *Everyday Chores and the Language of Dreams (Vardagsslit och drömmars språk),* quoted in *Inside Sweden,* ed. Eva Swedenmark, International Center of the Swedish Labor Movement, December 1986, p. 8.
10. Glann Boman, *Moa in Letters and Pictures (Moa i brev och bilder),* Stockholm, Askild & Kärnekull, 1978, p. 100.
11. Boman, *Moa in Letters and Pictures.*
12. Witt-Brattström in *Inside Sweden,* p. 8.
13. Forsås-Scott, p. 2. Virtually all information on Martinson's life and criticism of her work are available in Swedish only. For a brief review of changing literary opinion of Moa Martinson's novels, see my Afterword to my translation of *Women and Appletrees,* New York, The Feminist Press, 1985, pp. 199–213. For an overview of the male attitude that once prevailed about Martinson's artistry, see Maria Bergom-Larsson's three articles in *The Day's News (Dagens Nyheter),* November 2, 4, 6, 1975, reprinted in expanded form in her essay, mentioned earlier, in her book, *Women's Consciousness,* pp. 72–97. For particular criticism that reflects a patronizing male view, see Knut Jaensson, *Nine Modern Swedish*

Prose Writers (Nio moderna svenska prosaförfattare), Stockholm, Bonniers, 1943, and *A Swedish Literary Dictionary (Svenskt Litteraturlexikon)*, Lund, Gleerup, 1970, pp. 364–65. Two estimable and interesting exceptions to this view should be noted: Victor Svanberg, "Moa's Kingdom" ("Moas rikedom") in his book of essays, *Praise for the Present Day (Till nutidens lov)*, Uppsala, Lindblads, 1956; and Axel Strindberg, *People between Wars (Människor mellan krig)*, Stockholm, Kooperativa förbundets bokförlag, 1941, pp. 295–98.

14. Witt-Brattström in *Inside Sweden*, p. 8.

The Feminist Press at The City University of New York offers alternatives in education and in literature. Founded in 1970, this nonprofit, tax-exempt educational and publishing organization works to eliminate sexual stereotypes in books and schools and to provide literature with a broad vision of human potential. The publishing program includes reprints of important works by women, feminist biographies of women, and nonsexist children's books. Curricular materials, bibliographies, directories, and a quarterly journal provide information and support for students and teachers of women's studies. In-service projects help to transform teaching methods and curricula. Through publications and projects, The Feminist Press contributes to the rediscovery of the history of women and the emergence of a more humane society.

NEW AND FORTHCOMING BOOKS

Black Foremothers: Three Lives, 2nd ed., by Dorothy Sterling. Foreword by Margaret Walker. Introduction by Barbara Christian. $9.95 paper.

Families in Flux (formerly *Household and Kin*), by Amy Swerdlow, Renate Bridenthal, Joan Kelly, and Phyllis Vine. $9.95 paper.

Get Smart! A Women's Guide to Equality on Campus, by Montana Katz and Veronica Vieland. $29.95 cloth, $9.95 paper.

Islanders, a novel by Helen R. Hull. Afterword by Patricia McClelland Miller. $10.95 paper.

Library and Information Sources on Women: A Guide to Collections in the Greater New York Area, compiled by the Women's Resources Group of the Greater New York Metropolitan Area Chapter of the Association of College and Research Libraries and the Center for the Study of Women and Society of the Graduate School and University Center of The City University of New York. $12.95 paper.

Lone Voyagers: Academic Women in Coeducational Universities, 1869–1937, edited by Geraldine J. Clifford. $29.95 cloth, $12.95 paper.

My Mother Gets Married, a novel by Moa Martinson. Translated and introduced by Margaret S. Lacy. $8.95 paper.

Not So Quiet . . . : Stepdaughters of War, a novel by Helen Zenna Smith. Afterword by Jane Marcus. $9.95 paper.

Ruth Weisberg: Paintings, Drawings, Prints, 1968–1988, edited and curated by Marion E. Jackson. With an essay by Thalia Gouma-Peterson. $15.00 paper.

Sultana's Dream and Selections from The Secluded Ones, by Rokeya Sakhawat Hossain. Edited and translated by Roushan Jahan. Afterword by Hanna Papanek. $16.95 cloth, $6.95 paper.

We That Were Young, a novel by Irene Rathbone. Afterword by Jane Marcus. $10.95 paper.

Women Activists: Challenging the Abuse of Power, by Anne Witte Garland. Foreword by Ralph Nader. Introduction by Frances T. Farenthold. $29.95 cloth, $9.95 paper.

Women Composers: The Lost Tradition Found, by Diane P. Jezic. Foreword by Elizabeth Wood. $29.95 cloth, $12.95 paper.

For a free catalog, write to The Feminist Press at The City University of New York, 311 East 94 Street, New York, NY 10128. Send individual book orders to The Talman Company, Inc., 150 Fifth Avenue, New York, NY 10011. Please include $1.75 for postage and handling for the first book, $.75 for each additional.